All the Broken Places

ALSO BY JOHN BOYNE

NOVELS

The Thief of Time

Crippen

Next of Kin

Mutiny on the Bounty

The House of Special Purpose

The Absolutist

This House Is Haunted

A History of Loneliness

The Heart's Invisible Furies

A Ladder to the Sky

A Traveler at the Gates of Wisdom

YOUNG ADULT NOVELS

The Boy in the Striped Pajamas

Noah Barleywater Runs Away

The Terrible Thing That Happened to Barnaby Brocket

Stay Where You Are and Then Leave

The Boy at the Top of the Mountain

All the Broken Places

JOHN BOYNE

PAMELA DORMAN BOOKS ᴄ⁓ VIKING

VIKING
An imprint of Penguin Random House LLC
penguinrandomhouse.com

First published in hardcover in Great Britain by Doubleday,
an imprint of Penguin Random House Ltd., London, in 2022
First United States edition published by Pamela Dorman Books in 2022

A Pamela Dorman Book/Viking

LIBRARY OF CONGRESS CONTROL NUMBER: 2022945097

ISBN 9780593653067 (hardcover)
ISBN 9780593653074 (ebook)

Printed in the United States of America
5th Printing

Designed by Amanda Dewey and Claire Naylon Vaccaro

For Markus Zusak

Contents

Part 1

THE DEVIL'S DAUGHTER 1

London 2022 / Paris 1946

Interlude

THE FENCE 119

London 1970

Part 2

BEAUTIFUL SCARS 127

London 2022 / Sydney 1953

Interlude

THE BOY 259

Poland 1943

Part 3

THE FINAL SOLUTION 275

London 2022 / London 1953

EPILOGUE 375

Author's Note 385
Acknowledgments 389

Part 1

The Devil's Daughter

LONDON 2022 / PARIS 1946

ONE

If every man is guilty of all the good he did not do, as Voltaire suggested, then I have spent a lifetime convincing myself that I am innocent of all the bad. It has been a convenient way to endure decades of self-imposed exile from the past, to see myself as a victim of historical amnesia, acquitted from complicity, and exonerated from blame.

My final story begins and ends, however, with something as trivial as a box cutter. Mine had broken a few days earlier and, finding it a useful tool to keep in a kitchen drawer, I paid a visit to my local hardware shop to purchase a new one. Upon my return, a letter was waiting for me from an estate agent, a similar one delivered to every resident of Winterville Court, politely informing each of us that the flat below my own was being put up for sale. The previous occupant, Mr. Richardson, had lived in Flat One for some thirty years but died shortly before Christmas, leaving the dwelling empty. His daughter, a speech therapist, resided in New York and, to the best of my knowledge, had no plans to return to London, so I had made my peace with the fact that it would not be long before I was forced to interact with a stranger in the lobby, perhaps even having to feign an interest in his or her life or be required to divulge small details about my own.

Mr. Richardson and I had enjoyed the perfect neighborly relationship in that we had not exchanged a single word since 2008. In the early years of his residence, we'd been on good terms and he had occasionally come upstairs for a game of chess with my late husband, Edgar, but somehow, he and I had never moved past the formalities. He always addressed me as "Mrs. Fernsby" while I referred to him as "Mr. Richardson." The last time I set foot in his flat had been four months after Edgar's death, when he invited me for supper and, having accepted the invitation, I found myself on the receiving end of an amorous advance, which I declined. He took the rejection badly and we became as near to strangers as two people who coexist within a single building can be.

My Mayfair residence is listed as a flat but that is a little like describing Windsor Castle as the Queen's weekend bolthole. Each apartment in our building—there are five in total, one on the ground floor, then two on both floors above—is spread across fifteen hundred square feet of prime London real estate, each with three bedrooms, two and a half bathrooms, and views over Hyde Park that value them, I am reliably informed, at somewhere between £2 and £3 million apiece. Edgar came into a substantial amount of money a few years after we married, an unexpected bequest from a spinster aunt, and while he would have preferred to move to a more peaceful area outside Central London, I had done some research of my own and was determined not only to live in Mayfair but to reside in this particular building, should it ever prove possible. Financially, this had seemed unlikely but then, one day, like a *deus ex machina*, Aunt Belinda passed away and everything changed. I'd always planned on explaining to Edgar the reason why I was so desperate to live here, but somehow never did, and I rather regret that now.

My husband was very fond of children but I agreed only to one, giving birth to our son, Caden, in 1961. In recent years, as the property

has increased in value, Caden has encouraged me to sell and purchase something smaller in a less expensive part of town, but I suspect this is because he worries that I might live to be a hundred and
he is keen to receive a portion of his inheritance while he is still
young enough to enjoy it. He is thrice married and now engaged for
a fourth time; I have given up on acquainting myself with the women
in his life. I find that as soon as one gets to know them, they are dispatched, a new model is installed, and one has to take the time to
learn their idiosyncrasies, as one might with a new washing machine
or television set. As a child, he treated his friends with similar ruth-
lessness. We speak regularly on the telephone, and he visits me for
supper every two weeks, but we have a complicated relationship,
damaged in part by my year-long absence from his life when he was
nine years old. The truth is, I am simply not comfortable around
children and I find small boys particularly difficult.

My concern about my new neighbor was not that he or she might
cause unnecessary noise—these flats are very well insulated and, even
with a few weak spots here and there, I had grown accustomed over
the years to the various peculiar sounds that rose up through Mr.
Richardson's ceiling—but I resented the fact that my ordered world
might be upset. I hoped for someone who had no interest in knowing
anything about the woman who lived above them. An elderly invalid,
perhaps, who rarely left the house and was visited each morning by
a home-help. A young professional who disappeared on Friday afternoons to her weekend home and returned late on Sundays, spending
the rest of her time at the office or the gym. A rumor spread through
the building that a well-known pop musician whose career had peaked
in the 1980s had looked at it as a potential retirement home but,
happily, nothing came of that.

My curtains twitched whenever the estate agent pulled up outside, escorting a client in to inspect the flat, and I made notes about

each potential neighbor. There was a very promising husband and wife in their early seventies, softly spoken, who held each other's hands and asked whether pets were permitted in the building—I was listening on the stairwell—and seemed disappointed when told they were not. A homosexual couple in their thirties who, judging by the distressed condition of their clothing and their general unkempt air must have been fabulously wealthy, but who declared that the "space" was probably a little small for them and they couldn't relate to its "narrative." A young woman with plain features who gave no clue as to her intentions, other than to remark that someone named Steven would adore the high ceilings. Naturally, I hoped for the gays—they make good neighbors and there's little chance of them procreating—but they proved to be the least interested.

And then, after a few weeks, the estate agent no longer brought anyone to visit, the listing vanished from the Internet and I guessed that a deal had been struck. Whether I liked it or not, I would one day wake to find a removals van parked outside and someone, or a collection of someones, inserting a key into the front door and taking up residence beneath me.

Oh, how I dreaded it!

TWO

Mother and I escaped Germany in early 1946, only a few months after the war ended, traveling by train from what was left of Berlin to what was left of Paris. Fifteen years old and knowing little of life, I was still coming to terms with the fact that the Axis had been defeated. Father had spoken with such confidence of the genetic superiority of our race and of the Führer's incomparable skills as a military strategist that victory had always seemed assured. And yet, somehow, we had lost.

The journey of almost seven hundred miles across the continent did little to encourage optimism for the future. The cities we passed through were marked by the destruction of recent years while the faces of the people I saw in the stations and carriages were not cheered by the end of the war but scarred by its effects. There was a sense of exhaustion everywhere, a growing realization that Europe could not return to how it had been in 1938 but needed to be rebuilt entirely, as did the spirits of its inhabitants.

The city of my birth had been almost entirely reduced to rubble now, its spoils divided between four of our conquerors. For our protection, we remained hidden in the basements of those few true believers whose homes were still standing until we could be provided with the false papers that would ensure our safe removal from Germany. Our passports now bore the surname of Guéymard, the pronunciation of which I practiced repeatedly in order to ensure that I sounded as authentic as possible, but while Mother was now to be called Nathalie—my grandmother's name—I remained Gretel.

Every day, fresh details of what had taken place at the camps came to light and Father's name was becoming a byword for criminality of the most heinous nature. While no one suggested that we were as culpable as him, Mother believed that it would spell disaster for us to reveal ourselves to the authorities. I agreed for, like her, I was frightened, although it shocked me to think that anyone could consider me complicit in the atrocities. It's true that, since my tenth birthday, I had been a member of the Jungmädelbund, but so had every other young girl in Germany. It was mandatory, after all, just like being part of the Deutsches Jungvolk was compulsory for ten-year-old boys. But I had been far less interested in studying the ideology of the party than in taking part in the regular sporting activities with my friends. And when we arrived at that other place, I had only gone beyond the fence once, on that single day that Father had brought me into the camp to observe his work. I tried to tell myself that I had been a bystander, nothing more, and that my conscience was clear, but already I was beginning to question my own involvement in the events I had witnessed.

As our train entered France, however, I grew worried that our accents might give us away. Surely, I reasoned, the recently liberated citizens of Paris, shamed by their prompt capitulation in 1940, would react aggressively toward anyone who spoke as we did? My concern was proven correct when, despite demonstrating that we had more than enough money for a lengthy stay, we were refused rooms at five separate boarding houses; it was only when a woman in place Vendôme took pity on us and shared the address of a nearby lodging where, she said, the landlady asked no questions that we found somewhere to live. Had it not been for her, we might have ended up the wealthiest indigents on the streets.

The room we rented was on the eastern part of Île de la Cité and in those early days I preferred to remain close to home, confining myself to walking the short distance from Pont de Sully to Pont Neuf and back again in endless loops, anxious about venturing across bridges into unknown terrain. Sometimes I thought of my brother, who had longed to be an explorer, and of how much he would have enjoyed deciphering those unfamiliar streets, but, at such moments, I was always quick to dismiss his memory.

Mother and I had been living on the Île for two months before I summoned the courage to make my way to le Jardin du Luxembourg, where an abundance of greenery made me feel as if I had stumbled upon Paradise. Such a contrast, I thought, to when we had arrived at that other place and been struck by its barren, desolate nature. Here, one inhaled the perfume of life; there, one choked on the stench of death. I wandered as if in a daze from the Palais to the Medici fountain, and from there toward the pool, only turning away when I saw a coterie of small boys placing wooden boats in the water, the light breeze taking their vessels across to their playmates on the other side. Their laughter and excited conversation provided an upsetting music after the muted distress with which I had become familiar and I struggled to understand how a single continent could play host to such extremes of beauty and ugliness.

One afternoon, taking shelter from the sun on a bench near the boulodrome, I found myself consumed by both grief and guilt, and with tears falling down my face. A handsome boy, perhaps two years my senior, approached wearing a concerned expression to ask what was wrong. I looked up and felt a stirring of desire, a longing for him to put his arms around me or allow me to rest my head upon his shoulder, but when I spoke I fell into old speech patterns, my German accent overpowering my French, and he took a step back, staring at me with undisguised contempt, before summoning all the anger he felt toward my kind and spitting violently in my face and marching away. Strangely, his actions did not diminish my hunger for his touch but increased it. Wiping my cheeks dry, I ran after him, grabbed him by the arm and invited him to take me into the trees, telling him that he could do whatever he wanted with me in the secluded space.

"You can hurt me if you like," I whispered, closing my eyes, thinking that he might slap me hard, drive his fist into my stomach, break my nose.

"Why would you want that?" he asked, his tone betraying an innocence that belied his beauty.

"So I'll know that I'm alive."

He seemed both aroused and repulsed and looked around to see whether anyone was watching before glancing toward the copse that I had indicated. Licking his lips, he observed the swell of my breasts, but when I took him by the hand my touch insulted him and he pulled away, calling me a whore, *une putain*, and broke into a run as he disappeared out onto rue Guynemer.

When the weather was good I wandered the streets from early morning, only returning to our lodgings when Mother would already be too drunk to ask how I had passed my time. The elegance that had defined her earlier life was beginning to fall away now but she was still a handsome woman and I wondered whether she might search for a new husband, someone who could take care of us. But it did not seem that she wanted companionship or love, preferring to be left alone with her thoughts as she made her way from bar to bar. She was a quiet drunk. She sat in darkened corners nursing bottles of wine, scratching at invisible marks upon wooden tabletops while making sure never to cause a scene that might see her exiled to the street.

Once, our paths crossed as the sun disappeared over the Bois de Boulogne and she approached me unsteadily before taking my arm and asking me the time. She didn't appear to realize that it was her own daughter she was addressing. When I answered, she smiled in relief—it was growing dark, but the bars would remain open for hours yet—and she continued in the direction of the bright, seductive lights that dotted the Île. If I vanished entirely, I wondered, would she forget that I had ever existed?

We shared a bed and I hated waking next to her, inhaling the stench of sleep-infused liquor that poisoned her breath. On opening her eyes, she would sit up in a moment of confusion, but then the memories would return and her eyes would close as she tried to ease her way back into oblivion. When she finally accepted the indecency of the daylight and dragged herself out from beneath the sheets, she would give herself a rudimentary wash in the sink before pulling on a dress and making her way outside, happy to repeat every moment of the day before, and the day before that, and the day before that.

She kept our money and valuables in an old satchel at the back of the wardrobe, and I watched as our small fortune began to diminish. Relatively speaking, we were comfortable—the true believers had seen to that—but Mother refused to invest more in our accommodation, shaking her head whenever I suggested that we rent a little flat of our own in one of the cheaper parts of the city. It seemed that she had a simple plan for her life now, to drink away the nightmares, and as long as she had a bed to sleep in and a bottle to empty, nothing else mattered. What a far cry this was from the woman in whose embrace I had spent my early years, the glamorous society wife who had performed like a film star, sporting the latest hairstyles and dressing in the finest gowns.

Those two women could not have been more different, and each would have despised the other.

THREE

E very Tuesday morning, I cross the hallway to visit my neighbor, Heidi Hargrave, the occupant of Flat Three. Heidi will turn sixty-nine toward the end of the year, her birthday falling on the Feast of the Immaculate Conception, a rather ironic date as she never knew her biological parents and was adopted immediately after coming into the world. Heidi is the only resident of Winterville Court to have spent her entire life here, having been brought to Mayfair directly from the maternity ward and grown up with Hyde Park as her playground. She fell pregnant when she was a teenager and never married, inheriting her adoptive parents' estate when they passed away.

Despite being my junior by some twenty-three years, she is far less agile, both in body and mind. For three decades, she took part in the London Marathon but was forced to stop running when she developed a severe case of plantar fasciitis in her left heel, an affliction for which she has to wear night splints and receive regular steroid injections in her foot. It proved a terrible blow for such an active woman and I wonder whether this contributed to the gradual decline in her mental faculties, for she was once a person of great vitality, a highly respected ophthalmologist, but now she tends to wander in conversation. Her condition is not quite as severe as dementia or Alzheimer's, thankfully; it's more that she grows a little hazy from time to time, losing track of what we're talking about, mixing up names and places, or changing the subject so abruptly that one struggles to keep up.

On this particular morning, I found her studying some old photograph albums and hoped that I would not be forced to look through them with her. I keep no such scrapbooks myself and have never quite seen the point of littering one's home with family portraits. In fact, I have only two on display, a silver-framed image of Edgar and me from our wedding day and a picture of Caden upon his graduation from university. I don't display these for sentimental reasons, I should add, but because it is expected of me.

That said, on a shelf in my wardrobe, hidden toward the back, sits an antique Seugnot jewelry box that I purchased from a market stall in Montparnasse in 1946, constructed from fruitwood, trimmed in polished brass, with a mounted escutcheon on the front and a working key. Inside, I keep a single photograph and, although I haven't dared to look at it for more than seventy-five years, I believe I can recall its contents. I am twelve years old, my eyes are directed toward the photographer, and I'm doing my best to appear coquettish, for it is Kurt standing behind the lens, his finger on the shutter, his gaze focused entirely on me as I try not to betray my passion for him. He stands erect in his uniform, his slim, muscular frame, blond hair and pale blue eyes overwhelming me. I sense his cautious interest and am desperate to build upon it.

"Do you see this man, Gretel?" asked Heidi, pointing to a picture of an intelligent-looking fellow standing on a beach with his hands on his hips and a woodstock pipe hanging from his mouth. "His name was Billy Sprat. He was a dancer and a Russian spy."

"Is that so?" I said, pouring the tea and wondering whether this story might be one of her fancies—perhaps she'd been watching an old James Bond movie the night before and her mind was filled with espionage—although judging from the era of the photograph it was possible that she was telling the truth. There seem to have been rather a lot of Russian spies lurking around England back then.

"Billy was a friend of my father's and he got caught selling secrets to the KGB," she added breathlessly. "The security services were about to arrest him, but he found out that his cover had been blown and fled to Moscow. Terribly exciting, don't you think?"

"Oh yes," I agreed. "Very."

"They should have insisted that he come back to face the courts. There's nothing more provoking than the guilty escaping justice."

I said nothing, glancing across at the carriage clock that stood atop her mantelpiece and the small porcelain figurines next to it that she numbered among her treasures.

"Did you ever have any sympathies with the Russians?" she asked, taking a sip from her cup. "During the 1960s, I thought they might be onto something with their share and share alike philosophy. But once they started pointing nuclear bombs in our direction I rather lost interest. No one needs another war, do they?"

"I stay out of politics," I told her, buttering two warm scones and passing hers across. "I've seen what it does to people."

"But, of course, you were alive back then, weren't you?" she asked.

"The sixties?" I said. "Yes. But so were you, Heidi."

"No, I meant before that. The war. The . . . what do you call it?"

"The Second World War," I said.

"That's right."

"Yes," I told her. We'd had this conversation before, many times, but I had rarely gone into any great detail about my past and, when I had, it had mostly been the stuff of fiction. "But I was just a girl then."

Heidi put down the album before turning to me with a mischievous glint in her eyes.

"Any news from downstairs?" she asked, and I shook my head. This was one of those moments when I was glad that she liked to cast one topic aside in favor of another.

"Not yet," I said, putting a napkin to my mouth to wipe away some crumbs. "All quiet on the southern front."

"You don't think it will be darkies, do you?" she asked, and I frowned. One of the more distressing aspects of Heidi's increasingly muddled mind has been her tendency to employ phrases that are, quite rightly, no longer considered appropriate and that she would never, in her prime, have used. I suspect it's the language of her younger days staking its claim on the parts of her brain that are slowly dissolving. It's strange; she can tell me exhaustive stories about her childhood, but ask her what happened last Wednesday between six and nine o'clock and the fog descends.

"It could be anyone, I suppose," I replied. "We won't know until they show up."

"There was a lovely chap who lived down there for many years," she said, her face lighting up now. "A historian. He lectured at the University of London."

"No, Heidi, that was Edgar. My husband," I told her. "He lived with me across the hall."

"That's right," she said, winking at me, as if we shared a secret. "You have it now. Edgar was such a gentleman. Always turned out so well. I don't believe I ever saw him without a shirt and tie."

I smiled. It was true that Edgar had taken particular care in his appearance and, even on holidays, had not liked to "dress down," as they say. He wore a pencil mustache and there were those who said he looked a bit like Ronald Colman. The comparison was not unjustified.

"I tried to kiss him once, you know," she continued, glancing toward the window and, by the way she said it, I knew that she'd forgotten to whom she was speaking. "He was years older than me, of course, but I didn't care. He wasn't interested, though. Brushed me off. Told me that he was devoted to his wife."

"Is that so?" I said quietly, trying to imagine the scenario. I was not surprised that Edgar had never bothered to reveal this minor scandal to me.

"He let me down very gently and I was grateful for that. It was shameless behavior on my part."

"Has Oberon been to see you this week?" I asked. My turn to change the subject now. Oberon is Heidi's grandson, about thirty, good-looking but cursed with a ridiculous name. (Heidi's daughter, who tragically passed away from cancer a few years ago, had a passion for Shakespeare.) He works nearby—he's something high up in Selfridge's, I believe—and is kind to his grandmother, although I find him rather irritating in that whenever I'm in his company he addresses me in the loudest voice imaginable, enunciating every syllable, as if he assumes that I must be deaf. And I am not deaf. In fact, there is almost nothing wrong with me at all, which is both surprising and disquieting, considering my advanced years.

"He's calling in tomorrow evening," she replied. "With his girlfriend. He says he has news."

"Perhaps they're getting married," I suggested, and she nodded.

"Perhaps," she agreed. "I hope so. It's time he settled down. Like your Caden."

I raised an eyebrow. Caden has settled down so often that he must be among the most relaxed men in England, but I chose not to bother her with my son's rather careless approach to commitment.

"When you hear, you will let me know, won't you?" she asked, leaning forward, and I allowed my mind to scurry back through the conversation, wondering where she might have set up a temporary camp.

"When I hear what, dear?" I asked.

"About the new neighbors. We could throw them a party."

"I don't think they'd like that."

"Or at least bake them a cake."

"That might be more appropriate."

"What about Jews?" she asked after a long pause. "There was a time when buildings like this wouldn't accept Jews. I don't mind, myself. I'm open to all sorts. I've always found them a very friendly people, if I'm honest. Surprisingly cheerful, considering all they've been through."

I said nothing and, when her eyes closed soon afterward, I took the cup from her hands, washed the used crockery in the sink and departed, placing a soft kiss upon her forehead before closing the door behind me. In the hallway, I glanced down the staircase to the flat below. It remained, for now, as silent as the grave.

FOUR

The man's name was Rémy Toussaint and he wore a patch emblazoned with the Tricolor over his right eye, having lost that particular organ when a bomb he was planting exploded too soon. Despite his disfigurement, he was handsome, in a cruel way, with thick black hair and a sneer that masqueraded as a smile. He was younger than Mother by some eight years and could have had his pick of women, but he chose her and, for the first time since my brother's death, she seemed open to life's possibilities, curtailing her drinking and taking care with her appearance. She would sit by the grainy mirror in our room running a brush through her hair, and once suggested that this new romance was God's way of showing her that He did not hold her responsible for any crimes that had been committed in that other place. I, however, was less convinced.

"What you must understand about M. Toussaint," she told me, pronouncing his surname with such precision that she might have been interviewing for membership of the Académie Française, "is that he is a person of great refinement. His ancestral line is strewn with vicomtes and marquises, although, of course, as a committed *égalitariste*, he scorns such titles. He plays piano and sings, has read most of the important works of literature and, last summer, displayed some of his paintings at an exhibition in Montmartre."

"So what does he want from you?" I asked.

"He doesn't 'want' anything, Gretel," she replied, irritated by my tone. "He's fallen in love with me. Is that so difficult for you to believe? French men have always preferred women of a certain age to callow ingénues. They have the sense to value experience and wisdom. You mustn't be jealous; twenty years from now, you'll be grateful that this is the case."

She turned back to the mirror and, from my vantage point on the bed, I wondered whether this was true. Men, it seemed to me, valued attractiveness above all other things. And while Mother had always been a great beauty, she had lost much of her vibrancy since the end of the war. Her hair was less lustrous than it had once been, with flashes of gray intruding among the black like uninvited guests; tiny veins, too, had begun to peep forth across her cheeks like freckles, the result of her devotion to wine. Her eyes, however, remained compelling, a striking shade of Savoy blue that captivated anyone who sat across from her. It was not impossible that a man could still be enamored by her, I accepted. She was right, however, that I was envious. If a love affair was to play out, then I wanted to be at the heart of it.

"Is he rich?" I asked.

"He dresses well," she replied. "And eats at good restaurants. He carries a Fayet walking stick with his family crest on the collar. So yes, I assume that he is a man of some means."

"And what did he do during the war?"

She ignored this—it was as if I had not spoken at all—and walked toward the wardrobe, from which she removed a red silk dress, one that Father had given her as a gift on the night he told us that we would be leaving Germany. She put it on now and, where it had once clung to her body, accentuating her every curve, it was no longer quite so flattering.

"It needs a belt," she said, examining herself in the glass. She rummaged through the drawers and found one whose color contrasted well with the scarlet.

"And when will I meet him?" I asked, glancing out of the window at the people walking along the street below. Across from our lodgings was a haberdashery shop and there was a boy who worked inside, not much older than me, who had caught my attention. I often watched him as he went about his business. Like Kurt, he had blond hair, but his fell across his forehead and he seemed to be always stumbling over things, like a clumsy child, which endeared him to me. He was no dancer, but he was beautiful.

"When he extends the invitation," said Mother.

"But he knows that you have a daughter?"

"I've mentioned it."

"Have you told him my age?"

She hesitated. "And why would that matter to him, Gretel?" she asked, frowning. "As it happens, he has a daughter of his own. Much younger than you, of course. Only four years old. She lives with her mother in Angoulême."

"He's married then?"

"The girl is illegitimate. But, naturally, as a man of honor, he provides for her."

"Well, perhaps I could join you some evening," I suggested as she sprayed some perfume on her neck and wrists. This last bottle of Guerlain Shalimar had been given to her by Grandmother some seven years earlier on her birthday and it was now perilously close to empty. The scent brought me back to our farewell party in Berlin, when victory had appeared inevitable and the Reich seemed destined to survive for a thousand years. I saw my brother standing by the banister, observing the officers and their wives as they gathered in the reception rooms, both of us mesmerized by the uniforms and gowns that swept through the hallway in an orgy of color. Had that really been a mere four years earlier? It felt like so many lifetimes ago, and the two hundred weeks that separated that moment from this were sticky with blood.

"I think not," she replied, examining herself one last time in the mirror before leaving the room, ready for whatever adventures her night might bring.

I looked out of the window again and watched as M. Vannier, the haberdasher, stepped outside onto the pavement. A car had pulled up and the chauffeur opened the boot while the boy I liked appeared through the doorway carrying several boxes, each one perched perilously atop the next. Needless to say, he slipped as he negotiated the pavement and one of the boxes fell, followed quickly by the others. Fortunately, it was a dry evening so no damage was done, but M. Vannier reproached him anyway, swatting him about the head, and the boy put a hand to his ear to soothe the sting. Perhaps sensing that he was being observed, he glanced up and noticed me, then blushed scarlet and did a swift about-turn, making his way back into the shop just as Mother stepped over one of the fallen parcels and disappeared down a side street.

FIVE

I make great use of the Mayfair library on South Audley Street, a
pleasant ten-minute walk from my flat, where I have been a bor-
rower for many years. Edgar was a passionate reader and while many of
his books still sit on the shelves of what was once his office but is now
a guest room, his tastes and mine differed considerably. A historian
by day, my husband preferred contemporary fiction for his leisure
hours but, in general, I prefer non-fiction and it is to these titles that
I return time and again as I wander the stacks. I avoid anything to do
with the period of my childhood but am fascinated by the Greeks and
the Romans. I have a peculiar interest in the autobiographies of astro-
nauts, finding the desire to escape the planet, and the ability to see it
through, both eccentric and commendable. I'm not as voracious a
reader as Edgar was, but it's a character trait that Father, an equally
committed bibliophile, instilled in both his children.

My brother, of course, loved to read about explorers, insisting
that he would be one himself someday. Once, I overheard him talking
to Pavel, one of the waiters in that other place, about our Berlin
home and how he and his friends could spend hours exploring the
enormous attic filled with the bric-a-brac of many years, the dark,

labyrinthine basement, and the floors that had been designed to make the most of the architect's passion for inscrutable nooks and crannies. Pavel was probably not interested in any of this, but my brother rambled along with his usual disregard.

"Can't you do some exploring here?" asked Pavel, keeping his voice low, for Kurt was polishing his boots outside in the sunshine and had expressly forbidden him to speak to either of us. *You wouldn't converse with a rat, would you?* Kurt had asked me, and I, in my desire to please him, had burst out laughing and praised his humor.

"I'm not allowed," replied my brother sadly.

"And you're obedient to such a rule?" Pavel asked, a tired resignation in his tone. "Maybe you're afraid of what you'll discover if you look beyond the fence."

"I'm not afraid of anything," my brother insisted, sitting up in outrage.

"You should be."

A long silence followed, and I watched as my brother made his way back upstairs to his bedroom, considering these remarks. From the morning of our arrival, Mother and Father had been adamant that he was to stay close to home. They should have guessed that he wouldn't listen. Little boys seldom do.

Returning from the library on this particular morning, however, with a recently published biography of Marie Antoinette under my arm, I noticed an unfamiliar car parked outside Winterville Court and stared at it uneasily. There are only a handful of parking spots available on the street, each one so expensive that no one ever bothers. Residents have parking tags for a nearby garage and only a fool, a millionaire, or both would drive into London these days. Entering the lobby, I paused outside Flat One and pressed my ear to the door. I could hear movement from inside but no voices.

I tapped gently on the woodwork, that strange conflict of wanting to be heard but not wishing to disturb, and when the door was opened I found myself standing face to face with a young woman, perhaps thirty-five at most, dressed in what one might call an eclectic outfit, with a pink streak running through her platinum-blonde hair. I have to say, I rather admired her *elan*.

"Hello," she said, her expression open, and I mirrored it, extending my hand.

"Gretel Fernsby," I said. "Your upstairs neighbor. You're getting ready to move in, I see."

"Oh no," she said, shaking her head. "I'm just the interior designer. I'm here to measure the space."

That word again. The "space." Could we no longer call things what they were? It seemed to me that language was being torn asunder these days, with the most basic words being discarded as offensive. Perhaps "flat" was considered too bourgeois now. Or too proletariat. Really, it seemed that the safest thing was not to speak. In which case, perhaps the world had not changed very much at all.

"Alison Small," she added, introducing herself. "Small Interiors."

"A pleasure," I said, interrogating my emotions to discover whether or not I was disappointed by this. I'm a quick judge of character, she seemed a pleasant enough sort, and I felt that I would have been perfectly content to have her living beneath me. Her outfits alone would have kept me entertained. "I suppose you're measuring for curtains and sofas and what have you?"

"That's right," she said, stepping back into the flat and ushering me inside. "Come in if you like."

I thanked her and entered. I daresay she wouldn't have invited just anyone in, but people inherently trust the elderly. How dangerous could I be, after all? Still, it felt strange to be in Mr. Richardson's home now that all his effects had been taken away. As it was an exact copy of my own flat upstairs, I had an unsettling vision of what mine would look like when I was gone and everything that I owned, every small possession that I had accumulated over the years as proof of my existence, was consigned to a skip or an Oxfam shop, from the painting Edgar bought me as a wedding gift to the silicone spatula I used in my frying pan. Caden, I knew, would have the flat on the market before rigor mortis had even set in.

"Have you lived upstairs long?" asked Miss Small, and I nodded, surprised by how our voices echoed when there was no upholstery or furniture to dampen the volume.

"More than sixty years," I replied.

"Lucky you!" she declared. "I'd give my left arm to live in this part of London."

"Might I ask . . ." I paused for a moment, unsure how much she would be willing to divulge. "Your client. Or clients. They'll be moving in soon?"

"Yes, quite soon, I'm told," she said, pointing to an electronic device at one of the walls. It shot a red dot toward the paintwork and she glanced at its screen. I have no idea what the red dot signified or what information it revealed but, judging by how her forehead creased, it seemed of great importance. "So my team and I will have to get our skates on. Fortunately, I know exactly what they like. I've worked with them before."

"Them," I said, grabbing onto the word as a drowning man might seize hold of a buoy. "A couple, then?"

She hesitated. Her lipstick, I noticed, was rather thick. It made a smacking sound when she pressed her lips together.

"I probably shouldn't say, Mrs. Fernsby," she said. "Client confidentiality and all that."

"Oh, I'm sure they wouldn't mind," I replied, trying my best not to sound like the local busybody. "They will, after all, be living directly beneath me."

"Still. I know how much they value their privacy. As I say, they'll be here soon enough and you'll have a chance to meet them then."

I nodded, disappointed.

"I know it's nerve-wracking," she continued, recognizing my anxiety. "New neighbors to contend with when you've lived in a building for so long. The previous occupant was here for many years too, I believe?"

"Not really," I told her. "He only moved in in 1992."

She laughed; I didn't know why.

"Well, rest assured, you'll have no difficulty with my clients. They're a very . . ." She paused, searching for the right words. "How shall I put this? They're . . . Are you interested in the French Revolution then?"

I stared at her, baffled by the non-sequitur. My expression must have betrayed my confusion because she nodded toward the book that I was carrying.

"Marie Antoinette," she explained.

"Oh yes," I said with a shrug. "Powerful men and women have always fascinated me. I'm interested in how they wield power, whether they use it for good or for evil, and how it changes them when they do."

She seemed a little embarrassed. Perhaps this was a more detailed reply than she had expected. Lifting her contraption again, she pointed it at the wall that looked out onto the road and another red dot appeared in the window frame, doing whatever those red dots did. I wondered whether, if I outstayed my welcome, she might point the device at me.

"Well, I'd better get back to it," she said, dismissing me now, and

I nodded and turned away, making my way back toward the door. Before leaving, however, I tried once more.

"Just one last question," I said, hopeful that she might set my mind at rest on this issue at least. "Your clients. They don't have any children, do they?"

She appeared uncomfortable. "I'm sorry, Mrs. Fernsby," she said, and my heart sank as I waved goodbye before returning upstairs. It was only as I was brewing a pot of tea a few minutes later that I realized I couldn't actually be sure what her answer had meant. Was she sorry because she had been unable to answer my question, sorry because yes, there was a child on the horizon, or sorry because no, there wasn't, and an old dear like me might have been looking forward to a little youthful energy around the place? It was impossible to know.

SIX

On a sunny morning, as the light dappled through the leafy trees of the Île, I made my way across the Pont Marie toward the place des Vosges, where I occasionally sat with a book to observe the wealthier Parisians as they strolled past in their finery. I rather admired their shameless hypocrisy, this gaggle of erstwhile grandees who professed a belief in *égalité* but used clothes and jewelry to express their innate *supériorité*.

The war had proved a great leveler for the French, but there was a sense that the lower orders had done more to hijack the efforts of the Vichy government than the higher, and so a time of accountability had begun. A single word—*collaborator*—now incited the same levels of terror in the populace as another—*aristocrat*—had done a century and a half earlier. Witnessing the anxiety on the faces of the rich, I imagined it resembled the expressions on their ancestors' faces when the Estates General was summoned. Now, of course, it was the *épuration légale* that brought such people to the dock, leading either to executions or the lesser sentence of *dégradation nationale*.

It was at moments like this, left alone with my thoughts, that I struggled most with the complicated nature of my conscience. It had been three years since my brother died, and six months since my father was hanged, and I missed them both in different ways. My brother's loss was one I could scarcely allow myself to consider but my father's remained on my mind every day. I was slowly beginning to understand what he had been a part of—what *we* had been a part of—and the inhumanity of his actions contrasted so sharply with the man I thought I had known that they might as well have been two different people. I told myself that none of it had been my fault, that I had been just a child, but there was that small part of my brain that asked me, if I was entirely innocent, then why was I living under an assumed name?

As I watched, a man of substantial frame approached from the other side of the fountain and, when he drew closer, I recognized Mother's paramour, M. Toussaint. I turned away, hoping that he would not stop to talk to me. We had not yet been introduced—I had seen him only through the windows of the bars where he and Mother sat drinking—and I felt no great desire to make his acquaintance. But here he was, stopping before me now and removing his hat as he offered a graceful bow. His foolishness irritated me. Was he so vain as to imagine himself a modern-day Musketeer and I a distraught maiden on the road to Versailles?

"Do I have the honor of addressing Mlle. Gretel Guéymard?" he asked, and I looked up, the syllables of our fabricated surname still novel to my ears.

"You do," I said. "And you are M. Toussaint, are you not?"

He smiled, and I could see why a woman might fall so quickly into his arms. His face was unlined, his cheeks smooth, but a thin mustache that crept across his upper lip afforded him an air of mischief, accentuating the thickness of unnaturally red lips. His one uncovered eye was of a piercing blue and I wondered whether it would be pleasurable or unnerving to have it trained upon me. And yet, despite being of an age where my head was turned by the dozens of beautiful youths who passed me on the street every day, I found something disconcerting in M. Toussaint's gaze. He was handsome, certainly, but in a reversal of the myth, I saw him as Medusa and me as Perseus, guessing that it would be perilous for me to dwell on his countenance too long.

"Your mother has spoken of me then," he said.

"Once or twice," I admitted, regretting having played into his narcissism.

"Madame Guéymard is a fine lady and I'm delighted to meet her daughter at last. She talks of you often."

I wondered whether he was lying, for it seemed inconceivable to me that Mother would refer to me at all. Having a fifteen-year-old child would age her in any man's eyes and it was not as if I had a range of achievements of which she could boast.

"I doubt that," I said, challenging him, and I saw something in his eyes then, a flicker of interest, a small note of surprise that I did not merely simper beneath his compliments. I believed that I could hold sway over him by refusing to behave as he expected me to and had begun to realize that the power denied me since childhood was beginning to blossom.

"How did you know me?" I asked, and he shrugged his shoulders, as if I were famous throughout Paris.

"You resemble her," he replied. "Also, I've seen you late at night, spying on us, worrying that she might come to harm on the streets. You play the mother to her, I think, making sure that she returns to your rooms safely. Or is it me that you are watching?"

I did not like the fact that he had observed me without my noticing.

"I look nothing like her," I countered, ignoring his question. "I take after my grandmother, my father's mother, when she was young. Everyone says so."

"Then she must have been a great beauty," he remarked, and I rolled my eyes.

"Do these arrows ever find their target?" I asked. "You must think me awfully naïve."

He grew unsettled now, unaccustomed to ridicule, and enjoying myself enormously, I found that I could not stop.

"May I ask, are you a writer, M. Toussaint?"

"No," he replied, frowning. "Why would you think that?"

"Because you talk like one. A bad one, I mean. A writer of penny romances."

I stood up then, determined to walk away, but he grabbed me by the wrist, neither tenderly nor aggressively.

"You, Mademoiselle Gretel, are a young woman of uncommon rudeness," he declared, appearing rather satisfied by the remark. "Do you feel no guilt?"

I stared at him. "Guilt?" I asked. "Guilt over what?"

"Over your cruelty."

The silence between us seemed to last an eternity.

"I don't know what you mean," I said finally. "Cruelty toward whom?"

"Toward me. Why, who did you think I meant?"

I said nothing. I wanted to run as far from him as I could.

"You are unlike other girls of your age," he said. "Which makes me think that it would be quite something to know you in private life. There is a great difference between boys and men that I would be happy to show you." He reached up his other hand and his fingers caressed my cheek so gently that I felt my eyes close, as if he were placing me under a spell. Experience had made him so much better at this game than me.

Satisfied that he had asserted his dominance, he released me and turned to walk away, leaving me cursing at how easily I had surrendered my victory. When he had gone some distance he looked around, and laughed when he saw that I was still watching him.

SEVEN

Caden dropped by unexpectedly in the early evening, and as he stepped inside the flat I noticed that he'd put on weight. He'd never been a slim child but, in adulthood, when he began to work in the construction industry, his efforts on the building sites had helped keep him trim. Soon after his thirtieth birthday, however, he had started his own company using some money that Edgar and I had given him, and almost immediately began to go to seed, possibly because he then spent most of his time behind a desk, leaving the manual labor to others. It bothered me to see his stomach straining at the buttons of his shirt with such virulence.

"I've had a call," he said, collapsing into an armchair with a groan and rejecting the cup of tea I offered him in favor of a Macallan whisky.

"A call about what?" I asked.

"The flat."

"Whose flat?"

"Your flat. This flat." He looked around, spreading his arms wide, as if he were king of all that he surveyed and not simply the dauphin. "We've had an offer."

I took a moment to compose my thoughts, not wanting my temper to get the better of me.

"How could we possibly have had an offer on the flat," I asked, "when it isn't even on the market?"

"Sometimes people make enquiries," he replied casually, not daring to meet my eye. "There's a lot of demand for property in this part of London. They're offering three point one."

"Three point one what?"

"Three point one million."

"I don't think so," I replied, walking over to the cabinet and pouring a whisky for myself too. I would need one if we were to pursue this conversation.

"It's a lot more than I would have expected," he said. "It would be foolish not to discuss it at least."

"We are discussing it," I pointed out. "We're discussing it right now."

"I've taken a look at what's out there," he continued, ignoring this. "We could find you something very suitable for about one point five, leaving us one point six to play with."

"Us?" I asked. "Don't you mean me? And what would I do with £1.6 million? Put it on a horse?"

"You could invest it," he suggested. "I know some very good people who could advise you."

"I'm ninety-one years old, Caden," I replied. "It's not as if I need to start planning for a comfortable retirement. Anyway, you know I'm happy at Winterville Court."

"You don't think it's time for a change?"

"I don't, no."

He sighed.

"Father never liked it here," he muttered, sotto voce but loud enough for me to hear.

This remark took me aback, for Edgar had never expressed any dissatisfaction with our home. At least not to me.

"That's not true at all," I told him.

"Well, he was comfortable enough, I suppose," he conceded, waving my protests away. "But he never expected to grow old and die here. He wanted to find a little place in the country, a village with a cozy pub and a historical society, but you wouldn't allow it."

"You make me sound like a prison warden. And your father like my captive."

"You're the one who insisted on buying this flat when he came into his money, aren't you?"

"Well, that's true enough," I admitted.

"Why?"

"I had my reasons."

"And, as I understand it, you refused ever to consider living anywhere else in the years that followed."

"Also true."

"Why?"

"Again, I had my reasons."

He sighed. "I worry about you on the stairs," he said half-heartedly.

"And I worry about you pushing me down them," I told him, which made him smile. "Look, Caden, all I want, in the time left to me, is to enjoy the peace and security that comes from living in the place I've called home for more than sixty years. Is that too much to ask?"

"It's just . . ." He seemed uncomfortable now and I told myself that no matter how much pressure he put on me, I would not give in. "The truth is, the business has seen better days," he said finally. "Things are a bit tight at the moment."

"How tight?"

"Very tight. I've had all sorts of problems. First there was Brexit, and just when I thought I might be able to make a go of that, along came the pandemic. I took on new people to look after all the customs issues with Europe, but then I had to furlough them while still trying to keep the company afloat. I don't have to pay alimony to Amanda or Beatrice anymore, but Charlotte bleeds me dry every month."

One of the more unusual details regarding my son's checkered romantic history is that he appears to choose his wives in strict alphabetical order, much like the killer did in *The ABC Murders*. That said, his current fiancée is called Eleanor, so either he's "mixing things up," as they say, or old age has caused me to forget a Deirdre, Deborah, or Dawn.

"How is Amanda?" I asked, for his first wife was the only one I had ever really got along with and it had saddened me when they parted ways.

"She's fine," he said. "Well, I mean, she has cancer, but other than that she's fine."

"What?" I asked, sitting upright in my chair in shock. "What do you mean, 'she has cancer'?"

"Exactly what I say. Ovarian, I believe."

"And you're only telling me this now?"

"Mother, Amanda and I got divorced thirty years ago. There's no reason for me to keep you up to date on her various ailments. It's strange enough that I still have to hear about them."

"Cancer is not an ailment," I protested, appalled by how callous he sounded. "It's much more serious than that."

"I'm sure she'll be fine."

"What makes you sure? Are you a doctor?"

He said nothing.

"I don't see how you can be so dispassionate," I told him, raising my voice now. "Your marriage might not have worked out but there was a time in your life when, presumably, you loved her. You promised to spend your life with her, after all, before you reneged on that and promised to spend it with someone else instead. And then someone else. And now someone else again."

Caden said nothing. He hated to fail at anything, which explained why he never liked to discuss his ex-wives with me. A few months earlier, he had at least had the good grace to look embarrassed when he informed me about his forthcoming nuptials. And, if I'm honest, I'd been considering skipping this wedding entirely and holding off until the next.

"Would you just think about a retirement village?" he asked eventually, steering the conversation back to where it had begun. "There are some wonderful places out there these days. Whole communities of older people living happily alongside each other. There are dances and days out and—"

"Funerals every Monday and Thursday with a good lunch afterward, I know. I may be an old woman, but that doesn't mean that I have to live like one. I'm in excellent health for someone my age and if I went to live in a nursing home—"

"A retirement village."

"I guarantee that I'd be dead within the year."

"Oh no, Mother," he replied, sounding as if he could think of worse outcomes. "You'll outlive us all."

"Well, if I stay in Winterville Court, I might have a fighting chance."

I looked toward his glass. There wasn't much left in it, and I hoped he wouldn't ask for another. I was tired and wanted to settle down in front of a film. I finished my own, hoping he would take the hint.

"Downstairs went for three even," he said eventually, and I frowned. "Mr. Richardson's flat," he clarified. "Three million quid."

"How do you know that?"

"I'm in the building trade, Mother. I have my sources."

"Do you know who's bought it?" I asked. To my disappointment, he shook his head.

"I don't know his name."

"A man then?"

"Well, no, I just assumed—"

"Why would you assume that?"

He rolled his eyes.

"Fine. I don't know the buyer's name, or sex," he said. "But whoever it is must be pretty well off to be able to afford three even."

"Could you find out?"

"Find out what?"

"Who they are."

"I could try," he said. "Why, has the neighborhood grapevine gone into decline? No one around to give the branch a good shake?"

"I'd just like to know, that's all," I told him. "They had an interior designer around a few days ago and now there are painters coming and going at all hours. I want to know what I'm in for. That's not unreasonable, is it?"

"Have you asked the tradespeople?"

"Yes."

"And?"

"They know nothing. Or, if they do, they're not saying."

"You've tried offering them money?"

"Of course. But they're incorruptible."

"All right."

"So just see what you can find out, will you?" I asked.

I stood up now and he took the hint, draining the last of the whisky and rising to his feet before putting a hand to the base of his spine and groaning again. It felt strange to have a son who was showing these signs of old age. His father had enjoyed rude health throughout his life and maintained a slim figure until his passing. I walked Caden to the door and he kissed me on the cheek as he stepped outside.

"Have a think, that's all I ask," he said, turning back to me. "Three point one is—"

"A lot of money. I know. You said."

The door on the other side of the hallway opened and Heidi Hargrave looked out. By the condition of her hair, I could tell that she was not having one of her good days.

"You've grown fat," she said, pointing at Caden's stomach. "Fat as a fool."

And with that, she disappeared back inside, leaving my son and me to stare at each other. There was really nothing more to say.

EIGHT

The haberdashery store opened every morning at ten o'clock but I waited until noon, when M. Vannier disappeared for his regular two-hour lunch, before going downstairs and crossing the street.

Through the front window, which housed a pair of mannequins dressed in tired, pre-war tweed, I saw that the shop was quiet for this time of day. The boy was standing behind the counter, wrapping a shirt for a portly middle-aged man who was leering at him in a suggestive fashion. As he completed his task, the man removed a card from his pocket and handed it across. The boy stared at it for a moment, uncertain what was being asked of him, until the man leaned forward, his stomach pressing against the woodwork, and whispered something in his ear that caused him to frown and shake his head. Was it an invitation to a rendezvous? I wondered. If so, it was clear from the boy's expression that he was not inclined to accept. The man, shameless and nonchalant, simply shrugged his shoulders before placing his purchase beneath his arm and leaving the store.

I waited a few moments before going inside. It was my first time in the Vanniers' emporium and I was taken by the pleasant scent in the air, a fresh blend of sandalwood and lime. I imagined the boy spraying the fragrance around the shop each morning before unlocking the doors.

He looked up as my shoes sounded across the hardwood floor and seemed surprised to see a girl of my age on the premises but did not look away. Indeed, his gaze lingered longer than necessary.

"Can I help you, mademoiselle?" he asked, and I strode toward him, assuming an air of confidence.

"Buttons," I told him, the word sounding louder than I had intended. "I need some buttons. Have I come to the right place?"

He nodded and reached beneath the counter, using both hands to extract an enormous wooden box that he placed between us. When he lifted the lid, I let out an involuntary cry of delight. There must have been a thousand buttons within, all different shapes, sizes, and colors, the collection sparkling as the light from the lamps bounced off their glassy edges.

"Finding matching ones, that's the problem," he said. "But if you see one that you like, let me know and I'll help you find some more."

I plunged my hands deep inside the box. The sensation was wonderful, the buttons cool and hard against my skin, and as my fingers moved, so did they, like tiny sea creatures that my touch had brought to life.

"I do that sometimes too," the boy admitted, smiling. "It feels nice, doesn't it?"

"It does."

"I find it relaxing. Sometimes, when I'm annoyed or upset, I—"

He broke off, looking a little embarrassed.

"No, it is relaxing," I agreed. "I can see why you might. I'm Gretel, by the way. Gretel Guéymard." He blushed, inexplicably, when I told him my name, the color that came into his cheeks in stark contrast to the golden tumble of his hair.

"Émile Vannier," he said.

"*Emil and the Detectives*," I said, the jacket of the children's book appearing in my mind, for it had been a favorite of my brother's when we lived in that other place.

"But Émile with an e," he clarified. "At the end, I mean. Well, at the start too. Both ends." He was growing flustered now.

"You know the book then?"

"I read it when I was younger. Before Papa threw it away."

"Why did he do that?" I asked, surprised.

"Can't you guess?"

I thought about it. It did not take long.

"Because he won't allow books by German authors in the house," I said, and when he nodded, I grew anxious. I had worked hard to disguise my accent since arriving in Paris and, while I had done a good job of it, inflections from my past occasionally burst through to threaten my safety, as it had done with the boy in le Jardin du Luxembourg. The language itself had come easily enough, though. Mother, believing it to be the language of sophisticates, had insisted that my brother and I learn French from a young age, and Herr Liszt had continued those lessons when we lived in that other place.

"The war is over. We must put these things behind us," I said, hoping that he'd agree. Not that I truly felt this to be true. For me, the war lingered on, my own sense of culpability for the things that had taken place never far from my mind. His tie was hanging a little askew and, beneath the fabric, the second button of his shirt had come undone. I could see a whisper of skin beneath it and, from somewhere deep inside my body, a sigh emerged. I wanted to touch him. I had never touched a boy in a sensual way.

"In time, perhaps," he said. "But not yet, I don't think. The guilty must be punished."

He made his way toward a display of gentlemen's braces, which he proceeded to re-arrange carefully, while I continued to fish among the buttons, uncertain how to get him to show more interest in me. This was a new game to me and I was not yet skilled in it. My only previous attempts at seduction—with Kurt, when I was just a girl, and my attempts at flirting with M. Toussaint—had both ended badly.

"I've seen you, you know," I said finally, walking over to him, and he looked up again.

"Seen me?"

"From my window." I nodded toward the street, then pointed to the upstairs window of our lodgings. "That's my bedroom up there. I've noticed you coming and going. You fall over a lot."

"Papa calls me clumsy. My awkwardness annoys him. But I wasn't born to work in a shop."

"What were you born to do?"

He shrugged. He clearly hadn't thought this far ahead. "I don't know yet," he said. "I'm only sixteen."

"I'll be sixteen soon," I told him. "In a few weeks, in fact."

He looked at me with more interest now, the tip of his tongue emerging to press against his upper lip. I wondered whether he had ever kissed a girl and thought not. There was an innocence to him, but I guessed that, like a chained dog, he longed to be unleashed.

"Perhaps we could do something together," I continued after a painful silence. "I haven't been in Paris long and don't know many people here. No one of my own age anyway."

"And where were you before here?" he asked.

"Nantes," I replied.

"Then you'll know Mme. Aubertin," he said. "The dressmaker. She was a friend of my late mother's. She used to have a shop there before I was born."

I hesitated, knowing neither the woman nor the city and concerned that this might be a test of some sort.

"I'm afraid our finances have not allowed me to visit any dressmakers in recent years," I replied, avoiding a definitive answer. "But are there places that you go, Émile? When you're not working, I mean."

"There's a coffee shop that I like," he said. "I go there to read."

"To read German authors? Or are you too obedient to your father?"

"Sometimes I sneak them in," he admitted, then took a deep breath, as I waited for the invitation. "I could show it to you sometime, if you like," he said, and it seemed to take all his effort to make the offer. "The coffee shop, I mean. It's not far from here. They sell excellent pastries too."

"I'd like that," I said. "Perhaps tomorrow evening?"

"All right." He nodded. "I finish at four o'clock."

"I'll meet you by the front door."

Audacious, risking everything, I leaned forward and placed my lips against his cheek. His skin was soft and his body held the intoxicating scent of boy. When I stepped back and observed him, he seemed astonished by my brazenness, but also pleased. There was an unmistakable hunger in his eyes.

I turned away, however, smiling, then raising a hand above my head to wave as I made for the door. I had seen Marlene Dietrich perform this gesture in a film once and admired it.

"Until tomorrow then," I called out.

"But Gretel," he called after me. "Your buttons?"

"Don't be silly," I replied, laughing. "You don't really think I came in for them, do you?"

NINE

And then, at last, Madelyn appeared.

It was a Tuesday morning, perhaps a week since Caden's visit, and the previous day, the tradespeople and decorators had finished their work before lunchtime, returning Winterville Court to its usual state of calm at last. When I woke, an unusual acoustic in the air suggested there was at least one person downstairs who was new to our milieu. Having lived in the same place for so long, one becomes attuned to even the slightest variation in the atmosphere.

A few hours later, sitting in my living room, I tried to concentrate on Marie Antoinette but found my attention diverted to what might be going on twenty feet below me. I expected the sound of furniture being pushed a little this way or that, or the faint echo of music playing as cups, glasses, and crockery were put away. Doors opening and closing as the new occupants rearranged the rooms to their taste.

Finally, my curiosity at breaking point, I accepted that I would not be able to relax until I had seen their faces for myself and so, brushing my hair and applying a little scent to my wrists and neck, I placed some scones that I'd baked that morning on a plate and made my way down the staircase before knocking on the door of Flat One.

There was silence for a few moments, then the sound of bare feet padding across wooden floors.

"Good afternoon," I said, smiling at the woman who stood before me. "I'm Gretel Fernsby, your upstairs neighbor. I wanted to introduce myself. And to bring you these."

I held out the plate with both hands, like a religious offering, and the woman stared at it with a puzzled expression on her face. I felt as if I could read her thoughts, that she knew she should accept these scones but, having no idea where they had come from, what had gone into them, or how many calories they contained, she would have no choice but to throw them away later in the day, uneaten.

My new neighbor was in her early thirties, I guessed, quite tall, with striking features, and she carried her thick blonde hair in a sort of Dusty Springfield beehive that seemed simultaneously both out of step with the times and peculiarly fashionable. She had pale blue eyes, the left with a hint of green, long fingers of the kind a pianist might welcome, and the sort of slim, boyish figure that men seem to prize these days. She could have been a model, I thought. Perhaps she *was* a model. Even today, moving into her new home, she was dressed as if she was expecting to be photographed from several different angles.

"Oh," she said finally, taking the plate and looking past me as if hoping that there might be a carer lurking somewhere in the background ready to shuffle me back upstairs and settle me into a chair in front of daytime television. "How very kind of you."

"It was nothing, really."

We stared at each other. I determined to wait her out.

"Would you like to come in?" she asked eventually, conceding to manners.

"Thank you," I said—I was already halfway over the doorstep anyway—"I won't keep you, I'm sure you're very busy. I just wanted to say hello."

She closed the door behind me and I glanced around, taking everything in. Alison Small had done a fine job of turning Mr. Richardson's rather shabby flat into something that, as Caden might have said, looked every penny of three million quid. The furniture appeared deeply uncomfortable to sit in, but I knew this was the contemporary style, and it was distinctive in its way. It seemed not so much a home that one might live in as an apartment that might be featured in magazines or Sunday supplements, giving people unreasonable expectations as to what they might be able to afford if they simply buckled down and worked harder. I would have liked to spend a half-hour wandering around to see what other treasures might be on display but expected that I would get no further than the living room.

"Mrs. . . . Fernsby, was it?" said the woman, standing behind me, and I turned around to shake her hand as she placed the scones on a side table out of sight.

"Gretel, please," I insisted. "And you are?"

"Madelyn," she said. "Madelyn Darcy-Witt."

I nodded but felt inexplicably irritated by her reply. Not being English myself, I have a curious antagonism to names that sound as if they have emerged, fully formed, from the pages of Debrett's. She offered me a seat and I took it, again promising that I would not stay long, and to my surprise, the sofa, which looked as if it was made from granite, proved comfortable.

"Exquisite, isn't it?" she said, taking the armchair opposite me. By her sitting down, I assumed that I was not going to be offered tea. "The sofa is by Signorini and Coco. This chair is by Dom Edizioni."

"Mine is by John Lewis," I said, hoping this would make her smile, but it didn't. It wasn't by John Lewis anyway; Edgar, who liked nice things, had commissioned our furniture over the years from a company in Brighton and it had never seen us wrong.

"Of course," she said, and I wasn't quite sure what she meant by this.

"It looked uncomfortable," I said, caressing the sofa now as if it were a cat that might purr beneath my touch. "And yet it's anything but, isn't it?"

"It's deceitful," said Madelyn in a rather vicious tone, as if she and the sofa had suffered a falling-out and were only tentatively reconciled.

"Indeed," I replied. Looking around, I took in the small *objets d'art* that she must have been arranging on the shelves when I arrived. There were some framed pictures lying face down on an occasional table; I longed to see the images they contained. "You really get the light in here at this time of day," I added, for the sun was pouring in through the bay windows at the front, illuminating the room in a golden hue. I glanced up at the ceiling. I'd long grown accustomed to them, of course, but the extraordinary height of the flats in Winterville Court could not be faulted. A new chandelier hanging from the ceiling blinked at me, as if woken from slumber. Although there was no breeze, for no window was open, one or two of the prisms and crystal chains stirred like will-o'-the-wisps, as if to warn me off.

"Light is so important to me," replied Madelyn dreamily. "It was the first thing I mentioned to the estate agent. Light and height. When I was a child, my mother kept the curtains closed throughout the day to avoid bleaching the furniture and it drove me scatty. My friends would come to visit and say, 'Madelyn, why is it so dark in here? Why is it always so *dark*?' Then they stopped coming altogether. My mother was a nice woman, I should say. It's just that she never lived up to her true potential and was too concerned about other people's opinions." She paused for a moment, as if lost in a shameful memory. "My father was unkind to her, you see. His father was unkind to his mother too, and his to his, and so on. It's generational, don't you think?"

"I don't know," I said, a little embarrassed that she should be revealing so much when we'd only introduced ourselves a few minutes earlier. "Many people grow up to be utterly unlike their parents."

"Everyone likes to think that," she replied with certainty, shaking her head. "But underneath, we're all pale imitations."

I said nothing. I thought of my own parents. I was nothing like them, I told myself. I could never have done what they did. This woman, this strange woman, was talking utter nonsense. Perhaps she was mad, I thought.

"Have you lived here long?" asked Madelyn, and I nodded.

"Since 1960," I said.

She burst out laughing and I stared at her.

"Oh, I'm sorry," she said quickly, putting a hand to her mouth. "I thought you were joking."

"It's not *that* very long ago in the great scheme of things," I told her.

"You'll have to forgive me," she said. "I have a habit of laughing at inappropriate times. Only last week a friend of mine told me that her dog had been run over by an articulated lorry, and I was on the floor."

I wondered whether I should call a doctor and have her committed.

"I'm sorry," she repeated, frowning now and looking down at her feet as if realizing that she had committed a social transgression. "I don't know why I—"

"My late husband bought our flat about six years after we married," I continued, as if nothing untoward had been said at all. "He died . . . oh, almost fourteen years ago now."

"And you've lived alone ever since?"

"I have, yes."

"Sixty-two years," she said, tapping her index finger against her lower lip. "That's a long time to stay in one place."

"Not if you have a good reason to be there," I said.

"And do you?" she asked. "Do you have a good reason?"

"I do," I replied, and stared at her, challenging her to ask me what it was. Naturally, I never would have told her, but I enjoyed the unsettling nature of the moment. I hadn't liked the way she'd said that it was "a long time to stay in one place," as if she judged me unambitious or lacking in curiosity. That would have been unfair, for Edgar and I had traveled extensively during our marriage, visiting all the continents, save Africa, which was on our list before he passed away.

"Well, I'm glad to hear it," she said. "I doubt I'll be here as long, though."

"Possibly not, but you'll be here after I'm gone, I'm sure," I said, laughing a little, and she shook her head, leaned forward and took my hand in hers, telling me that I must not say such a thing, that I must never say such a thing.

"But I have been happy here," I told her, taking my hand back. "This is a wonderful building. The residents keep mostly to themselves but there's a consideration too. If you were in any difficulty, for example, then you could knock on any door."

"Quiet is important to me," she said, and I noticed that she swallowed nervously as she said this, looking around as if she was expecting some loud bang to disturb her serenity. "Honestly, Gretel, I would have preferred to move to the country, with lots of open space and only the sound of mooing cows for company, but Alex insisted. He has to be in town for work, you see. I don't work. I did, of course, once. But I don't anymore. I'd like to, again, someday, perhaps."

It felt as if she was justifying a position that I had not asked her to defend. Naturally, I picked up on the name instantly.

"Alex," I said. "And he is . . . ?"

"My husband."

So. There was a husband. She was not alone.

T·E·N

I waited until I saw Émile emerge from the haberdashery store before making my way downstairs and stepping out onto the street.
When he caught sight of me, he offered an awkward bow and his
thick, dark hair, which was brushed away from his forehead and held
in place by pomade, tumbled into his eyes. He swept it back with his
fingers and smiled.

"You look handsome," I said, for he did, and he blushed a little,
then repeated my words back to me before correcting himself.

"Beautiful, I mean," he said. "You look very beautiful."

Through the window, I became conscious of M. Vannier's hostile
gaze, which combined an unsettling mixture of concern and contempt. Was he so protective of his son, I wondered, that he could not
bear to see him taking up with a girl? Our eyes met and I expected
the man to turn away, but no, he held my stare and only when it
became too much to sustain did I concede defeat. In that other place
where I had lived, no man would have dared even to look in my direction, let alone with such an attitude of scorn.

Once inside the café, it was easy to see why Émile felt so comfortable there. Most Parisian teashops had retained an air of tense
austerity since the end of the war but this one had a sense of the

bohemian about it, as if it were deliberately reverting to the atmosphere before hostilities began. At least half the tables were filled with good-looking young men reading books, smoking or flirting with pretty girls. We took a seat in the corner, by a window, ordered coffee and pastries and, recognizing Émile's bashfulness, I took the lead in the conversation, asking whether he enjoyed working in his father's shop.

"I haven't given the matter much thought," he said. "But it will be mine one day, so I need to learn the business. Otherwise, it will fail, and so will I."

"You don't intend to work there forever, surely?" I asked.

"I expect so."

I considered this. Did I want to live out my days above a haberdashery store? I thought not.

"But you're too young to make such irrevocable plans," I told him. "Wouldn't you like to travel? To see the world? There's life beyond these streets, you know."

"I could never disappoint my father," he said.

"Why not? Fathers disappoint us all the time."

"The truth is," he continued, "the shop was meant to go to Louis. He was older than me by four years and Papa always intended that he would inherit."

"You have a brother then?"

"I did. But not anymore. He's dead. The war, of course."

I should have expected this reply. I glanced out of the window and sipped my coffee, allowing a respectful silence to mark the boy's memory. The pangs of grief for my own lost brother simmered within. I closed my eyes for a moment, pushing them away to a place where they could not hurt me.

"He fought with the Resistance," he said, sitting up straight now, as if to ensure that he did not show any disrespect to this sacred organization. "He killed his first German on the day the Nazi tanks rolled into Paris. Afterward, he helped to organize a chapter here in the *quatrième* and was captured twice and tortured before making his escape. He remained loyal to the end, however, never revealing names, no matter what they did to him."

"And what did they do to him?" I asked, but he shook his head, unable to say. Tears pooled in his eyes and he wiped them away with a handkerchief.

"Terrible things," he said at last, the words catching in his throat. "After they shot him, they threw his body into the street for the dogs to fight over. Soldiers stood guard with guns so we could not intervene. It was a week before we were allowed to take what remained of him and give him a decent burial. I wish I had been older. Then I could have fought too. I would have killed every last one of them. I would have stuck my knife into every German soldier's neck and dragged it slowly across."

"I'm not sure any cause is worth giving your life for," I said, disturbed by the brutality of his words.

"Of course it is," he insisted.

We sat silently for a few moments.

Finally, I reached across and placed my hand on top of his.

"I'm just glad that you're alive," I said.

"Sometimes I'm not sure that I am."

"You are," I said, squeezing his fingers now. "I can feel you. And it's over now. The war, I mean. You mustn't keep thinking about it."

"It isn't over," he replied, taking his hand back. "It won't end for many years yet. The newspaper articles, they're shocking. Have you read them? The things they're saying?"

"I avoid them," I said. "I refuse to live in the past."

"It can't be true, I don't think," he continued, frowning, his face lost in despair. "What they say about these camps, about the things that went on there." He paused and seemed at a loss for words. "It can't be true," he repeated. "Who could ever imagine such things? Who could ever create such places? Run them, work in them, kill so many people? How can there be such a collective lack of conscience?"

I pushed my chair back, the metal scraping against the tiles, and excused myself, making my way toward the bathroom while avoiding the eyes of the young men who looked me up and down. Safely inside, I locked the door and placed both hands upon the marble sink, staring at my reflection in the mirror. I found myself struggling to breathe and loosened the belt around my dress and the collar at my neck.

Examining my face, I saw Father's shadow there, his unsympathetic expression, his determination to remain true to the things he had spent his adult life believing. A memory came to me. I was standing outside his office, eavesdropping on a conversation that he was having with my brother, who wanted to know who those people we saw every day from our windows were. The ones on the other side of the fence.

"Those people," Father said, sounding almost amused by the question, "well, they're not people at all."

My brother was unsatisfied with this answer and, later, he asked me. I told him it was a farm. I said it was a place where animals were kept.

I closed my eyes now and threw some water on my face, drying it off with a dirty towel. I had hoped to continue my seduction, but the conversation had taken a turn I was not enjoying. For the first time, I fully understood that I would have to lie about everything, every day, for the rest of my life, if I was to survive.

When I returned to our table, Émile had decided to turn to more cheerful subjects, recounting stories about some of the more eccentric characters who frequented the shop. He made me laugh and so I

invented things to entertain him too, strange people I had encountered on the street, a dog walking on its hind legs, a set of twins who
finished each other's sentences. I was from Nantes, I lied. My father
had died when I was just a child, I lied. My mother had been a seamstress in the town, I lied. We had only come to Paris because she felt
she was too young to live out her days in the place where she was
born, I lied. I had left three close friends behind me, Suzanne, Adèle,
and Arlette, but they wrote regularly, I lied. I had left my cat, Lu-
cille, in the care of Arlette and she had been pining for me ever since
my departure, I lied.

Now it was his turn to reach a hand across the table, and he
pressed his fingers against each of mine. His touch excited me.

"When you kissed me the other day," he began, looking down at
the table, his face coloring a little.

"It was forward of me, I know," I said.

"But I was glad of it."

He glanced around to make sure that we were not being observed
before leaning forward across the table and kissing me again. This
time, on the lips. When we separated, he seemed lost in thought.

"Shameless," he said, and I expected him to laugh, but no, he
looked at me without any affection at all. It was almost as if he re-
viled me. Was this how boys felt toward the girls they kissed? I wondered. That they wanted us but despised us the very moment that
desire was reciprocated.

"And you have no brothers or sisters?" Émile asked as we returned home along quai Voltaire a little later, glancing across the
bridges to where the Jardin stood on the other side.

"No," I said.

"Then you're lucky," he said. "To lose a parent, well, that's the
nature of life. We've both experienced it and survived. But to lose a

brother? This is a thing that will haunt me forever. You are fortunate not to have suffered such a loss."

Walking toward us was a mime artist who seemed to have finished his work for the day, for while he wore the traditional black-and-white striped top, the dark beret, a pair of braces and had a face covered in white makeup, he was smoking a cigarette and appeared furious with his diminished place in the world. Passing me, he flicked the cigarette away so it landed before my feet and threw me a look of utter contempt, as if he might be silent to the world but he knew exactly how many lies I had told that day.

ELEVEN

You have a husband," I said, more to hear the words spoken aloud than anything else. "How nice. And have you been married long?"

"Eleven years," she replied, and, for some reason, her tongue pressed against her cheek when she said this and her expression changed, as if she could scarcely believe that it had been so long herself. "Yes," she continued after a moment. "Eleven years now."

"Good Lord! But you're so young!"

"Oh no, I'm ancient," she replied. "I'll be thirty-two next month. Of course, I married very young," she conceded. "Alex was ready to settle down—he's ten years older than me—and he says that I just happened to be the lucky girl he was dating at the time." She burst out laughing as if this were somehow humorous. "Don't you think that's funny?" she asked.

"Not particularly," I said. "Does he mean it as a joke?"

"Oh no," she replied, frowning. "No, my husband doesn't joke."

"And do you mind if I ask what he does?"

"He's a film producer," she said.

"Oh, how exciting!"

"I suppose. Well, people generally think it is anyway."

"What kind of films does he make?"

"All sorts."

She listed half a dozen and, although I rarely go to the cinema these days, I had heard of some of them. They were the kind of films that attracted big stars and won awards. I searched my brain for his name. Alex Darcy-Witt. Had I heard it before? I didn't think I had. But then, as most directors are anonymous to the public, producers are hardly likely to get a look-in.

"I'm very rude," I said after a moment. "Asking what your husband does and not asking about your life first. You said that you used to work. What was it you did?"

"I was an actress," she replied. "That's how I met my husband. I was in one of his films. He made his interest obvious early on and I found him hard to resist. I was terribly innocent at the time, I should add. Terribly naïve. Would you believe that I was a virgin? Well, not really, but close enough."

I was uncertain how to respond to such an intimate revelation.

"Still, eleven years," I said, avoiding her question, which I hoped was rhetorical. "That's a long time by current standards. Clearly it was meant to be."

She frowned, then bowed her head.

"I should go," I continued, placing my hands on my knees and preparing to stand, but to my surprise, she shook her head.

"No, don't go yet," she said. "If you go, I'll have to keep on opening boxes and putting things away and, quite honestly, I haven't the energy."

"All right," I said, happy to stay a little longer. I hoped she might offer tea, but hospitality seemed to be unforthcoming.

"You're not English, are you?" she asked, and I felt my body stiffen a little. It had been many decades since someone had asked me this. I'd lived in London for so long that I imagined I spoke no differently to anyone else here.

"How did you know?" I asked.

"When I was acting," she told me. "When I was at acting school, I mean, I did a lot of work with accents. My teachers said that I had a gift for them. I find now that I can identify something at the back of people's voices, something that gives away their past. There's a hint of Central European in your speech. If I had to guess, I would say German."

I smiled at her. She intrigued me. "You're right," I said. "In fact, I was born in Berlin."

"I love Berlin," she said enthusiastically. "I played Sally Bowles there once. The perfect city for it."

"Indeed."

"People said I was very good," she added, and, for the first time, I wondered whether she might be taking some form of medication. It was as if she drifted away with her thoughts and became introspective, forgetting that she had company.

"My late husband and I went to the theater a lot," I said, and Madelyn startled in her chair. "More than we ever went to the cinema. I prefer the theater, don't you?"

"Don't say that to my husband. He'd have you taken out and shot."

"People are better behaved in the theater, I find. They don't arrive laden down with food and drinks as if there's a possibility that they might die of starvation or dehydration before the curtain call."

"I would have liked to have stayed working in the theater," she replied. "But my husband insisted that I concentrate on film. Not that it got me anywhere in the long run."

"You've stopped acting then?" I asked.

"Something like that," she replied, an answer that was not an answer at all.

"Would you like to go back to it?"

She looked across at me, as if surprised even to see me there. "That wouldn't be possible," she said. "It's too late. I'm too old."

I burst out laughing. "You're thirty-one," I said. "You're a child! These days, people don't seem to settle on anything until they're closer to forty."

"No," she said. "No, it wouldn't be possible. How did he die? Your husband, I mean."

I stared at her. It was the most extraordinary change of subject, worthy of Heidi Hargrave.

"He suffered terribly from asthma," I told her. "He was hospitalized for it several times. Then, in 2008, during hay-fever season, we came back from a walk in Hyde Park, and he sat down to read, but the moment he picked up his book he started sneezing. It went on and on and I made a joke of it at first, but then it became obvious that he was struggling to breathe. I fetched his Ventolin, but it did no good. He started to choke. His lungs became filled with fluid, you see. I called an ambulance. They were here within minutes but couldn't revive him. He died in the living room. Between arriving home from our walk and the ambulance taking his body away, no more than twenty minutes must have passed. But within that time, my entire life changed." I paused and looked down at the floor. "And that was that," I said. "Such is life. Such is death."

"I'm sorry," she said, and she meant it too. She was staring right at me, as if she were examining my features for any trace of a lie. I wondered whether it was something she had learned in acting school. "Did you love him?"

"Of course I loved him," I snapped, shocked by the rudeness of the question. I had been there long enough now. I wanted to leave.

"Of course I loved him," I repeated, raising my voice, angered by any suggestion to the contrary. "He was my husband."

"I'm sorry, I didn't mean anything by that."

I controlled my temper. She looked drained, the poor creature.

"No, I'm sorry," I said. "Anyway, I'm sure you want to get on. You don't want to listen to anymore of my stories."

I stood up, determined to leave this time, even if she begged me to stay, but she seemed content for me to go. She walked me to the door.

"And your husband," I said. "He'll be joining you this evening?"

"No, he's in LA," she said. "He won't be back for another week."

"Then you're all on your own," I replied. "Well, it will give you a chance to get settled in. That can be nice in itself."

I waited, knowing that I would finally have my answer. Actually, I knew it the moment she shook her head.

"I won't be alone," she said. "My son will be here later."

"Your son," I repeated quietly.

"Yes. Henry. He's just started in his new school today." She glanced at her watch. "He'll be home around three thirty."

I nodded. A boy. "How old is he?" I asked as she held the door open and I stepped back out into the lobby.

"He's nine," she replied. "It was so nice to meet you, Gretel," she said. "I hope we become friends."

"I hope so too," I said as she closed the door, but then I realized that no, I hadn't said that at all, I had simply thought it. I hadn't been able to get the words out. I wondered whether this was how Edgar had felt, in those final moments of his life, knowing that he had to breathe in order to live but finding himself incapable of letting any air into his lungs. The panic. The dread. The fear of what was to come.

TWELVE

When Mother announced that M. Toussaint had proposed an afternoon's punting along the Seine, I was surprised to be included in the invitation.

"Are you sure he meant both of us?" I asked.

"Perfectly sure," she told me, sitting before the mirror and applying powder to her face before brushing her hair. Mother always maintained that a woman's hair was her most important characteristic, more than just an accoutrement, indeed the first indication of her femininity. "He's eager to meet you. He claims that he's heard me speak of you so often that it's as if he already knows you."

Naturally, this remark surprised me. So M. Toussaint had not revealed that we had already become acquainted, our paths having crossed at the place des Vosges some weeks earlier. But then, nor had I.

"It looks too cold for punting," I said, rising now and opening the curtains, for I felt instinctively that I did not want to take part in this outing. I looked down toward the street and M. Vannier's haberdashery and was surprised to see Émile looking up at me, as if he'd been waiting for me to appear. I waved, but he turned away, disappearing back into the shadows of the shop. Had he not noticed me standing there? I wondered.

"Nonsense," said Mother. "The sun is out. There's a slight chill, yes, but we'll dress warmly. Come along, Gretel, have a bath and get dressed. I don't want to keep Rémy waiting."

As I washed, I wondered what the purpose of this trip might be. Was it possible that M. Toussaint wanted to get to know me so he could decide whether to propose marriage to Mother? After all, it would be one thing to take her into his home but another thing entirely to welcome a dependent child.

Later, while dressing, I asked Mother what she thought M. Toussaint's intentions were toward her, and her face lit up with hope, recalling for a moment the woman she had once been. The Mother of Berlin, the Mother I had loved, the Mother who had cared for my brother and me and promised that no harm would ever come to either of us.

"I think," she began, then closed her eyes for a moment, correcting herself. "I *hope* that he means to marry me."

"Has he spoken of it?"

"Not in so many words, no. But I believe we have formed an understanding. We have so many interests in common and . . ." She hesitated. "Well, you're old enough now to understand that we have become lovers. And I feel that we are *simpatico*."

I blushed a little, turning around as I fastened my shoes, not wanting to betray my innocence. Sensing my embarrassment, Mother stood up and came over to the bed, sitting next to me. It was as if I was a child again and needed comforting.

"You must understand, Gretel," she said quietly. "There has never been any man in my life other than your father. None before and none since. Until now, that is. I wouldn't want you to think poorly of me. I may have made mistakes in the past, but my virtue has never been in question."

I turned to look at her and recognized the humility in her face, but still, it amazed me that of all the things we had been through she would think the matter of whether she had taken lovers would be the thing that would shatter my faith in her.

"When we were there," I said. "In that other place."

"Yes?"

"Lieutenant Kotler?"

Now it was her turn to blush. She looked away, unable to meet my eye.

"Kurt was just a boy," she said. "Handsome, of course, but just a boy."

"So there was no dalliance?"

My brother had suspected one, he had whispered of it to me, and when he had, I had wanted to hurt him for even suggesting it. I had wanted to punish him. I *did* punish him.

"As I said," she replied. "He was just a boy."

I remained silent. This was no answer.

"I loved your father very much," she continued. "I didn't want him to accept that position. In fact, I begged him not to."

"No, you were excited about it," I protested. "The party we held. Before we left Berlin. You were—"

"I put on a good show," she replied. "Remember who was there. So many important figures. I couldn't possibly have put my doubts on display. It would have been disastrous for all of us, for your father especially."

"Still," I said, standing up and walking toward the mirror, where I examined myself from head to toe. I looked fine, but there was a glow missing from my face, for I was apprehensive about what lay ahead. "You agreed to it. And you brought us there. Me and—"

"Don't," she said, her voice low, almost breaking in grief. "Don't, Gretel," she implored. "Don't say his name."

I sat down next to her once again.

"I'm sorry," I said, taking her hand.

"I can't have his name spoken."

"I know."

"I'm afraid, you see," she said, turning to me now, and there were tears in her eyes. "I'm afraid for me, for you, for our future. Yes, we have some money, but how long will it last? Another year at most? And then what? What will become of us?"

"We could get jobs," I said, as if it were the most obvious thing in the world.

"I wasn't brought up to work," she said, shaking her head. "I have no skills, that's the truth of it. No, if I am to survive, then I need to marry again. Rémy is wealthy. He has a good position. He will take care of us."

"We could take care of ourselves," I suggested. "I could educate myself, find a career, make my own money."

"No, you will need to marry too," she said in a determined voice. "Not yet, of course. But in a few years' time, when you're nineteen or twenty, we will find a good match for you. With M. Toussaint's support, the young men will flock to you." She took my hand and gripped it tightly. "A friend told me that she saw you walking with the boy who works in the shop across the road," she said. "I hope she was wrong?"

"He doesn't just work there," I protested. "He's the son of the owner. It will be his one day."

"He is not suitable," she replied, rising and taking the key to the front door from the side table. "He's pleasant to look at, I will admit, but I don't envision your future as a shop girl. Flirt with him, if you must—I know the days can be tedious here and you find yourself idle and friendless—but no more than that. Is that understood? You must not allow your reputation to be compromised. Do all you can to impress today," she continued, holding me by both shoulders and looking me directly in the eye. "Be amusing and conversational, but do not dominate. Laugh at his jokes and compliment him on his skill with the pole. Ask no personal questions but be open if he asks some of you."

"How open?" I asked her. "How much does he know, after all?"

"He knows what I have told him."

"That we come from Nantes."

"Exactly."

"And, should you marry, are we to maintain this fiction for the rest of our lives?"

She turned away. "It's no longer a fiction, Gretel. Tell a story often enough and it becomes the truth."

Her accent slipped a little as she spoke, the French giving way to the German, and she heard it, continuing with more conviction.

"This is not just about money, you understand that, don't you?" she asked me.

"Then what is it about?" I asked, for if it were not this, then I was at a loss to understand what the point of it all was.

"It's about staying alive," she told me. "One slip, just one tiny slip, Gretel, and that might be it for both of us. Remember that. These people are unforgiving."

"Does that surprise you?" I asked.

"What?" she replied, frowning.

I laughed bitterly. "I mean, do you honestly think either of us deserves forgiveness?"

She stared at me. I was not privy to the workings of her mind and wondered whether she felt as much guilt as I did. I know she shared the grief. When she spoke again, her tone was low and insistent.

"I deserve happiness," she said. "I did nothing wrong. And neither did you."

We made our way down the staircase, and I observed our landlady seated in her armchair. In her hands was a copy of the new newspaper, *Le Monde*. She turned the pages, and, for a brief moment, I saw a word in a large font spread across the front page. I had heard Father use this word with Kurt on several occasions and could recall him visiting the place at least twice.

Sobibór.

So, I told myself as we stepped out onto the street. They are writing about all the death camps now, big and small. What a world we had created, families like mine.

THIRTEEN

I was about to hail a cab outside Fortnum & Mason when I heard a voice calling my name. I looked back in surprise, but Piccadilly was rather busy and I could see no one I knew until I noticed a man approaching in great haste. I froze, fearing that I was about to be mugged in broad daylight. Or worse, that I had been recognized. Such a thing had never happened across more than seven decades, but it was an idea that haunted me. The idea of passing an elderly person in the street and having them stare in horror before pointing a finger and denouncing me.

"Mrs. Fernsby!"

The man slowed down as he got closer, bending over a little with his hands on his hips to recover his breath, and I realized that I did, in fact, know him.

"Oberon," I said, for it was Heidi's grandson, he of the Shakespearean name. "You gave me a fright! Where did you spring from?"

"I was on my way to see Granny," he explained, "and then I saw you coming out of the store. Can I help you with your bags?"

"I was looking for a taxi," I told him. "But if you're happy to carry them, then we could walk?"

"Of course."

I handed my shopping over gratefully and we continued along together. Our paths hadn't crossed in some months but I was always glad to see him. He had what I believe are called "movie star good looks," and charm to equal them.

"How are you?" I asked as we strolled through the side streets.

"Quite well," he said. "Busy. Did Granny tell you my news?"

I cast my mind back to the conversation I'd had with Heidi where we'd speculated that he might be about to marry. I had forgotten to ask her, since then, whether we had been right.

"And what news might that be?" I asked.

"I'm moving to Australia," he said.

I took a deep breath before saying anything. I had been to that continent myself, once, and had I never set foot in a certain pub on Sydney's Circular Quay, I might have lived out my days there. But my stay had ended badly and, in the decades between then and now, whenever I'd seen the city on the television I'd immediately changed the channel. I didn't want to be reminded of it. Or of him. He was probably dead by now, but still.

"Are you indeed?" I asked. "And what's brought this on?"

"I've always fancied it, if I'm honest," he explained. "I did my gap year there and have been back a couple of times since. I like the people, the climate, the beaches. A job came up, quite a good job, in fact, as deputy manager of their biggest department store. I applied and, well, I got it."

"Congratulations," I said. "You must be very excited. Your grandmother will miss you, though. She's terribly fond of you."

He remained silent for a moment, as if lost in thought, and switched my carrier bags between his hands.

"How have you found her lately?" he asked.

"Reasonably alert," I said. "Is it just me or do there seem to be more good days than bad at the moment? I wonder whether her illness has . . . what's the word . . . plateaued? Perhaps it won't become as debilitating as we feared."

"Still," he said. "It's not as if she'll improve, is it? She'll either stay the same or decline."

"Yes, I suppose that's true," I said, disappointed by his pessimism. "Will you be able to come back to see her often? Australia is so far away."

"Well, that's one of the things I wanted to talk to you about."

I glanced at him, wondering whether we had met by chance at all, as I had assumed, or whether he'd been lying in wait for me. My routine was quite a regular one, after all.

"The thing is," he said, "I'd quite like to take Granny with me."

"To Australia?"

"Yes."

I burst out laughing. The idea of Heidi ascending the Sydney Harbour Bridge or rambling the beaches of Bondi struck me as absurd. She was almost seventy, after all, and moving to a strange country on the other side of the world, where even the bank notes would be alien to her, would only exacerbate her confusion.

"I'm serious," said Oberon, smiling.

"But is that a good idea?" I asked. "After all, everything she knows is here. She's never traveled far."

"All the more reason for her to see something of the world, don't you think?"

"If she were twenty years younger, perhaps," I replied, unconvinced.

"The thing is," he continued, "I was hoping that you might talk to her for me."

"Talk to her about what?"

"What I'd like to do, you see, is sell the flat—"

"Whose flat? Your flat?"

"No, her flat."

"I see."

"And for her to come with me when I leave. Come with us, I mean. My girlfriend's joining me. She's had enough of life here too. First Brexit, then the pandemic—"

"You know that she's lived in Flat Three her entire life, yes? Her adoptive parents brought her back there when she was a baby. That she's never lived anywhere else?"

"Of course. So she must be sick of it by now, right?" he asked, grinning, but I did not entertain the joke. I could see exactly where this conversation was going, and it irritated me. Did all these men just sit around waiting for the moment they could monetize the deaths of their parents or grandparents?

"Those flats are worth a fortune," he continued. "Well, you know that, of course. Caden's told you."

"Caden—" I began, but was unsure how to finish the thought. Had Caden and Oberon been speaking behind my back? Comparing notes about how profitable it would be if Heidi and I were out of the way?

"I'm looking at buying in Mosman, which is pretty expensive," he said. "It's on Sydney's North Shore, near—"

"I know where Mosman is," I said.

"You do?"

"I lived in Sydney," I told him. "A long time ago now. But I'm familiar with it."

"You're a dark horse."

"Darker than you know. But look, I just can't imagine Heidi living in a house so far away."

"Oh no, you misunderstand me," he said. "I wasn't thinking that she would move in with Lizzie and me. No, I've done some research and found the most fantastic retirement village nearby. She'd make lots of new friends, there are plenty of activities and, of course, the weather is—"

"The weather, the weather, the weather," I said, waving a hand in the air dismissively. I had always been irritated by English people's determination to bring every conversation back to this most tedious of subjects. "It's not the only important thing in life, you know."

"No, but—"

"And what does your grandmother think of this great plan?"

"She's not keen," he admitted.

"I should think not."

"Which is why I was hoping to get you on board."

"To what end?" I asked. "You're hoping that I might persuade her?"

"Surely you can see that it makes sense. If I'm going to be 17,000 kilometers away—"

"I don't do kilometers," I told him. "How much is that in real money?"

He thought about it. "Maybe 10,000 miles?"

"Fine. Continue."

"If I'm going to be 10,000 miles away, then it just makes sense that she should come with me. I'm the only family she's got, after all."

"Which could also be seen as a reason for you to stay."

"I can't, Mrs. Fernsby," he said, shaking his head. "It's a great opportunity for me. I need a new adventure. I'm too young to settle down in Selfridges and just play out every day, week after week, year after year, until I retire."

This was not unreasonable, and I nodded, relenting a little. We were approaching Winterville Court now and paused by the steps that led to the front door.

"I'm not trying to cheat her out of anything, if that's what you're worried about," said Oberon. "It's not like I want to sell the flat and pocket the money myself. Although I won't pretend that it wouldn't be useful to have some of my inheritance now, when I really need it. I would never abandon my grandmother. But I don't want to walk away from a chance like this on her account. I'm trying to figure out a way to make it work for all of us."

"When did you speak to Caden?" I asked.

"I'm sorry?"

"When did you speak to Caden?" I repeated. He'd heard me well enough the first time and was only playing for time.

"We *have* spoken," he admitted. "But more by chance than anything else. The two matters aren't related."

"What two matters?"

"My plans and . . ." He had the good grace to look somewhat embarrassed. "His own, I mean, your own plans for, you know, your flat."

I looked away, glancing toward the bay window that faced out onto the street and behind which, presumably, sat Madelyn Darcy-Witt. A small shadow appeared, darkening the curtain. The face of a child. A small boy. So, he was at home. I had yet to see him in the flesh but had heard his voice as he and his mother left or entered the building. He seemed like a quiet sort, and I wasn't sure if this was a good or a bad thing.

"So, will you talk to her?" asked Oberon, and I took my shopping from him now, my mind elsewhere.

"I will," I agreed. "But only to find out what she wants to do and where she'd prefer to live. I won't try to persuade her either way. It's not my place to do so. But I am glad for you, Oberon, truly. You're right, it does sound like a tremendous opportunity and it's good of you to factor your grandmother into your plans."

He seemed satisfied by this, and I made my way into the building, closing the door behind me. For a moment, I stood quietly in the lobby, hoping to hear sounds from Flat One, but all was silent. And yet, for some inexplicable reason, I felt certain that the boy was standing on the other side of the door with his ear pressed against the woodwork. Or, perhaps, standing on a chair and watching me through the spyhole.

It was only when I went upstairs that it occurred to me that Oberon hadn't stopped in to see his grandmother after all. He'd simply dragged me into his plans and then continued on his way.

FOURTEEN

M. Toussaint collected us in an ostentatiously styled red car which attracted the interest of every passerby. I had no idea where his wealth came from but assumed that it was Old Money, carefully hidden away during the war and now, with the advent of the liberation, given permission to play outside once again. Despite my suspicion of him, I found it exciting to climb into such a vehicle. From across the street, Émile stepped out of the haberdashery store with an envious stare.

"You're not going away, are you?" he asked, leaning over the metalwork and studying the leather seats and polished interior. Mother threw him a look as she climbed inside, annoyed to see us conversing.

"Just for the day," I told him. "Punting, I'm told." I rolled my eyes to feign disinterest, although I was rather looking forward to the expedition now. "It wasn't my idea."

"If your grubby hands sully my paintwork, Émile, you'll be charged with washing it later," said M. Toussaint, stepping into the driver's seat. Émile made a great show of wiping the door with his handkerchief, offered a polite bow, then wandered back into the shop. As we pulled away, I glanced around, hoping that he would continue watching until we had disappeared from view, but no, to my disappointment, he'd already gone back inside.

M. Toussaint kept the hood of the car down and it felt wonderful to feel the wind on my face as we drove along. It had been such a long time since I'd been driven anywhere. Naturally, when we lived in that other place, Father had a car, and Kurt, more often than not, was assigned as his driver. Indeed, I had experienced thrills of desire for the young lieutenant while seated behind him, mesmerized by his thick blond hair and the way his comb left lines in it, like a freshly tilled field. I could see him still, standing by Father's vehicle in the sunshine, wearing a sleeveless white vest over his trousers that drew the eye to his tanned, muscular arms. I had been flirting with him in my childish way when my brother interrupted us, insisting that as I was only twelve years old I should stop pretending to be more grown up than I really was. Kurt had pulled away from me then, and I wondered whether he had been made more anxious by my youth or the fear of Father's displeasure. I had been so angry with my brother at that moment. It was the first time that I had actively wished him harm.

"Where are we going anyway?" I asked now, but neither M. Toussaint nor Mother answered. They were too busy laughing and talking to each other. I raised my voice and tried again. "M. Toussaint?" I called, my voice forcing its way through the wind. "Where are you taking us?"

"A place called Saint-Ouen," he said, not turning around but keeping his eyes on the road ahead. His left hand, I noticed, rested in Mother's lap. "It's not far, perhaps a thirty-minute drive. There's a park nearby where we can eat lunch and, afterward, we'll take a boat out on the river."

"Is it safe?" I asked.

"Oh, Gretel," said Mother, laughing in an entirely false way. "Rémy would hardly take us somewhere that held any danger, would you, darling?"

"I would sooner sacrifice a limb," he declared, and I chose not to pursue the conversation any further, preferring to be left alone with my thoughts. My hair blew out behind me, I opened the top two buttons of my dress to allow the air at my skin, and closed my eyes, tilting my head back. When I opened them again, I saw M. Toussaint observing me in the rear-view mirror and our eyes met. I wanted to turn away but couldn't. Mother glanced across, saw how we were watching each other and placed a hand gently on his arm. He turned to her then and smiled, before returning both hands to the wheel.

M. Touissant had brought a picnic basket with him, and we sat on the dry grass of the Grand Parc des Docks eating ficelle, cured meats, Tomme de Savoie, and a cake I had never tasted before, pitted with sun-dried tomatoes and olives, all of which was washed down with glasses of wine. It was not very busy but there were a few young couples strolling around, exchanging fond glances, as well as some families with small children and even smaller dogs. I wondered what scene might have presented itself here just a year or two earlier. Would the park have been filled with soldiers or had the people continued their daily lives much as they had before the invasion?

"You dress with great elegance, M. Toussaint," I said, and Mother turned to frown at me, somewhat inexplicably, as she had told me to be polite to him, and what was a compliment if not the height of courtesy?

"Thank you, Gretel," he replied. "That's kind of you to say."

"I suppose you have a personal tailor?"

"I do, as it happens," he admitted.

"Is it M. Vannier?"

He paused for a moment. "But who is M. Vannier?" he asked.

"He owns the haberdashery shop across the road from where we live. I thought perhaps you shopped there."

"No," he replied. "My tailor resides in Faubourg Saint-Germain."

"Then you've never been inside M. Vannier's store?"

"I'm afraid not," he said, shaking his head. "Would you recommend it?"

"I fear that Gretel is falling in love with the boy who works there," said Mother, her tone growing nasty now as the alcohol took hold. "He's entirely unsuitable, of course."

"Unsuitable in what way?"

"Well, he's in trade. A mere shop boy."

"Is he handsome?" asked M. Toussaint.

"But you know him, surely?" I asked.

"I don't," he said, appearing entirely innocent. "As I said, I've never been inside the shop."

I decided not to pursue this any further. Had I misheard him earlier? But no, I could recall his words distinctly. *If your grubby hands sully my paintwork, Émile, you'll be charged with washing it later.* If he didn't know the shop or its owners, then how could he possibly have known Émile's name?

"And now, I think we've eaten and drunk our fill," he said, standing up and brushing himself down. "Time we set about hiring one of these boats, don't you agree?"

"Oh yes!" exclaimed Mother as she gathered up the picnic plates and cutlery, returning them to the hamper. "Come on, Gretel, help me with these things."

I folded the rugs in half and half again and gathered up the empty bottles of wine.

"Are you a reader, Gretel?" M. Toussaint asked me as we returned to the car to pack the hamper away. Mother had gone in search of a public convenience, and it was just the two of us now.

"Yes, I love books," I admitted.

"Have you read *Thérèse Raquin*?"

I shook my head. I had heard of Zola, of course, but had yet to make his acquaintance on the page.

"An interesting story," he told me. "The three characters at the heart of the novel come to this very place, to Saint-Ouen, for a day's punting. Thérèse herself, her sickly husband, Camille, and her lover, Laurent, who is the best friend of Camille. Unknown to the unhealthy young man, the lovers plan on pushing him off the boat into the river. They wish to drown him in order to be allowed to marry themselves."

"How cruel," I said, wondering why he was telling me this. "And do they succeed in their plan?"

"They do," he replied. "But their happy ending is frustrated. Camille returns every night in their dreams to haunt them. His soul cannot rest at peace with the knowledge of their dastardly crimes and it determines to make them pay."

"And how does their story end?"

"I wouldn't want to spoil it for you," he said, smiling, showing me his sharp white teeth. "But let's just say that justice is served."

"Do you believe that?" I asked. "That the souls of those we have wronged are looking over us, waiting for a moment of vengeance?"

"As much as I believe that the world is round and day follows night," he said. "But you have nothing to worry about, do you, Gretel? A girl your age could have wronged no one. Your conscience is clear, yes?"

"What are you two gossiping about?" Mother asked, rejoining us now and looking from one of us to the other in a rather suspicious way.

"Murder," said M. Toussaint, continuing to look me directly in the eye. "Deceit. Revenge."

"Far too philosophical a topic for a day like today," she said, shivering a little. "Come along, Rémy," she added, linking his arm. "Let's find a boat. It won't be long until the sun starts to hide behind those clouds."

They walked on in the direction of the quay, but I remained by the car for a moment. Only when Mother turned around and called my name did I follow them.

FIFTEEN

Of course, it was only a matter of time before I met Henry.

At the rear of Winterville Court stands a long garden, some fifty feet by thirty, encased by trees, an idyllic enclave with a pair of wooden benches facing each other on the east and west sides and, in the far corner, a picnic table. Edgar and I had often sat out during the summer months, reading peacefully or simply enjoying the sunshine, and when Caden was a boy, he ran wild in it with his friends. As I've grown older, however, I've spent less time there and, on the day that our paths first crossed, it might have been four months since I'd last set foot in it.

It was a warm morning and I'd opened all the windows to air out the flat but was feeling a little claustrophobic, so I took my sunglasses from their drawer and went downstairs with Marie Antoinette, setting up camp on one of the benches with a bottle of water by my side. The overhanging trees provided some welcome shade from the sun, and I picked up where I had left off, with the young adventuress becoming Dauphine of France by marrying Louis-Auguste, a neat trick, considering the groom didn't have the courtesy even to show up for the ceremony.

I had been reading for no more than twenty minutes when I began to sense that I was being watched. I looked up, and around, but all was silence, so I returned to my book. Then, at last, the back door that led from the building to the garden opened and a small head poked out. I steeled myself, recognizing the inevitability of the moment, and prepared to make the boy's acquaintance.

My great fear when Caden was born was that he would remind me of my brother—it was one of the reasons I had hoped for a girl— but, to my relief, he bore no resemblance to him, taking after his father's side of the family instead. Everything about Henry, however, took me back eighty years and I had to reach out to grip the arm of the wooden bench to steady myself.

Like my brother, the boy was small for his age, with a mop of dark brown hair and a clean, blemish-free face. He wore a pair of brightly colored shorts and a polo shirt and, even from a distance, I could see how blue his eyes were. As we each considered the other, we remained frozen in our separate positions. For me, it was as if a ghost had risen from the ashes to confront me. Finally, with great caution, he started to walk toward me.

"Hello," he said, when he drew close.

"Hello," I replied.

His left arm, from the wrist to the elbow, was sheathed in a fiberglass casing and the arm itself rested in a sling. When he glanced up toward the trees, I wondered whether he enjoyed climbing and if some misadventure in his previous home had led to his injury.

"My name's Henry," said the boy.

"I'm Gretel."

He appeared surprised by this, then laughed a little.

"I can't call you that," he said.

"Why not?"

"Because I have to call you Mrs. Whatever-Your-Name-Is. It's good manners."

"Well, in that case, you should call me Mrs. Fernsby," I told him. "But I don't mind if you want to call me Gretel. I prefer it, actually. I don't stand on ceremony."

"Like Hansel and Gretel?" he asked.

"I suppose so, yes. You're familiar with that story?"

He nodded. "They get captured and locked away by a horrible old witch. Then she fattens them up and tries to cook them in the fire."

"She does," I agreed. "But she doesn't succeed."

"Do you have a brother called Hansel?"

"No," I said.

"You don't have a brother, or you don't have one named Hansel?"

I didn't reply. Perhaps this talk of stories made him look at the book on my lap, and he pointed toward it.

"What are you reading?" he asked.

"It's a biography of Marie Antoinette," I told him, lifting it to show him the cover.

"Who's she?"

"Who *was* she," I replied, correcting him. "She was Queen of France, oh, it must be more than two hundred years ago now."

"And what happened to her?"

"She had her head cut off," I said.

Henry's eyes opened wide and his mouth made the shape of an O. I hoped I hadn't scared him.

"Why?" he asked breathlessly.

"The people rose up," I explained. "The citizens, I mean. They felt that the king and queen were not treating them very well so they staged a revolution."

He was listening intently now, and something told me that he was probably a good student in school, that he was interested in the world around him, the things that had happened in the past, and the things that were yet to occur.

"How did they cut her head off?" he asked, and I smiled now. Little boys did so enjoy hearing the more gruesome details.

"There was a machine called the guillotine," I told him. "Have you ever heard of it?"

He shook his head.

"It was very tall, made of wood, with an angled blade hanging from the top. The revolutionaries made their enemies lie down inside it and the blade fell from above. It sliced through the neck and the head fell into a basket. Apparently, women would sit in the front row and get on with their knitting while they watched. I don't know if that's true or just something invented by Hollywood."

"That's horrible," he said, but I could tell that a part of him was thrilled by the dreadfulness of it.

"It is," I agreed. "Although they say that it was painless. It was supposed to be humanitarian."

He frowned. "What does that mean?" he asked.

"It means being nice to people," I said.

He considered this, then turned around, dragging his trainers in the grass, much like a bull preparing to charge. Unexpectedly, he ran to one corner of the garden—carefully, so as not to upset his injured arm—then ran back, as if he'd experienced a sudden need to burn off some energy. When he started talking again, it was as if none of that had taken place.

"Do you live here too?" he asked, and I nodded, pointing up to the first-floor window.

"I live directly above you," I told him. "In Flat Two."

"I live in Flat One."

"I know. And are you enjoying it here?"

He shrugged his shoulders, as if one place was much the same as another to him.

"Do you have a nice bedroom?" I asked.

"I have a poster of Harry Potter on my wall," he told me. "And I have all the books and eleven of the action figures."

"Have you read them?"

"Twice," he said. "But now I'm reading this."

Until this moment, I hadn't even realized that he too was carrying a book, under his good arm, but here it was now, extended toward me.

"Mummy says I have to read something different before I can read *Harry Potter* again."

It was as if someone had slapped me. When Caden was a boy, I hadn't allowed him to borrow the book that Henry held from the library, even though the title intrigued him. He could choose anything he wanted, I told him, a book for any age group, except this one.

"What's wrong?" asked Henry.

"Nothing," I said.

"Your face has gone all funny."

"I'm old," I explained.

"How old are you?" he asked.

"I'm one hundred and twenty-six," I said, and he seemed to accept this as a perfectly reasonable reply.

"I'm only nine," he said.

At the other end of the garden, the doorway opened, and Madelyn stepped outside, her face filled with concern. When she saw us talking, or rather when she saw that Henry was alive and well, she put a hand to her breast, as if whatever horrors his absence had inspired in her imagination had been assuaged.

"There you are!" she called out, and the boy spun round.

"That's my mummy," he said, and I nodded.

"Yes, I know," I said. "I've met her."

"Henry, stop bothering Mrs. Fernsby!" she shouted. "Come back inside."

He did as instructed without complaint and I was impressed by how obedient he was.

"Goodbye, Gretel," he said, walking away.

"Goodbye, Henry," I replied, and then, before he could go so far that he wouldn't hear me, I called after him. "Oh, Henry!" I shouted.

He turned and looked back at me, a quizzical expression on his face. The door was still open, but Madelyn had disappeared, presumably returning to her own flat.

"What happened to your arm?" I asked.

He stared at me, then at the limb in question. I saw him try to formulate an answer, and his eyes scrunched up, as if he couldn't quite remember what he was supposed to say. Then, without another word, he turned and ran back inside, slamming the door behind him.

It was only then that I realized that he had left his copy of *Treasure Island* on the bench.

SIXTEEN

A few days after the punting expedition, I called into M. Vannier's store in search of Émile but was met by his father, who greeted me without much politeness. This was the first time we had found ourselves in conversation and I could tell from his expression that he didn't take kindly to my presence in his son's life.

"He was supposed to be back here at two o'clock," he said, taking a pocket watch from his waistcoat and tapping the glass. His fingernails were too long for a man, and I stared at them with a certain revulsion. "And see, it's ten minutes past the hour already. He's an unreliable boy."

"But he works so hard," I replied, defending him. "He's devoted to both his job and to you."

M. Vannier muttered something incomprehensible under his breath. It seemed that he was in no mood to be appeased.

"It's Gretel, isn't it?" he asked finally, and I nodded.

"Yes, Gretel Guéymard," I said.

"Guéymard," he repeated slowly while staring directly at me. I looked away, not wanting the expression on my face to betray the fact that the name had been mine for only a short time.

"And tell me, what is it you want with my son, Mlle Guéymard?" he asked.

"His friendship, that's all," I replied, surprised by the question.

"A boy and a girl of your age cannot be just friends. There will always be feelings that intrude. You have designs on him, I think?"

I shook my head, annoyed that he dared to address me in such a condescending fashion, the way Mother might have spoken to our maid, Maria, when we lived in Berlin or that other place. I was still arrogant enough to believe that I should be treated with particular respect. "We're getting to know each other, that's all."

"I don't want him distracted from his work," said M. Vannier.

"Everyone needs a distraction from time to time," I said, my courage building now. M. Vannier opened his mouth to argue but, before he could make his case, the bell over the door sounded and we turned to see Émile stepping inside. He brushed his hair away from his forehead and paused in the middle of the shop, looking from one of us to the other, unsettled to see us engaged in conversation.

"Papa," he said, nodding toward his father. "Gretel."

"You're late," replied M. Vannier, making his way behind the counter, where he took his coat from a stand.

"I was delayed. I'm sorry."

His father grunted and, without another word to either of us, left the shop to take his lunch. Émile turned back to me with an embarrassed smile.

"I'm sorry about that," he said. "He gets grumpy when he's hungry."

"It's fine," I said. "I don't think he likes me very much, though."

"It's just his way. He worries about me."

"He thinks I'm leading you astray."

"No, that's not it."

I frowned, waiting for him to explain, but instead he came toward me and we kissed rather awkwardly.

"You haven't been to see me since Sunday," I said. "When M. Toussaint took Mother and me to Saint-Ouen."

"I'm sorry," he replied. "I've been busy here. Did you have a nice day?"

"Not particularly. He acted as if he was an expert on boats but, honestly, he nearly overturned us on more than one occasion. Possibly because he'd drunk too much wine. Mother screamed and everyone on the river turned to stare at us. I was mortified."

Émile laughed. "I would have liked to have seen that," he said.

"I wish you had been there. I think . . ." I paused and he stepped closer to me. I looked down at the ground, hoping it would encourage him to reach out and place his fingers beneath my chin. When he did, I glanced up, staring directly into his eyes.

"You think what?"

"That M. Toussaint might be in love with me."

It was impossible not to notice the expression of amusement on his face. It was as offensive as it was infuriating.

"You think I'm joking?"

"He's an old man," protested Émile. "Thirty-five at least. And you're just a girl."

"Men of that age like girls my age," I told him. "They appreciate our innocence."

"I'm not sure that's the word I'd use to describe you," he said.

"Why not?" I asked, surprised by his tone, which seemed antagonistic, but he remained silent. I stared at him. Had I been too forward in my advances?

"You're being unkind," I told him.

"I'm just joking," he said, placing his hand gently on my forearm. "There's no need to be so sensitive."

He made his way over to a box by the counter, hoisted it onto the work surface and ran a sharp blade across the seal. It opened to reveal a vast array of socks in a rainbow of colors. I found it hard to imagine any man wearing something so flamboyant and it irritated me that Émile had returned to his work while I was still there. I wanted his attention. All of it. I demanded it as my right.

"So," I said finally. "When will we see each other again?"

"We're seeing each other right now," he replied.

"You know what I mean," I said. "Perhaps you could take me to that coffee shop again. Or we could go for a walk. Or maybe some evening we could . . ."

I stopped talking and he looked up, recognizing my suggestive tone. "We could what?" he asked.

"Well, your father isn't home all day and night, is he? We could spend some time together. Upstairs." I glanced toward the door at the rear of the shop, which, I assumed, led to a staircase that in turn led to their living accommodation and his bedroom. He followed my gaze and when he turned back to me I could see the desire on his face. It was so easy, I realized, to regain the attention of a boy.

"Really?" he asked, his voice cracking slightly.

"Really," I said, offering a half-smile. I didn't care whether this degraded me in his eyes. It was important that I maintained his interest and, anyway, I wanted to experience this rite of passage with him. I had wanted it from the moment I first laid eyes on him.

He walked back to me now and kissed me more passionately. As he pressed himself against me, I could feel his ardor and put a hand to his chest.

"I didn't mean right now," I said.

"Then when?"

"Another time. Next week. When would be best?"

He thought about it. "Thursday," he said. "My father visits his friend on Thursday evenings and he's always gone for hours."

"What sort of a friend?"

"A lady friend," he replied, looking both embarrassed and repelled by the idea. "They have an arrangement. He goes out reeking of cologne but returns stinking of perfume."

"Then he could hardly blame us, could he?" I asked. "Have you . . ." I hesitated, uncertain how far I could pry into his past when I was so secretive about my own. "Have you been with a girl before?"

He nodded. "Only once," he said. "The night the war ended. She was older than me. I'm not sure I acquitted myself to her satisfaction. And you? With a boy?"

I shook my head. He seemed surprised and put a hand to my cheek, his thumb tracing a soft path across it. It was all that I could do not to drag him upstairs at that moment, but I knew better than to do that. I wanted to sleep with him, yes, but I wanted more than that. I needed him to fall in love with me, to marry me, to take me away from Mother and help me to build a new life that might erase my past. Was I wrong, I wondered, to promise myself to him so soon when I might achieve my ends better by making him wait? But I had agreed to Thursday and would not go back on that. I was many things, but I was not a tease.

We kissed a little more and when I finally left the shop a thought came into my head.

"Do you think I'm wrong about M. Toussaint then?" I asked. "That he's falling in love with me?"

Émile shrugged his shoulders. "He falls in love with every girl he meets," he said. "Old or young. They say that he has an insatiable desire for women."

"You know him well then?"

"I've known him since I was a child. Although he was older, he was a great friend of my brother. Louis looked up to him. He was a hero in his eyes. He only joined the Resistance because of Rémy."

I considered this as I made my way onto the street, where the cold wind blew in my face, harsh and brittle now. So, he did know him, after all. Or, rather, they knew each other. Why, I wondered, had M. Toussaint lied to me?

SEVENTEEN

Heidi Hargrave was having one of her good mornings. We were sitting over coffee in her flat while a tradesman repaired her oven. She'd phoned me the moment he arrived because she didn't like to be left alone with strange men. An incident had occurred perhaps a decade earlier when a man claiming to be from the gas board had inveigled his way into her front room and taken £200 from her, and she'd never quite recovered her confidence afterward.

"Have you met the new neighbors?" she asked me in a confidential tone, and I nodded.

"I've met the wife," I told her. "And the little boy. I haven't met the husband yet. Apparently, he's a film producer."

"I met him last night," she said. I wasn't aware that Mr. Darcy-Witt had returned from Los Angeles and had seen or heard nothing to indicate his presence at Winterville Court. "I did," she insisted, noticing my skepticism. "I'm not making it up. Wait till you see him."

"Why?" I asked.

She smiled and put a hand to her chest, fluttering her eyelashes in such a girlish way that I couldn't help but laugh. "You know Richard Gere?" she said.

"The actor? Yes."

"Well, he reminded me of him," she told me. "Only better looking. I was downstairs, collecting my post, and he came out to check
his box. We had a very nice conversation."

"About what?"

"About Winterville Court. About films. He smells like he's been
dipped in sandalwood. I didn't know a man could smell that good.
And his teeth! Gretel, I don't know if they're real or not, but they're
white as snow."

"Veneers, I imagine."

"Not the sort of teeth you see on your average Englishman, that's
for sure. You'd know he worked in pictures. Oh, if only I were twenty
years younger!"

"And the boy?" I asked. "Have you spoken to him?"

"No, but I've seen him playing outside." She nodded toward the
window, which, like my own, looked over the garden. "I don't have
much use for boys," she added dismissively.

"Mrs.," said the tradesman, entering the room now and holding a
large screwdriver in his hand in a rather threatening fashion. "I need
to replace not just hob but socket and wiring too. This is okay
with you?"

"Yes, yes," she said, waving a hand in the air. "Just so long as I can
boil an egg. That's all I care about."

He nodded and left the room. I stared after him.

"Where's he from?" I asked, lowering my voice so he wouldn't
hear me.

"I don't know, I didn't ask. Somewhere in Europe, I imagine.
Why?"

"No reason," I said. "So, you liked him then? He seemed friendly?"

"Who? The man fixing my oven?"

"No, Mr. Darcy-Witt. From downstairs."

"Oh, yes. His name is Alex."

"Yes, she told me that."

"Alexander, I suppose."

"Probably."

"What's the wife like?"

I thought about it. "Hard to say," I told her. "She seemed a bit lost to me. Rather distracted. Or overwhelmed by all the drama of moving into a new home."

"Does she seem happy?"

"Not especially, no. She doesn't work. She implied that her husband doesn't want her to. She was an actress originally. That's how they met."

"She's pretty," said Heidi. "I'll give her that."

"I thought you hadn't met her?"

"I haven't. But I've seen her. I always look out the front window when I hear the downstairs door opening. I like to keep track of the comings and goings."

I frowned, wondering whether she wrote down everyone's movements in a notebook. Maybe she'd started doing it after being robbed.

"She's a bit young just to be sitting around doing nothing, don't you think?" I asked. "A young woman like her should be out in the world making a living for herself. Not relying on her husband."

"She's hardly just sitting around," protested Heidi, who had enjoyed housewifery more than I had and wouldn't hear a word said against it. "She has the child to look after, for one thing."

"He's nine," I said. "I expect he's in school most of the time. Perhaps she's one of these women who spend their mornings in the gym and then meets friends for lunch and is blotto on cocktails by teatime." This was rather unkind of me, but I was in that sort of mood.

"I haven't met the boy," she repeated.

I sipped my coffee and said nothing. I found it curious how Heidi could slip in and out of a conversation like that, one moment so lucid and then just a fraction away from it, like a photograph taken a millisecond after its subject has moved. Not quite out of focus but just slightly blurred.

"Now," I said, changing the subject to what I really wanted to talk about. "What's all this I hear about Australia?"

"What about it?" she asked, frowning. "What's happening in Australia?"

"Well, I ran into Oberon," I told her. "And he told me that he's planning on moving there and taking you with him."

She stared at me as if I'd gone mad.

"He told you what?" she asked, sitting forward in her chair.

"That's what he said," I replied with a shrug. "It's not true then?"

"He told me about his job offer, yes," she agreed. "And he did mention something about me going with him, but I told him in no uncertain terms that they'd be carrying me out of here in a box. Me! In Australia! Can you imagine?"

"Oh good," I replied, feeling greatly relieved. "I was worried that we were going to lose you."

"Gretel, I'm almost seventy years old," she said, laughing now. "Do you really see me out there in New Zealand playing with kangaroos and wallabies and what have you?"

"Australia," I clarified.

"The idea is ridiculous."

Before I could utter another word, I heard the sound of a door opening below and we both glanced out of the window. Henry had emerged into the garden and was making his way toward the bench. He sat down, opened his book—I had left *Treasure Island* by the door to Flat One, assuming he'd find it there—and started to read. Perhaps sensing that he was being observed, he looked in our direction and we both turned away, as if caught doing something we shouldn't.

"Oberon seemed keen that you should join him," I continued now, choosing my words carefully. I didn't want to upset her or cause any mischief between grandmother and grandson, but neither did I want her to be taken advantage of. "I think he feels that it would be financially helpful if you did."

"He's after my money, you mean."

"Well, not quite. He's a good boy, I know that. He's always been very solicitous. I suppose he feels that, with your help, he could start off a little better than he otherwise might."

"He can whistle," said Heidi dismissively. "I love Oberon, I do, and I'll be very sad if he moves away, but the answer's no. If I went to Australia, I'd be dead within a month. I wouldn't understand the people, the money, the language—"

"They do speak English there, Heidi."

"But do they, Gretel?" she asked, frowning. "Do they?"

"Well, yes. They do."

"Still. It would be like moving to Mars. No, I'm staying exactly where I am. Oberon will inherit this flat one day and that will set him right, but it won't be for a few years yet, I hope."

My bad mood evaporated instantly. There was no confusion here; she could not have been any clearer in what she was saying. The tradesman reappeared and informed her that the work had been completed, her oven was once again fit for purpose, eggs could be boiled, fried or poached, and he handed her a docket to sign. She thanked him and stood up to see him out. When she returned, I was on my feet too and told her that I'd see her soon. We did not kiss; we don't do that. We're not French.

When I stepped out into the hallway between our flats, the tradesman was still there, leaning against the staircase, studying something on his phone. He glanced up at me and nodded, then returned his attention to the screen.

"Do you mind if I ask where you're from?" I said, standing by my door, the key already in my hand. His accent had seemed familiar to me, but I couldn't quite place it.

"Holborn," he said.

"Yes, but before that."

He hesitated. I wondered if he thought I was going to make some unkind remark about immigrants.

"Poland," he told me.

"Where in Poland?"

"Town called Mikołów, in the south. Near Katowice. You know Poland?"

I shook my head. I was not about to reveal that I had lived there as a girl. He glanced at my arm, but I was wearing a long-sleeved blouse. My right arm instinctively covered the place on my left where a tattoo would have been, had one been scarred into me.

"My grandmother," he began, but I shook my head quickly, cutting him off.

"No, no, not that," I said, wishing that I had never initiated this conversation. It was shameful of me to have led him to think that I had been an inmate, even if that had not been my intention. "No, you misunderstand me."

I forced the key into the lock and practically threw myself inside, breathing heavily, feeling claustrophobic. I made my way toward the bay windows and opened them both, inhaling heavily as the breeze made its way inside. From below, Henry looked up from his book and stared at me.

Then, to my bewilderment, he slowly raised his right arm and pointed his index finger in my direction. His lips didn't move but he held the hand there until, frightened, I turned away.

EIGHTEEN

I took a long bath that Thursday evening, using so much hot water that our landlady banged on the door and shouted that if she heard the tap turn on one more time she would throw both Mother and me out onto the street. But I wanted to be clean for Émile, to feel as pure as possible.

Later, seated at our dressing table, I applied some of Mother's unguents and perfumes before drawing the brush through my hair, and stared at my reflection in the mirror. I knew that I was pretty—I attracted more than my share of approving glances in the street—but I felt as if all the life had disappeared from my eyes. Once, when I was a girl in Berlin, Grandmother had told me that they were my best feature, that men would fall in love with me because of them, and, in my vanity, I had longed for the day she would be proved right. Now they were the color of barbed wire, of rusty ovens, of smoke and ash.

For days, I had been concerned that I might have offered myself to Émile too soon. Mother had warned me that men did not want what she called "spoiled goods," that a husband expected his wife to be a virgin on their wedding night, although no such expectations were made of them, of course. From the moment I'd laid eyes on him, I had made Émile a pawn in my plan to achieve some independence from the only family I had left, but if I allowed him to make love to me, would he cast me aside afterward for someone he considered more wholesome?

It was too late to change my mind, however. I would not be the type of girl who promised herself to a boy and then disappointed him.

I put on my finest dress, the one good item of clothing I had taken with me when we left that other place, then placed a hand upon my stomach, trying to settle my nerves. I felt sick with anxiety, but also experienced a tingle of excitement. Watching the street now, I waited until I saw M. Vannier leave for his regular appointment and then slipped down the staircase, crossed the street, and tapped on the door of the haberdashery shop.

"You came," said Émile, who had been hovering by the mannequins in anticipation of my arrival. He seemed to be trembling slightly as he undid the latch to let me inside. It took him several attempts to lock it behind me, the key unsteady in his hand.

"I said I would," I replied, trying to sound sophisticated.

I could tell that he was pleased, although his expression made me take a step back. I couldn't tell whether he wanted to kiss me or kill me.

"Should we go upstairs?" I asked, and he nodded, leading the way through the shop and turning off the lights as he went. He took my hand as we ascended the staircase toward the small apartment that he shared with his father and I looked around, intrigued to see how well the two men kept house. It was perfectly orderly, as neat as the shop downstairs, which didn't surprise me. I took M. Vannier for a fastidious man, one who would be offended by any disarray.

On an occasional table stood a framed portrait of Émile's parents—I assumed the woman was his mother—on the day of their wedding. They appeared utterly miserable.

"It's terrible, isn't it?" said Émile, laughing a little as he watched me. "They look like they're going to a funeral."

"Were they unhappy together?" I asked, turning back to him.

"Not at all," he said defensively. "They loved each other very much."

"Perhaps they were just nervous," I suggested.

"Or they had some premonition of what their future would hold. My father fought in the first war, of course. And then had a son who died in the second."

I looked away. I hated talking about the war.

"Will you give me a few minutes, Gretel?" he asked after an un-comfortable silence. "I've been working all day and I should probably bathe."

"Of course," I said, a part of me wishing that he would stay as he was, with the smell of the day's work infused in his skin. He slipped into another room and I heard the rush of bathwater, followed by the sound of clothes tumbling onto the bathroom floor. It excited me to imagine the boy naked, washing himself as he prepared to be with me.

There were a few more photographs scattered around the room and I went from one to the other, examining them. The first was of Émile when he was just a child, smiling at the camera. Then one of an older boy, who I assumed was his brother, Louis. He was strik-ingly handsome, with dark hair, determined eyes, and a chin that he pushed forward, as if to assert his masculinity. He wore a worker's cap, not the type one could purchase in M. Vannier's haberdashery, more the sort that a factory worker might don when attending to his duties. He had not shaved in some days and the stubble only added to his allure. Here was a strong man. Here was a man who would defend his country to the death. Returning the picture to its place, I imagined him standing before the firing squad, one arm in the air, even as the bullets tore through his young body.

From the bathroom, I heard the sound of the bathwater being emptied and I left the living room, making my way quickly along the corridor. There were two bedrooms, one with a double bed and another with twin beds, and it was this room that I entered. One of the beds had been stripped entirely; even the mattress was gone. All that remained was an iron frame and the springs stretched across the support rails. The other had been carefully made. I wondered whether Émile paid such careful attention to it every day or whether he had prepared it especially for me. There was only enough space between the two beds for a narrow locker and on top of this stood another picture, this one depicting the brothers standing together. They each had an arm around the other's shoulder, but while Louis was laughing directly into the camera lens, Émile was looking at his brother with an expression close to devotion on his face. There was such reverence there that I wondered how he could continue to survive without him. I had loved my brother too, of course, but lost him when we were both just children. Had he lived, I daresay our relationship would have grown in time and we would have become close too. But that would never happen now. He was gone. Louis was gone. Millions were gone.

A sound from behind startled me and I turned to see Émile standing in the doorway, naked but for a towel wrapped around his waist. I was surprised to see him in a state of such undress and my face grew red. His chest was lean and hairless, and the muscles were defined. I longed to know how his skin would feel beneath my fingers. Sensing this, he smiled and stepped toward me. We kissed and I could feel his excitement grow.

"Before we do this," he said, pulling away for a moment, and the dampness of his skin, the scent of it, made me close my eyes as I breathed in his musk. I had never felt so weak in the hands of another. At that moment, he could have asked me to do anything, to leap through the window, to set myself on fire, and I would have obeyed. "Before we do this," he repeated, "there's something I need to ask of you."

"Yes?" I said, looking up at him.

"This Sunday. Three days from now. You will meet me that evening?"

"Of course," I said, moving to kiss him again, but he held me back.

"I need you to promise," he said. "Sunday at six o'clock. No matter what happens between now and then, you will not let me down?"

I frowned, uncertain why he was focusing on something so trivial at such a moment. "I promise," I said. "Sunday at six o'clock. I'll meet you outside the shop. Why? Where are you taking me?"

He smiled and shook his head.

"It's a surprise," he said. "You just have to trust me."

"I do trust you," I said. "I trust you with everything."

He seemed satisfied by this response and began to undo the buttons at the top of my dress while my trembling hands loosened the knot of his towel. He kicked the door closed behind us with his bare foot and led me, more confidently than I had expected, to his small bed.

And yet, as he lay on top of me, his face buried in my neck, his body thrusting inside my own, I found that I could not take as much satisfaction from his love as I had hoped. The empty bed beside us seemed a judgment on my past. I could hear the voice of his brother, or his brother's ghost, goading Émile on, telling him not to spare me, to take as much gratification as he could while denying me any.

To hurt me if it so pleased him.

NINETEEN

I knew there was something wrong the moment I woke.

Unlike many people of my age, my sleep pattern is rarely upset. Typically, I retire after the ten o'clock news and, although my alarm is set for seven, my brain is so attuned to waking at that hour that my eyes open a few minutes before it goes off, and I reach out and press the button to prevent its beep from being my introduction to the day.

On this particular night, however, when I jolted back into consciousness, the room was still dark. I turned on my bedside lamp and glanced at the clock. Just after 1 a.m. I sighed, not feeling sleepy but dreading the idea of remaining awake for hours. I considered making some chamomile tea in the hope that it might knock me out but, before I could decide, I heard a noise rattling through the building and climbed out of bed to investigate. It was most unusual for anything to disturb the peace of Winterville Court at this hour, but the sound had been so loud that I imagined I wasn't the only one who had heard it. A door had been slammed with such ferocity that it must have been almost taken off its hinges. I put on my dressing gown and made my way into the living room, reaching for the light switch, but then decided against. Perhaps it would be better, I thought, to remain in darkness.

I stood very still, waiting to hear what might happen next, then heard shouting coming from the flat beneath me. It was Henry, I was sure of it. In some distress. I walked toward the window that faced onto the street and drew back the curtain only a little. The street-lights were on, bathing the road in a peaceful yellow glow but, to my astonishment, I was confronted by the most extraordinary sight.

Madelyn Darcy-Witt was sitting on the curb, her head buried in her knees, her long hair falling down over her legs. She was wearing nothing but a bra and panties, a matching set. From the way her body rocked back and forth, I guessed that she was crying. I turned away, looking around my living room as if I would find an answer to her behavior there.

Uncertain how to react, I parted the curtain once again and peered out. Now she was standing up, holding herself fully erect, with her arms raised in the air, her left leg lifted from the pavement, and she appeared to be performing some sort of yoga pose, the palms of her hands touching each other above her head. She held this pose for a few moments before her body seemed to collapse and she stumbled, almost falling over. Was she drunk? I wondered.

She looked around—other than her, the street was entirely empty—before picking up a stone that was lying on one of the flower beds, holding it in her right hand and examining it for a few moments before suddenly, without warning, dragging it across her forehead. She didn't hit herself hard, enough to bruise but not to tear the skin, and I let out an involuntary cry before turning around, ready to run downstairs and onto the street before she could injure herself more seriously. Before I could, however, I heard the front door being flung open and the voice of a man crying out a single-syllable obscenity in a loud, angry voice while marching toward her. I stood back from the window as he approached Madelyn—I felt certain that I did not want him to see me—but was still able to observe him as he wrapped one arm around her thin waist and picked her up. She let out a scream, cursing and wailing, her legs kicking in the air, but as soon as she was back inside she went quiet, and I wondered whether he had put a hand over her mouth.

The door to Flat One slammed shut, echoing up the stairwell, and then, all was silence.

I remained exactly where I was, disturbed by what I had witnessed, before making my way to the drinks cabinet, where I poured myself a small whisky to ease my nerves. The incident had left me shaken.

It was another twenty minutes before I felt I could return to bed but, just as I stood up, the door from downstairs opened once again and I heard the man shouting. Angry now, I considered going downstairs and inviting him to think about the other people who lived in Winterville Court, but I did not have the courage to do so. Instead, I listened as lighter footsteps ran through the building and out toward the back of the house. Returning to my bedroom, I took up position there, staring out into the garden.

A motion sensor had been placed outside a few years before after some robberies in the area. Fortunately, it ignores any midnight visitors from the animal kingdom and bursts into light only when disturbed by a person. It was on now. I observed a small movement in the trees. It was Henry. His feet were bare and he wore a pair of striped pajamas, the whiteness of his sling catching the light. He looked terrified, and I felt equally frightened for him. And then a voice called out:

"Henry!"

A man, the same man who had dragged Madelyn inside, was out there too, wearing jeans and a white shirt, his sleeves rolled up to reveal strong forearms. Even from this distance I could see that he was muscular and would be an intimidating presence to anyone, let alone a child.

Henry retreated into the foliage as the man continued to call out his name, his voice irrational with rage. I watched as the little body moved once more, in search of a more secure hiding place. I pressed myself against the windowpane and my movement must have alerted him, for he looked up then and saw me. The light from the sensor caught his face and I could see both the fear and the desperation in his eyes. Using the index finger of his good hand, he pressed it to his lips, urging me to remain quiet, but this was enough for his father to notice because he strode toward him now and, even though the boy backed away, scooped him up as if he were as light as a bag of flour.

Mr. Darcy-Witt lifted him awkwardly, however, pressing too tightly against his son's injured arm, and Henry let out a cry of pain, at which point his father dropped him on the ground. He hovered over the boy and, for a moment, I was certain that he was going to kick him, but no, the pair remained locked in this frightening tableau for a few moments, until Alex lifted him once more and held him in a more cautious embrace, one at odds with the ferocious expression on his face.

I wanted to look away but couldn't. The entire scene had proved so upsetting that I felt only by remaining completely motionless would I be able to preserve my anonymity. But perhaps there was something that alerted Mr. Darcy-Witt to being watched because he paused before entering the building, held himself very still, and then looked directly up at me, his eyes meeting my own. His expression was one that I had seen before, when I was a child and living in that other place. The soldiers had worn it, almost to a man. A desire to hurt. An awareness that there was nothing anyone could do to stop them. It was mesmerizing. I could not look away and nor, it seemed, could he. We held this mutual gaze for perhaps twenty seconds before I stumbled backward, tumbling awkwardly onto my bed. From below, I could hear the sound of the door closing and being locked from the inside and then footsteps making their way back toward the lower flat. The child, it seemed, was being returned to his mother. I heard a voice say, "Keep him here."

All was quiet then until, to my horror, the footsteps began to ascend the staircase. I made my way as quietly as I could through the living room and toward my front door, ensuring that it was both locked and latched. I could feel my heart beating heavily in my chest as the steps came closer, and I pressed my eye to the small spy hole that gave a distorted view of the hallway outside.

Alex Darcy-Witt was standing there, looking straight at me. I dared not move. I wondered whether he could see the slight shadow of my feet beneath the door. He took a step forward and then, raising his right hand, pressed his thumb against the spy hole, holding it there for the longest time so my view was obliterated. I stepped back, retreating into the living room, uncertain what to do. Should I call the police? Or Caden? But he lived so far away. I had Oberon's number in my phone, and he lived closer, but I couldn't think straight. I hadn't been able to feel truly frightened yet, although that emotion would come soon enough.

Finally, after remaining still for no less than ten minutes, I made my way slowly back toward the door and, dreading what I might see, looked through the spy hole once again. The hallway was empty now and my only view was the familiar one of Heidi's door on the opposite side.

The rest of the night, mercifully, was steeped in silence. I know, because I lay awake throughout all of it.

TWENTY

Did I feel different after sleeping with Émile? I did not regret it, I knew that much, but I could not say that I had enjoyed the experience. During the act itself, he had been brutal and aggressive, insensitive to the fact that he was clearly hurting me. Twice, I had asked him to be more gentle and, while he'd relented somewhat, it had not taken long for him to return to a more unforgiving rhythm. I knew that it was natural that I would bleed a little, but the near violence of his lovemaking, if it could be called that, left a more substantial stain on the linen than seemed normal and I was in a great deal of pain afterward. When he was finished, to my dismay, he seemed indifferent to me, the complete opposite of the sensitive, caring boy I believed him to be, and as I gathered my clothes to leave he became once more preoccupied with our plans for Sunday evening. Back home, alone in the bed that Mother and I shared, I wept, my spirits as low as they had been since my arrival in Paris.

Still, three days later, having avoided him in the meantime, I convinced myself that he had not meant to behave in so pitiless a fashion. After all, he was almost a novice too and perhaps it took time for a boy to understand that he needed to learn tenderness. I considered asking advice from Mother but was uncertain how she would receive the news. She was far too busy preparing for her own evening, as M. Toussaint was taking her out to dinner, to listen to any of my concerns.

"He said this is a night that I will remember for the rest of my life," she told me, beaming in excitement. "I think he's going to ask me to be his wife, Gretel. In fact, I'm sure of it. Then all our troubles will be over."

I questioned my true feelings about this. It would be wonderful to leave this small room, of course, and to move somewhere I could have space for myself, but I did not much care for the idea of a stepfather, particularly not this stepfather.

"And you will say yes?" I asked, my tone betraying my anxiety.

"Of course," she replied. "And then I'll no longer have to pretend to be the widowed Madame Guéymard but will be the married Madame Toussaint, a woman with a respectable position in society once again."

"And what did that ever bring us in the past?" I asked.

"It kept us alive, didn't it?"

"Some of us, yes."

She looked at me as if it was taking every fiber of her being to stop herself from slapping me.

"What's wrong with you?" she snapped. "Don't you want to live in a big house and have pretty dresses and a better suitor than that shop boy across the street?"

I struggled to find an answer. Yes, there was a part of me that did want all those things—I could not deny that I had enjoyed being my father's daughter—but it frightened me too. I knew how transitory such things could be.

"We could always leave," I said.

"Leave?" asked Mother, frowning. "Leave where? Leave Paris?"

"Yes."

She stared at me as if I had lost my mind. "Leave Paris when we're about to get everything we came here for? Don't talk nonsense, Gretel! Where would we go?"

"Anywhere. We could start again. With our old names."

"Do you want to go to prison?" she shouted, becoming angry now. "Because that's what would happen. Do you want us both to be dragged to Nuremberg to answer for your father's crimes? To have the eyes of the world upon us, condemning us, calling us the most terrible names?"

"My father's . . . ?" I began, amazed that she could so easily dismiss her part in what had happened. And mine.

"Yes, your father's crimes!" she shouted. "His. All his. Not mine. Not yours."

"But we're . . ." I said, shaking my head, sinking onto the bed in dismay.

"We're what?"

"We're guilty too," I told her, and this time she did not hesitate. I didn't even see her draw her hand back before she hit me. It took a few moments for the sting to become painful, but I did not touch it. I wanted her to see the mark that she had left.

"We're guilty of nothing," she said, spitting out the words.

"But we are," I replied, the tears starting to fall down my cheeks, even as I tried to wipe them away. "You must have known."

"I knew nothing," she insisted. "And neither did you."

"I was there," I said. "I went inside, remember? With Father and Kurt."

"Shut your mouth, you stupid girl," she hissed, looking around as if she feared that some unsuspected presence might be listening in to this conversation, overhearing every word. "I was a wife who obeyed her husband's commands, as I promised to do on the day we were wed. And you were a child. As for those Jews . . . those filthy Jews . . ."

"Don't, please," I begged her.

"All the trouble they caused before the war. And now all the distress they're causing since it ended. I don't care for politics, you know that, but God in heaven, when you look at what's happening, at the revenge they're taking, don't you think that the Führer's case has been proven? These people! Your father was right. They're not people at all."

I looked at her in disbelief, her eyes glowering, her cheeks red with anger. I let out a sigh and a phrase emerged from my mouth that I had never intended on saying, had never even thought until now. And yet, I meant every word of it.

"I wish it was me who had died," I said.

She said nothing. The silence between us went on for so long that I wondered would we ever speak again. Finally, she smiled, turned around and took one final look at herself in the mirror, as if this entire conversation had never taken place.

"Stay up for me tonight, if you like," she said at last, her voice perfectly even now. "I hope to return with good news. And then, my darling girl, we can start again. The past will no longer exist. It will be as if we have both been reborn."

It was almost an hour later before I tapped on the door of M. Vannier's store, and when Émile emerged I reached up to kiss him, but he avoided my lips. He seemed distracted, nervous even, and I asked him whether anything was wrong.

"No," he said as he led the way through the streets, taking me in an unfamiliar direction.

"But you're so quiet."

"I have things on my mind, that's all."

"What things? You can tell me."

He shook his head and led me down rue des Carmes, past the Panthéon, and into a busy conclave of side streets that I had not yet explored during my time in the city. Although I felt anxious, he seemed to know exactly where he was going. I had to walk quickly to keep up with him.

"Where are you taking me?" I asked.

"Somewhere special," he replied. "Trust me, this is a night you will remember for the rest of your life."

I frowned. This was the same phrase that M. Toussaint had used to Mother to describe their evening ahead. Could it be a coincidence or was something more at play here? I grabbed him by the arm, and he pulled up short.

"What?" he asked me, looking frustrated as he brushed the hair out of his eyes.

"There's something I need to ask you," I said.

"Go on then."

"M. Toussaint called you by your name that day at the car, when he drove Mother and me to Saint-Ouen. He claimed he didn't know you, but you told me that you've known him for years. Why did you lie?"

He smiled, but this was not a smile that I could decipher. There was something bitter there. Something cruel.

"I could explain," he said, pointing to a door to our left. "But we've arrived anyway. So let's wait a moment, yes? Let's go inside. Then everything will become clear and you will understand."

"No, tell me now," I insisted. "Why did you lie?"

He hesitated before looking left and right on the street, as if he were deciding how much to reveal. Then he walked to the door, which was a fairly nondescript affair, a gray iron entrance that led into what appeared to be some sort of warehouse. I followed him, demanding an answer, and he shrugged his shoulders and looked me directly in the eye.

"You think I lied?" he asked, his tone perfectly calm now.

"I know you did."

"But tell me this, Gretel," he said, leaning forward and taking hold of my arm, his fingers clenching it so tightly that it caused me to cry out. "Why would I ever tell the truth to a *putain* like you?"

I froze, unsure that I had heard him right. Had he really spoken to me in this way? Before I could protest, however, he pulled open the door and physically flung me inside, closing it firmly behind us as he pushed me bodily into the building. I stumbled, confused about what was going on, before spinning around, determined to leave, but he ignored my protests as he pulled a latch across, barring anyone else from entering. I had heard voices as we entered, but they had grown quiet now. Turning around, Émile dragged me forward, out of the shadows. When he let go, I stopped still, confused by the scene laid out before me.

There were perhaps forty people gathered there. Old men, old women, younger men, younger women. Judging from their clothing, they came from all stations in life, rich and poor, tradesmen and gentry. They turned to look at me, revulsion on their faces. In the center of the room two chairs had been set out next to each other.

One was empty and, in the other, sat Mother.

I turned to Émile in bewilderment and he dragged me forward mercilessly. I tried to pull away, but another man grabbed me by the arm, and I saw that it was M. Vannier, Émile's father. Looking around, there were others I recognized too. The butcher who sold us meat from his shop at the corner of our street. The girl who served behind the bar at one of Mother's favorite haunts. And there in the corner, even our landlady, who, we had been assured, did not care where her tenants came from as long as they paid their rent. I looked from one to the other, feeling as if I had been drawn into some horrible, surreal nightmare, and only when Mother slowly lifted her head to look at me did I dare speak.

"What's happening?" I cried out. "What's going on here?"

Mother looked at me with abject terror in her eyes and I saw that she had been struck with even more force than she had hit me earlier. Dried blood was stuck to the right-hand side of her mouth, descending in a narrow rivulet toward her chin, while her cheek showed the colorful beginnings of a bruise. Her eye was swollen too.

"Gretel," she said, shaking her head, her voice drifting off into a low moan. "No, no, no. Not my daughter, please. She has no part in this."

A man I did not recognize took me roughly by the neck and threw me into the chair next to Mother. As he tied a rope around my waist to keep me still I noticed that she had been similarly bound. When I tried to stand, another man used his boot to push me back into the chair, winding me. I had never been assaulted like this in my life.

And then, from out of the shadows, emerged Rémy Toussaint.

He looked from Mother to me and back again with such contempt on his face that we might have been demons. Then he turned to the gathering, who immediately fell silent.

"My name is Rémy Toussaint," he declared in a clear voice bristling with authority. "My brother's name was Victor Toussaint. He was hanged from a tree after he opened fire on a German battalion outside Brussels. As the noose was placed around his neck, the Nazis stabbed him with their bayonets, as the Romans did to Christ on the cross."

I turned to Émile, pleading for an explanation as to what was happening, but the moment I caught his eye he stepped forward too and spoke.

"My name is Émile Vannier," he said. "Brother of the murdered Louis Vannier, who was captured and tortured by the Nazis, his body thrown into the street to be eaten by dogs."

"And I am Marcel Vannier," declared his father, his voice cracking with emotion. "Louis was my son."

One by one, every person present spoke his or her name and told us of their dead loved ones. Some had fallen as soldiers, some had been captured as members of the Resistance and brutalized before death, and some, of course, had died in the camps.

"We had nothing to do with any of this," groaned Mother. "You have the wrong people."

"You are—," said M. Toussaint, pointing an accusatory finger at her and using her real name. "Your husband was the devil of—." And here he named that other place where we had lived after Berlin. "And you are Gretel," he continued. "The devil's daughter."

"No, it's not true!" cried Mother.

"It is true!" screamed a woman who had spoken of two dead sons who'd been forced to play a game of Russian roulette by their captors. She rushed toward us, tearing at Mother's face with her fingers, and had to be pulled away.

"No," said M. Toussaint, his arms wrapped around the devastated woman as he gently soothed her. "That is not what we do, Marguerite. We have a way to deal with these monsters, you know that. They will pay for their crimes."

I stared at him and in that moment believed that this was the night that I would die. Mother was protesting her innocence, but I felt a strange sense of calm, content to take whatever punishment came my way, as long as it was quick. I closed my eyes, praying for a bullet. I imagined there would be no pain with a bullet. One moment I would be here and the next, gone.

But no.

When I opened my eyes again two large men were walking toward us and, without warning, ripped our dresses open, tearing at the fabric until we were seated in only our underwear. That humiliation alone was more than I could endure.

"Did you think that we did not know?" asked Rémy, and his composure was almost as terrifying as the assault we were enduring. "Did you think that we are not always watching out for strangers with inconsistent histories who might be connected with the devils? That we do not have a network of spies intent on discovering the true identities of anyone we suspect? You," he said, turning to Mother. "With your cheap dresses and pathetic attempts to cover your accent. You're no actress, I promise you that. And you're stupid too. So stupid. Do you know how many times you confused Nantes with Nice?" He laughed.

Mother didn't reply. She knew, as I did, that there would be no reprieve from whatever they had planned.

"And you," continued M. Toussaint, turning to me. "Trying to flirt with me when we met in the place des Vosges. A silly child. A repellent brat. You did this with your father, perhaps? Fluttered your eyelashes and tried to be more than you are? You want to join him, don't you? Burning forever in eternity?"

I nodded. "Yes," I said, as calmly as I could. "Yes, I do."

He frowned, not having expected this reply, but there was no sympathy in his expression. A silence fell on the room and I looked up as two elderly women approached M. Toussaint and Émile, each one holding a straight razor. They flicked them open and the sharp, silver blades appeared. I heard Mother take a long gasp of breath before crying out loud.

"No, we don't kill women," said Émile, sensing what we thought, and I turned to look at him. He was a stranger to me now. "We do this instead."

He walked over slowly, accepting a razor from one of the women. Then he marched toward me, and I panicked, waiting for it to rip through my skin. I lost control of myself and felt the contents of my bladder spilling from between my legs and pooling around my feet as Émile took a step back in disgust. This same boy who had been inside me a few evenings earlier.

The blade did not, however, fall across my throat. Instead, Émile pressed it against my forehead, at the very start of my hairline, and dragged it back, mercilessly, taking my hair with it while cutting into the skin. I screamed louder than I thought possible and heard Mother screeching too as M. Toussaint performed the same action on her. With a flourish, my barber scattered the first strands of hair upon the ground, into the piss, black spider strands among the yellow, and then he began again, drawing another streak, the blade lacerating my skull in unforgiving slashes. I could feel the blood trickling into my eyes as he shaved me, making sure that he hurt me enough that I would feel everything. I vomited into my lap and saw that Mother, next to me, had fainted. A woman came forward and slapped her hard to wake her, and only when she was revived did Rémy recommence his shearing. We would be conscious throughout our ordeal. I stared at her, her beauty destroyed, replaced by a gruesome head, half bare, with clumps still standing and blood seeping down her face. She breathed in deeply then let out a cry that was neither human nor animal as Émile attacked me again, from the rear this time, and I shouted too, although I knew that resistance was futile, that they were committed to their work and that our cries were nothing more than a discordant accompaniment to their task.

Finally, they were done. We were not entirely bald; there were too many hideous clumps and strands remaining to make us look as disfigured as possible. My skull felt as if it were on fire, the blood running so deeply into my eyes that I could make out my jury only through a viscous red screen. Our ropes were untied and I fell from the chair, crawling along the ground, uncertain where I was going. I pleaded for mercy. Had others done that, I wondered, while I was safely in my house in that other place, playing with my dolls, flirting with Lieutenant Kotler, ordering Pavel to make my lunch? Had others begged like me? Their pleas had gone unanswered, despite their innocence, so why should mine be heard?

"Help me," I whispered as I dragged myself along the stone floor, my legs and knees scraping on the gritty surface, the pain meaning nothing to me now. "Help me, please. Someone. Help me."

And then, at last, from out of the darkness, emerged a familiar face.

He was here.

He was here at last.

My brother. Trapped forever at nine years of age, wearing his favorite shorts, a white shirt, and a blue jumper. He had been standing in the center of the group, it seemed, throughout it all, watching me, and he approached me now with no emotion on his face. In his left hand he was carrying his beloved copy of *Treasure Island*.

I dragged my body toward him and called out his name, wondering whether I too was dead now and he had come to claim me for the afterlife. I threw my hand out to him. I wanted him to hold on to it, to take me wherever he had been taken and to whatever place he was returning. But it was covered in blood and he simply stared at it, shaking his head, as if he were disappointed that I could disgrace myself so badly before the world, before him, and before God.

Interlude

The Fence

LONDON 1970

Although the doctor assigned to my case was of a similar age to me, she experienced very little hardship during the war, having been evacuated to a farm in Wales in early 1940 and, if the stories she told me were to be believed, spending a rather idyllic time there. Her father fought, but survived, and an older brother lost a hand but was left otherwise intact.

"And you, Gretel," she asked repeatedly during my first months in the hospital. "What experiences did you have? We were all scarred by it one way or another, don't you agree?"

I told her little, but then I spoke little. When I did feel the need to say something, I remained loyal to the fiction that Mother had invented almost a quarter of a century earlier, recounting stories of my youth in Nantes, where I had supposedly witnessed none of the fighting and led a mostly humdrum existence. What I did not reveal was how difficult our relationship had become, for while the events in Paris made me consider for the first time my own culpability, and begin to accept it, it had the opposite effect on Mother, who grew increasingly hostile to any criticism of the Nazis. Indeed, for someone who had remained mostly uninterested in politics, even while the war was being waged, the humiliation and injury we had received at the hands of our self-styled jury appeared to harden her stance immeasurably, making her so loyal to the fallen regime that our relationship grew progressively fractured. Over time, she began to speak of Hitler as a martyr to a cause that had been unjustly defeated, and I learned not to contradict her, for our arguments became so venomous that I feared she would physicilly attack me.

"I don't think you're being honest with me," replied Dr. Allenby, looking disappointed. "I'm good with accents and I don't hear much French in your voice."

"It's long gone," I told her. "I spent some time in Australia in the early 1950s before settling in England. And I've been here for seventeen years now. It's natural that my voice would have changed."

At moments like this, she would simply smile and make notes on her pad, clearly not believing a word of it but choosing not to argue. Perhaps she felt that, in time, I would learn to trust her and unburden myself of my secrets, which was testament to how little she knew me.

"I have a theory," she told me on one occasion, "that those of us who were children during the 1940s will spend our lives coming to terms with the trauma of so much bloodshed. We all lost someone, didn't we? We were confronted with grief at an early age. And guilt."

"Why would we feel guilt?" I asked her, surprised by the remark. I knew why I should feel it but couldn't understand why she would.

"Well, for not being old enough to fight, I suppose," she said. "Survivor's guilt, if you will."

This was the kind of remark that made me feel I had no business being in the psychiatric ward at all. If Dr. Allenby thought she had any concept of what guilt was, then she was fooling herself. Guilt was what kept you awake in the middle of the night or, if you managed to sleep, poisoned your dreams. Guilt intruded upon any happy moment, whispering in your ear that you had no right to pleasure.

Guilt followed you down streets, interrupting the most mundane moments with remembrances of days and hours when you could have done something to prevent tragedy but chose to do nothing. When you chose to play with your dolls instead. Or stick pins in maps of Europe, following the armies' progression. Or flirt with a handsome young lieutenant.

That was guilt.

And as for grief. Well, perhaps that was a shared emotion. None of us had a monopoly there.

I spent almost a year in the hospital but remember little of my early months there. Subsequently, I learned that I refused to speak at all at the start, ate almost nothing, neither read nor interacted with the other patients, and either lay in bed staring at the ceiling or sat in a bath chair in the garden observing the birds. I do recall a certain sense of contentment, though, a feeling that I had somehow managed to escape the world at last and could be left alone now with my thoughts until I grew old and withered away. It was a pleasant enough idea, even though I was not yet forty. I think I had been seeking that kind of peace for the best part of thirty years and believed that, if I was forced to remain alive, then it was better that I should be kept away from civilized society.

In retrospect, it's hard to believe that it took so long for me finally to have the breakdown that had been coming on for decades. When it hit me, however, it was not directly related to the past but to the present. And not to my brother, but to my son.

From the moment I learned that I was pregnant I knew that I would be a terrible mother. For four months, I chose not to consult a doctor or tell Edgar, hoping that I might be mistaken. I considered having an abortion, but the idea of some filthy, back-street pseudo-clinic terrified me and I was far too much of a coward to indulge in any of the popular wisdom about how to end an unwanted pregnancy.

I prayed instead that I would miscarry, but no, my body seemed determined to see the business through. In the end, I had no choice but to inform Edgar that he was going to be a father and, of course, he was thrilled. By now, I had made my peace with the inevitable, but hoped that the child would be a girl. On the day that I went into labor, I did not scream as other women did; that is, until I was told that I had, in fact, given birth to a son.

My fear was that, as he grew, he would resemble my brother, that he would behave like him or share some of his characteristics. I had spent so many years trying to forget the past that I did not want to be reminded of him in any way.

Edgar's mother, Jennifer, was a great help. She didn't much care for me, but she did love her son and grandson and, as soon as she realized that I was entirely unfit for the task at hand, she took over with brisk efficiency while having the decency never to say so. I refused to breastfeed and avoided taking the baby for walks in his pram. I wanted as little to do with him as possible and left everything to my husband and mother-in-law.

In those early years, there was very little resemblance—in fact, he took after the Fernsby side of the family—but then, when he turned seven, I started to see signs of my brother that showed themselves in less physical ways. His love of books, for one thing. His interest in explorers. His determination to get out of the flat and run into the wooded area behind Winterville Court, which in those days had not been developed to the extent that it has been today, and see what he might discover over there.

It was when Caden turned nine that the builders came in and started work on the land behind us, which was ripe for development.

While they left us the thick front of trees that made us feel that we were in a more rural location than we actually were, they constructed a fence further beyond them and Caden regularly ran toward it, looking across, fascinated by what was taking place on the other side. He was utterly captivated by the demolition and construction equipment, the workmen in their yellow hats and hi-visibility jackets.

Although the site was well secured, I did not like the idea of him being there so often. It was a noisy place, a filthy place, and whenever he disobeyed me and made his way toward the fence he would return covered in dirt and debris. I would have to throw him into the bathtub to scrub him clean. No matter how furious I grew with him, he didn't seem to care and no threats that I made could keep him away from the place.

And then, one day, he simply disappeared.

He had run off after finishing his homework and, when I searched for him in his bedroom, I knew exactly where he had gone and stormed down the garden in search of him, furious that he had disobeyed me yet again. When I arrived at the fence, however, he was nowhere to be seen. I wandered up and down, calling out his name, but there was no answer, and the men on the other side, wandering around in their workwear, began to stare in my direction as if I had lost my mind. I was about to turn back for Winterville Court and phone for the police when I noticed a small gap in the base of the fence, big enough for a child his age to crawl beneath. It had been raised from the ground and I knew immediately that he had entered the site.

For a moment, the world swirled around me and I thought that I was going to faint. I imagined what Mother and Father had felt like, all those years ago, when they had stood at their own fence and discovered my brother's pile of discarded clothes upon the ground. I tried to scream, imagining that I had lost Caden as my parents and I had lost my brother, but no sound would emerge from my mouth.

My hands pulled at the fence, and I crawled through, lacerating my face and arms. When I emerged on the other side, I found myself running in all directions, shouting my son's name as the men watched me in bewilderment.

It took only a minute to find him, standing with one of the foremen, who seemed to be enjoying explaining the details of a large schematic of what the site would one day look like, when it was completed. Caden was wearing a protective hat and, somehow, had found a jacket of his own. I ran toward him, calling out his name, and he turned, frightened by my intensity. I confess that I laid hands on my son, although this was the only time, slapping him so hard that he fell to the ground.

Much of what happened after that remains a mystery to me, but soon, Edgar was called, then a doctor, and I was brought to hospital. From there, to a more specialized unit, where I was sedated for several weeks and accommodated in my own room. I was worn thin by fevers and nightmares, unaware of whether I was in seventies London or forties Poland. The two blended. Caden and my brother became one and the same in my head. Father and Edgar too. The past and the present merged.

In the end, it was decided that I should see no member of my family for three months, and I worked exclusively with Dr. Allenby, who guided me through my troubles. Edgar visited twice a week for the year of my confinement. His mother took over my duties at home, leaving me to recover in peace. There was a lot to unravel. Berlin, that other place, Paris, Sydney, London. The people whose paths had crossed with my own. The mysterious cruelty of my life. By the time I finally emerged I was a very different woman to the one who had entered.

But, unlike so many others, at least I was able to go home.

Part 2

Beautiful Scars

LONDON 2022 / SYDNEY 1953

ONE

Only a ten-minute walk from Winterville Court stands a pub called the Merriweather Arms with a pleasant garden to its rear. Occasionally, on a warm afternoon, I like to wander down there and take a seat beneath one of the parasols, reading a book and enjoying a glass or two of rosé. It's a nice break from the flat and, these days, I prefer not to venture too far from home.

I found myself there a few days after the troubling late-night events in Flat One. I was wearing my prescription sunglasses while continuing with Marie Antoinette, who was now scandalizing France with the Diamond Necklace Affair. The garden itself was about a third full and, at one point, I happened to look up and noticed an actress best known for her stage work seated on the opposite side with a man who, when I looked more closely, I was certain was Alex Darcy-Witt. The pair were engaged in conversation and she was laughing at some remark he'd made. Perhaps accustomed to being stared at, even feeling it her due, she did not turn my way, but he sensed something and glanced in my direction, at which point I quickly returned to my book. His presence made me anxious, however, and I found myself reading the same paragraph over and over, barely taking in the words. When a waiter approached to ask whether I wanted another drink, my instinct was to say no and return home as rapidly as I could, but I did not want to walk past the pair and so changed my mind and ordered another. When he brought it, I noticed the actress rising behind him and kissing Mr. Darcy-Witt on both cheeks, before waving in a deliberate fashion as she departed, the same wave I had once offered Émile in imitation of Dietrich. He, however, did not follow her, and it took only a few moments for him to come over to my table.

"Excuse me," he said, and I glanced up, pretending that I had been completely oblivious to his presence all this time. "I'm sorry to interrupt, but I think we might be neighbors."

"Really?" I asked. "Are you sure?"

"I live in Flat One, Winterville Court. I think you live above me? You've met my wife and son."

"Oh yes, of course," I said, employing all my own acting skills to pretend that I had not recognized him.

"Do you mind if I join you? There are two things I hate in life: leaving a beer half full and drinking alone."

He laughed, as if this were a great joke, and, unable to think of a reason to say no, I indicated the seat opposite me. He retrieved his glass, which was in fact about two thirds full, and sat down.

"Gorgeous day, isn't it?" he asked, looking around and smiling widely.

"Very pleasant," I agreed.

"I suppose we should introduce ourselves."

He stared at me and I realized that he expected me to go first.

"Gretel Fernsby," I said, extending my hand.

"Alexander Darcy-Witt," he replied, shaking it and holding the fingers a little more tightly than necessary. "Alex." Close up, the resemblance with Richard Gere lessened.

"I understand that you're a film producer," I said.

"For my sins, yes," he said, nodding. "You probably saw me talking to—." And here he named the actress who had just left. "I've been trying to persuade her to play a grandmother in a film I'm making and she's proving a lot harder to convince than I expected. It's a good part and she'd be working with a great cast but she's worried that, once you start playing older roles, that's it. There's no way back."

"I wouldn't know anything about that," I told him. "But I've seen her on stage a few times. She's terribly good. You'd be lucky to have her."

"I would, yes," he said, sipping his beer. "So, tell me a little about yourself, Mrs. Fernsby. It is Mrs., I assume?"

"It is, yes," I said. "Although my husband, Edgar, died some years ago."

While my first instinct whenever anyone addresses me by my married name has always been to invite them to call me Gretel, I chose not to on this occasion, preferring to maintain our distance.

"What would you like to know?" I asked. "If you're hoping to cast me as a great-grandmother, then I'm afraid I'll have to disappoint you. I have no skills in that department."

He looked as if he was judging me silently.

"Have you lived in Winterville Court long?" he asked.

"Most of my adult life," I told him, although I suspected that he knew this already. Madelyn, I guessed, would have imparted to him all the information that I had given to her.

"Doesn't it get rather lonely for a widow?"

"Sometimes," I admitted. "But that's not the fault of the building, is it? It would be the same wherever I lived."

"Still," he replied, looking away. "All those memories. That can be hard, I imagine. Were you and Mr. Fernsby soulmates?"

I was taken aback by the intimacy of the question, declining to answer and turning it on him instead.

"Why, is that how you would describe your relationship with your wife, Mr. Darcy-Witt? Soulmates?"

"Call me Alex, please," he said. "I hope we are. I'm lucky to have married her. Well, you've met her, so you'll understand. I genuinely think she's the most beautiful woman I've ever met in my life."

I frowned, irritated that this was the greatest compliment he could pay her. Her beauty. But somehow, it didn't surprise me.

"Henry is charming," I said. "Before you moved in, I was a little worried about a child living in the building—they can be terribly noisy, of course—but I never hear him at all. He's very well behaved."

Alex laughed and shook his head. "You don't know him," he said. "He can be an absolute nightmare when he gets going."

It was true that I barely knew the boy, but somehow I doubted this. It seemed obvious to me that Henry was an introvert. A shy boy, bookish and quiet.

"I'm glad I've run into you actually," said Alex finally, after an uncomfortable pause. "I think we might have frightened you the other night."

"I don't know what you're talking about," I said. I really didn't want to discuss the events I'd witnessed.

"I think you do."

I lifted my rosé and took a rather large mouthful, eager for the alcohol to offer me the courage I needed. I looked behind him. Somehow, without my noticing, the beer garden had almost entirely cleared out and there were only four other people present now, sitting at some distance from us. I began to feel rather nervous.

"Madelyn throws little tantrums from time to time," he continued. "You mustn't think badly of her, but she's been like that for some years now. She takes medication for it, of course, but when I'm away, she tends to forget. Or she claims to forget anyway. It's hard to know whether she does it on purpose. When I'm home, I give her the tablets first thing in the morning and then I hold her mouth open afterward to make sure she's swallowed them."

I remained silent. This seemed an extraordinary thing to admit. Again, I was brought back to the hospital and the morning, afternoon and evening rituals that, I was told, would help to make me better but which, in fact, only made me feel less connected with the world than I had before.

"Anyway, I think she might have forgotten to take them for a few days," he continued. "The fact is, when I came back from LA, she was all over the place."

"I see."

"She's better now."

"I'm glad to hear it."

"The last thing I needed was a repeat of the last incident."

I tried not to betray my curiosity. I refused to ask, waiting for him to explain it in his own time.

"Henry's arm," he said finally. "This must be two months ago. I was attending a film festival and she went off her meds. When I got back, well, something unfortunate had taken place. I think she got a bit rough with him. Unintentionally, of course. She's a wonderful mother when she's behaving herself. A wonderful wife too," he added after a moment. "When she's behaving herself."

I didn't know which part of this speech to investigate first. "She broke his arm?" I asked, surprised and disbelieving at once.

"Not intentionally," he said, leaning forward and sweeping a few fallen leaves from the tabletop. "As I said, Henry can be a handful, and he acts up even worse when I'm not around. He knows better than to pull any of his stunts when I'm *in situ*. I suppose one thing led to another and . . . snap." He'd picked up a small twig that had fallen onto the table and broke it between his hands. "Children's bones can be brittle, Gretel. We forget how fragile they are."

"Do we?" I asked, noting how he was employing my first name anyway, despite not having been invited to do so.

"Anyway," he said, finishing the rest of his beer in one draft. "I just wanted to explain and to assure you that there will be no further incidents of that kind."

"As I said, Mr. Darcy-Witt," I told him. "I don't know what you're referring to. I haven't been disturbed since you all arrived."

He smiled again and looked me directly in the eye. "For someone who thinks she has no skills in the acting department, you, my dear, have the one thing that every actress needs above all others."

I stared at him. I had no choice but to ask.

"And what is that?" I asked.

"The ability to lie."

TWO

At the beginning of 1952, when I was twenty-one years old, I made the long journey by ship from France to Australia. Mother had died three weeks earlier, her liver corroded by alcohol, her mind addled by the multiple griefs she'd endured. I bought my ticket on the very day that I buried her. I wanted to get as far from Europe as I possibly could, and there was nowhere more distant, after all, than the Antipodes.

After the traumatic events in Paris, we had been flung mercilessly out into the streets, having been told by the erstwhile Resistance members that they would not even waste a bullet on us, and had fled within days, making our way to Rouen, our shaven scalps disguised beneath head scarves. I took classes in English from a Norfolk woman who had lived there since her marriage, knowing that I would need to speak the language if I was to survive in my chosen destination.

I had few belongings of value but had saved enough money from my job as a seamstress to afford a passage on board a ship, and treated it like a wonderful adventure, even though there was almost no privacy on board. The women in steerage all slept in enormous dormitories at one end of the ship with their children, while the men had their cots at the other. It was a time of emigration and many of the passengers were British—the ship had begun its voyage in Southampton—some of whom wore black to mark the recent passing of their king. They had grown weary of their bleak homeland, which had found austerity a poor substitute for the peace that had existed before the war. Like me, they were hoping for sunshine and new opportunities on the other side of the world.

For the first day or two, there was excitement and optimism on board. People talked to each other and formed quick, tentative friendships, although it did not take long for fatigue to set in, at which point our six-week voyage became fractious. Several people—men and women alike—ended up in the makeshift prison cells that the officers kept belowdecks, and the remains of at least half a dozen others were wrapped in shrouds and cast into the ocean when they failed to survive the journey.

There were romances too, furtive couplings late at night in hidden corners of the ship, although I steered clear of such intrigues. It had been six years since I'd given my innocence to Émile and I had felt only fear and distrust of every boy I'd encountered since then. Some made advances toward me, and there were a few to whom I was drawn, but I could not allow my defenses to drop. My rejections made me equally unpopular among men, who saw me as stand-offish and frigid, and women, who believed I thought myself too good for the boys on board. I longed for a cabin of my own, where I could avoid their stares and gossip, but it would have been a foolish extravagance to waste money on one. A new life awaited me in New South Wales, and I would need to be solvent if I was to make it work.

In time, however, I became friendly with an Irish woman named Cait Softly, and we took to wandering the decks together for exercise and eating in each other's company. I liked Cait. She was only a year older than me and had left Ireland in search of a better life when she found herself pregnant and unmarried. Upon learning of the scandal, her father had kicked her so hard in the stomach that he killed the child.

I liked the sea. I had not grown up around water and I found it soothing. The sailors said that ours was not a bad crossing, that the weather and the waves were proving more favorable to us than they often did, but while both Cait and I had strong stomachs and did not succumb to the early sea-sickness that plagued much of the ship's manifest, it still seemed at times that we might be pulled beneath the waves on stormy nights when the ship, which had seemed so substantial on shore, revealed its true insignificance within the infinite landscape of the ocean. The salt water often proved painful to me too. Although my hair had long since grown back, there were still scars upon my skull and they stung when splashed with water. At least it *had* grown back, though, unlike Mother's; she had to wear a headscarf day and night until her death. For a woman who prized this aspect of a woman's beauty above all others, it served as an unhappy daily reminder, rebuke and accusation.

"We'll get a place together, will we?" asked Cait one evening as we sat by the railings, watching the sun set on the horizon. "For the company, I mean, and so we have another girl to rely on."

I considered it. I'd planned on living alone and taking no other person into my confidence, but it seemed now that it would not be a bad idea to have a friend in a strange land.

"It'd be cheaper too," she added. "All we'd need is a bedroom, a place to sit in the evenings for the chat and a bit of a kitchen."

"All right," I agreed. "Have you thought about what you'll do, then?" I asked. "To earn money, I mean."

"I haven't a notion," she said, laughing into the breeze. "Do you have any skills yourself? I can sing a bit and I can pour drinks. I'd like the barmaid's life, I think. The sociability of it. Daddy owned a pub, you see, the malignant ol' bastard, and he had me in there cleaning from the time I could hold a mop."

"I can sew," I told her. "That's about it."

"Sure, there's always a need for seamstresses," she said, nodding. "There's jobs that'll never go out of fashion, no matter if the world is up or down, and that's one of them. Undertakers, there's another."

I smiled and she pulled a pipe from the pocket of her dress, lighting it up. I had been shocked the first time I'd observed her doing this but now it rather amused me, and I liked the scent, which was an intoxicating blend of rose, cloves, and cinnamon.

"Will you have a puff?" she asked, taking a few herself before pointing the stem in my direction.

"I won't, but thank you."

"It'll put hairs on your chest."

A couple of young men strolled by and when one of them whistled in our direction Cait sent them away with a flea in their ears. I wasn't so sure. She often chatted with the men on board, and they danced attendance on her, for while I was pretty, Cait was beautiful. She stood at almost six feet in height and had the sort of body that pin-ups were made of. Defying stereotype, her long thick hair was not red but black, and even though we had precious few opportunities to wash, it seemed to shine every day.

"Will you be looking for a husband over there, do you think?" she asked another night, and I shook my head.

"No," I said, before adopting my best Greta Garbo accent. "*I vant to be alone.*"

"Men are the very devil," she said, puffing away at her pipe. "I've no use for them at all."

"And the fellow who . . . ?"

I glanced at her empty stomach.

"He was a bowsy," she said. "A good-for-nothing. How I ever let him near me is a mystery even to myself. No, the fellas can stay away, as far as I'm concerned. We'll be a pair of spinsters, will we?"

Although I smiled, I didn't care for the concept in my head. The truth was, despite my distrust of men, I still felt a desire to fall in love and to marry. I barely admitted this to myself, let alone to Cait, but when I fell asleep at night I dreamed of an Australian man who might take me in his arms and tell me that he would take care of me forever, if only I would take care of him too, and that he didn't care who I was or what I'd done because it wasn't the past that mattered, it was only the future.

"So, are you going to tell me?" Cait asked on our last night as the crew mingled with the passengers for the final time and what remained of the caskets of wine were opened.

"Tell you what?" I asked.

"The secret you're hiding. I know there is one. I've known it from the start. You can trust me, you know. I don't judge. I have my own share of skeletons. You'd find less in a graveyard."

"I don't know what you mean," I said, wondering whether I wore the great shame of that other place on my skin so obviously.

"You do indeed, so don't be lying to me. It's all right. You don't have to say if you don't want to. But you'll tell me one day, probably when we're both in our cups. And then I'll tell you mine too."

"You have a secret?"

"I do, of course."

"Go on then."

"Not a chance, missy. But someday, if you're lucky."

We stood together, holding hands, on the morning that our ship rounded Watsons Bay and passed by the rocky peninsula where the wife of a New South Wales governor had once sat to watch the transported convicts arrive to serve their sentences. Unlike them, of course, we were not prisoners. We were free people. But considering the thousand or more souls on board, it was hard not to wonder what multitude of sins we'd committed between us that we had chosen this distant land as the place to wash them clean.

As the ship finally dropped anchor, and the passengers and crew let out a great cheer, I asked myself whether I could really expect to find forgiveness on this youthful continent. At the back of my mind, I knew that it would take more than 10,000 miles to achieve absolution.

THREE

I t's called Autumn Valley," said Caden, handing me the brochure
for the retirement village. I flicked through it quickly. The pages
were filled with photographs of remarkably attractive elderly people
who looked almost hysterical with joy, as if their entire lives had
been a mere preface to their journey to this Utopia. "They have book
clubs and sewing circles. Movie nights and—"

"Winter Valley would be more appropriate, don't you think?" I
asked, looking up at him. "The residents are coming to the end of
their metaphorical year, so to speak, rather than just starting to notice that the nights are beginning to close in."

"I suppose that might make it seem rather bleak," he replied. "It
looks very nice, don't you think?"

"Are you considering moving there?" I asked. "You'd be young to
enter such a place, you're only sixty-one, but if you feel it's necessary,
then of course you must do so. Is sewing something you've been interested in taking up?"

He smiled. "Ha ha," he said. "You did say you'd think about it,
Mother."

I handed him back the brochure and poured us both another cup of tea. "And I did think about it," I told him. "And decided it wasn't for me."

"Eleanor's uncle retired to Autumn Valley," he continued. "And he said it was the best decision he'd ever made."

"I'm surprised you didn't bring him along to convince me."

"Can't. He's dead."

"Well, there you are," I said, sitting back in my chair, triumphant now. "We all die sooner or later, but in places like that, people just give up the ghost. No, I'm sorry, Caden. I've made my decision and I don't want this to be an ongoing conversation. I'm not leaving Winterville Court, and that's the end of the matter. And, by the way, I don't appreciate you talking to Oberon Hargrave about it. I prefer to keep my business private."

He did his best to look innocent. "I don't know what you're—"

"Yes, you do, so don't play the innocent. Remember, I've known you all your life and you can get nothing past me. You and he are in cahoots, trying to force two old ladies out of their homes, and I won't stand for it. If, for some reason, I become completely incapacitated or start insisting that Mrs. Thatcher is still prime minister, then you can have the men in white coats carry me off. But until then, I'm staying right here, and that, as they say, is that."

He knew me well enough to accept that once I had made my mind up about something there would be no changing it.

"Now, as for your business problems," I continued. "I've had a think about that too and have decided that I'm willing to make an investment."

"Oh?" he asked, brightening up now. "How much?"

"That's what I love about you, Caden," I said. "No pussyfooting around. Always straight to the point."

"I'm sorry, I just—"

"It's fine. I'm only teasing." I wasn't entirely; he really was shameless.

"On a scale of one to ten, how serious are your difficulties? And be honest with me. Don't be greedy."

He thought about it for a long time before answering. "I'd say a solid six," he said. "But a six that could swiftly turn into an eight if I don't make some serious changes soon."

I nodded, then walked over to my writing desk and removed my check book from the upper drawer. Glancing out of the window toward the street, I saw Heidi locked in conversation with Madelyn Darcy-Witt and longed to know what they were talking about. I watched them carefully, hoping they wouldn't sense they were being observed, until Madelyn threw her head back in laughter, which struck me as odd, as Heidi was not known as a great wit. I sat down at the desk but, before writing anything, turned to look at my son, who was watching me with unapologetic eagerness.

"I thought £100,000," I told him, removing the cap from my fountain pen. "Will that keep the wolf from the door?"

His expression was a curious melange of relief and disappointment. Perhaps he thought I would offer less; perhaps more. But it was a substantial amount. A full ten percent of my net worth, excluding the value of the flat itself.

"It's very generous of you," he said. "That will help enormously. I'll pay you back, of course, when—"

"There's no need for that," I told him, filling in the figures and signing my name. "Everything will come to you in time anyway, so let's just call it an advance, all right? But this is all I can give you, Caden, is that understood? I have a nest egg, yes, but it's only so big and this makes a dent in it. So use it wisely."

He had the good grace to look embarrassed as I handed it over— in fairness, it must be humiliating for a man of his age to ask for money from his mother—and I returned to my armchair.

"So," I said finally, as he folded his ill-gotten gains in half and tucked the check away in his wallet. "I suppose the wedding is still going ahead?"

"Oh yes," he replied. "But we've decided to keep it small. No fuss. Just family and a few close friends."

"Very sensible," I told him approvingly. Caden's weddings had always been a little extravagant in the past, as if he needed to prove to others the measure of his success. But if things really were as tight as he said, then he could hardly afford to be profligate.

"We're looking at about six weeks from now," he added. "A registry office. I'll keep you informed. You will be coming this time, I presume?"

"Don't be like that," I said. "I've only missed one."

He nodded and, when he caught my eye, neither of us could help it; we both started laughing. We carried on for a full minute until I had to take a handkerchief from my pocket and wipe the tears from my eyes. It was at moments like this, when I could tease him and he seemed to rather enjoy it, that we had some degree of closeness.

"You're a terrible old woman," he said, shaking his head, and I agreed that I was. He looked around the room, delivering a deep sigh, and I wondered whether he was calculating how long he needed to stay now that our financial business had come to an end. "Oh, I meant to ask you," he said. "How are things going with the new neighbors?"

"They're a curious bunch," I said. "She seems as if she has her head in the clouds most of the time and he seems rather a bully. Or maybe it's just the environment he works in. You do read stories about these intimidating film producers, don't you? How they terrorize their staff and harass vulnerable young actresses. Perhaps they treat their families with a similar disregard."

"And the child?"

"Quiet. I like him."

"That's good. I know you're not great with small boys."

I looked at him, but nothing in his expression suggested that he had been intending to hurt me. Still, I understood how he could say it. After all, neither of us could pretend that I had been the perfect mother and I knew that he'd been bullied terribly when his friends discovered that his mother was holed up in what they called the loony bin.

Later, when he left, he kissed me on the cheek and thanked me again for helping him out.

"You're very welcome," I said. "But if I hear that you and Oberon have even so much as picked up the phone to talk to each other, I will cancel that check. So be warned."

"Oh, Mother," he said, winking at me and laughing. "It would be too late by then anyway. I'll have this lodged in my account within the hour." He skipped off down the stairs then, with as much elegance as a man of his girth can skip, and I smiled as I returned indoors. The truth was, had it not been for his remark about my not being good with small boys, it would have been one of our friendliest encounters in years.

FOUR

Having only previously lived in Europe, I was unprepared for how oppressive the temperature could be in Sydney. My skin, naturally pale, burned easily, my scarred scalp singed and, for several weeks, I was so exhausted by mid-afternoon that I would fall asleep wherever I was and then have difficulty sleeping through the night.

Cait and I found lodgings on Kent Street, close to the harbor, in a Queenslander house made from timber with a veranda extending around the upper floor. The lower part of the building was occupied by three middle-aged bachelor brothers who left early every morning in tradesmen's clothes and returned home drunk late at night. At first, I was worried that they might prove bothersome to Cait or me, but in fact they scarcely acknowledged our presence other than to make their disdain for women keenly felt, particularly women who had the audacity to live without the protection of a father or husband.

Employment opportunities were abundant, and I found myself working in a ladies' clothing store at the north end of George Street, under the tutelage of a woman some twenty years my senior called Miss Brilliant, which I thought a wonderful name. Miss Brilliant—I never did discover her Christian name—had inherited the shop from her mother and, when she told me this, I thought of Émile and his inheritance, and just as quickly tried to dismiss him from my mind. So I was a shop girl after all, I told myself when offered the job. Everything that Mother had always felt was beneath me.

Miss Brilliant was not, I felt, cut out to work with the public. She despised the ordinary working women who made up the bulk of our clientele, most of whom could afford to purchase a new skirt or blouse only a couple of times a year or perhaps a pair of nylons on the rare occasions when we could get them in stock. She had what could only be called aspirations, regaling me and her other employees with tales about the grander Sydney stores where wealthy women shopped and how she should have preferred their patronage.

It wasn't often that an Aborigine woman would risk stepping through our doors, but it happened occasionally. Black women too, and sometimes the immigrants from the Samoan Islands or Papua New Guinea. Miss Brilliant called them "wogs" and let out a roar when any of them entered, demanding to know what they wanted, telling them that they were being watched and that she would see them in prison if they stole anything. She did not object to taking their money, of course, but always put on a pair of silk gloves when accepting it. When the customer left, rather than placing the cash in the till, she would hand the notes or coins to me before sending me down the road to the bank to lodge the money directly into her account.

While I endured life under Miss Brilliant, Cait found a job that she adored, working in a pub called Fortune of War that stood on the edge of the harbor, with clear views across to Bennelong Point, where, long after I had left Australia, the opera house would be built. The pub had an open frontage and a bar that ran down the center with high stools placed on either side. The men would gather there after work, enjoying the cool breezes that drifted in from the water as they sank schooner after schooner of ice-cold beer. Toward the rear was a smaller room that held a half-dozen tables, where the younger men took the women they were courting. Despite the long hours, Cait loved it and soon became a favorite of the regulars, not just because she was easy on the eye but for her quick tongue and her ability to make everyone feel welcome. Our different working hours benefitted us both as she worked well into the night, giving me the freedom of our flat in the evenings, while I started early, affording her some privacy in the mornings. It was a perfect arrangement.

Occasionally, in need of company, I would make my way there when I left work and sit at the bar, drinking a glass or two, even chatting on occasion to some of the other patrons. An old man called Quaresby, who claimed to have been one of those who built the Harbour Bridge, took a shine to me and often sat on the stool next to mine, calling me "darl" and "sweetheart," while trying to put a hand on my leg, but I made it clear that I was not interested in his attentions. Once, when I emerged from the ladies' room, he was waiting for me outside and tried to shove me back through the door, insisting that he had something important that he needed to impart to me, but I refused, pushing him against the wall, where he hit his head against the corner of a painting. He left me alone after that, ignoring me for a full calendar month before growing friendly again and behaving as if nothing untoward had ever taken place.

It was on one such evening, some months into my stay, that I sat in my regular spot as Cait handed an envelope to me, her share of the monthly rent, which I intended to deliver to our landlord on my way home. On the opposite side of the bar was a man wearing a tan bush hat and, next to him, a boy of about seven. His son, I assumed. I'd seen them both there before. The man, Cait had told me, often came in after work with the boy in tow. He'd drink an orange juice and it was obvious that he loved sitting at the bar with the grown-ups. I was counting my own money into the envelope when I heard another man's voice emerging from the side of the bar that led into the snug.

"Another James Boags, please, miss," he said.

"Coming up," replied Cait, turning away from me and strolling over to the tap to pour it. Without being certain why, every sense in my body was suddenly on high alert.

"Warm today, yes?" continued the man in a friendly tone as Cait topped off the glass, and she turned back to him cheerfully.

"They say it'll get hotter by the weekend. It'll be like a steam box in here. Anything else, darling?"

"No, thank you," he replied.

"What's beer taste like?" asked the boy, and there was a slight hesitation before the man answered.

"I'd let you taste it," he said, "but your father might object."

"No skin off my nose," said the other man. "If he wants to be sick, it'll be on him."

"All right then, little man," replied the first. "One sip."

It was with the use of this phrase—"little man"—that I felt my stomach clench and held on to the counter to steady myself. I wanted to turn around but dared not, instead keeping my eyes focused directly on my shoes. The man had done all he could to disguise his accent, but I could hear the Teutonic strains underneath. When Cait returned, having taken payment, my expression appeared to startle her.

"Gretel," she said, her voice rising in concern. "What's happened? You look as if you've seen a ghost."

Only then did I look up and dare to glance across the bar. The man was gone now, returned to the small room in the rear, and I couldn't see him from my vantage point. Still, I stared at the woodwork that separated us, as if by doing so I might be able to burn a hole through the joinery and recognize the face on the other side.

"Gretel," she repeated. "What's wrong, love? Do you want some water? Hold on, let me get you some."

She returned a moment later with a glass filled with iced water and I drank it down.

"I'm fine," I said, the words catching in my throat. "Something just . . . something came over me, that's all."

"The curse, is it?" she asked, lowering her voice a little.

"Yes. Something like that."

"Well, this heat doesn't help," she said, looking at me with real concern on her face. She reached out a hand and pressed it against my forehead to check my temperature, but I pulled away. I didn't like to be touched.

"You're not getting ill, I hope?" she asked. "Maybe you should go home and have a lie down."

I nodded and got to my feet uneasily. "Yes, I'll do that," I said. "Don't worry about me, I'll be fine."

Cait was summoned again, and she stared at me a moment longer before moving away to serve her customers. As I gathered my things and turned in the direction of the street, however, I knew that I could not possibly leave without being certain. It wasn't possible, I insisted to myself. We were many thousands of miles from Europe, and from Poland, after all. It couldn't be him. But that voice, I knew it so well. Quietly, hoping that I would not be observed, I made my way slowly toward the back room and stood in the shadows of the doorway, looking around until my gaze fell on the man seated alone at a table, his back turned to me, his thick blond hair neatly combed, his suit pristine. He was reading a newspaper while drinking his beer and, for now at least, seemed oblivious to my presence.

After a moment, however, he raised his head and turned it just a fraction, not quite looking behind him but offering the slightest hint of a profile. If he knew that he was being observed, then he did not intend to present himself to his onlooker. He sat very still, however, and I found myself almost unable to breathe. Despite being surrounded by people and conversation, for a moment it seemed as if we were the only two people there. He continued to hold his position and now I knew that he could sense my eyes upon him. But still, he did not turn. Finally, I could stand it no longer, turned and made my way back out to the street.

I could not be absolutely certain, of course. I had only heard a voice and seen a partial profile, but still, I knew in my heart that it was him.

FIVE

The urgency of the knock took me by surprise, and I sat up abruptly in my chair. I'd been watching an old movie on television, but it had proved rather dreary, and I'd started to nod off. The banging summoned me back to life, however, and I made my way to the door, anticipating a confused Heidi seeking help with another domestic issue. However, to my surprise, it wasn't my neighbor from across the hall, but from the floor below.

"Madelyn," I said, looking her up and down, and it appeared as if she, and not I, was the one who had just been woken from sleep. Her hair was unkempt, and her eyes were struggling to focus, mascara streaked beneath the lids. She looked utterly disheveled. "Is everything all right?"

"I forgot him," she replied, slurring her words. "I forgot Henry."

It was obvious that she'd been drinking, and I glanced at my watch. Ten minutes to three. I wondered what time she'd started.

"My dear," I said, standing back. "Do you want to come in? Can I make you some coffee, perhaps?"

"I forgot Henry," she repeated. "Forgot all about him." She shrugged, then laughed a little, putting a hand to her mouth. "You must think I'm the worst mother in the world."

"I don't think anything of the sort," I said, not entirely certain what she was talking about. "You forgot him? What do you mean, you forgot him?"

"School," she said, glancing up the staircase toward the top floor of Winterville Court, where an award-winning novelist and a prominent literary critic live across the hall from each other, writing for each other's displeasure. "He gets out at three. I won't make it in time. I don't feel well, Gretel. I need to go back to bed."

"Oh dear," I replied, uncertain why she was involving me in any of this but silently agreeing that sleep might be the best thing for her. "Does he have a key? Are you worried that he won't be able to get in? I can keep an eye out for him if—"

"I need you to collect him," she said. "He's not allowed to walk home on his own. He's too young. Someone might take him."

I stared at her. It was fantastical that she expected me to be responsible for bringing the child home. I wasn't his grandmother, after all. Didn't she have any friends or family that she could call on in times of crisis?

"Your husband," I said. "Mr. Darcy-Witt. Where is he?"

She rolled her eyes. "Who knows? In a hotel suite somewhere, I imagine. Auditioning actresses." She made inverted-comma symbols in the air with her fingers when she uttered the penultimate word, and I frowned. I thought that kind of behavior had been well and truly brought to a halt a few years earlier.

"And you can't contact him?" I asked. "Doesn't he have a mobile phone?"

"No," she said, increasingly anxious now. "I mean, yes, he has one, of course, but no, I can't call him on it. He hates me disturbing him during the day. Anyway, he'd kill me if he knew that I'd forgotten him." She shook her head, looking annoyed with herself. "Forgotten Henry, I mean. Not Alex. Sorry, I feel like I'm not making any sense."

"My dear, I'm ninety-one years old," I said, surprising myself by using my age as an excuse to get out of something. "You can't expect me to go traipsing around London in search of a little boy. There must be someone else you can ask."

"There's no one," she said, breathing heavily through her nose, as if trying to regain control of her senses. "I'm not allowed to have any friends of my own, you see," she added, then started laughing again. "I used to have them, of course. I used to have lots of them. Men and women. But he says they get in our way, that they're jealous of me and they gossip about me behind my back. They're full of spite, he says. Has anyone ever been jealous of you, Gretel?"

"Not that I can recall," I said. "I've never been the type of woman that others envy."

"I bet you were quite the beauty when you were younger," she said, looking me up and down. She smiled now, and I thought for a moment that she was going to fall over. "I can see it in your face. You have wonderful skin for someone so ancient." She frowned and put a finger to her lips and her face scrunched up in confusion. "What did I come up here for?" she asked me. "I've completely forgotten."

"Henry," I reminded her. "He needs to be collected from school."

"Fuck, that's right," she said, and I winced a little at the word. She had raised her voice and shouted it out loud and, from the other side of the hallway, Heidi's door opened, and her head poked out.

"What's going on?" she asked. For some inexplicable reason, she was wearing a red paper hat, the type one finds in a Christmas cracker, even though Christmas had come and gone months ago.

"Nothing, Heidi," I said, waving her away. "Go back inside. It's a lot of fuss over nothing."

"Who's that?" she asked, and Madelyn spun round irritably.

"Didn't you hear what Gretel said?" she snapped. "She said go back inside and mind your own business."

I closed my eyes briefly. Of course, I hadn't included that addendum but, by the expression on her face, Heidi clearly believed that I had, and she retreated into her flat, looking wounded. I would have to call on her later, I decided, and hope that she'd forgotten all about this. One advantage of her illness was that she overlooked the occasional slight.

"I can't stand busybodies," said Madelyn, turning back to me now. "So. Can you collect him for me, Gretel?" she asked. "I don't think I can. I'm in no state. If you don't, he'll be on his own and frightened."

I sighed. Really, this was too much, I thought, but I had no choice in the matter. One could hardly leave the poor boy sitting on his own for the rest of the afternoon, waiting for his mother. If one believed what one read in the papers, there were all sorts out there, just waiting to grab a child like that and take him away for nefarious purposes.

"Fine," I said with a deep sigh. "What school does he attend?"

She told me the name and I scribbled it down on a notepad, along with the address. It wasn't too far away but I had no intention of walking, particularly as the carriage clock above my mantelpiece had just chimed the hour and so the children, presumably, were already being let out.

"You're very kind," said Madelyn, turning around and making her way back down the stairs. She held on to the banister carefully, and I watched her, hoping she wouldn't fall.

"Perhaps I'll give him his supper," I suggested, calling after her. "You might not want him to see you in this condition. Is that all right?"

"Yes, yes," she said, without looking back. "That's very kind of you. I will have a little nap, I think. It's been such a day!"

I went back into my flat and retrieved my shoes, coat, and bag and checked my face quickly in the mirror. I had no idea what the poor unfortunate boy would think when he saw me arriving to collect him and I knew that I would have to think up a convincing reason for my presence.

As I stepped outside Winterville Court, ready to hail the first cab that came along, Madelyn's door opened once again and she came flying out, almost knocking me over in her urgency. She had already poured herself a fresh glass of wine and it came perilously close to spilling.

"Don't tell him," she whispered, clinging on to my arm, and the look on her face was chilling. I couldn't remember the last time that I'd seen anyone so frightened. "Promise me you won't tell him."

"I won't," I said irritably, peeling her off me. "I'll just say that you had an appointment you couldn't get out of. I'm sure he'll believe me. Children that age rarely question what they're told."

"Not Henry," she hissed, rolling her eyes as if I were the stupidest woman in the world. "Alex. Don't tell Alex. He'll kill me. I mean it. He could actually kill me."

SIX

"You're out of sorts," said Cait on Sunday afternoon as we took a long walk out of the city in the direction of North Head. It was cool that day, although I kept a hat on my head, for I was fearful of the damage the sun could do to my hidden scars. "What's the matter with you?"

"Nothing," I said, but it must have been obvious from my tone that I was lying.

"It's not nothing," she told me. "Is it a fella? Do you have your eye on someone, is that it?"

I shook my head. I was indeed thinking about a man, but not in the way that she meant it.

"Are you sure? Because it's usually a fella," she continued, marching along. She had long legs and, of the two of us, was usually the one who set the pace on these expeditions. It was all that I could do to keep up with her. "Not that you have much choice of them in that shop of yours. It's all women in there, isn't it?"

"Yes," I said.

"Lucky you," she replied, and I frowned, uncertain what she meant by this. "The fellas make a disgrace of themselves in the pub," she explained. "There's not one of them can hold their drink. Four or five beers and that's it, they're telling me what their daddies did at Gallipoli in the first war, what they did in the second, and believe me, you don't want to see the condition they leave the toilets in when they're in that state. Considering all they have to do is aim and shoot, it's a mystery to me how not one of them can hit his target. How they ever managed a gun is beyond me. And who has to mop it all up afterward? Muggins, that's who."

I laughed. Cait loved to talk disparagingly about her patrons, but I never once heard her complain about having to go into work.

"Actually, there was someone I wanted to ask you about," I said tentatively as we made our way along the rocky promontory.

"Oh yes?"

"There was a man I noticed in there when I came to collect the rent from you last week."

"You filthy article," she said. "You said there was no fella involved and here you are asking me about a—"

"No, it's not like that," I said, interrupting her. "I don't have any . . . romantic interest in him."

Didn't I? I wasn't entirely sure.

"You know most of the people who come in there, don't you?"

"Well, the regulars, yes," she admitted. "It keeps things friendly."

"The man I saw—"

"At the bar?"

"No, in the back room."

"Ah, that's a different type altogether. The working men all sit up at the bar because they get to flirt with me and the other girls as we pour their drinks. The bosses, the rich lads, the fellas wearing ties, they all sit in the back because they want to be left alone with their newspapers. I serve them their drinks and they don't say an awful lot. What did he look like, this fella of yours?"

"He was in his late twenties, perhaps," I said. "Tall, slender. Thick blond hair. Very handsome." I thought about it, wondering whether I could add any other description, but all I could do was reinforce what I'd just said. "Very handsome," I repeated.

"Australian?"

"No. Although he does his best to sound like one. Central European, I think. German."

She nodded. "I know who you mean," she said. "A regular in his way. He's not much of a one for the chat. And he's not German. He was waiting for his drink one time when a barrel was being changed and he asked me where I was from, and I told him Cork and I asked the same question in return."

"And how did he reply?"

"Prague."

I raised an eyebrow. He was no more Czech than I was.

"He shows up twice a week, Wednesdays and Fridays, like clockwork," continued Cait. "Always at the same time, around a quarter past six, so I suppose he comes directly from work. Someone told me he's a banker. He has the look of one anyway."

I nodded. This seemed like the kind of profession he would have entered. It had all the things that mattered to him. Power. Influence. Money. "And do you know his name?"

"Kozel," she replied. "That's his surname, anyway. I don't know his first. Do you fancy him, is that it? Because you'll be on to a loser there. He has a wife. She came in one time, dressed up to the nines and looking like a film star."

"Was she Australian?" I asked, trying to ignore the shameful feeling that I was actually jealous that such a woman existed.

"Yes, I think so." She stopped walking and turned to me now, her hands on her hips. "What's all this about, Gretel?" she asked. "Did you have something going on with him that I know nothing about? You kept it quiet if you did."

I hesitated. I was fond of Cait, we'd become fast friends, but I knew better than to trust anyone with the secrets of my past. We rarely spoke about the war, and I sensed that neither of us wanted to discuss how we had spent those terrible years. But even if we had been connected by blood, I could not see myself revealing to her, or to anyone, the truth about my childhood.

"No, it's nothing like that," I said. "I'm just . . ." I shook my head. "It's silly of me, I know. But he reminds me of someone, that's all."

"Someone you liked?"

"Yes," I admitted. "Someone I liked very much."

"Well, if you want my advice," she said, turning away from the view and leading me back in the direction from which we had come, "I'd steer clear of him. He's very polite, I'll give him that. Never gives me any trouble, unlike some of them. And yes, he's easy on the eye, if you like that sort of thing. Which I don't. But there's something under the skin, something that frightens me a little. And if you know me at all by now, Gretel, you'll know that I don't frighten easily. But that fella? He's no good."

SEVEN

Perhaps I should not have been surprised that one cannot simply show up at a school these days, select a boy at random, and take him home with you. It turns out that the teachers like to feel you have some actual connection to the child.

My taxi pulled up outside Henry's school at twenty minutes past three, but there was no sign of him outside. I paid the fare and looked around, wondering whether he might be wandering up and down the street in search of his mother, but the road was empty and so I made my way inside toward reception, where I was greeted by a young woman seated behind a glass divider who glanced up as I approached her.

"How can I help?" she asked, and I glanced around, hoping that I wouldn't have to go into too many details.

"My name is Gretel Fernsby," I told her. "I'm looking for Henry Darcy-Witt. I'm to take him home."

She ran a finger down a sheaf of documents that sat before her, then picked up the phone, dialing a three-digit extension and muttering a few words that I could not hear through the glass. When she replaced the receiver, she indicated that I should take a seat in one of the four colorful armchairs that adorned the reception area.

I chose not to sit, however, instead examining the class photographs that hung upon the walls. A decision had been made to display some of the oldest pictures there and I found myself staring at the ghostly faces of boys who had been aged around nine or ten in the early 1930s. They all sat perfectly still, backs straight, hands on their laps, expressions stern. At the edge of each portrait was a different master, adorned in cape, hat, and pencil mustache. It was difficult to look at them and not think about the world in which they were growing up. Each of these boys would have come of age when Mr. Chamberlain returned to London with the promise of peace for our time. They would have been courting their first sweethearts and thinking about their careers just as the Führer sent his tanks into Poland. I reached up a hand and found my index finger touching the cheeks of these lost boys. The quiet buzz of the school was replaced by the sound of trains arriving late at night. The cries of boys and girls being separated from their parents. And then that other boy, the boy I had met only once, who I encountered when he was stealing a set of clothes. He'd begged me not to report him. *He'll kill me*, he had said, and I'd stared at him, asking who he was referring to. He'd looked beyond the hut toward the car, where Kurt was sitting, waiting for Father. I'd never seen such terror as I saw in that boy's eyes. What was his name? He had told me and, for years, I had remembered it. Then, for decades, I had tried to forget.

A voice sounded from behind me and I snapped out of my reverie and spun around.

"Mrs. . . . . Ferns, is it?" asked a young black man in a green pullover, so youthful and smooth-cheeked that it was hard to tell whether he was part of the student body or one of the teachers.

"Fernsby," I corrected him. "I'm here to—"

"Are you quite all right?" he asked, and I frowned.

"Yes, I think so," I said. "Why do you ask?"

"I can get you a handkerchief if you like," he said.

"Why would I need a handkerchief?"

He seemed almost embarrassed by the question.

"Because you're crying," he said.

I reached a hand up to my cheeks and, sure enough, they were damp with tears. Had I started weeping while examining the pictures? I must have, I supposed, although it astonished me that I had not noticed. Shocked, even a little frightened, I reached into my bag and removed a tissue to wipe them dry, choosing not to reply.

"I'm here for Henry Darcy-Witt," I told him when I had composed myself.

"Yes, I'm Henry's teacher," he replied, clarifying his position at least. "Jack Penston."

"Nice to meet you, Mr. Penston," I said. "I'm sorry I'm late, only I had to get a taxi and—"

"The thing is, it's usually Henry's mother who picks him up," he said.

"Yes, I know, but I'm afraid she's indisposed today," I said, glancing behind him, hoping to see the child emerge from the shadows. I didn't like schools and didn't want to stay in this one any longer than necessary. There was a familiar scent, a mixture of chalk, rubber, disinfectant, and boy, which, added together, was not a perfume I found particularly intoxicating.

"Nothing's happened to her, I hope?" he asked, and I shook my head.

"No, no," I replied. "She was taken ill, that's all. Women's problems." I generally found this phrase was enough to shut men up, but Mr. Penston seemed unperturbed, so I was forced to continue. "I advised her to take a nap. I live in the same building as the Darcy-Witts, you see. In the flat above theirs. I imagine she's sleeping now," I added, certain that this would not be the case. If anything, I suspected that Madelyn was stretched out on her sofa, making further inroads into a bottle of wine. "She asked me to collect him."

"Right," said Mr. Penston, frowning a little and stroking the place where his beard might one day be. "Only, you're not on the list, Mrs. Fernsby."

"What list?" I asked.

"The list of approved people. Parents make a list of the adults who are permitted to take the boys from school. Most of them include a grandparent or two, sometimes an uncle or aunt. Someone they trust."

"Oh," I said, nodding. "No, I won't be on that list."

"No," he agreed.

"But she did ask me," I assured him. "I promise you that."

"I don't doubt you for even a moment," he said, reaching out as if to touch my arm, then thinking better of it and returning it to his side. He looked nervous. I expect he wasn't accustomed to denying the requests of elderly ladies. "But you must understand, I can't let Henry go with you without parental approval."

I nodded. This was not unreasonable, but it certainly presented a problem. Now, at last, from the end of the corridor, a small head appeared, and I smiled when I saw him, relieved that he was still alive at least.

"Hello, Henry," I said, offering him a small wave. He smiled and waved back.

"Hello, Mrs. Fernsby," he replied, apparently unsurprised to see me there.

"Well, at least you know that I am who I say I am," I said, turning back to Mr. Penston. "Although I do have my bus pass too, if that's helpful at all."

"You know Mrs. Fernsby?" asked the teacher, ignoring this remark as he turned to the boy.

"Her bedroom is above my bedroom," he said. "I can hear her when she turns off her lights at night and goes to sleep. We're friends."

I stared at him, mildly surprised that this was how he would describe me. He was right about the geography too. It made sense that my bedroom would be above his as the layout of our flats was exactly the same and I had moved to the smaller room after Edgar's death.

"I'll just phone Mrs. Darcy-Witt, if you don't mind," said Mr. Penston, and I nodded, although I worried whether she would be able to hold a coherent conversation. He went behind the glass divide and, tapping away on a computer, presumably looking for the right number, picked up a phone and dialed. Henry came over and looked up at me.

"Where's Mummy?" he asked.

"She's at home," I replied. "I needed to stretch my legs because I'm one hundred and twenty-six years old and I get arthritis if I just sit around all day. I asked her whether I might collect you and walk you home, just for the exercise, and she very kindly said that I might. You don't mind, do you?"

He narrowed his eyes. He didn't seem entirely convinced.

"You're not really one hundred and twenty-six years old, are you?" he asked.

"One hundred and twenty-seven at my next birthday," I said. "Can't you tell? When I was a girl, we didn't even have boys. They weren't invented until the 1960s."

He giggled and seemed torn between believing me and not. He reached a hand out slowly, toward mine, then, like his teacher, thought better of it. What was that about? I wondered.

"Will I get my coat and bag?" he asked, and I nodded.

"Please do," I said. "When Mr. Penston is finished on the phone, I'm sure he'll give us permission to leave."

Quick as a flash, he scampered off back down the corridor and I felt a strange urge to follow him and see what classrooms looked like these days. Very different, I imagined, to the austere wooden desks and formal rows that had been part of my education in Berlin. And Jack Penston seemed a lot livelier than Herr Liszt, the teacher who had visited my brother and me every day when we lived in that other place.

The door to the office opened and Mr. Penston reappeared from behind the glass.

"All is well," he said, smiling.

"Oh good," I said, relieved. "She wasn't asleep then?"

"Actually, I couldn't reach Mrs. Darcy-Witt," he said. "She wasn't answering her phone. So I called Henry's father instead."

I tried not to allow my face to betray my anxiety, even though I could still see the expression on Madelyn's and the frightened way that she had said, *Don't tell Alex. He'll kill me. I mean it. He could actually kill me.*

"I see," I said. "And he was happy for me to collect the boy?"

"He seemed surprised. But he said it was fine. When I next see Mrs. Darcy-Witt, I'll ask her whether we should place you on the approved list for the future."

"Oh, I wouldn't bother with that," I said, as Henry returned, buttoned up now in his coat and carrying a backpack that must have weighed almost as much as he did. "This won't be a regular occurrence. It was just an emergency, that's all."

Henry waved goodbye to his teacher, and we set off toward the doors, the eyes of the dead boys following me with every step I took.

"Now, we need to find a taxi," I said as we stepped outside.

"I thought you wanted to walk," replied Henry. "Because of your arthritis."

I looked down at him. Not much got past this boy, I had to admit.

And, *Shmuel*, I thought. That was the boy's name. In that other place. The one who had begged me not to report him to Kurt for stealing clothes.

He'll kill me, he had said.

Yes, that was it.

Shmuel.

A name that sounds like the wind blowing.

EIGHT

Cait had said that the man she referred to as Mr. Kozel visited Fortune of War twice weekly, so I feigned illness the following Wednesday and asked whether I might be allowed to leave work early. Miss Brilliant was distrustful of any girl who made such a request, believing she simply wanted to go home to change for a rendezvous with her young man, so in order to reinforce my case I spent the morning rushing back and forth to the bathroom so she might believe that I was out of sorts. However, in the late afternoon, when I asked whether I might go, she took me into her office, where she looked me up and down judgmentally, paying particular attention to my stomach.

"Is there something you want to tell me?" she asked, her face stern, her tone filled with suspicion.

"Only that I must have eaten something that didn't agree with me at breakfast," I said. "I'm sure I'll be fine in the morning. I just need to sleep it off, that's all."

"I want to make one thing perfectly clear, Gretel," she said, holding her hands before her, the fingers interlaced as if in prayer. "I don't ask much from my girls, just honesty, punctuality, good hygiene, and politeness to our clientele. But this is a respectable establishment, and I will not allow an assistant without a ring on her finger to work in my shop if she finds herself in the family way."

I stared at her, baffled by this declaration. I had never heard the phrase before and had no idea what it meant.

"I beg your pardon?" I said.

"Are you expecting a Christmas surprise?" she asked, and I wondered whether she had gone mad. "Because if you are, then I would appreciate if you would tell me now, so I can start interviewing for your replacement."

"I'm sorry, Miss Brilliant," I said, and the expression on my face must have made it clear that I had no idea what she was talking about. "I don't—"

"Are you going to have a baby?" she snapped angrily, and I felt my face burn scarlet at the idea.

"No!" I cried. "No, of course not. You've got the wrong idea entirely!"

"But you've been sick all morning and—"

"Miss Brilliant, I assure you that I am not pregnant. There is simply no possibility of that being the case, at least as far as I understand the basics of biology. I keep myself very tidy. I just have a sick stomach, nothing more."

It seemed that she believed me now, and was relieved, and she even had the good grace to look embarrassed as she allowed me to go. As I gathered my bag and coat and made my way down George Street, I couldn't help but laugh at the misunderstanding. I'd had just a single lover in my life—Émile—and our one evening of passion had taken place seven years earlier. It was true that other men had propositioned me since then, but I had never given in to any of their advances, even when I had felt desire of my own. This was not owing to any particular sense of morality on my part but simply because I did not and could not trust men. Still, that did not mean that I did not have longings, and here in Sydney, the boys were rugged, handsome, and bronzed from the sun. My eyes often wandered over their bodies and longed for some intimacy with them, but I had restrained myself, certain that this self-imposed abstinence needed to last forever.

I made my way toward Fortune of War shortly before six o'clock but did not immediately go inside. Instead, I chose to observe the entrance from a distance, crossing the road to stand by the steps that led down to First Fleet Park. The streets were busy at this time of day with people coming and going as the Rocks faced an influx of men who wanted to spend an hour or two after work among friends, drinking beer and gossiping without a foreman breathing down their necks. I was worried that I might miss Kozel among their number but the fact that these were mostly working men, dressed in short trousers and singlets, meant that he would likely stand out from their number.

And so it was. I had been waiting no more than fifteen minutes when I saw him approaching. He carried a briefcase and wore a hat, which was surely unnecessary in this climate. He was alone and stopped for a moment at a stall to buy a newspaper, handing across some loose change and remaining in the street briefly to scan the headlines. Then, folding it and placing it beneath his arm, he entered the pub, and I watched as he made his way toward the rear, stopping for only a moment to place his order at the bar, before disappearing into the back room.

If I had been feigning illness before, I felt it for real now, my stomach turning somersaults as I considered my options.

I could walk away, exile myself from Cait's place of employment forever and never cross paths with him again. Or I could go inside and talk to him. But what would I say after all this time? When we were both pretending to be people we weren't.

At last, I took a deep breath and walked across the road, my legs so uncertain beneath me that I almost marched into the path of an on-coming car. I didn't so much as raise a hand in apology, striding straight into the pub before I could change my mind. Cait was nowhere to be seen, but her colleague Ben was behind the bar and greeted me by name, asking whether I wanted a beer. I nodded and held on to the wooden counter as he poured it, watching the cold, golden liquid bubbling and fizzing as it entered the glass, then placed a few coins on the bar and took the drink with me into the back room.

It was empty except for him and, as before, he was seated quietly, reading his newspaper. I moved to the other corner and sat down, staring at the table itself, before lifting my eyes and glancing in his direction. There was no doubt in my mind now. It was him. Almost a decade older, certainly, but there could be no mistake.

Sensing my interest, he looked up for a moment and turned in my direction. I waited to see whether his expression would change, but no, it appeared that he did not recognize me. In fact, he smiled a little, as if he was accustomed to young women looking at him appreciatively, then nodded his head in greeting, and I felt myself flush. He returned to his reading, the self-satisfied smirk still on his face, but then, after a moment, something changed. He glanced at me once again, but for only a moment, then looked away, his smile very slowly disappearing, replaced by a hardening of his jaw, as if he was clenching his teeth tightly. On his tabletop was a cheap pen and, after what seemed like an eternity of silence between us, he picked it up and removed the lid, before writing something on the top of his newspaper.

Anxious now, I reached out for my drink, but my hands were so unsteady that I knocked the glass and it fell, the glass breaking, the beer spilling across the table. Ben came over immediately with a dishrag that he used to wipe down the table, and chatted amiably to me about trivial things, although I was incapable of focusing on anything he said. Instead, I stared at the ground and only when he left, taking the shards with him, did I dare look up again and glance toward the other table.

But it was empty now and I was alone in the snug. The man's hat and bag were gone and all that remained of his presence were the newspaper and the pen.

Standing up, I walked across the room and lifted the paper from the table. They were not words that he had been writing; rather, it was a drawing of some sort. At first, I didn't understand it. It appeared to be nothing more than a series of lines criss-crossing vertically and horizontally. But then I noticed what appeared to be leaves of grass dotted about the base, and I knew that he had intended it as a message to me. Or a warning.

Kurt Kotler, the former Untersturmführer in that other place, personal aide to my father, and the boy with whom I had first fallen in love, had drawn a fence.

NINE

What does one give a nine-year-old boy to eat?

It had been many decades since I'd last entertained a child in my flat and I had no idea what type of food a boy like Henry might enjoy, so I poached a couple of eggs, placed them on two slices of toast with some baked beans on the side, and he seemed perfectly content with this rather mundane meal. I prefer low-fat milk, but he pulled a face when he tasted it, so I substituted it for a can of fizzy orange, which I keep in the fridge for when my blood sugar feels a little low, and he was much happier with this.

I sat next to him, nursing a cup of tea, and watched as he ate. Arriving back at Winterville Court, I had glanced toward the windows of his own flat, hoping Madelyn would not be lying in wait for us and insist on taking him back in her drunken state, but all was quiet, so I brought him upstairs, composing a short note to explain his whereabouts and sliding it under the Darcy-Witts' front door. I was worried about what might happen when she awoke. She had made it clear that the boy's father was not to be told that I was collecting him and, while the matter had been taken out of my hands so I could hardly reproach myself for it, he was now fully aware of it.

"Are you enjoying that?" I asked, and Henry looked up with a satisfied smile. I noticed that he moved his right arm a little carefully and wondered whether it still felt sensitive, even though his cast had now been removed.

"You're a very good cook, Mrs. Fernsby," he replied, in such a mature tone that I couldn't help but laugh.

"It's not really cooking," I told him. "Anyone can put a plate like this together. Don't they feed you at school?"

"There's a canteen, yes," he said, pulling a face. "But I can't eat anything there. It all tastes like sick."

"Oh dear! What do they serve?"

"Chicken nuggets," he replied. "Pasta. Pizza. There's big trays of vegetables too, but they're all shriveled up."

"In my day, we had to bring our own food to school," I told him. "Maria used to make two halve hahns and put them in a brown paper bag with an apple for me every morning before I left the house."

"Who's Maria?" he asked.

"A young woman who worked for my family when I was a girl," I said at last. "A maid, I suppose you'd call her. People don't really have maids anymore, do they, but back then, families with money would have at least one. Sometimes more."

He ate more slowly now as he thought about this.

"My daddy has lots of people working for him," he told me.

"They're probably assistants," I said. "Or secretaries, perhaps. Maids work in the home. They make beds and they clean. And, in our case, prepared lunches for my brother and me."

He seemed satisfied with this explanation, but he wasn't finished yet.

"And what's halve . . . halve . . ."

"Halve hahn," I said, repeating the phrase. "Maria was from Cologne, you see, and it's popular there. It's fairly simple, really. Just a bread roll filled with cheese, pickles, and onions. But quite tasty."

"I don't like cheese, I don't like pickles, and I don't like onions," he said determinedly.

"Then you probably wouldn't like a halve hahn," I said, and he smiled and returned to his baked beans.

"Do you have a maid here?" he asked after a few moments, and I shook my head.

"Oh no. I have no need of one. There's only me, after all. I haven't had a maid since I was a girl."

"And where is Maria now?"

I stared at him. I didn't know the answer to this question and, in truth, hadn't thought about her in years. After Mother and I left that other place, she came with us only as far as Berlin, and then we parted. Mother wanted her to stay with us, but she made it clear that she wouldn't even consider it. She said some unkind things and I was shocked by how much contempt she had felt toward both my parents. Had she not been nervous of drawing attention to herself, I feel certain that Mother would have struck her. Still, despite that incident, I had missed her at first, although once we reached Paris, there was no time to think about such luxuries.

"I'm afraid I lost track of her many decades ago," I told him. "Of course, she's probably dead. She'd be almost one hundred if she were still alive."

"The queen is almost one hundred," said Henry.

"Yes, but the queen has people to wait upon her hand and foot. It does make life a little easier. Also, I suspect that she's immortal."

"What's immortal?"

"It means you never die."

He raised an eyebrow. "Everybody dies," he said.

"They do. It's true."

He finished eating and pushed his plate away with a smile on his face.

"I really enjoyed that," he said, sounding like a grown man in the body of a small child—he even ran his hand in circles over his belly as he leaned back—and now it was my turn to laugh.

"I'm glad," I said, standing up and taking his plate to the sink. "I suppose you'd like something sweet now?"

"Yes, please," he said, beaming.

I rooted in another cupboard, certain that I'd find something appropriate, and opened a packet of chocolate biscuits before handing him one. Then, changing my mind, I offered him a second.

"Thank you," he said, nibbling around the edges first, like a mouse, to remove all the chocolate exterior. I sat down again and continued to watch him. He seemed so self-contained, so insular.

"Are you glad you moved here?" I asked him finally. "To Winterville Court, I mean?"

He shrugged. "We move a lot," he said. "I've lost count of how many houses I've lived in. It's exhausting."

I smiled. His tendency to use grown-up expressions that he'd obviously overheard from his elders reminded me of my brother, who had been notorious for listening at keyholes and behind closed doors. He called me "the Hopeless Case," I remember. He must have heard either Father or Mother describe me thus and adopted the phrase as his own. And, of course, this was exactly what I had worried about when Mr. Richardson died and his flat was put up for sale. That uncomfortable memories would resurface.

"And your mummy and daddy," I asked. "They enjoy this nomadic lifestyle?"

His forehead frowned into creases.

"They like moving around," I clarified. "Not staying in one place too long."

"I think so," he said. "We lived in America for a year. And then we came back here. But we were here before that too. And I think we lived in Europe when I was very small, but I don't really remember it."

"Where in Europe?" I asked.

"France."

"I lived in Paris for a time," I said.

"You're not English, are you?" he asked. "I can tell by your voice."

"You're very perceptive," I said. "Not many people notice my accent anymore. No, I'm German. Although I haven't been back there since I was twelve."

"Don't you have family there?" he asked. "People you want to visit?"

I shook my head. "No," I told him. "My only family is here. My son. Although he's old himself now. In his sixties."

"You don't have many photographs," he said, looking around.

"I don't care for them," I told him.

"Why not?"

"I choose not to live in the past."

He frowned as he considered this. Of course, I did not tell him about the single photograph I kept in the Seugnot jewelry box in my wardrobe. He would surely insist on seeing it and, having not dared to look at it myself in so many decades, I had no intention of taking it out now.

"Don't you have any grandchildren?"

Before I could answer, the doorbell rang and I smiled at the boy.

"I bet that's your mother," I said, feeling a little disappointed that we would not be able to continue our conversation longer. He grew immediately uncomfortable, as if he would prefer to stay here and talk to me a little longer yet. I made my way to the front door, opening it without looking through the spy hole, expecting to see Madelyn standing there, with luck looking reasonably sober.

But it wasn't Madelyn. It was Alex. He was typing something on his phone and looked up at me without so much as a smile or a hello when I opened the door.

"I believe you've kidnapped my son," he said.

TEN

Walking into the kitchen the next morning to eat breakfast, I was surprised to discover an unfamiliar woman sitting at the table smoking a cigarette and drinking coffee. She wished me good morning, as if she had every right to be there, while I stared at her, wondering who she might be and how she'd got in. Wary of strange men breaking into our flat in the middle of the night when they left the nearby pubs, both Cait and I made a point of always locking our front door before going to bed.

"You must be Gretel," said the woman in a strong Sydney accent.

"That's right," I replied.

"I'm Michelle," she said. "But you can call me Shelley. Everyone else does."

I was at a loss for what to say but fortunately, at that moment, Cait appeared in the doorway, her hair unkempt, looking a little flustered.

"Gretel," she said, a sprinkling of red appearing in her cheeks. "I thought you'd be gone to work by now."

"I'm running a little late," I said, pouring water into the kettle and turning it on. I didn't eat much first thing, but I needed tea if I was to function at all. "Miss Brilliant will kill me."

"This is Shelley," she said, nodding at her guest.

"Yes, she said."

"Shelley's a friend of mine."

I nodded. I knew that Cait had made some friends through her work in Fortune of War but had yet to be introduced to any of them and I'd never heard her mention anyone by this name before.

"Sit down, darl'," said Shelley, taking the cigarette from her mouth and tapping the ash onto a newspaper, as if this were her home and not mine. "You're making me nervous, hovering about like a blue-arsed fly."

I did as instructed, taking my tea with me, and glanced from one to the other, hoping for some type of explanation, but when none was forthcoming and the silence became excruciating Cait finally spoke.

"I heard you were in the pub yesterday evening," she said.

"Briefly," I told her.

"Ben said you left in a hurry. That you seemed a bit upset over something."

"It was nothing," I said. "I'm fine now." I had considered confiding in Cait about my two encounters with Kurt, but, if I was going to discuss him at all, it would certainly not be in the presence of a stranger.

"Do you dance?" asked Shelley, and I turned to her, surprised by the question. I noticed that she had a tattoo on her right forearm, an image of Betty Grable taken from the rear, wearing only a corset and high heels, her hair done up in a beehive as she looked back and winked.

"Do I dance?" I repeated the question. "I mean, I have danced. I don't . . . since I came to Sydney, I haven't. Why do you ask?"

"Just making conversation, darl'," she replied, lighting another cigarette and blowing the smoke toward me before using her left hand to wave it away, which only made it worse. "Katie and I went dancing last night, didn't we, darl'? We had a fine time of it."

"Where did you go?" I asked, not particularly interested but willing to appear sociable.

"Miss Mabel's Rooms," said Shelley. "You ever been there?"

"I can't say that I have."

"It wouldn't be your sort of place, Gretel," said Cait, looking a little embarrassed, but I had also noticed how she smiled when Shelley referred to her as "Katie."

"Why not?" I asked.

"It just wouldn't. Let's just say that it's not intended for girls like you."

I frowned, uncertain whether she meant this as a slight. It hurt me to think that she considered Miss Mabel's Rooms, whatever and wherever they were, too sophisticated for me.

"Why not?" I asked.

"You're not another Irish girl like Katie," said Shelley. "Where you from, then?"

"The European mainland," I replied, unwilling to narrow it down to a more precise location than this.

"That's a bloody big place," she replied. "I've never been outside New South Wales myself. No, I tell a lie, when I was a girl, my dad took me and my brother to Melbourne for a weekend, but I can't remember much about it. No plans to go back there, neither."

"I see," I said, not seeing at all.

"I'm gonna get going, darl'," said Shelley, putting her cigarette out now but squeezing it closed at the tip as it were only half smoked, before placing the fragment behind her ear, which I thought terribly gauche. "That was a hell of a night, though. I'll love you and leave you."

She stood up and moved around the table, leaned over, and then, to my astonishment, kissed Cait full on the lips while placing her left hand on the back of her head. This was not a quick peck from one friend to another but a lingering kiss, and I turned away, not knowing where to look.

"Nice to meet you, Gretel," said Shelley with a wink as she left.

Silence descended on the kitchen in her wake, and I sat there, sipping my tea, wanting the ground to swallow me whole. Finally, I dared to glance at Cait, who looked equally uncomfortable.

"I'm sorry about that," she said, looking down at the table. "I hadn't intended you to meet in this way."

"It's quite all right," I said.

"I suppose you've figured out my secret, then," she added, offering a half-smile.

"I think so," I replied.

"Are you scandalized?"

I thought about it. I felt that I should be. I had never known any woman—or man, for that matter—who was interested in romantic relationships with people of the same sex, but I found, to my surprise, that I didn't much care. It all seemed so trivial compared to the traumas we had survived over the last thirteen years.

"You might have told me before now," I said.

"It doesn't matter to you then?"

"Not in the slightest," I said.

"That's good of you," she replied, smiling and reaching across to take my hand. I hated myself for the fact that I grew slightly anxious as she touched me, wondering whether she thought that I might have similar inclinations, and she let go quickly, perhaps sensing my discomfort, before standing up to wash the breakfast things.

"Anyway," said Cait from the sink. "What happened to upset you last night? Why did you go running off like that?"

"I went in to see that man," I said, turning around on my chair to face her as she rinsed out the cups.

"What man?"

"The one I told you about. The one you call Mr. Kozel."

"You still chasing after him then? I told you, he's married."

"I'm not chasing after him," I insisted, raising my voice in irritation. "I told you, I thought I recognized him, that's all. I think I knew him when I was younger."

"No," she said, shaking her head. "You told me that he reminded you of someone." She sat down next to me. "What is it, Gretel? Who is he?"

"I can't tell you," I said. "I want to, but I can't."

"Haven't I told you something personal?" she asked. "Women have been put in prison for what you've found out about me today. Whatever secret you're hiding, it can't be anymore shocking than that, can it?"

I said nothing. I couldn't.

"He didn't hurt you in some way, did he?" she asked. "He didn't . . . you know . . . do something to you that you never asked for and didn't want?"

I shook my head.

"No, it's nothing like that," I said. "It's more complicated." Despite myself, I started laughing. "There was a time in my life when I was convinced that I was in love with him, if you can believe it."

"But he didn't take advantage, you promise me? Because if he did—"

"He didn't, I swear it," I assured her, reaching out to take her hand now, and then, as if to prove my friendship and show that nothing between us had changed, I leaned forward and kissed her on the left cheek and then the right. "You're a good friend, Cait," I said, standing up. "I'm lucky to have you in my life." I hesitated for a moment as I walked away, then turned back with a mischievous smile on my face, adopting my broadest Australian accent. "Or is it Katie, darl'?" I asked, and Cait stuck her tongue out and threw a tea towel at me.

ELEVEN

Eleanor was in her mid-forties and quite pretty but wore a little more makeup than I thought necessary. I had avoided meeting her during the ten months of her and Caden's courtship, assuming that she would not be in the picture very long, but now that the wedding date had been set, it seemed I had no choice but to make her acquaintance.

My son's first wife, Amanda, had been my favorite of my daughters-in-law. I'd assumed that we would be in each other's lives forever, so had made a great effort to cultivate a friendship, which was reciprocated, and I was deeply saddened when they separated. Beatrice, his second, was a rude woman who showed little interest in me and constantly pleaded with Caden to sell his construction business and move into a career more suited to her delusions of grandeur. I only met Charlotte, his third, a few times and I don't think she ever forgave me for skipping their wedding, but her disdain had not bothered me in the slightest. I could tell from the start that their relationship was doomed. And now, here was Eleanor.

After much wrangling over dates, I found myself dragged to a busy Chelsea gastropub on an overcast Sunday afternoon. To my surprise, I rather liked the surroundings, which were cozy and welcoming, with high ceilings, wide spaces between the tables—a holdover, I assumed, from the pandemic—and music playing at a sufficiently discreet volume that it did not interfere with conversation. Eleanor, I understood, lived nearby, and Caden had arranged a taxi to bring me back and forth to Winterville Court, pointing out that he would be drinking—"I'll need it," were his exact words—and would therefore be unable to drop me home afterward.

As I gave my coat at the door, I spotted the happy couple seated in a corner booth, Eleanor studying her phone while Caden read the menu with such intensity that he might have been a diplomat reviewing an international trade agreement. A waiter led me toward the table and, when they saw me, they both stood up, Caden kissing me on the cheek and Eleanor reaching out a hand to shake my own.

"So nice to meet you at last, Mrs. Fernsby," she said, dropping into a half-curtsey, as if I were an aging royal. I was about to invite her to call me by my first name but then decided against. Let's keep the formality a little longer, I thought, and see how familiar I want us to be.

"You got here all right then?" asked Caden. "Taxi driver didn't give you any problems?"

"None at all," I said, nodding toward the waiter, who walked over as I studied the drinks menu. "Although he told me that if I recognized him, it was because he'd been on a television singing competition seven years earlier. I didn't, in fact, recognize him and told him so, and he seemed to take that rather badly."

I ordered a glass of rosé and Eleanor decided to join me, so we switched to a bottle.

"Of course, there was a time when I would have walked this distance without giving it a second thought," I continued. "Nowadays, though, I'd be worried that I'd get caught short along the way."

Caden frowned. "I don't think you mean caught short," he said.

"Don't I?"

"Caught short means, you know, needing to use the lavatory."

"Oh," I said. It struck me as strange that, even after all these years, I could still get things slightly wrong and inadvertently reveal that English was not, in fact, my first language. "I meant that I might get tired and need to sit down."

"Walking is so important," said Eleanor. "I try to get in 20,000 steps every day."

She stretched her arm across the table and showed me a small watch-like accessory in a lurid pink color wrapped around her wrist. Tapping the screen, an image of two feet appeared, with a small number above them.

"Eleven thousand, four hundred already today, and it's only twelve thirty. Actually, that's below my average, I'll need to get some more in later."

"Eleanor takes good care of herself," said Caden proudly, almost proprietorially. "As you can see."

"I can," I admitted, for there was no question that the woman was in excellent shape, although she carried a little extra upholstery, shall we say, about the chest area. I wondered whether that was what had attracted my son to her. Men can be rather shallow in these things, I've always found, and I'm sure it was no coincidence that my previous daughters-in-law were all equally blessed in the bosom department.

"Are you a walker, Mrs. F.?" she asked, and I smiled at her, surprised by the familiarity of the sobriquet but, somehow, not offended. There was an innocence to her tone, a genuine curiosity, that I liked.

"I'm sure Caden's told you that I live opposite Hyde Park," I replied. "I have done for many decades. So it's a rare day that I don't go walking there. In my younger days, of course, I could do two hours at a stretch sometimes and I wouldn't think anything of it."

"Which explains why she was never home when I got back from school," said Caden, and I turned to look at him, analyzing his tone, but he didn't seem to have any malicious intent. Perhaps he had meant it as a joke.

"You should get one of these," said Eleanor, displaying her wrist again.

"What is it?" I asked.

"It's called a Fitbit."

"Oh yes, I've heard of them."

"You tell it how many steps you want to do every day and it records them and you get little bonuses every time you achieve your target."

I smiled. It was a harmless enough toy, I suppose, and I've always had an ordered mind and rather liked the idea, so wondered whether I might, indeed, invest in one. It would help me to be a little more active in my exercise, which would keep me alive longer, although that would rule out Caden's chance of inheriting for a few more years yet.

The waiter came by again and we ordered. Steak, chips, and eggs for Caden, a kale and beetroot salad for Eleanor and a chicken pie for me. The bottle of rosé was almost half gone already, and I had a feeling that, between us, Eleanor and I could make inroads into at least one more.

"So, you've set the date, I understand," I said finally, smiling at Eleanor, who looked genuinely delighted.

"We have," she said. "May sixteenth."

"How lovely. Your family must be terribly excited."

"They are, yes. They're very fond of Caden."

I felt a certain irritation that he had got to know them while she was only meeting me for the first time, but I let it pass. After all, that had been almost entirely my choice.

"And this will be your first marriage? I asked.

"My second," she said. "My first husband passed away five years ago."

"Oh, I'm sorry to hear that. Can I ask what happened?"

"Cancer."

"Ah. But you don't have any children?"

She shook her head and looked a little sorrowful. I wondered whether this was by choice or fate, but it seemed intrusive to ask.

"Well, you've struck gold here," I added, patting Caden on the hand from across the table. I didn't want to appear unsupportive, although, in truth, I wondered why he was going through with this. It wasn't as if he was still going to be married to her in three years' time, let alone five or ten. All that would happen is that she would take a chunk of his money, be another recipient of monthly alimony, and leave him distraught once again. The last time around, he'd become deeply depressed. And I might not be around to pick up the pieces when Eleanor moved onto pastures new.

"And don't I know it," she said, leaning over and kissing him on the cheek. Caden beamed and, I must admit, they both looked happy. Perhaps she was fond of him, at least. It was a start.

TWELVE

It wasn't difficult to track Kurt down to the Commonwealth Bank—I simply had to wait by the ferries in the morning until he arrived and follow him to his place of business—and, on my day off, I waited across the street until just after six o'clock for him to emerge. When he did, he looked handsome in his tailored suit and I followed him back toward Circular Quay, where he boarded a ferry heading in the direction of Manly, and I, keeping some distance from him, did the same. I did not know, as yet, what I wanted with him or whether I would even dare speak to him should we find ourselves alone, but I did feel a need to keep him in my sights in an effort to learn more about his life. It was almost as though I believed that, by keeping track of him, I could prevent him from doing any further harm.

I wondered what he told the people he worked with about his past life. I pictured him eating lunch with his colleagues, laughing at their stories, then returning home to his wife, leading an entirely normal life without any thought for who or what he was. Did he sleep well at night, or did he have nightmares, like me? I was sure that he would have convinced himself of his innocence in much the same way that I had tried to do, but how well had he succeeded?

The evening was sunny, and he sat outside on one of the benches that lined the deck of the boat while I remained inside, trying not to stare as he read his newspaper. The ferry was busy, but this was a one-stop service, so I knew there was no possibility of losing him. A young man sat next to me and asked for a light for his cigarette and, when I told him that I didn't smoke, he took a match from his pocket and struck it against the sole of his shoe, an action I had only ever seen performed in films.

"If you had a match," I asked him, confused by his behavior, "why did you ask me for one?"

"Because I wanted to talk to you," he said, before placing his hand upon my knee. I shook him off and stood up, annoyed by how he felt he could just grab me like this, but he simply shrugged his shoulders and laughed, and some of the other men nearby smirked too and whistled at me as I changed seats, moving toward the rear of the vessel and directing my attention toward the waves.

Traveling on ferries had become my favorite aspect of living in Sydney. Some days, when I was not at work, I would board one at random, visiting Parramatta, Pyrmont, or Watsons Bay, sitting outside to read my book with the wind in my hair and the light spray of water dancing up from the waves. I would spend an afternoon at some quiet café before returning to the city, struck by the spirit of adventure. At such moments, Berlin, Paris, and that other place felt as if they were part of a different universe entirely, a nightmare which I had shaken off.

As the ferry pulled into Manly Wharf, I joined the crowds waiting to disembark, keeping a watchful eye on my prey. Taller than most, he was easy to keep track of and as we emerged onto dry land he turned right and continued along the esplanade, before turning onto Cove Avenue toward Addison Road. Finally, he stopped at a pleasant-looking timber-framed house facing the water, opened the latch on a picket-fence gate and stepped inside. I maintained my distance, hoping that he had not noticed me, and watched as the front door was flung open and a small boy, aged around five, ran outside and flung himself into his arms. A moment later, a young woman emerged, as blonde as Kurt, wearing shorts and a bikini top. He smiled and leaned forward to kiss her. To my shame, I felt a stab of jealousy as I watched this display of affection, and was glad when the little boy hauled him away toward the side of the garden, which was partly hidden by trees.

I could no longer see him from where I was standing and was nervous of getting any closer, but I wasn't ready to leave just yet and so made my way slowly along the opposite side of the road, doing my best to seem as if I belonged there. Kurt's wife glanced across the street and, when our eyes met, I smiled, and she offered a small nod in return before disappearing back inside the house, leaving the front door ajar. When I reached the end of the road, at Smedley's Point, I turned back, a neighbor out for an evening stroll, but slowed down, the better to observe the activity in the garden.

A picnic table stood in the center of the grass and Kurt had removed his jacket and tie, throwing them upon it. He was standing behind his son, his shirtsleeves rolled up, his shirt open at the neck. The child was seated on a swing, and Kurt was pushing him, the boy wearing a wide, excited smile as he gripped the chains, crying out in excitement every time the seat rose.

"Higher, Daddy, higher!" he shouted, and he acceded to the boy's request, pushing him with such vigor that I feared the child would fall. I paused by a tree, a memory stirring, and in a moment, I was back at that other place, recalling the far more rudimentary swing that my brother had set up in our garden years before. I remembered him approaching Kurt in search of a tire and Kurt, as was his way, belittling him.

Cautiously, I stepped closer to the house now and watched the pair, imagining what would happen if I were to let out a scream. Would the little boy leap from the seat in surprise, fly through the air and fall to the ground? Perhaps he might even impale himself upon the fence. I reached out to touch it. It was made of wood, not wire, and there was no one standing in a watchtower nearby, ready to shoot anyone who attempted to cross it. So why did it frighten me so? Fences like this, I knew, existed all over the world. How long would Kurt stand there, I wondered, before he rushed to his fallen son?

Kurt slowed the swing down now and it gradually came to a stop. From inside the house, his wife called out to say their dinner was ready, and hand in hand, the little boy and he walked toward the front door. The child, still full of energy, raced ahead as Kurt kicked off his shoes, his shadow dark in the sunny entranceway. A moment later, he closed the door behind him and the Kotlers—the Kozels— were left in peace.

That was when I realized that my left hand was damp with blood from where it had been clutching the fence. Splinters, though, not barbed wire.

THIRTEEN

The food, when it arrived, was rather good. I enjoyed my chicken pie and Caden made short work of his steak, although Eleanor seemed more interested in deconstructing her salad and moving its component parts around her plate than ingesting any of it.

"You're a nurse, aren't you?" I asked her, when the conversation seemed to have run a little dry, and she shook her head.

"A doctor," she told me. It was undoubtedly an unfair prejudice on my part, but I doubt anyone would have taken her for a doctor. Frankly, she looked like some sort of showgirl.

"What sort of a doctor?" I asked.

"A heart surgeon," she replied, and I stared at her in surprise before turning to Caden, who was mopping up the remaining ketchup on his plate with his chips. I couldn't believe that he hadn't told me this before.

"But that's an extraordinary thing to do," I said, leaning forward, interested now. The revelation made me see her in an entirely new light, which was terrible narrow-mindedness on my part. "You must have brains to burn. Caden, why didn't you tell me any of this?"

"I did," he said.

"No, you didn't. You told me she was a nurse."

"Wrong," he replied. "Don't you remember making a joke about her capturing my heart?"

I frowned. I didn't remember this at all. Perhaps, like Heidi, I was losing my marbles.

"Well, I'm very impressed," I said, sitting back again and looking at Eleanor with a new-found respect. "In my day, of course, such things would have been impossible."

"Did you have an interest in medicine then, Mrs. F.?" she asked, and I shook my head.

"Oh no," I said. "No, I could never have done something like that."

"She could barely put a bandage on my knee when I fell over," muttered Caden, reaching for his beer.

"That's not true," I said, wounded by the remark, however true.

"Dad took care of all my injuries," he continued, looking directly at me. "You know he did."

I turned back to Eleanor, making a vague attempt to laugh this off. "The truth is, I'm not good with blood, dear," I told her. "I don't know how you do it."

"Oh, you get used to it," she said. "It's the deaths that bother me most."

I said nothing. I had assumed that one became immune to them.

"Before a patient goes in for heart surgery, he or she has usually had quite a long relationship with the operating team," she explained. "We're not supposed to see them as anything but 'clients' these days, of course, we're supposed to take all sentimentality and emotion out of it, but I just can't do that. None of us can, to be fair. And most people are fine after their operation—maze surgery, aneurysm repair, coronary artery bypass grafting—whatever it might be. But, of course, occasionally, we lose someone. And that does get to me, yes. The older doctors, they're better at dealing with it—it's just another day at the office for some of them—but for me . . . well, it's awful feeling culpable but, honestly, I hope I never get so inured to it that I lose that sense of guilt."

I stared at her. My mouth felt dry, but I found that I couldn't quite reach for my glass.

"And is that something you feel?" I asked her. "Guilt?"

"Of course."

"But why? You're simply doing what's been asked of you."

"I suppose I think that I haven't done all I could to save them," she said. "These patients have come into my care, or our care, and put their faith in us. And we've let them down. I've participated in hundreds of operations over the years and lost fifteen patients. I can't remember the names of those that survived, but I remember each one that died."

I remained silent, thinking about this. I could tell already that this deep sense of ethics defined her, both as a woman and as a doctor, and that she would remember those fifteen people, and whoever was unfortunate enough to be added to that list, until her dying day. Was there something missing in my psychological makeup that meant that I did not share it? I wondered. When I looked at my past, so much of it was built around evasion and deception, the impulse to protect myself over others.

"But you mustn't feel that any of that was your fault," I said finally, my tone almost beseeching her.

"But I must," she replied softly, even kindly. "If I am to live a good life."

"If I was going under the knife," said Caden, his voice crashing into the conversation and overpowering both of us, as men will, "I would prefer a female surgeon to a male. They're more caring."

"Keep eating all those steaks and you might get your wish," said Eleanor, smiling at him, and he smiled back, not in the least insulted.

Instead, he reached across and took her hand, squeezing it a little. I watched this small interaction and felt moved by it.

"Well, good for you," I said at last, ready to move on from this subject now. I could have discussed it with her all afternoon, had there been only the two of us, but with my son there, it seemed impossible. "Now, Caden will undoubtedly insist that he's already told me this too, but how did you two meet?"

"At a party to mark the retirement of one of London's best architects," she replied. "My uncle. Caden had worked with him on and off over the years."

"And you hit it off immediately?"

"Your son is a gentleman, Mrs. F.," she said, smiling at him again. "He swept me off my feet."

I found this rather hard to imagine but was willing to give her the benefit of the doubt. In fairness, Caden's previous wives had also testified to his chivalrous nature. Before they divorced him, that is.

"And, I'm not being funny, but did you ever work?" asked Eleanor, looking directly at me, and I shook my head.

"I didn't," I admitted, sensing no judgment in her tone. "Well, I was a mother, of course. The most important job of all, as they say."

"Ha!" said Caden, and I turned to look at him. It seemed that he was in a bad mood with me this afternoon, but I had no idea why. Perhaps it was the beer. He was already on his fourth.

"I did my best," I protested weakly.

"You did," he said in a somber tone. "I don't doubt that."

"Perhaps I should have got a job outside the home," I continued, returning my attention to Eleanor, "but the truth is, I didn't have much of an education. Girls often didn't in those days. It's not as if I never worked. I worked in a department store before I met Caden's father. In fact, that's where our paths first crossed. I wasn't on the shop floor but in accounts. And I rather enjoyed that, to a point, but I never saw it in career terms."

"Was this in Berlin?"

I frowned, surprised by the question. "Why would it be in Berlin?" I asked.

"Caden told me that you grew up there."

I cast a look toward my son, who avoided my eye. He knew that I didn't like it when he told people even the smallest details about my past. The fewer who knew anything, I had decided long ago, the better.

"Well, I lived there until I was twelve," I said. "I'm not sure if that counts as 'growing up' there. After that, I became a rather peripatetic sort, moving from country to country until I settled in England."

"Which countries?" she asked. "I love to travel. Not that I get to do much of it."

"France for a time," I told her. "Then Australia."

"And Poland," said Caden quietly. "Don't forget Poland."

"Yes, Poland too," I said, surprised that he would mention this. He was aware that I had spent some time in that country, but I had always been purposely vague about the circumstances and he had never inquired too much. Or at least, he hadn't asked anything of me. It crossed my mind now that he might have asked Edgar. "I don't really think about that time," I continued, dismissively. "I spent several years in Paris after the war and then, in 1952, emigrated to Sydney. Originally, I thought I would live out my days there."

"But it didn't work out?"

"It didn't, no."

"Why not?" she asked.

I did my best to offer a nonchalant shrug. "Oh, who knows?" I lied. "I was so young. And the weather was intolerable. Perhaps I wasn't ready to settle down in one place just yet. Still, I have strong memories of France and Australia, although I've never returned to either."

"I'm sure you'd have strong memories of Poland too," said Caden, "if you put some time into recalling your days there." I refused to look at him. Whatever game he was playing, I was not going to indulge it. But it frightened me.

"I went to Poland once, actually," said Eleanor, pushing her plate aside now, having eaten no more than half the food upon it. "As part of a school trip. They took us to Kraków for three days and, on the middle day, we visited Auschwitz."

I reached for my glass of rosé, drained it, and pointed at the bottle so Caden would pour me a refill.

"It frightened me," she continued, shivering a little. "I've seen all those movies, of course. *Schindler's List, The Pianist, Sophie's Choice.* And I've watched a few documentaries and read a few books. But you don't really get a sense of it until you're actually there, do you? Have you ever been, Mrs. F.?"

I said nothing.

"I have," said Caden, and I turned to him in surprise.

"No, you haven't," I said.

"I have."

"When?"

"Before Dad died."

"Nonsense!"

"It's not nonsense," he said, his tone remaining perfectly calm. "In fact, we went together."

I stared at him, mystified by what he was saying. "But . . ." I began, uncertain how to finish the sentence. "But you didn't. You didn't."

"We did, Mother," he said. "You remember that trip Dad and I took to Warsaw before he passed away?"

I thought back. Caden had a contact there who was going to help him import steel at a significantly reduced rate. He'd gone over for four days and invited his father to accompany him. I had thought it was a very nice gesture at the time. And Edgar had been delighted.

"I remember," I said.

"Well, we visited then."

"Edgar never said."

"Didn't he?"

I knew from his tone that he knew he hadn't.

"No," I said.

Turning to Eleanor now, he said, "Dad died only a year later. It was good to spend that time with him. We really opened up to each other."

"But why?" I asked, not wanting him to continue this thought. "Why there? Why that place?"

Caden ignored my question and simply stared. I watched, counting the seconds between each blink. The silence was horrible. For a moment, I thought I was going to scream out loud. To let out such a cry that everyone in the restaurant would stop talking and clutch their children tightly to them.

The monster, they would think.

The monster is here among us.

"What part of Poland did you live in?" asked Eleanor finally, and I turned to her, flustered.

"What?" I asked.

"Poland," she repeated. "What city were you in?"

"You wouldn't know it," I said, feeling as if I needed some fresh air or I might pass out. "Quite a small town."

"My grandfather received a promotion at work," explained Caden, turning to her. "So he, my grandmother, and my uncle all had to up sticks and move with him. And Mum, of course."

"You have an uncle?" asked Eleanor, raising an eyebrow in surprise. "You've never mentioned him."

"I never met him," he said. "He died during the war."

"Oh," she said, turning to me again. "You lost a brother? I'm sorry to hear that."

"It was many, many years ago," I told her.

"Still, you never get over something like that, do you?"

"You'd know, would you?" I snapped, my tone unnecessarily harsh, and she reared back a little in the seat, surprised.

"Mother," said Caden, cautioning me.

"I would, as it happens," she said. "I lost a brother too. When I was six and he was eight. He ran out onto the road without looking and got hit by a car. My mother was never the same afterward. Nor my father. They had three other children, but it always felt as if we couldn't make up for Peter's loss."

"I'm sorry," I said, putting my hand to my eyes, keeping them closed. I no longer wanted to be there. I wanted to be at home. I wanted to be dead. "I didn't know that."

"No reason why you should," she replied, smiling a little to make me know that she did not feel insulted. "I don't remember him well, of course, because I was so young at the time. But I still think about him. I often wonder what he might have done with his life. Mum says that he loved planes so I like to think that he might have become a pilot. Was your brother a soldier, Mrs. F.?"

"No," I told her. "No. What? No. He was just a little boy. He was only a child."

"And were you close?"

I nodded.

"What was his name?"

I didn't reply. Caden told her. I hadn't spoken that name since the day he'd crossed to the other side of the fence. Not once in seventy-nine years.

"And if you had worked," said Eleanor, as the waiter took our plates away. "If you could have done any job in the world, what do you think it would have been?"

I searched my brain for an answer. It seemed terribly sad to me that nothing came to mind. The truth was, I didn't feel there was anything I could have done. It wasn't the way I was brought up.

"There was nothing," I said eventually, feeling myself close to tears. I reached out, and I think I frightened her when I took both her hands in mine, clutching them tightly. "There was nothing I could have done," I told her. "Don't you see that? Don't you understand? Even if I had wanted to, it would have been impossible."

FOURTEEN

I waited until the following Tuesday, my half-day from work, to visit again, but this time with a clear plan in mind.

Disembarking the ferry shortly after 1 p.m., I made my way back along the esplanade, secure in the knowledge that Kurt would not return home for at least another five hours, by which time I, and my prize, would be long gone. Despite my malevolent intentions, I felt strangely calm as I approached the house, possibly because I was no longer stalking an unpredictable prey but had become a more focused predator. As I drew closer, I heard voices and caught sight of his wife and son in the garden. Passing by on the other side of the street, I saw her seated beneath the shade of the porch, reading, while the little boy sat close by, issuing what appeared to be a detailed set of orders to a collection of soldiers, all of which were standing to attention along the patio, preparing for battle. I walked on as before, as far as Smedley's Point, and then retraced my steps. Once I was close enough to be seen, however, I began to move unsteadily on my feet and emitted as distressed a cry as I could, stumbling against the fence.

Immediately, the woman leaped from her seat and ran out onto the pavement, while the child watched, intrigued by this unexpected moment of drama.

"Are you all right?" she asked, reaching out a hand to help me up.

"It's the heat," I said, shaking my head and doing my best to look weakened. "I left home without breakfast, which wasn't very clever on my part. But I'm fine, thank you. You're very kind."

"Come and sit down," she said, indicating the porch. "Let me get you some water."

"I couldn't," I began faintly, but as I had expected, she refused to hear any protest.

"I insist," she said, and I allowed her to lead me back toward the house, where she sat me down in the second chair before disappearing inside. It only took a few moments before I heard water running in the sink. The boy watched me, a look of suspicion on his face, before returning to his soldiers.

"What are you playing?" I asked him.

"War."

"Is that a game?"

"It's the best game in the world."

"And are you winning?"

"I won't know till it's over."

"And perhaps not even then."

"Here you are," said his mother, reappearing now and handing me an ice-cold glass, which I accepted gratefully, taking a large gulp at first to reinforce how badly the heat had affected me.

"Thank you," I said as she sat down next to me. "I feel ridiculous now."

"No need," she said. "These things happen."

"But I'm disturbing your day."

"Stay as long as you like." She waved a hand in the air. "It's just me and my son and, to be honest, I could do with a little adult company."

I glanced toward her as she replaced her sunglasses on her face.

She was once again dressed in the minimal required clothing and it could not be argued that she was not a beautiful woman. There wasn't much of Kurt in the boy's face, however, except perhaps around the eyes.

"I'm Cynthia, by the way," said his mother. "Cynthia Kozel. And you?"

I hadn't thought this far ahead and, despite having an entire universe of names at my disposal, I found it difficult to settle on one.

"Maria," I said at last.

"Are you from Sydney?"

"I live here," I said. "But no, I'm from Europe originally. France."

"Oh, I love Europe," she said in a theatrical tone.

"You've been there?"

"Well, no, but I want to. Someday, perhaps. When this little bugger is a bit older. It's probably not the best time anyway. They're still rebuilding, or so I read in the newspapers. After all that unpleasantness, I mean."

I felt as if I might laugh out loud. It was an extraordinary way to refer to six years of war, countless millions of deaths, and all the broken places that had been left behind.

"And you?" I asked eventually. "You were born here?"

"Melbourne," she replied. "Ever been?"

I shook my head.

"I miss it sometimes. Sydney's nice, of course, but Melbourne's home."

"You have a lovely house," I said, looking around, although it was fairly standard and hardly worthy of comment.

"Aren't you sweet?" she said.

"And what's your son's name?" I asked, pointing toward the child.

"Hugo," said Cynthia.

"I'm five," announced the boy, turning to look at us the moment he knew he might become part of the conversation.

"Good for you," I said.

"I'll be six in October."

"You hope."

Cynthia turned to look at me, her eyebrow raised, perhaps surprised by the remark, but I did not attempt to justify it or even acknowledge her confusion. Instead, I simply looked around the garden and sighed contentedly. I could understand why she enjoyed sitting out here like this. It felt like another Eden, removed from the realities of the world. "Is it just me or does it get hotter every year?" I asked.

"Strange that you should say that," said Cynthia, brightening up again. "I was only saying the same thing to my husband last night. He doesn't seem to feel the heat, even though he's not Australian."

"Oh no?" I asked. "Where's he from then?"

"Europe. Like you."

"What part?"

She hesitated for a moment. "Well, he's German," she said in a hushed tone, putting a finger to her lips. "But we don't really tell people. We say that he's Czech. There's still a lot of anti-German sentiment around here since the war ended. It's over, I tell people. Move on. But they don't. If grudges were an Olympic sport, there'd be a lot of people competing for gold."

"I'm sure."

"The truth is, when we first met, he told me that he was from Prague. It was six months later when I saw his passport and the truth came out."

"Not good to start on a lie," I said.

"I suppose not."

I said nothing for a long time, not wanting to appear too eager with my questions.

"Was he . . . was he a soldier then?" I asked eventually. "In Germany?"

She looked shocked by the suggestion and shook her head. "Kurt?" she asked. "Oh Lord, no! He's far too gentle for any of that. No, he was one of those—what do you call them?—conscientious objectors. He got out of the country just as the war broke out. Moved to England and helped with the war effort from there. He hated Hitler and all those terrible men."

I didn't blame Kurt for denying his past—Mother and I had done the exact same thing—but it was another thing entirely for him to present himself as something of a hero.

"Do you think he's still alive?" she asked me.

"Who?"

"Hitler."

I was so tired of reading stories in the papers that suggested the Führer had not really killed himself in his bunker, or been cremated outside of it, but was in fact living a splendid existence somewhere in South America, secreted by his true believers, ready to launch himself on the world again at an appropriate moment.

"I hope not," I said.

"I think he is. We haven't heard the last of that bugger, you mark my words."

"And you've been married long?" I asked.

"Five years," she replied, then nodded toward the boy. "I know, I know. But we did the right thing in the end, that's all that matters, isn't it? My dad, he wasn't too happy about it. Threatened to knock Kurt's block off. That's why we came to Sydney. Now all my parents want to do is visit their grandchild." She sat up. "Will you excuse me for a minute? Call of nature. And then I have to put a chicken in the oven to roast for later. Keep an eye on this one, would you?"

I nodded as she disappeared into the house, and I took another long draft of the water before placing the glass on a side table.

"I see you have a swing," I said to Hugo, and he looked around and nodded. "Would you like me to push you on it?"

Utterly trusting, he nodded, and we made our way toward it, me taking up the same position that Kurt had held when I had been spying on them the previous week. I pushed him gently and he rose in the air.

"You were walking up and down the road last week," he said in a clear voice. "I saw you."

Now it was my turn to be surprised.

"You were watching me," he said.

"Not really."

"Yes, you were."

"I promise I wasn't."

I pushed him higher now, my hands harder against his back, and I could feel his small body tense a little every time he returned to me, as if he was anxious about being hurt.

"Then you must have been watching Daddy," he said.

"Is he a nice man?" I asked. "Your daddy?"

"Of course!" he cried, his voice raising as he swung ever higher.

"You know that some men just pretend to be nice," I told him.

I stopped pushing now and came around to the front of the swing, keeping a safe distance from him to avoid being kicked as he slowed down.

"Why do they do that?" he asked, his face creasing up in confusion.

"Because inside, they're monsters," I said.

He slowed to a halt now and gripped the sides of the swing tightly, his shoes planted firmly on the ground.

"My daddy's not a monster," he insisted.

"But who's to say?" I asked him, reaching into my bag and removing an envelope with the name Kurt Kotler written across the front and placing it on the next seat along, weighing it down with a stone from the flower bed, before reaching forward to take the boy from the swing and holding him firmly by the hand.

"Come with me," I told him as I led us both back onto the street. "You and I are going on a great adventure."

FIFTEEN

My next encounter with Madelyn Darcy-Witt came almost a week after I collected her son from school. I had expected her to knock on my door the following day to thank me but, somewhat to my relief, it had been silence from downstairs. It took until Tuesday, as I was returning from my walk, for me to notice the curtains twitching in Flat One and, ten minutes later, when I was back upstairs with my shoes off and the kettle on, for a knock to come on the door. I sighed, knowing exactly who it was and wishing that she would simply leave me alone to get on with my day, but of course she had seen me ascend the steps to the building so I could hardly pretend not to be at home.

"Madelyn," I said when I opened the door, and I feigned a smile. "How lovely to see you."

"Hello, Gretel," she replied, extending both hands toward me. I looked down and saw that she was carrying a small box of expensive chocolates.

"For you," she said. "To say thank you for collecting Henry last week."

"There was really no need," I said, putting the gift down on a side table. "I was happy to help."

"Yes, but it was wrong of me to ask. You shouldn't have to get involved with any of my bullshit."

I was taken aback both by her choice of words and by the fact that she sounded as if she was reading them from a script. My irritation turned to concern, and I invited her in, offering her a seat but no tea; I didn't want her staying too long.

"Are you all right, dear?" I asked, sitting opposite her. "You seem rather out of sorts, if you don't mind my saying."

She shuddered and rubbed her arms with her hands. "I'm fine," she said. "I haven't been sleeping well, that's all."

"Midday naps are not a good idea, I find," I told her. "They play havoc with the sleep cycle. You need a good eight hours every night and plenty of exercise."

She smiled but didn't offer a reply.

"And Henry," I asked. "How is he?"

"Oh, he's fine. Back in school. Don't worry, I'll collect him later." When she laughed, it was tinged with a certain hysteria.

"I wasn't worried," I said.

"I'm supposed to thank you for feeding him too."

I frowned. "You're supposed to? Whatever do you mean?"

"Just that . . . well, you gave him his tea, so thank you for that. I don't think I had anything in. I rely too much on delivery firms, you see, and forgot to place an order. Alex says that I should do more home cooking."

"Perhaps Alex should do more home cooking," I suggested. "I understand that men are just as capable of turning an oven on as women. Yes, I'm sure I read that somewhere."

"No, he wouldn't do anything like that," she said, shaking her head. "He's far too busy to bother with minor domestic tasks."

"I'd hardly say that preparing a meal for his son is a minor domestic task," I said.

"Anyway, he's gone away again for a few days. Scouting a location in Paris. Or so he tells me."

I hesitated for a moment. I didn't wish to pry, but I was intrigued. "You say that as if you're not entirely convinced," I said. "Do you have reason to suspect he's lying to you?"

"If you . . ." She looked a little embarrassed by what she was about to say but surmounted it bravely. "If you had a bottle of wine open, maybe we could have a glass? Or you could come down to mine."

"My dear, I haven't even had my lunch yet," I said, laughing a little. "It's barely past noon."

"Of course. You're right."

Still, she looked at me, hoping that I might relent, but I had no intention of starting drinking at this time of the day, nor did I want to encourage her in doing so.

"I should probably go," she said finally, although she showed no sign of standing up.

"Madelyn, are you quite all right?" I asked. "You look rather shaken."

"I'm fine. Well, maybe not entirely fine. To be honest, I made a terrible mistake last week. Which was why I had to ask you to collect Henry. I did ask you not to tell Alex, you know."

"And I didn't. It was the school that did that. You weren't answering your phone."

"I suppose. But still." She didn't seem convinced, which irritated me no end. "It was stupid of me, I know, but I think I should explain."

"You don't owe me any explanations," I said, curious to know what she was referring to but certain that more knowledge would only drag me deeper into her affairs.

"I think I do," she said. "You must have thought me a terrible mother, just showing up like that and demanding that you collect my son. And I'd been drinking. Well, I don't think I need to tell you that."

"No," I admitted, for it had been quite obvious. "What happened?"

"I ran into an old friend, you see," she said, not looking at me but staring down at the floor, her hands twisting in and out of each other anxiously. "Around a week before. It was quite by chance; I hadn't planned it. He's not someone I've stayed in touch with. I was in a bookshop on Oxford Street, you see, and suddenly there he was. Standing in front of me."

"Would this be an old boyfriend?" I asked.

"Yes," she said. "From a hundred years ago, of course. We were at drama school together, but my friend, Jerome, he wasn't a very good actor, if I'm honest, and moved into directing. He really found his niche there. He's directed a few plays in the West End and has just made his first film."

She named the film in question, and I was rather impressed. I'd heard of it, read a series of unanimously positive reviews in the newspapers, and because it was set during the Raj, a period of history that has always interested me, Heidi and I had gone to see it at the cinema.

"We were close all those years ago," she continued. "But I did the dirt on him, you see, and that was that."

I frowned. "The dirt?" I asked.

"I cheated on him."

"Oh. I see."

She shrugged.

"Alex says I was such a slut back then," she continued, looking around at the wallpaper, as if she might find answers to her problems there. "I suppose he's right."

"How old were you at the time?" I asked.

"Eighteen. Nineteen. Something like that."

"As far as I understand, young people flit from person to person at that age," I said. "It doesn't cheapen them in any way. It's part of growing up."

"Alex says differently," she said. "Anyway, it was just so lovely to see Jerome again. He suggested a drink and we spent a few hours together in the end, just talking about old times, remembering people that we once had in common."

"And did some indiscretion take place between you both?" I asked. "Is that what this is all about?"

"Oh no," she said, shaking her head. "No, nothing like that. He wouldn't have been interested in me that way. He's gay now, you see. Well, I suppose he always was, but he slept with women in those days and he doesn't anymore. Anyway, the point is, we got along so well, and it was just like old times, and he asked me . . ." She closed her eyes briefly and her fingers started tapping the cushion of her seat. "He told me that he was casting for his new film and there was a part in it that he thought I'd be perfect for. He claimed he'd even been thinking of me for it and wondering how to get in touch so it was serendipitous that we should just run into each other in the way we had. He wanted to know whether I'd be interested in auditioning."

"But that's wonderful, Madelyn," I said, brightening up. "I hope you said yes."

"I did. But I shouldn't have, you see. Not without speaking to Alex, I mean."

"But if you wanted to do it—"

"He's my husband, Gretel," she said, and again it sounded as if these were words that she was parroting rather than thinking for herself. "I shouldn't make decisions like that without consulting him first."

"Oh, for heaven's sake, it's not the 1950s," I pointed out. "You don't have to run every decision you make by him."

"Anyway, I said yes, I told him that I'd love to audition," she continued, ignoring this remark. "And so I went along the next day to his office and read with another actor. It went very well, I thought. Surprisingly well. I was nervous, of course—it had been so long since I'd done anything like that—but the script was brilliantly written so the lines were a joy to speak. I just fell into the part. Afterward, Jerome was delighted. He said he couldn't make a decision just yet, that there were other people to consult, producers and so on, but he definitely wanted me to come back to read again. It wasn't a lead or anything, you understand, it was a supporting role, but a really good one, I think. The kind of part that, if you played it right, could get you noticed. I used to get noticed all the time, of course, but not anymore. Not since I let myself go and put on so much weight."

Needless to say, the woman hadn't an ounce of fat on her.

"Anyway, when I left, I felt like I was walking on air. And then Alex found out."

She went silent.

"You told him?" I asked.

"No, he read an email that came for me."

"Does your husband regularly read your emails?"

She pressed her tongue into the side of her mouth, considering this. "I must have left my laptop open," she said. "And he just happened to see it."

I remained silent. This seemed unlikely to me.

"And he wasn't happy?" I asked finally.

"No."

"It seems to me that a loving husband would be thrilled that his wife was finding a little success and happiness of her own, independent of her family."

"Alex doesn't think that way," she said. "He said I'd gone behind his back, although I hadn't. I really had run into Jerome by chance.

Although, I suppose he's right that I went for the audition without telling him. That was wrong of me."

"Or you simply wanted to explore the opportunity privately, without any pressure," I suggested. "And if things went well, then you could let him know the good news."

"It doesn't matter now anyway," she said. "The part went to someone else in the end."

"Why?"

"Alex said I shouldn't do it. He was right, of course. It could have been terribly embarrassing. I mean, look at me, I'm not the skinny young thing I once was, and the camera adds so many pounds. I'd have looked like an elephant on screen. He didn't want me to be humiliated."

"But my dear, you're wasting away," I said gently.

"That's kind of you to say, but no, I'm not. Anyway, I knew he was right, but I was too embarrassed to call Jerome, so Alex did it for me, and he even organized to get an actress he's worked with recently, a real up-and-comer, an audition, and she got the part instead. That was the day I forgot Henry. I was a bit upset when I found out, you see, so I opened a bottle of wine. And then another. It was wrong of me, and so unfair on Alex."

"On Henry, you mean."

"I promise it won't happen again. I'm a terrible mother. Really, I am. I ought to be taken out and shot."

She stood up so suddenly, before I could even contradict her, that I startled in the chair.

"I'd better go," she said. "I just wanted you to have the chocolates. And to say sorry."

"I'm just glad I was able to help," I said, standing now too and walking her to the door. There was a lot more that I wanted to say to her, but it didn't seem like the right moment. A part of me wanted her to stay, to find some protection within my walls. While another part wanted her to go back downstairs, close her door behind her and never bother me again.

"Thank you, Gretel," she said as she left, surprising me by turning back and giving me a kiss on both cheeks. As she embraced me I caught the scent of her perfume, but there was something stale underneath, as if she hadn't washed in a day or two and was masking her body odor with deodorant rather than bothering with a shower. As she walked toward the stairs, she raised a hand in farewell and her long sleeve fell backward, almost to the elbow. Heidi had appeared from her flat and was watching her leave.

"What happened to her arm?" she asked me when she'd disappeared out of sight. "That was a horrible bruise."

SIXTEEN

I made my way quickly back along the esplanade, holding tightly to Hugo's hand, and purchased two tickets for the return ferry to Sydney. From time to time, the boy would turn to look in the direction of his house, but, to my relief, he did not seem particularly anxious that a stranger was taking him on a boat without either his mother or father accompanying him. He asked me several times to slow down, but I assumed that, by now, Cynthia would be frantically searching for her son, and I couldn't risk our still being at the wharf if she followed us there.

Hugo had been on the ferry many times, he told me, and preferred to sit upstairs, in the direction of travel.

"Are we going to see Daddy?" he asked me when the bridge appeared on the horizon.

"Not this evening," I replied. "Daddy is working late and he's taking your mummy out for dinner later. That's why they asked me to look after you."

He frowned, growing suspicious now. "But Mummy doesn't know you," he said.

"Of course she does. We're old friends."

"But when you fainted outside our house," he said, unwilling to let it go, "you and Mummy told each other your names."

"I meant that your father and I are old friends," I said, which, strictly speaking, was not untrue. "And he asked this favor of me."

"But shouldn't we have told Mummy that we were leaving?"

"Oh, I wouldn't worry about that. She wanted to have a bath and make herself pretty. Just think of this as a great adventure, Hugo. Do you like that idea? Imagine you're Captain Cook, exploring the city for the first time."

"I'd love to be an explorer," he said enthusiastically, and I was surprised by how brutally this comment took me back in time.

"I had a brother who wanted the same thing," I told him, staring at the water as the ferry cut through it.

"And did he become one?"

"No."

"Why not?"

"Something bad happened to him."

He looked at me now, his eyes wide open in interest.

"What?" he asked breathlessly.

"He died," I said.

"Oh! Was he just a little boy?"

"Yes. Older than you, but not by very much. He was nine when we lost him."

"My neighbor, Mrs. Hamilton, died last year," he said, looking down at his shoes. "She used to let me play with her dog, but after her funeral someone came and took the dog away."

"That's a pity," I said. "Although I'm sure he went to a good home."

"I asked Daddy for a dog for my birthday."

"And do you think you'll get one?"

He shrugged his shoulders and sighed heavily, as if he had the weight of the world on his shoulders.

"What time will we be going home?" he asked eventually.

"Actually, Hugo, you won't be going home tonight," I told him. "You're going to stay with me. In the city."

He frowned. "Overnight?" he asked.

"Yes. That's all right, isn't it?"

"But I've never slept anywhere but at home," he said, and he looked utterly confused by the concept. "Am I allowed?"

"Yes. Think of it as a special treat. You can tell all your friends about it later."

He went silent now and seemed to be considering all of this in his head. I suspected that he knew instinctively that there was something suspicious about what was going on here but was willing to accept that there must be a reason for it. Children, I knew, were generally trusting of adults, assuming that whatever plans they were making were for the best. Which was ironic, really, considering that adults are the very last people who should ever be trusted.

When we docked at Circular Quay, I took him by the hand once again and led him over to one of the ice-cream stalls to buy him a treat, which perked him up enormously. It wasn't a long walk from there to Kent Street and, when we arrived, Hugo sat at the table while I poured him some milk. I had hoped that Cait would already have left for work, but she was still in our flat and when she emerged from her bedroom, she looked surprised to see a five-year-old child sitting in the kitchen. Still, it didn't worry me or upset my plans and, I reasoned, at least she would know the boy's name when she, inevitably, became the person to discover his body.

"And who's this then?" she asked, a half-smile on her face as she looked from one of us to the other.

"His name's Hugo," I told her, taking her into my bedroom and keeping my voice low so he wouldn't hear us. "His mother works with me at the shop. She's been having a bit of trouble with her husband lately so she asked whether I might look after him for the night."

"You?"

"Why not me?" I asked, frowning.

"Well, you don't know much about kids, do you?"

"How hard can it be?" I asked. "He's not a baby. He's five. Almost six. He'll fall asleep early enough, I imagine, and then I can put him to bed."

"And where will he sleep?"

"In here. With me. Then I'll bring him back with me in the morning."

"Seems a funny sort of arrangement," she replied. "Doesn't he have any family who can look after him?"

"I don't think so," I said, hoping that she would not challenge me any further and, to my relief, she let it go, returning to the kitchen and chatting to the boy for a few minutes before leaving for work. I kept an ear out for the sound of the telephone ringing from downstairs. It surely wouldn't be long now. Cynthia would have found the note when she was searching for her son and, most likely, would have called Kurt at work, who would have taken it from there. I wondered what she thought when she saw the surname Kotler inscribed on the envelope. And how her husband would explain this to her. He might be panicking about the abduction of his son, but this could potentially frighten him even more. And inside the envelope, no note. Just a telephone number to call. I wanted to speak to him one last time before my plan reached its conclusion. I imagined Cynthia insisting on phoning the police, but he would have enough sense, knowing the danger, to insist that she leave this matter to him.

"Can I go home now?" asked Hugo after we had eaten, and I rather regretted not buying a few toys or some children's books to keep him entertained.

"You can't, I told you," I said, trying to keep my voice kind so as not to frighten him unduly. I had no desire, after all, to cause the child any unnecessary pain, and planned on waiting for him to fall asleep before carrying him into the kitchen and laying him down on a blanket on the floor, next to me. At which point I would simply turn on the gas and leave the oven door open. It seemed like such an appropriate end for us both. "It's just for one night. And you'll be able to tell Mummy all about it tomorrow."

He appeared downcast and upset now, wiping a few tears from his eyes. It was at that moment that I remembered the little girl who lived on the ground floor of the house next door. She had a dog, and he'd mentioned that he was fond of them. I wondered whether she might be willing to let Hugo play with it.

"Let's go downstairs," I said, and taking him by the hand, I stepped outside and looked across the fence, where my neighbor was throwing a ball for a friendly Labrador.

"Sarah," I called, and the girl glanced over. "This is my friend Hugo. Would you let him play with you for a while? He loves dogs."

Sarah, in the way of children, was uncertain whether she wanted a stranger coming over, but Hugo appeared so excited at the prospect of the animal that she gave in. I watched for a while as they ran around the garden together, relieved that I had thought of something for him to do.

"I'll come back down for you shortly," I said, before returning upstairs and retrieving the rolls of masking tape I had purchased the day before and using them to seal the windows in the kitchen and the ventilation shaft. It didn't take long until the room was completely airtight. I fetched some spare blankets then and lay them down on the floor. This was where I would take him when the moment came. I would close the door, seal it too, take him in my arms, and we would lie down and simply fall asleep together.

It was a strange, liberating feeling knowing that the end was in sight. I was relieved, but frightened too. I didn't know whether I believed in heaven, but I knew that I believed in hell. After all, I had lived there once.

And then the phone rang.

My heart skipped a beat as the loud ringing sounded. I walked over to it, took a deep breath, and lifted the receiver, but remained silent.

"Hello?" said a voice on the other end, and I smiled a little. He was doing his best to adapt to this new country, but his accent was still there.

"Kurt," I said at last, trying hard to keep my voice steady.

"Gretel," he replied. "I knew it was you."

SEVENTEEN

I was surprised to receive a phone call from Eleanor, informing me that she planned on catching up with a colleague over lunch in Piccadilly on her day off and wondering whether I might like to meet her afterward. It had only been a few days since she, Caden, and I had met for lunch but, not wishing to appear stand-offish, I agreed, and got a taxi to Fortnum & Mason for three o'clock. We arrived at the front door at the same time, which felt a little awkward as we had to make small talk as we made our way toward the tea salon, Eleanor insisting on walking through the ladies' clothing section first to tell me that I'd look "absolutely gorgeous" in some item that was clearly meant for a woman in her third or fourth decade, instead of her tenth.

"My days of looking absolutely gorgeous are well behind me," I said when we finally sat down and I consulted the menu. "Nowadays I'm happy to settle for well preserved or neatly turned out."

"Nonsense," said Eleanor, waving away my self-effacement. "If I look half as good as you when I'm your age, then I'll be a happy woman. And Caden will be delighted."

"My dear," I said, smiling a little. "If you're unlucky enough to live to my age, then Caden will be almost one hundred and ten years old and unlikely to have any opinion on the matter at all."

"True," she said. "Maybe I'll go the other way then. I'll be ninety-nine but I'll have a twenty-two-year-old boyfriend."

I chose not to remark that I was not quite that old.

"It was kind of you to invite me," I said, after we'd ordered.

"I want to get to know you, Mrs. F.," she said. "You are going to be my mother-in-law, after all."

"True."

"Did you get on with the others? Caden's first three wives, I mean."

"Some," I admitted. "His first, Amanda, was lovely. I didn't know the other two very well. Which was probably for the best, in retrospect. It would have proven a waste of energy."

"I can't believe I'm going to be the fourth Mrs. Fernsby," she said, although she didn't sound remotely put out by the fact.

There was something open about Eleanor, something that I liked, and I thought she would not mind if I expressed my curiosity on her choice of husband.

"Do you mind if I ask you something rather personal?" I asked.

"You're going to ask why someone my age is marrying your son."

"I mean no offense to Caden," I told her. "He has many sterling qualities. But he's not exactly in the first flush of youth, is he, while you're still a young woman."

"I'm forty-five!"

"My dear, that is young."

"Thank you, but it doesn't feel it," she replied, more serious now. "I'm already at the invisible stage to most men. Although you're not the only one who's asked me that. My friends have too—I'm sure they're all gossiping behind my back. I can't seem to get it through to them."

"Get what through to them?"

"That I love him."

I nodded, considering this. The waiter returned with our teas and scones, and I waited for him to go away before speaking again. "I'm glad that you love him," I told her. "As it happens, I could see that you did when we met on Sunday. But why exactly?"

"Isn't that a strange question for a mother to ask?" she asked. "Don't you love him?"

"Well, of course I do. But a mother will always love her child, won't she? It's in one's DNA."

"I know you've struggled over the years, the two of you," she said, and I looked down at the small pots of jam, not wanting to catch her eye and wondering just how much my son had told her about his childhood. I tried not to think about that year away but guessed that, even after such a long passage of time, it was something that still bothered him. Although I didn't like to think of it, I was certain it had had some unfortunate effect on his relationships with women. A psychologist, I imagined, would have a field day with it.

"I was not," I said eventually, my voice betraying a deep sigh, "entirely cut out for motherhood. Experiences I had in the war did something . . . unhelpful to my mind. I'm not good with children, that's the truth of it. Can I tell you something? Something I've never confided in anyone, not even my late husband?"

She leaned forward, intrigued, and I wondered why on earth I was doing this. Perhaps I was growing to like her.

"When I lived in Australia," I said, "I did a terrible thing."

"What?" she asked, pouring our teas.

"I kidnapped a child."

She sat back now, her eyes opening wide. "You did what?" she asked.

"I kidnapped a child," I repeated. "A little boy."

"But why?"

"I knew his father, many years earlier. He'd been part of something that had brought great loss into my life. I wanted him to know how it felt to lose someone you love."

"Was this during the war?"

I nodded.

"You gave him back, right? The little boy."

"Oh yes. The following day."

"So, you just took him for a night? That's not so terrible. I mean, it's not great but—"

"The thing is, Eleanor, I hadn't planned on giving him back at all."

"What had you planned on doing with him?"

"Killing him. And myself."

To my surprise, she did not seem shocked by this revelation. Perhaps her years of medical training had made her immune to such revelations. Who knew what appalling things she had seen in her time at the hospital?

"But you obviously didn't do it."

"No."

"Well, that's something at least. What was his name? The little boy, I mean."

"Hugo. Hugo Kozel."

"And did you . . ." She looked around, in case we were being overheard, and lowered her voice. "Did you go to prison?"

"No," I said. "There were, shall we say, extenuating circumstances. His father didn't report me to the police, for one thing, although I daresay his mother wanted to. And I left Sydney a few days later, sailing to England, which, of course, is where I settled. I thought it too dangerous to stay in Australia."

"In case the police caught up with you?"

"They were the least of my worries. There were others who might have found me and punished me for what I had done. To come up against them could have led to . . . well, a great deal of unpleasantness."

She thought about this for some time, sipping her tea. "Does Caden know about any of this?" she asked.

"No one does," I said. "The boy's father, well, I assume he's dead by now. He was older than me. And the little boy, he was only five at the time, I'd be surprised if he has any memory of it at all."

"So why are you telling me?"

"Because I need you to understand that I have been a terrible mother and have often wondered whether Caden's lack of success with women in general—"

"He's had three wives," she protested.

"But isn't that a sign of failure in itself?" I asked. "His inability to hold on to them? I'm not trying to sound unkind, I know that he's always done his best, but somehow, despite positive starts, he always seems to end up alone. I've wondered whether it's all my fault. Because I wasn't there for him. Because I abandoned him."

"You asked me why I love him," said Eleanor, reaching forward now and taking my hand in hers. "Part of it must be because of the man you created. He's kind, Mrs. F. And he's funny. And he's interested in me. He asks questions about my life and he listens when I answer. He's not just asking for the sake of it. He's hard-working, and I admire that. I need that in a man. And he makes me feel safe. He's hopeless with money, I think we both know that, but other than that, he's a godsend."

I felt tears coming to my eyes at this description of my son that I didn't really recognize. Perhaps I had not been such an awful mother after all. Or was it that Edgar had compensated by being a particularly good father? It was hard to know.

"Why did you leave him, though?" she asked. "I mean, you don't have to tell me, of course, if you'd rather not. But if you wanted to, I'd be willing to listen. It might give me some more insight into him."

I thought about it and sighed. Perhaps it would be a relief to finally get this off my chest. I looked down at our teacups, which were almost empty.

"I don't suppose I could tempt you to a glass of wine, Eleanor, could I?" I asked.

EIGHTEEN

Of course, I could never have killed him. Or myself. Had I enjoyed that level of courage, I would have taken my life in Paris long before, suspending a rope from the ceiling of our room, tying it around my neck and kicking a chair out from under my feet. And when Kurt asked to see me, I agreed immediately. After all, from the time I was twelve years old, I had wanted nothing more than to be in his company. A decade might have passed since our last encounter, but some things, it seemed, never changed.

He wanted to come into the city that same night, but I refused him, insisting that Hugo would stay with me until the morning, at which time I rose earlier than usual to bathe, wash my hair, and apply makeup, an indulgence I rarely bothered with. I wore a light summer dress, yellow with white polka dots, aware that it displayed my body at its best, and when I studied myself in the mirror, it was not Gretel that I saw looking back at me but a younger version of Mother, when I was still a child in Berlin and her beauty was at its peak. Before my brother was born. Before that other place even existed. Before all of it.

We arranged to meet at ten o'clock in a small café called the Dandelion, a short walk from Kent Street. Cait agreed to watch over

Hugo while I was gone and, to my relief, the boy seemed more re-laxed after a night's sleep, perking up considerably when I told him that Cait would take him to be reunited with his father in a couple of hours.

"I thought you said his mum was one of the girls in your shop," Cait said, as I put on my earrings and applied a fresh coat of lipstick.

"That's right," I told her. "But her husband is going to collect him."

"And what's with all this?" she asked, looking me up and down. "The whole get-up. Anyone would think you were going on a date."

"Is it a crime to want to look nice?" I asked, raising my voice a little. I was nervous, excited, and frightened all at once and didn't feel the need to explain myself. All I wanted was to be outside in the fresh air, composing my thoughts.

"All right, all right," she said, showing me the palms of her hands. "No need to bite my head off, I was only asking."

"I'm sorry," I said. "It's just . . . I have things on my mind, that's all."

"I don't understand why you're having coffee with his father," she said, her forehead creasing in bewilderment. "Seriously, Gretel, there's something not right here, and I wish you'd—"

"Just trust me," I said, pleading with her now. "I'll explain every-thing later this evening, I promise."

Twenty minutes later, I found myself seated inside the café, wait-ing for Kurt. I thought back to the moment when I'd first laid eyes on him, only a few hours after arriving at that other place, when he'd appeared in full uniform, marching into Father's office to introduce himself to his new commandant and, for the first time in my life, I had understood what it was to feel desire. I was only twelve, of course, and had scarcely given any thought to boys at all, but he was tall and handsome, his blond hair swept away from his face, and I was certain that I'd never seen anyone so beautiful in all my life. It was like being in the presence of a god.

Father had introduced us and Kurt had looked at me with stony indifference. I had wanted to say hello, to shake his hand, to know how my own hand would feel inside his, but it was as if I had forgotten how language worked. Instead, I had run from the room and upstairs, sitting on my new bed in a state of utter confusion, breathless, telling myself that this—*this*—is what I had been reading about in books since I was a child. It was real. All of it was real.

I was so lost in these memories that I almost didn't notice when the door opened and a small bell rung above it to announce a customer entering. He stepped inside and looked around before spotting me at the last table by the window. Cocking his head to the side, he stared at me for a few seconds, a half-smile on his face, before turning to speak to the girl behind the counter and ordering a coffee. He was not dressed in the formal attire he wore to the bank every day but in a pair of white trousers and an open-necked shirt with the sleeves rolled up. His skin was tanned, and the color suited him. It crossed my mind that he had taken as much care with his appearance today as I had with mine. Collecting his cup, he walked slowly toward me.

"Gretel," he said, reaching for my hand and lifting it to his lips. "*Du wirst es vielleicht nicht glauben, aber ich habe immer geahnt—*"

"No," I said, interrupting him, feeling an immediate panic at the sound of my native tongue, terrified that someone might overhear us. "No, not German, please. English. Always English."

He looked into my eyes and there remained that strange mixture of beauty and cruelty that had entranced me since our first encounter.

"*Wie du möchtest,*" he said, sitting down opposite me. "This might surprise you, but I always suspected we would meet again someday."

"You've thought about me, then?"

"Not often, no. But sometimes. And you?"

"Not often," I lied. "But sometimes."

He nodded and took a sip from his coffee. I mirrored him, not wanting to feel that it was my responsibility to talk first.

"We're a long way from—" he began, and I cut him off immediately.

"Don't say it," I said. "I hate the word. I never use it."

"But we must call it something."

"I call it that other place."

"Your brother. He used to call it Out-With, if I remember correctly."

I felt a surge inside my stomach when he mentioned my lost sibling.

"Out-With," he repeated quietly, shaking his head and offering a slight laugh. "Rather silly, don't you think?"

"Lieutenant Kotler," I began, placing my hands on my lap now, for they were trembling slightly and I didn't want him to notice my discomfort.

"If I cannot use the name of that other place, as you call it," he said, "then you cannot call me by a name that I have long since shrugged off. Lieutenant Kotler, as you knew him, no longer exists. He died somewhere in Germany toward the end of the war. I am Kurt Kozel."

"It always felt impertinent calling you Kurt back then," I told him. "Father and Mother insisted that I speak to you with all the formality of your rank."

"But you disobeyed them."

"I don't know what to call you now. Kozel feels like a lie."

"Kurt is fine," he said. "But before we go any further, and as much as I'm enjoying these nostalgic memories, you must tell me: Where is Hugo? Where is my son?"

"He's safe," I told him. "He's with a friend of mine. As soon as we're finished talking, I'll return him to you."

"You haven't hurt him?"

"I would never hurt a child," I said.

"Which of us could?" he asked, smiling, and I felt my face harden.

"Please, don't be facetious."

"Gallows humor," he said with a shrug. "Nothing more."

"It's not funny."

"I suppose not. But if you have injured even a—"

"Kurt, he's fine, and you know he is. He'll be here later. After we've talked."

He seemed to accept this, relaxing a little, before adding some sugar to his coffee and stirring it slowly.

"So," he said at last. "You might as well tell me what is it you want from me? Is it money? I don't have much."

"I don't want your money."

"How did you find me, anyway?"

"By chance. I wasn't looking for you. If I had been, then I daresay I'd never have got within a thousand miles of you. The truth is, I moved to Sydney earlier this year. One evening, I was sitting in Fortune of War, talking to a friend, and I heard a voice that I recognized. I would have known it anywhere. I thought I'd got away from all that—"

"So did I."

"But there you were. Ordering a drink without a care in the world."

"And then?"

"I followed you. I sat near you in that same pub one evening."

"I remember," he said. "I was aware that I was being watched but I wasn't sure who it was. Whether you had been an inmate, perhaps. Or were a hunter. It never occurred to me that it might be you. I left a message, though; did you find it?"

"The drawing of a fence," I said.

"That's right."

"Why that?"

"It's always felt to me like a symbol of that time. One that any of us who were there, on either side, would remember."

"Are you worried about being discovered?"

"Of course," he said. "But I have no intention of being captured, Gretel. I remain on my guard at all times. I expect I will have to do so for the rest of my life."

"I followed you to Manly another evening, and you didn't see me. I wasn't sure what I wanted. Until I saw you with your son."

"His mother has been driven crazy overnight," he told me. "It was all that I could do not to get her to call the police."

"How did you stop her?"

He smiled a little, that same brutal, sensual smile that had always had the power to draw me in. "Cynthia knows that it's best to abide by my decisions," he said, choosing his words carefully.

"You're cruel to her," I said, more of a statement than a question.

"No, I don't think so," he replied. "I love my wife. But I have a traditional side to me too. I believe in the husband being head of his household. Your father held similar beliefs."

"You're nothing like my father," I said.

"No, my name will not live in infamy, as his will. After all, he was the one in charge, wasn't he? A grown man, in his forties. I was just . . . what is the word? An accomplice. A teenage boy playing dress-up and enjoying the power that had somehow landed in my lap. Your father was a monster. I was just the monster's apprentice."

I glared at him. This was not what I had meant, but it would have been difficult to contradict him.

"That said," he continued, "Cynthia is not made of infinite patience and I won't be able to keep her from phoning the police if I am too long delayed."

"I told you, I'll return him to you," I said. "And I don't lie."

"Of course you lie," he said, bursting out laughing. "You must have lied every day of your life for these last seven years. What are you calling yourself here, after all?" I told him, and he laughed again. "So, you kept your first name, just as I did. But changed the surname, just as I did. We're not so different after all, are we?"

"It would have been impossible to keep my birth name," I said.

"When did you change it? On the boat to Australia?"

"No. As soon as the war ended. Mother and I moved to Paris once it was safe to travel out of Berlin."

"And how did that work out for you?"

"Not well," I said, feeling a slight tingling in my scalp at the memory of the razor blade, the blood seeping down my forehead, the ugly clumps of hair that remained in its wake. "I try not to think of the past."

"And you fail, I imagine?"

"Of course. Don't you?"

"No," he said. "But then, I'm one of those people who somehow succeeds at whatever he puts his mind to."

I turned to look out of the window, uncertain how I could break down his wall of confidence. Some schoolchildren were passing by, holding hands in pairs, large hats on their heads to fend off the sun. They looked impossibly innocent.

"I didn't expect to survive, you know," he said after a moment, his voice quieter now. "Your father sent me to the front."

"I remember."

"But do you remember why?"

I did, or thought I did, but waited for him to tell me.

"Your grandfather, I recall, had come on a visit. I was invited to join the family for dinner. And I let slip that my own father had been reluctant to embrace the Reich. You remember now?"

"I remember you kicked Pavel to death."

"Who?"

"Our waiter. That was his name. Pavel."

"Oh yes. The Jew," he said. "He spoke back to me, I think."

"No, he didn't say a word. He would have been too frightened. He simply spilled some wine on the table."

Kurt smiled. "I think it very unlikely that I kicked a man to death for spilling wine."

"But you did," I said. "I recall it vividly. My mother begged my father to intervene, but he said nothing, simply sat there calmly, continuing his dinner."

Kurt looked down at the tablecloth and ran a palm across it. I watched him carefully. To my surprise, he seemed conflicted by this memory.

"I've never forgotten it," I said, the words catching in my throat. "I'd never seen something like that happen before me."

"And yet you cried when I was sent away."

"I did," I admitted. "I was so confused. Of course, I had feelings for you and I didn't yet have the maturity to cope with them, but then you did that and—"

"Many things happened in that other place, as you call it," he said. "But I too was punished, for what my father had done. A price that you have not paid, I might add. I had been loyal to the commandant and he sent me away. All because of that. What, was he worried that if others found out it would reflect badly on him?"

"I don't know," I said. "He would never have discussed those decisions with me."

"The fact is, what he issued me was a death sentence. And I was terrified, I'll admit it. I was just a boy, after all. But I didn't die. Somehow, the soldiers around me fell one after one, but I endured. They could not kill me, you see. I was shot, once, but in the shoulder. After that, I was sent back to Berlin, where I was given a job behind a desk. It was a good position for me. Had I known that I would find myself working in such an environment, I would have asked someone to shoot me long before. I might even have asked you."

"And you weren't arrested?" I asked. "Afterward, I mean? When the war ended."

He shook his head.

"We knew the Allies were coming, of course," he said. "It was obvious that it was only a matter of time before they would break through. The Führer came to the building where I was stationed al-most every day and seemed increasingly broken, increasingly unrea-sonable. His anger was alarming to behold. Most people did their best to stay out of his way, but I liked to observe him."

"Why?" I asked.

"He fascinated me," replied Kurt with a shrug. "Well, he fasci-nated all of us, remember?"

"I remember," I said, for it was true: he had.

"It was like being in the presence of something otherworldly. So I watched, from a distance, trying to learn from him. And then, one day, we were informed that he had retreated to his bunker. Some of the officers went with him. The secretarial staff too. Cooks and so on. I received a message that he had left a pair of spectacles on his desk, and I was to bring them to him. Hitler's spectacles, can you imagine it? I took them and made my way out of the building, but the armies were already closing in—it was obvious that they'd be upon us in a day or two at most—and so I ran. I ran as fast as I could."

"And where did you go?"

"North, toward Denmark at first, and then onwards to Sweden.

I spent a few years there, changed my identity, my voice, my accent. When an opportunity arose to relocate to Australia, I took it. It seemed like a good way to make a fresh start."

"And to shake them off," I suggested.

"Who?"

"Those who might have your name on a list. Those who want to find you and bring you to justice."

"If there are such people, then they are looking for Lieutenant Kotler," he told me. "They have no interest in a mild-mannered banker named Kozel who lives a quiet life with his beautiful wife, Cynthia, and their son. Some are here, of course. Nazi hunters, I mean. But they're few compared to those who are searching North and South America. I think they've forgotten about Australia."

"They'll remember some day," I told him.

"Perhaps. And what will you do then?"

"Me?"

"I'm fairly insignificant in the great scheme of things. You, on the other hand . . ."

"I had nothing to do with any of it," I protested, leaning forward. "I was just a child."

He raised an eyebrow.

"Your father was the commandant of the most notorious concentration camp of them all," he replied. "And you've chosen not to present yourself to the authorities in the years between the liberation of that camp and today."

"That was Mother's decision, not mine."

"Of course. Always an excuse. But don't you think the courts would wish to speak to you too?"

"Why? What could I tell them?"

"Something. Anything. Every tiny piece of information could provide some relief to the families of those we . . ." He stopped himself and bit his lip. "You can pretend otherwise, Gretel," he said after a moment. "But you, like me, are what's called a person of interest. And they would surely find some way of suggesting that you were as guilty as any of us. No matter how young you were."

I felt a mixture of emotions inside. I had spent so long trying to convince myself that I was innocent, but he was right in what he'd said. I had encountered many Jews in my time there, not just Pavel, and I knew a lot regarding how they had been treated and the manner in which their lives had ended. I could have told the authorities all of this. But if they caught up with me, I knew that I would do exactly as Kurt had done that day in Berlin. I would run.

He reached into the breast pocket of his shirt now and removed a small pair of spectacles—narrow arms with small circular frames—and placed them on the table before me. I looked at them, uncertain what he meant by this, before understanding and letting out a gasp of horror.

"These belonged to him?" I asked, looking up.

"Yes."

"And you've kept them all these years? Why?"

He shrugged. "A memento, perhaps?" he suggested. "Something to remind me that I did not dream it all. That it was real and that, once in my life, I was a part of something very beautiful. Speaking of which, you've grown into an extremely attractive young woman, you know," he added, reaching across and running a finger across my cheek. I closed my eyes. There was a time that I would have crawled over broken glass to feel that hand upon my skin.

"Would you like to try them on?" he asked quietly, and I stared ahead, seeing and hearing nothing around me but him.

"What?"

"His spectacles. Try them on. See the world through his eyes, so to speak."

I glanced down at the table and watched as my hand moved toward them. The Führer's glasses. I touched them with the tip of my finger, almost expecting to receive a shock of some sort when they made contact with my skin. I felt sick. I felt excited. I felt faint. I felt powerful.

"Try them on, Gretel," repeated Kurt, leaning forward now, his voice almost a whisper.

"I can't," I said.

"You want to. I know you do."

"No."

Time seemed to stand still as I stared at them. I could hear his voice in my head. The sound of heels clicking together. My father hailing his name loudly.

I reached out again, my hands visibly trembling, and lifted them by the arms. I felt disgusted to be holding them and, to my intense shame, privileged.

Could I wear them? Did I dare? A moment later, they were on my face and a sound, a sigh of pleasure or a groan of dismay, emerged from my mouth.

"It's thrilling, isn't it?" asked Kurt, blurry to me now, for the prescription was far too strong for my eyes. "Tell me how you feel."

It was too complicated to put into words. That potent mixture of authority, horror, and guilt all at once.

"You can sense his presence, can't you?"

"Always. But never more than now."

"And how does it make you feel?" ·

"Disgusted. Repulsed. Ashamed."

"And?"

I stared at him.

"The truth, Gretel."

"Excited," I whispered.

He smiled, reached out and gently removed them from my face, setting them down once again between us.

"Tell me you don't miss him," he said in a low voice, leaning forward. "Tell me you don't wish he'd seen it all through and that we'd achieved victory. Imagine the world we'd be living in now. How different everything would be. I wanted it so badly. For the Reich to last a thousand years, just like he promised. Be honest with yourself, Gretel. You wanted that too, didn't you?"

NINETEEN

When I returned to Winterville Court from my afternoon with Eleanor, I found Henry seated on the staircase, reading a book. Not *Treasure Island* this time; he must have finished that and was now engaged in *Chitty Chitty Bang Bang*. I rather admired that he seemed to prefer classic children's fiction to contemporary and wondered whether it was his mother, his father, or a school librarian who furnished him with his reading material. He looked up when he saw me and offered something that blended an embarrassed smile with relief that a responsible adult was, at last, on the premises.

"Hello, Henry," I said.

"Hello, Mrs. Fernsby."

"Is there a reason you're sitting on the stairs? I don't mind, you understand. If you're comfortable there, then good luck to you. I'm just wondering."

He seemed reluctant to explain but then gave in, avoiding my eye by focusing his attention on his fingers. "Mummy's taking a nap," he said. "I didn't want to wake her up by knocking too loudly."

I sighed, wondering what condition Madelyn might be in behind the locked door.

"And how did you get home from school?" I asked.

"I walked."

"On your own?"

He nodded.

"I thought you weren't allowed."

"It seemed easiest," he said. "No one showed up for me."

I glanced toward Flat One, concerned about what might have happened to the boy along the way.

"Would you like to come up to mine?" I asked, and he considered this for a few moments before shaking his head.

"I'm fine here," he said. "She'll be awake soon."

"All right," I said, feeling no great desire to push the issue. I made my way toward the staircase, and he moved to one side to let me pass. When I reached the top, I looked back down at this tiny creature seated alone with no one to take care of him. He seemed so undersized and lonely. I wondered whether boys in his class made fun of him for being small.

"Can I bring you a glass of milk?" I called down. "Or a biscuit, perhaps?"

"No, thank you," he said, not looking around, and I moved on. It was unusual for a child of his age to reject treats, but I wasn't going to dwell on the matter.

I was only in my flat a few minutes, however, when a knock came on my door and I smiled, assuming that he'd changed his mind. However, when I opened it, it wasn't Henry standing there but Heidi Hargrave's grandson.

"Oberon," I said, surprised to see him. "Hello."

"Mrs. Fernsby," he replied, his tone cold. "Can I have a word?"

I nodded, waiting for him to speak, but he looked over my shoulder and, as it was obvious that he wanted to talk in private, I reluctantly stepped back and ushered him inside. Something in the way he walked reminded me of Father, which was unsettling.

"Are you aware that there's a small child sitting on the staircase?" he asked as I closed the door.

"That's just Henry," I told him. "He comes with the building. Now, what can I do for you?"

"I have a bone to pick with you," he said. I had just been about to offer him a seat but changed my mind now. If he was going to prove argumentative, then I would be happy to show him out just as quickly as I had shown him in.

"Do you indeed?" I asked. "Would you care to tell me why?"

"Granny says that you're discouraging her from moving to Australia."

"Granny is correct," I agreed.

"Might I ask why?"

"Because I think it's a terrible idea," I told him. "You may be her grandson, Oberon, but I've known her considerably longer than you. Her life is here. Her friends are here. She asked whether I thought it was a good idea for her to move halfway across the world and I told her no, that she wouldn't understand the culture or the people or the climate and that she was better off in Winterville Court. Would you have preferred that I had lied to her?"

"I'd have preferred that you didn't interfere."

"But you asked for my help! And if a man knocked on her door and said he was from the gas board and wanted access to her flat but wasn't willing to show his credentials, would you rather I didn't interfere then too?"

He rolled his eyes, which made me want to slap him.

"That's hardly the same thing," he said. "I'm not a man from the gas board. I'm her grandson. I only want what's best for her."

"And you believe that you're in the best position to decide that?" I asked.

"I do, as it happens, he said. "She's doolally," he added, rolling a finger in a circular motion around his temple. "She doesn't know what's best for her."

"Then, fortunately, I do," I replied.

"I'd rather you stayed out of it," he said, his tone angry, and I found my own temper rising now. I had had enough of being bullied by men. It had been happening all my life, from the moment I had first drawn breath.

"She won't live forever," I said acidly. "I'm sure you'll receive your inheritance in due course, if that's what you're worried about."

"You think this is about money?" he asked, but he was a poor actor. His attempts at sounding insulted were wasted on me.

"I do," I admitted. "Awful of me, I know, but then I'm ninety-one. I'm probably half doolally myself. Now, if you don't mind, I'll have to ask you to leave. I have things to do."

He glared at me, annoyed, wounded even, and I wondered whether I'd been unfair on him.

"Yes, I'm sure you have a busy afternoon of appointments," he said.

"There's no need to be rude," I replied.

"I'm sorry," he said, opening the door. "I know you mean well, but I'd ask you to stay out of our affairs in future," he said. "I believe I know what's best for my own grandmother."

"Yes, yes," I said dismissively, ushering him through the door and closing it behind him, but not before glancing down at Henry, who was seated exactly where I had left him but was looking up now, observing the action and clearly troubled by the sound of raised voices. He had enough of those in his life, I assumed.

I made some tea and read for an hour or more, before turning on the radio and listening to the news. I was beginning to wonder what I might have for supper when a thought occurred to me. I dismissed it, thinking no, it wouldn't be possible, but then, curious, even anxious, I opened my front door and glanced downstairs once again.

He was still there.

"Henry," I said, and he turned to look up at me. He'd been crying, I could tell, but he wiped his cheeks and eyes; he didn't want me to see how upset he was. "You're not still sitting there."

"I've knocked," he said plaintively. "But she's not answering."

"Oh, for pity's sake," I said with a sigh and made my way downstairs. This was really too much. I knocked on the door myself, so loudly that I'm sure the people in the next building could hear it.

"Mrs. Darcy-Witt," I called at the top of my voice. "Madelyn. Are you in there? Can you open the door, please?"

No sound came from within, and I pressed my ear to the wall, hoping to hear her feet making their way across the wooden floors.

"Madelyn!" I called again, rapping on the woodwork once more. "Madelyn, open up!"

Still nothing.

I turned to look at Henry, who wore a haunted expression on his face. For the first time, I noticed that he had a large bandage on the side of his right hand.

"What happened here?" I asked him, reaching out to touch the wound, but he quickly moved it out of sight.

"I got burned," he said.

"How?"

"On the oven."

I stared at him, wanting to ask more, but unsure whether I should. I knocked on the door once again as Heidi opened hers upstairs and peered down.

"Gretel," she cried. "What's the matter?"

"The poor boy can't get in," I said. "His mother's . . . I don't know . . . well, she's not answering."

Heidi made her way downstairs now too. She looked as if she was having one of her good days.

"He's been sitting out here for hours," I told her.

"Don't you have a key?" she asked, turning to the boy.

"I'm not allowed to have one," he said, and I could see that he was close to tears again.

Heidi frowned, then her face lit up, like she'd had a eureka moment. She reached up and ran her hand across the top of the door. It came away empty but dusty, and she blew the filth away, in my direction. I coughed and flapped a hand before my face.

"What on earth are you doing?" I asked.

She didn't reply but turned toward the plant pot that stood outside the door instead, plunging her hand into the soil. When it emerged again, it held a silver key.

"Mr. Robertson always left a spare here," she said, holding it out toward me in triumph.

"Mr. Richardson," I said, correcting her, as I wiped the dirt from the key. "Will it work, do you think? Might they have changed the locks since moving in?" I handed it back to her.

"Only one way to find out," she said, putting the key into the lock and turning it. The door opened.

"Hurrah!" I cried. "Clever you, Heidi!"

She beamed, delighted with herself, and strode in as if she owned the place. I was less eager to march in uninvited, but Henry leaped to his feet and ran in before me. I followed him and stood in the living room, looking around. Everything seemed as it should. Henry threw his school bag on the ground and made for the kitchen. He was hungry, after all. I didn't know where Heidi had gone but, before I could go in search of her, she emerged from the corridor that led to the bedrooms.

"Gretel," she said, her face pale. "You need to call an ambulance."

TWENTY

"I met him too, you know."

Kurt raised an eyebrow as he returned the spectacles to his lapel pocket.

"You met who?" he asked.

"The Führer."

He raised an eyebrow, as if he didn't believe me.

"It's true," I said. "He came to dinner in Berlin. It was the night he gave Father his new orders, the ones that would bring us there. I tried to impress him by telling him that I could speak French. He looked at me and asked me why I would ever want to. I couldn't think of an answer."

"I never spoke to him," replied Kurt, his tone tinged with regret. "Even when he passed my desk and glanced in my direction, I didn't dare address him."

"You could sell those, you know," I said, nodding toward the glasses. "There are collectors who would probably pay a fortune for them."

"Some day, I might," he replied. "Perhaps I should think of them as my pension."

It seemed surreal to be speaking like a couple of old friends catching up after years of being out of touch. There were a few other people in the café, along with the woman behind the counter, and I wondered what any of them might do if they knew the truth about our real identities. I felt a curious desire to tell them, the same sense of danger one feels when looking over a precipice and, although never previously harboring any thoughts of suicide, experiencing an overwhelming desire to jump.

"You haven't told me about the rest of your family," he said after a time, and I looked at him, shaking my head slightly as if I had been woken from sleep. "Your father was hanged, wasn't he?"

I nodded.

"I read about it," he said. "Were you—"

"We'd gone into hiding by then," I told him. "We read about it too."

"Were you upset?"

"He was my father."

"And your mother?"

I shrugged. "Her mind was focused solely on staying alive."

"Did she come to Australia with you? She's not the person looking after my son, is she?"

"My mother is dead," I said.

He seemed surprised by this.

"Really? And so young."

"She never recovered."

"From what?"

"From all of it."

"I suppose she claimed she knew nothing of what was going on."

I nodded.

"It would have been impossible," he continued. "She knew. They all knew. It was their generation that started it. And ours that paid."

"You're not counting yourself as a victim, I hope," I said, and he shook his head quickly.

"No, not that," he said. "But—"

"But what?"

"But I don't remember making any conscious decisions about my life. It was all laid out for me so young."

"The things you did," I began, but he breathed in deeply, clenching his hands into fists, and I found myself unable to continue, dreading the idea that he would turn this back on me and I would be forced to confront the fact that, as he had already pointed out, we were not so very different.

"And your brother?" he asked after a moment. "He didn't like me very much, did he?"

"No."

"What was his name again? I forget."

I closed my eyes, swallowing hard. I never said my brother's name. I couldn't bear to. I hoped he wouldn't ask again.

"Oh, wait," he said, clicking his fingers. "I remember now." When he uttered the word, a chill ran through me at hearing those two syllables spoken aloud. "And where is he? He was too young to fight so, let me guess, I imagine he's a student somewhere. He had a bookish bent, didn't he? He always had that copy of *Treasure Island* with him. He read it over and over."

"He loved it," I said.

"So am I right?"

"He died too," I told him, and, for the first time, I saw a flicker of surprise on his face, even shock.

"Really?" he asked. "How?"

I shook my head. "I can't talk about it," I said.

I looked down at the table and, for a moment, considered lifting the knife that sat there and driving it straight into his eye. It could be done in a moment, before he even had time to react. The worst of it was that I could still feel his lips upon my hand, from when he had kissed me earlier, and wanted him to do it again.

"All right," he said at last. "But I think we have to decide something, don't you?"

"What's that?" I asked.

"Here we both are, and we both know each other's secrets. So, what are we going to do about it?"

"It's not obvious?" I asked.

"Not to me."

"You need to pay for what you did."

"And what did I do?"

"You know exactly what—"

"I know what you think I did. But I'd like to hear you describe it."

"You were part of it," I said. "A big part of it."

"Part of what?" he asked, his voice betraying a certain irritation now. "Really, Gretel, I don't know why your father employed Herr Liszt to educate you when you seem so incapable of translating your thoughts into words."

"You say that my mother knew what was going on," I told him. "But you did too. And you did nothing. You approved of it."

"The killing, you mean."

"Yes."

"Why do you struggle to call things what they are? All this obfuscation. We had Jews. We had gas chambers. We had crematoria. We had killing. You won't say your brother's name. You won't say any of these—"

"Stop!" I insisted, my forehead wrinkling in revulsion. "You knew about it from the start."

"Of course I did. It's the reason I was sent there. To help facilitate the exterminations."

"Was there no part of you that thought it was wrong?"

His forehead creased. I could tell that this was something he did his best never to think about.

"It was . . . difficult at first," he said. "I am a person. But I seemed to forget in time . . ."

"Forget what?"

"That they were people too."

"You took pleasure in it."

He shook his head. "No," he said.

"You did. I remember."

"I took pleasure in the power that was in my hands. It was exciting and frightening at the same time. What would you have had me do? I was a soldier. And soldiers obey orders. If I'd refused, I would have been taken out and shot. I was just a boy of nineteen. I wasn't going to give up my life that easily. I'd been indoctrinated as far back as I could remember. At ten years old I was forced to join the Deutsches Jungvolk. Four years later, I was part of the Hitlerjugend. I knew nothing about anything. I simply did what I was told to do. And from there I was moved along the ranks until I was a fully established member of the SS."

"You said your father was opposed to—"

"My father was weak!" he said, raising his voice now. "A weak man. I didn't want to be him. I wanted to be stronger than him. So it did not strike me as a bad solution to the question."

"What question?" I asked.

"The Jewish question. It was ambitious. Probably too ambitious to have ever truly succeeded."

"You feel no regret?"

"I regret that we lost," he told me. "I would have liked to continue my army career. I think I could have risen quite high in the ranks, had things gone differently. It still surprises me. For a couple of years, things were looking very positive. Don't you wish that we had won?"

I stared at him, uncertain how to respond.

"Be honest with me, Gretel. If you could click your fingers so the Allies would have been defeated, wouldn't you do it? Your father, your mother, your brother, they'd still be with you. You'd be a popular girl, the daughter of a man of enormous power and influence. Just imagine the life that you might have led. Tell me, if you had that ability, wouldn't you do it?"

"I wouldn't," I said. "I couldn't."

"You're lying."

"No."

"You are. I can see it in your face. You need to tell yourself that you wouldn't so you can feel a sense of moral superiority, but I don't believe you for even a moment." He reached out and grabbed me by the wrist. "You would click your fingers, Gretel, to win back all that you have lost, even at the expense of millions more lives. You can deny this if you choose, but I know it's a lie."

I pulled my hand back. The wrist felt sore from where he had gripped it and I rubbed it with the fingers of my left hand.

"You only want to talk about me so you won't have to face up to your own part in things," I said.

"No. If you think my conscience is clear, you're wrong. It isn't. It never will be. But I choose not to let it control me."

"You were cruel."

"I was obedient."

"The children."

"Of course, we must feel more sympathy for the children," he said, rolling his eyes. "The sainted children. Why should I care?"

"I heard you once, you know," I told him.

"Heard me what?"

"You were with my brother in the kitchen. You'd brought another boy in, to help clean glasses for a party. You said his fingers were small enough to do the job correctly. He ate something, I think, from the fridge. My brother gave it to him, but he denied it and you punched the boy. He couldn't have been more than nine years old, and you punched him in the face."

Kurt shrugged. "I don't remember that," he said.

"You have a son of your own now. How does it make you feel?"

"Don't talk about Hugo."

"What if Hugo had been on one of those trains?"

"Shut up," he hissed.

"I was listening on the stairs that day. I was too frightened to come down and stop you."

"What do you want from me, Gretel?" he asked, leaning forward, his face filled with rage. "Do you expect me to break down and cry? Because it would be a performance, nothing more, if I did. Something theatrical to appease your pathetic guilt. I refuse to live my days thinking about these things."

"If you, and others like you, had only said no. If you'd stood up to—"

"You're living in a dream world," he said, sitting back again and regaining his composure. "A utopian ideal where man exists for no other purpose than to help his fellow man. It's not natural, can't you see that?"

"But why not?"

"Because it's not how we're designed. It starts in the schoolyard, with small boys fighting among each other. In the 1930s, the Reich found a people to hate. Now, twenty years later, it's us who are hunted down. When they discover one of us, they bring us to a courtroom so the world can hear of our crimes but, really, all they want is to shoot us, hang us, kill us in any way they can. We're all just trying to survive.

You as much as anyone. Why are you here, after all? In Australia. So far from home. The truth is, you're afraid of being caught too."

He was right, but I hated to acknowledge it.

"I live every day with what my father did," I told him.

"Ah, you're still protesting your innocence? You saw the trains arrive. You watched as the people disembarked. There were only so many huts and yet we continued to fill them, even though you never saw anyone leave through the front gates. And you're telling me— me, of all people—that you never questioned any of this? The smell of the burning bodies; you weren't aware of it? The days when the ashes would fall on our heads like black snow; you were inside on those days, were you, playing with your dolls?"

I felt the tears come to my eyes now.

"I didn't know," I insisted.

"You can lie to me, if you wish, but to lie to yourself? I know why you're here. You're here to transfer all the guilt in your soul onto me. But you can't do that, Gretel, because I refuse to accept it. I have my own guilt to contend with."

"If I can do something good," I insisted. "If I can just make up for—"

He shook his head. "You're a fool," he said. "You were an empty-headed girl back then and you're an empty-headed woman now. Now, are you going to tell me how this interview ends, or do I have to keep guessing?"

"I wanted to look at you, to talk to you, before I report you," I said, sitting erect now and trying to maintain some level of composure. "I'm going to the police to tell them who you are."

"And I will be arrested and tried. And, most likely, incarcerated for many years. I don't believe that's what you want."

"I want you to pay for your crimes."

"While you escape yours. But I will be just another death on your conscience. Don't think I don't understand how powerful that feels. Nothing matches it. You think giving life is a wonderful thing? It is, of course. But it is nowhere near as exciting as taking it."

Movement from outside the window caught my eye. It was Cait and Hugo, arriving across the street. I held my hand up to tell her to remain there for now, and she nodded. Kurt glanced across the road too, saw his son and waved at him, exhaling a deep sigh of relief. At this same moment, the door to the café opened and two policemen stepped inside, making their way to the counter and looking up at the menu on the wall.

"How fortuitous," said Kurt, glancing in their direction and then smiling back at me. "Your chance has arrived to cleanse your ruined soul. Will you call them over, or will I? You can tell them every-thing. I won't run. I'll admit it all, as long as you take responsibility for your own actions too. You've said all these brave things, Gretel, but this is the moment your life has been leading toward. It's the work of only a few seconds to summon them over and tell them who I am and who you are. Let them arrest us and we can both watch as the international legal system captures us within its grasp. For me, it will inevitably lead to my death. And for you? Well, who knows? But it will be very interesting to observe your journey."

"But I'm innocent," I protested.

"Even if this were true, it counts for nothing. Your life will no longer be your own. Do you really believe that your father's one sur-viving child will be absolved of all responsibility by a world con-sumed by shock? Within days, your photograph will be on the front page of every newspaper across the planet and, believe me, there'll be far more interest in you than there will be in me. They'll talk about me for a while, but they'll write books about you. And that's what you always wanted, isn't it?" he asked, reaching across and tak-ing both my hands in his. "For you and me to be linked in some way.

Oh, Gretel, the things I could have done to you back then, had I chosen to," he added, musing now. "You would have let me do anything I wanted. But it turns out I had some decency, after all."

"But not in this way," I said, taking my hands back.

"Your life will be destroyed. And his," he said, nodding through the window toward his son. "And if, one day, you have children, then their lives will be ruined too." He reached out and ran a finger gently along my cheek. "You have the most beautiful scars, Gretel," he said. "Some inflicted by your family; some, perhaps, by me. But this is the moment for you. You say that you live with torment, well, you can ease it now. You tell me that you're filled with regret, then unburden yourself of it. My life is in your hands. Just as, all those years ago, the lives of all those innocent people were in mine."

I found myself simply staring at him. Everything he had said was the truth. I could expose him, but in doing so I would have to expose myself too. Was I willing to do this? Could I sacrifice my own life simply to bring retribution to his? It seemed as if hours passed before he spoke again.

"So, there we are," he said, standing up now. "It turns out that we're exactly the same, you and me. The world would never forgive either of us for what we have done, so what is the point of exposure?"

I stood up now too and, to my surprise, found that we were somehow locked in a kiss. It was the kiss that I had longed for since I was twelve years old and, as my lips parted, I found that I could forget the world entirely in his embrace. And then, almost as quickly as it had begun, it was over. He took a step back, offered a courtly bow, and smiled.

"Goodbye, Fraülein Gretel," he said. "It was a pleasure to be in your company once more, but it is the final time. We won't meet again."

I watched as he walked casually out of the coffee shop, wishing the police officers a good morning as he passed them, and then crossed the road, exchanging a few words with Cait, who laughed uproariously at something that he said, then took his son by the hand and disappeared down the street.

L ess than forty-eight hours later, I rose early in the morning, left a note of apology for Cait on the kitchen table, along with a month's rent, and made my way to Circular Quay, where I boarded a boat for Southampton. My last act before departing Australia was to post a letter to Cynthia Kozel in which I explained my full history with her husband in detail, from the morning my family departed Berlin to the moment Kurt left the Dandelion. I left no detail out, admitting who I was, who my family had been, and the activities that Kurt had participated in. Of course, in retrospect, I see that I was simply abdicating responsibility once again, leaving it to a stranger to decide whether I should be punished while knowing that, should she choose to expose me, she would likely be inviting trauma into her own life. For what guarantee did she have that I would not expose her husband in return?

In traveling halfway across the world to Sydney, I had done all that I could to put the past behind me, but I knew now that this was impossible. I could be in France, Australia, or England, I could find myself living on Mars, but no matter where I was, those beautiful scars that Kurt had spoken of would always drag me back to that other place. I could never escape it.

Interlude

The Boy

POLAND 1943

M other protested, but Father insisted.

Now that I was twelve, he announced, I was old enough to understand his work, particularly since I was ostensibly a member of the Jungmädelbund but had the misfortune of being unable to attend any of their meetings or participate in their activities due to what Mother liked to call our "exile" in Poland. It was Father who had given me the picture of Trude Mohr that I kept on my bedroom wall, and I idolized her, in the same way that he did the Führer himself. Had we still been living in Berlin, I would certainly have been a leader in the organization due to Father's elevated status, perhaps even an Untergauführerin or a Ringführerin, but in that other place, the only person over whom I could exert any power was my brother.

"I don't see why you get to go and I don't," he said as I brushed my hair that morning, having put on the blue skirt and middy blouse uniform that I had rarely had an opportunity to wear.

"Because I'm twelve and you're only nine," I said.

"But I'm a boy. So I matter more."

I rolled my eyes. There was little point arguing with him.

"There are matters to do with Father's work that you wouldn't understand," I continued, determined to be as patronizing as possible, even though I was scarcely anymore informed on this subject than he was. "One day you will, when you're a little older, but until then—"

"Oh, shut up, Gretel!" he snapped, jumping off my bed and stamping his foot on the floor. "You're the most annoying sister in the world!"

"You shut up," I retorted, growing tired, and returned to beautifying myself while he sat cross-legged on the floor in frustration. For all our arguments, we spent more time in each other's company than we did anyone else's.

"I understand more than you know," he said, his voice low and secretive now.

"Do you indeed?" I replied.

"I could tell you stories about what goes on over there, but you wouldn't believe me."

"Over where?" I asked.

"On the other side of the fence."

"It's a farm," I told him. "I've explained that to you before."

"It's not a farm," he said.

"Then what is it?" I asked, turning around to look at him, curious to know how much he might have learned. We had both spent much of our time since arriving trying to figure out what we were doing there, what the purpose of this place was, and when we might be allowed to leave.

"I don't know," he conceded finally. "But I'm working on it."

I shook my head, standing up and adjusting my skirt. I was very happy with my appearance and planned on sneaking some of Mother's Guerlain Shalimar perfume onto my neck and wrists before going downstairs.

"You know nothing," I said, leaving him alone now. "Now be a good boy and look after Mother while we're gone."

It was only as I was going downstairs that I heard him shout from his room.

"But it's not a farm!" he roared. "I know that much!"

Lieutenant Kotler drove us to the entrance of the camp in an open-topped car, but we did not speak on the short journey as Father, in the front passenger seat, was busy reading through one of his files. The barrier lifted for us and the soldiers jumped quickly into line, offering the familiar salute and declaration at the top of their voices. I had perfected the gesture myself, practicing it time and again in my bedroom mirror, and, while Father simply tipped a finger to his cap, I returned it with gusto, making Kurt glance at me in the rear-view mirror with a half-smile.

We pulled up outside one of the officer's buildings and Father instructed me to wait in the car while he spoke to one of the men inside. When he disappeared, I asked Kurt whether I might join him in the front seat. He glanced a little nervously toward the staircase that Father had ascended before shrugging his shoulders.

"If you like," he said, and I jumped out and took my place next to him on the one long seat, allowing our bodies to press close together. When I sat, I made sure to pull my skirt up a little so my knees, which I considered shapely, were on display. I noticed his eyes flicker toward them before he lit a cigarette and looked out of his window.

"Do you like it here, Kurt?" I asked when the silence between us became unbearable. It was clear that he was not going to be the one to break it.

"It's not a matter of liking, Gretel," he said. "It's a matter of doing what is asked of me."

"But if you weren't here, if there was no war, what do you think you'd be doing instead?"

He thought about it and took another drag of his cigarette. "I expect I'd be at the university," he said. "I'm nineteen, so it would seem like the natural place to be."

"Like your father."

"I'm nothing like my father."

A tension had fallen on the house in recent days since an upsetting dinner when Kurt had been invited to eat with my family and had stumbled into revealing that his father, a university professor, had abandoned Berlin for Switzerland in 1938, a year before the war broke out, because of personal disagreements with the policies of the National Socialist government.

"What reason did he give," my own father had asked, his tone remaining unnaturally calm as he ate, masking the danger of the question he was posing, "for leaving Germany at the moment of her greatest glory and her most vital need, when it is incumbent upon all of us to play our part in the national revival?"

Kurt's disclosure had been unplanned, and he'd found himself at a loss for how to reply, insisting that he and his father had never been close, that they disagreed on many things, and that his own loyalty to the Party could not be called into question, but the damage had been done. The tension around the table came to a head when a waiter, one of the men who was taken from the other side of the fence to serve us at our meals, made an error as he served him. Wine was spilled, then blood. A brutal encounter. I remember my brother screaming while I tried to cover his eyes. Mother appealed to Father to make Kurt stop, but he ignored her, continuing to eat, oblivious to it all.

"And if you were at the university," I asked. "What would you study?"

"Economics, I think," he said. "I'm interested in the concept of money, how we use it, how it uses us in return. When the war is over, I might like to work in the Ministry of Finance, and in time become an economist for the Reich. There will be a world to rebuild and, of course, not only will we have to run it, but we'll need to make plans for those countries we have vanquished. That will be complicated."

"We should let them rot," I announced, eager to please. "For daring to oppose us at all."

"No, Gretel," he said, shaking his head. "In victory, one must have humility. Think of the great leaders throughout history—Alexander, Julius Caesar. They didn't seek to degrade their conquests, and the Führer is surely among their number. It might take a generation or two, after all, for these nations to accept their new status within the Reich, and I see myself playing a part in that." He paused and smiled, displaying his white teeth. "Generals come and go, but financiers— that is where the true power lies."

I nodded. This seemed like a fine idea, and I fantasized about us living together in a grand house in Berlin, hosting extravagant parties that the Führer himself would attend, along with all the great men of the Reich and their wives. We would have five or six children, each of whom adored their father and honored him in their actions. I knew it would take a few more years before this could be realized, but I longed for it.

Awkwardly, shyly, my heart beating fast in my chest, I moved my right hand out and allowed it to find its place within his left. He allowed me to do this, didn't pull away, but neither did he turn to look in my direction. Instead, he simply continued to stare out at the camp, smoking his cigarette. When his fingers finally closed around mine, however, I experienced a moment of excitement unlike any I had known before and watched as his face changed, a small smile appearing across his lips, the tip of his tongue appearing when he looked at me, his eyes roaming the contours of my body. Within the connection of our locked hands, his middle finger began to move, stroking

the inside of my palm, and I leaned back, sighing. I could hardly believe that this was happening. It was all that I had longed for since
my arrival there.

"Kurt," I said. For the first time in my life, I understood what it
was to feel desire.

In a moment he pulled away and I opened my eyes, returning to
the real world, as I saw Father emerge from the building and walk in
our direction. He didn't seem to notice that I'd changed seats and
simply gestured at me now to follow him. Stepping out of the car,
somewhat unsteady on my feet, I glanced at the palm of my right
hand, where Kurt's fingers had touched mine. Perversely, I moved it
slowly to my face, inhaling the scent, then kissing it.

I looked back at the young lieutenant, who was watching me intently with an expression on his face I couldn't read. I hoped he did
not already regret the moment of intimacy we had shared. We had a
secret now and the idea of that thrilled me, although, perhaps, it
frightened him. He finished his cigarette and, in a movement, flicked
the spent butt out onto the gravel.

"Now, Gretel," said Father as we walked along, and my attention
turned to what was before me. "You must never be frightened of this
place. The world is being reborn here. Think of it as somewhere that
sick animals are brought to be put down, so they can no longer be a
threat to decent men and women."

"Of course, Father," I said. We turned a corner and I noticed a
railway line running north through the camp and, to my right, an
enormous plot of land with rows of long huts stretching out farther
than I could see.

"This is how they arrive," he said, nodding toward the rail spur.
"And that is where we house them."

"Who, Father?"

"*Die Juden*. And over there," he added, pointing toward a group of men walking slowly in single file, each one pushing a wheelbarrow filled with wood, "is how we make sure that they are of use during their time here. The Reich will not permit indolence. We feed these people, if you can call them that, but they must work to earn that bread. You agree?"

"Everyone must work," I replied. "The Führer says that work will set us free. Every man, every woman, every child must contribute, and bread costs money."

"Indeed it does, Gretel," he said, tousling my hair, and I smiled, for I liked to please him.

"And what is that building?" I asked, pointing to a stone edifice about five hundred yards from where we were standing. It had an austere feeling to it.

"We call that the chamber," said Father. "Would you like to see it?"

I nodded.

"Very much," I said.

"It's not in use today, so we picked a good time."

"What happens in there?"

He smiled. "Something very beautiful," he said. "Come, let me take you inside and I'll show you. One day, you will tell your own children about it. Now, you mustn't be frightened, though. Think of it as—"

Before he could finish his sentence, however, a young soldier came running toward us and whispered something in Father's ear. He frowned and nodded, then turned back to me.

"Stay here, Gretel," he said. "I'll be back in a minute or two. There's a phone call from Berlin that I need to take."

"Yes, Father."

I watched as he made his way back in the direction of the office, then looked around again. Everywhere I turned I could see people wearing their uniforms of blue-and-white stripes. There were men and women but almost no children. Everyone seemed exhausted, lifeless, drained of energy. They were filthy too, which disgusted me. Why could they not take better care of themselves? It would have been impossible to count the number of people shuffling around in the fields ahead of me. Were there a thousand? Two thousand? I felt as if everyone's eyes were turned to look directly at me, that they were consumed with fear by my presence, as if a single word from me could mean the difference between life and death.

And it was at that moment that I saw the warehouse.

The warehouse, as I would come to think of it whenever I tried to banish this scene from my memory, was no larger than one of the huts that dotted the landscape but clearly served a different purpose from the accommodations. I ran to the side of it, eager to be out of sight of those people I had been watching, then pulled open the doors and stepped inside. It was cool in here, and quiet, a little light peeping in from the gaps in the slatted roof, and I stood there, hoping for a moment of solitude. I don't like this place, I told myself. I had wanted to, but no. It frightened me.

I glanced around and, as my eyes adjusted to the dark, I realized that this was where the uniforms were kept. Not the uniforms of the soldiers, but those of the inmates. Blue and white, gray and white. Shoes. Yellow stars. Pink triangles. Why, I wondered, was everyone forced to dress the same? Where were the clothes they had arrived in?

In the corner, out of sight, I heard a sound, and looked over in fright. Was it a mouse? I wondered. A rat? Or something worse?

"Is someone there?" I asked, keeping my voice low. Loud enough to be heard but not so loud that anyone outside would be alerted to my presence.

All remained silent for a few moments, but this silence was not a true silence. It contained a hidden treasure. I stepped forward cautiously, narrowing my eyes in the gloom.

"Hello?" I whispered. "Come out, whoever you are."

More silence, and then a slight rustle from behind the clothing before, to my surprise, a small boy emerged. I stared at him and he looked down.

Neither of us spoke for a moment. Finally, older and determined to assert the fact that I was in charge, I found my voice.

"Hello," I said.

"Hello," said the little boy.

He was staring at the ground with a forlorn expression. He wore the same striped pajamas that all the other people on that side of the fence wore and a striped cloth cap on his head, although he whipped this off quickly, pressing it to his chest in an act of supplication toward me. He wasn't wearing any shoes or socks and his feet were rather dirty. Sewn into his uniform was a yellow star.

"Who are you?" I asked.

"I'm Shmuel," he said.

"What are you doing here, Shmuel?" I asked, the word unfamiliar on my tongue. I found myself unable to pronounce it with as much care as he had.

"Hiding," he said.

"Hiding from whom?"

"From everyone."

I looked at him and felt a sudden pang of sympathy for him. He was painfully thin, his eyes almost bulging from their sockets. I could see how his cap was trembling in his hands and so I sat down, cross-legged, on the ground, hoping he would do the same and that it might soothe him. A moment later, he did, looking up at me now with a shy expression on his face.

"How old are you, Shmuel?" I asked.

"I'm nine," he said. "My birthday is April fifteenth, 1934."

I frowned. This was the same day my brother had been born. In a different time and place, they might have been twins.

"How old are you?" he asked in return.

"Twelve."

"That's old."

"It's not really."

"It's older than nine."

"Yes," I said. "But when you're twelve, you won't feel old. You'll still feel that no one notices you or listens to you."

"I'll never be twelve," he said quietly.

His words sent a chill through my body. Why shouldn't he be twelve? We all turned twelve at some point, and he would too. I was certain of it.

"My name's Gretel," I said at last.

"You live over there, I expect," he said.

"Where?"

"With him. On the other side."

"With who?"

This frustrating child was so difficult to talk to.

"He comes to visit me."

"Who does?" I asked.

"The boy."

I shook my head, wondering whether I should leave.

"You know, you're the first child I've met here," I said.

"There aren't many of us."

"Where are the rest of them?"

He exhaled deeply through his nose, then looked around the warehouse, trying to formulate an answer.

"There were more when we arrived," he said. "My family and me, I mean. There were lots of us on the trains. But then they took them away."

"Who did?"

"The soldiers."

"Where did they take them?"

He stared at me with such a penetrating glance that I had no choice but to look away.

"Why didn't they take you too?" I asked.

He held up his hands. "My fingers," he said. "They're so small and thin. They said that sometimes they keep someone like me to clean the bullet shells. It's how I spend most of my days. But when I get bigger, I won't be able to clean them anymore. There's no food to eat, so I might die. But when there is food, if I eat it, I might get fat. And then I'll die too."

"Nonsense," I said. "No one would let a child your age die."

He shrugged and looked away, with neither the energy nor the interest to contradict me.

"This will all end soon," I told him, anxious to be reassuring. "We're winning the war. When we have, then everything will return to normal. Only it'll be a better normal than it ever was before."

"Are you going to hurt me?"

"What?" I stared at him, wondering if he'd gone mad. "Of course I'm not going to hurt you."

"Are you going to tell on me?"

"Tell on you about what?"

"That I hide in here sometimes."

"Who would I tell?"

"Lieutenant Kotler."

I stared at him and shook my head. "I won't tell anyone, Shmuel," I said.

"Then can I go?"

He looked at me with such beseeching eyes, and there was a part of me that wanted him to stay, to help me understand the things about this place that I did not, but I suspected that Father was looking for me by now and, if he found me in here with this boy, there would be trouble. Some for me; a lot for him.

"You can go," I said.

He stood up and put his cap on his head once again before making his way to the door.

"Tell him to come and see me again," he whispered, before opening it to go back outside. "At our usual place."

"Tell who?" I asked.

And then he said my brother's name, and I understood. This was where he disappeared to on those afternoons when he said he was exploring the woods. He was coming to the fence. He was meeting Shmuel. I felt angry but also confused and hurt that he hadn't told me. He had made a friend when I had none.

"I'll tell him," I said finally. "Goodbye, Shmuel," I added.

"Goodbye, Gretel," he replied.

It was a few months later. Kurt was gone by now, dispatched to the front, leaving me in the traumatized certainty that he had been killed. My brother, of course, was delighted that he'd been sent away and teased me about it relentlessly.

And I hated him for it.

Hated him so much that when he eventually confided in me

about his meetings with Shmuel I pretended to think it was wonderful that he had a friend to talk to.

And when he told me that Shmuel's father had gone missing, and that the boy wanted him to climb under the fence to help him look for him, I said that he should. That was what friends were for, I told him.

"But what if I'm spotted?" he asked, and I shook my head.

"There's a warehouse," I told him. "Your friend will know where it is. They keep all the uniforms in there. He can get an extra set for you and you can change when you meet him. No one will notice you then."

I wanted him to get caught.

I wanted him to get into trouble.

Maybe, like Kurt, to be sent away.

"That's what Shmuel suggested too. Won't it be dangerous?" he asked.

"Of course not! You can help him find his father."

He seemed uncertain but didn't want to be seen to be frightened.

"All right," he said. "That's what I'll do."

To me, the entire thing was a joke. A petty way to get my revenge on him.

It was only one day later that Mother opened the door of my bedroom, looking nervous and frightened.

"Gretel," she said. "Have you seen your brother? I can't find him anywhere."

Part 3

The Final Solution

LONDON 2022 / LONDON 1953

ONE

Marie Antoinette had long since lost her head and I was now, unusually for me, reading a novel, about a group of senior citizens solving a murder in their retirement village, when the back door to Winterville Court opened and I heard footsteps approaching. Seated on the bench beneath the oak tree, I sensed a certain malevolence in the resolve of the tread but told myself not to glance up. Only when my visitor stood directly before me did I bother to put my book down.

"Mr. Darcy-Witt," I said. "How nice to see you."

He was dressed more casually than he had been on our previous encounters, wearing a pair of pale yellow shorts that looked rather expensive and a white polo shirt. His footwear resembled something one might wear on the deck of a luxury yacht, rather than the back garden of a well-appointed London apartment building. It had been almost a week since I had called an ambulance for his wife, who had taken an overdose of sleeping pills in what I assumed was an attempt to kill herself and, while he had come and gone every day since, taking Henry to school and hiring a young woman to bring the boy home again, he had not thanked me for saving Madelyn's life or to update me on her condition. Fortunately, I had a spy in his camp—Henry himself—who had kept me informed, for he'd taken to coming upstairs when he could. I welcomed his visits, a far cry from when I'd feared the idea of a child moving into Flat One. As it turned out, it was the adults that I should have been nervous of.

"Mrs. Fernsby," he said. "I thought you'd like to know that Madelyn will be coming home later today."

"I'm pleased to hear it," I replied. "She's better then?"

He smiled but said nothing, easing himself down onto the bench beside me. Although it would comfortably fit three people, I felt rather hemmed in by him, perhaps because he was a big man, muscular and tall. It seemed like something of an imposition for him to take a place close to me like this and made me long for the days of social distancing. I considered standing but didn't want him to feel that he had any power over me.

"'Better' might be going too far," he said. "But they're not willing to hold on to her any longer. It was an accident, of course. She didn't mean to take so many pills. She gets confused."

"Well, let's hope that she doesn't get confused again."

"She won't," he said. "For one thing, she won't have access to any medication from now on. I'll take control of that myself."

"Of course you will," I replied.

He turned his head to look at me and offered a half-smile, as if he were humoring a child.

"That seems like a loaded remark," he said.

"Not at all. It's just that, before her accident, as you put it—"

"How else should I put it?"

"Before that, she did seem rather . . ."

I found myself growing cautious about how to finish this sentence.

"She seemed rather what?"

"Frightened," I told him defiantly, shifting a little in the seat to maintain some distance from him. "She seemed to me like a frightened woman."

"Such a choice of words," he said, shaking his head. "I wonder that someone of your status, having spent a lifetime in what I assume has been luxury, could even understand the meaning of that word. I grew up with nothing, did you know that?"

"Why would I?"

"My father beat my mother, they both died of alcoholism. I was shifted from foster home to foster home until I was seventeen, and you don't even want to know what that was like or the things that went on there. Do you have any idea what fear really is?"

It took all my self-control not to laugh.

"My dear man," I said, keeping my voice steady. "I have witnessed fear in ways that you could not possibly imagine. In your wildest dreams, in the most vivid fantasies of the cinematic entertainments that you throw together, you could not even come close to understanding the traumas that I have seen. Do I have any idea what fear is? I'm sorry to say that I have more idea than most ever will."

He turned to look at me now, perhaps intrigued by the melodramatic nature of my response. I immediately regretted my words. I had gone too far, I could see that, and had only succeeded in making him curious. I was old, of course, and the fear of discovery that had haunted my youth and middle years had long since diminished, if not disappeared entirely, but still. It was not like me to put myself at such risk. He glanced toward my arm, but I was wearing long sleeves.

"You know something?" he asked. "I actually believe you. Tell me, Mrs. Fernsby, what is it that you've seen? Or maybe it's something that you've done? Remind me, where did you grow up?"

I turned away, wishing he would go away, never bother me again and leave me alone with my octogenarian sleuths.

"Is there something I can help you with, Mr. Darcy-Witt?" I asked in as cold a tone as I could muster, and he nodded.

"The thing is, I know that you and my wife have become friendly since we moved in," he began, but I interrupted him.

"We really haven't," I said. "We've become acquainted, that's all, in the way that neighbors do. And we've talked a few times, as you know, but I would not go so far as to say that we're friends. The reality is, I barely know the woman. And she barely knows me."

"I suspect that very few people know you," he said. "You play your cards close to your chest, don't you?"

"I play no cards at all, Mr. Darcy-Witt. I'm not a gambler."

"You really have to call me Alex. Mr. Darcy-Witt is too big a mouthful. Although it's obvious that you have a big mouth."

"You're a very rude man," I said after a suitable pause.

"No, I'm just direct, that's all," he said. "There's a difference. Anyway, whatever the nature of the relationship is between you and Madelyn, I would prefer if you drew a line under it now. If you see each other in the lobby, then it's perfectly reasonable that you will say hello, but let that be where it ends. No enquiries after her health. No advice regarding her ridiculous ambitions about returning to acting—"

"But why shouldn't she if she wants to?" I asked. "Are we living in some bygone era where the husband determines what the wife might and might not do with her life?"

"And there'll be no further need for you to enter our home," he continued, ignoring my question just as I had ignored his. "I've changed the locks, of course, so whatever keys you've squirreled away from the previous tenant will be useless to you now."

"I haven't 'squirreled away' any keys, as you put it," I protested. "Mr. Richardson's spare key was left inside the plant pot. And it was Heidi Hargrave who discovered it, not me. You owe her a thank you, by the way. Were it not for her, your wife might have died."

"There's also no need for you to have any engagement with my son."

"Henry. He has a name."

"He's not your concern. Madelyn and Henry belong to me. She's not your surrogate daughter. And he's not your surrogate grandchild."

"I assure you, Mr. Darcy-Witt, and I'll stick with the formalities if you don't mind, that I have no designs on either of them fulfilling those roles. I live a quiet life and keep myself to myself. I always have done. It is your family and your endless dramas that have rather foisted themselves upon me, not the other way around. I'm quite content for you and your caged bird to make each other miserable without involving me in any way. And as for Henry, if the boy likes to call on me, if he finds a certain peace in my flat that he's missing in his own, then I'm not going to—"

Quick as a flash, he reached over and took my left wrist in his grip. He squeezed, not tightly enough to bruise but enough to hurt.

"Let go," I insisted, shocked by the assault. "You're hurting me."

"You talk too much, Mrs. Fernsby," he said, his voice low but hissing venom. "Do you know what I can't fucking stand? It's women who won't shut the fuck up. And you won't shut the fuck up."

I stared at him. Tears were starting to build behind my eyes—a rare humiliation; I am not an emotional woman—and yet I found that I did not want to challenge him any further. I had begun to understand how Madelyn felt. And Henry. How easy it was for a dominant man to instill fear in even the hardiest of souls.

"I just want to be sure that we understand each other, that's all," he continued. "You leave my family alone and I'll leave you alone."

"Let go!" I repeated, pulling my hand free. I was determined not to give him the satisfaction of frightening me away. I'd been seated out here first—reading quietly, disturbing no one—and I would still be here when he left.

To my relief, however, he stood up, looking at me as if to suggest that he was disappointed in me, that I had let him down.

"And also," I added, hating to hear how my voice cracked. "No one belongs to you. People don't—"

"Yes, we're done here," he interrupted in a tired voice, rubbing at his eyes as he began to walk away. "Just bear in mind what I've said."

I watched as he made his way back toward the door but, before he reached it, he turned again and looked at me.

"Fernsby," he said. "It's an unusual name, isn't it?"

"It was my husband's name."

"And yours?" he asked. "Your maiden name? What was it?"

I said nothing, but I could feel the blood rush to my face. He could sense that I was reluctant to answer him. Not that I knew what answer I would give. There was my real name, of course, the one that I had been born with and used both in Berlin and in that other place. Then there was Guéymard, the name I had employed in Paris and Sydney; there was Wilson, which I had used when I first came to London, not wanting to sound so French, and this was the name by which Edgar had known me. Were there others? I could scarcely remember. My life was so littered with cast-off identities that it was almost impossible at this point to remember who I really was.

"Never mind," he said, turning away again. "I'm sure I'll be able to track it down. You strike me as an interesting woman, Mrs. Fernsby. Someone who is not entirely honest with the world. As a film-maker, a storyteller, that intrigues me."

TWO

The first person with whom I exchanged words upon my arrival in London was the Queen.

It was shortly before Christmas and I had been in England for almost a week, having arrived by boat into Southampton and chosen to spend a few days there in order to readjust to life on land. My mood was wildly different than it had been when I traveled to Australia earlier in the year. The voyage out, after all, had been filled with the optimism of starting a new life. The fact that I was journeying back toward Europe only eight months later proved that this was an impossibility. Several young men and women made friendly overtures toward me on the crossing, but I spurned them all, not wishing to connect myself with someone as I had done with Cait Softly. Now, I preferred to remain alone.

I arrived in Central London by train on December 23rd, and as I carried my suitcase through the concourse, I noticed a crowd gathering to one side and a group of policemen watching the people carefully. Not immediately keen to step out into what looked to be a very wet afternoon, I wandered over to see what all the fuss was about and, to my astonishment, saw the Queen walking along the platform, accompanied by the Duke of Edinburgh, two men in uniform, and a couple of ladies-in-waiting. She was in conversation with one of the men but, as she passed me, I was so surprised by this unexpected encounter that I offered a greeting and she turned her head and smiled at me, saying hello and wishing me a happy Christmas. She was very beautiful, with perfect skin, and carried herself with both an awareness of her role and a slight embarrassment at the absurdity of it. Like most Londoners—which I now consider myself to be—I've seen her a dozen or more times over the decades since, driving past in a convoy of cars when I happen to be on the street, but it's this memory that lingers.

Of course, we had something in common, Elizabeth and I. As I made my way to a cheap hotel that evening, I wondered how she would have reacted had she known my identity. True, neither of our fathers had been killed fighting, but the war had effectively seen them both off. I knew I could not compare my father's death with her father's, but still, we were the daughters left behind, one to preside over a Commonwealth of nations and an unruly family, the other with only a few pounds to her name and no relatives at all.

In those early months, I struggled to adapt to the English weather. I had not been born into a particularly warm climate, but Sydney had given me a taste for sunshine and every day here seemed cold, wet, and miserable. After a few days of staying in cheap hotels, I found lodgings in a shared building off the Portobello Road. A landlady presided over the tenants from her ground-floor flat, above which five girls lived in five bedrooms spread across three floors, with a single shared bathroom between us all. We were served something tasteless every evening at seven o'clock and, if we were not there to receive it, it would be given to the dog. I hated the place but could not afford anything better. The other girls considered me stand-offish as I preferred to keep myself to myself.

Enough time had passed for me to assume that Cynthia Kozel had decided not to act upon the information I had given her, for no policemen showed up at my door demanding answers and no journalists stopped me in the street requesting interviews. I began to relax and tried to convince myself that I had done the right thing in inviting exposure into my life and could hardly be blamed that it had not taken place. Of course, I was not foolish enough to fall for such pathetic self-deception, and my guilt continued to simmer within, waiting for the moment when it might be brought to the surface and cause untold damage.

Using my experience in Miss Brilliant's clothes store, I was fortunate enough to find work in Harrods and soon impressed my supervisor so much that I was recommended to the higher-ups. I took an evening course in payroll and, to my delight, was promoted to the offices, where I worked with two other girls, organizing the weekly pay for the staff, accounting for days off, holidays, and various other matters that would now be considered part of a Human Resources department. I enjoyed the work very much, the elegance of the numbers, the necessity of making my accounts balance, the relative authority I had, and the sense of responsibility that came with it.

There were difficult moments, of course. My immediate superior was a Miss Aaronson, a quiet, efficient woman, who I liked immediately and who treated me with great kindness, remaining patient as I adapted to the particular routines of office life. As the weather improved, she took to wearing blouses with shorter sleeves and, one afternoon, as she reached across me to explain an error I had made in an employee's wage packet, I noticed the numbers tattooed upon her arm and reared back in my seat in fright. Moments like this, appearing unexpectedly, had the power to distress me greatly. I felt as if they had been sent from God to remind me that I could experience peace and happiness in my daily life but that I should never forget my part in the horror, for my culpability was scarred just as deeply into my soul as those numbers were upon Miss Aaronson's arm.

"You mustn't be frightened, dear," she told me when she saw how pale I had grown. "But I refuse to hide them away. It's important that people see these numbers and remember."

"And your family?" I asked, the words catching in my throat.

"All gone," she told me, an expression crossing her face that blended sorrow with resignation. "My parents, grandparents, two brothers, and a sister. There's just me now. But let's get back to this wage packet. We can't see the poor man deprived of his rightful pay."

I could not think of anything to say in response but, upon returning to my lodgings that night, wept with as much force as I had since my arrival in England and, although I felt incapable of harming myself, I fell asleep on nights like that praying that I would not wake in the morning.

However, it was while working in Harrods that I met both David and Edgar, and it was the latter to whom I first spoke when he stopped me one afternoon on the shop floor, as I was passing through Gentlemen's Evening Suits in search of an assistant who had failed to tell me that he had been overpaid by a pound the previous week. As I looked around in search of the mendacious young man, a fellow wearing a blue suit approached me, raising a hand in the air as if I were a passing omnibus.

"Excuse me, miss," he said. "Do you work here?"

"I do," I admitted. "But I'm not shop floor, I'm afraid. I'll see if I can find an assistant for you."

"Actually, I'm not buying," he said. "I'm looking for a friend of mine. Perhaps you know him? David Rotheram. We're supposed to have dinner together. You haven't seen him about, I suppose?"

I shook my head. I did know David, he was an assistant manager on this very floor, having risen in the departmental ranks at a furious rate, but somehow we had never, as yet, engaged in conversation. All the girls in the office had a crush on him because he was a ringer for Danny Kaye but, while he had glanced in my direction once or twice, offering what appeared to be an approving smile, I had been too shy to return the look and neither of us had as yet found any reason for social intercourse.

"Mr. Rotheram is usually lurking around here somewhere," I said, turning my head to scan the floor and immediately regretting my choice of verb. Edgar started to laugh.

"Lurking," he said. "You make him sound like a fellow with bad intentions."

"No, I didn't mean that," I replied, blushing a little. "I just . . . I do apologize. Please don't tell him I said that. He might take it amiss."

"My lips are sealed," he said, making the zip sign across his mouth, and I smiled. Although he was of average good looks, he had a kindly face with warm eyes and his pencil mustache offered a certain *joie de vivre*. A scar running beneath his left ear made me wonder whether he had acquired it in the war, but I dismissed this idea quickly, for he could not have been more than a year or two my senior so would have been only fourteen at the height of the hostilities. "Oh, here he is anyway," said Edgar after a moment, seeing his friend stroll toward him, and I turned and watched as David crossed the floor.

"Edgar," he said, grinning happily. "Sorry to have kept you waiting."

"It's quite all right. Your colleague here, Miss . . . ?"

"Wilson," I said.

"Miss Wilson was keeping me company."

"Then you're a lucky man," said David, smiling at me now. "For Miss Wilson never keeps me company. She seems to make a point of avoiding me, in fact."

"No, I don't," I said, wondering why he would even think such a thing, let alone say it aloud.

"Well, we never talk, do we?"

"We've just never had an opportunity, that's all."

"Should I leave you two alone?" asked Edgar. "You can sort the matter out between you."

"No need," I said.

"What brings you down here anyway, Miss Wilson?" asked David. "You don't normally mingle with the hoi polloi."

"I'm looking for a man," I said.

"Miss Wilson!"

"One of the assistants, I mean. Mr. Deveney."

"You'll talk to that young tyke, but you won't talk to me?"

I stared at him, unsure what to say. I wasn't competent enough in repartee to keep up the pace of it.

"He needs a telling-off," I said eventually. "Mr. Deveney, I mean. And I'm here to deliver it."

"What's he done?"

"I'd rather not say."

He nodded and didn't pursue the topic, pointing toward the opposite side of the floor. I thanked him, said goodbye to Edgar, and continued on my way, but before I could get very far, David had run after me and caught me by the arm.

"I'm very sorry, Miss Wilson," he said, looking apologetic. "I may have been a little rude back there. I was trying to be funny, but it came out all wrong."

"I don't know why you would suggest that I avoid you, that's all," I told him. "I've never done any such thing."

"No, of course not," he replied. "The truth is, it's me who's been avoiding you."

"Why?" I asked, frowning.

"In case I said something stupid. I didn't want to embarrass my-self and make you think me an idiot. And now it rather looks as if I've done that anyway."

I felt the blood rush to my face. Was he flirting with me? It had been so long since anyone had done such a thing that I wasn't certain I would even recognize the signals.

"That's quite all right," I said, simultaneously wanting to stay and leave.

"So you don't think me a fool?"

"I don't think anything at all."

"Then if I were to ask you out for a gin and tonic sometime, would you come?"

"What makes you think I drink gin and tonics?" I asked.

"Most girls do."

"I'm not most girls."

"All right then, what do you drink?"

"Beer," I said. Which was true. I was German, after all.

He frowned. I could see there was a part of him that thought this was a rather unladylike preference, but I didn't care. He could take me as I was or not at all.

"Then if I were to ask you out for a beer sometime, might you come?"

He glanced back toward Edgar before looking at me again.

"It's just that if I don't ask you now, then I'm pretty sure that my friend will, and he's ten times the man I am so I'll lose my chance."

I looked over at Edgar and then back at David. Two men inter-ested in me. This was a turn up for the books.

"Thursday night," I said. "Come and find me in Payroll at six o'clock and we'll go somewhere quiet."

And then, anxious not to lose any advantage I had gained in the conversation, I went directly back to my office, where I sat, giggling a little, extremely pleased with myself. It was hours later, when I was already in bed, that I realized I'd forgotten to track down the dishonest Mr. Deveney, but I dismissed this now, deciding that he could hold on to his pound. He might have done me the most terrific favor and so had earned every penny of it.

THREE

B y choice, I have resisted building a circle of friends throughout my life, but I felt the lack of them now that a confidential ear was needed. The conversation that had taken place in the garden between Alex Darcy-Witt and myself had left me frightened and unsettled and I desperately wanted to speak to someone about it. There had been a time, perhaps, when I might have knocked on Heidi's door to discuss it, but those days had long since passed.

Seated in my living room, I scrolled through the contacts list on my phone and regretted that it was not fuller. For a moment, my finger hovered over Caden's number, but I decided against calling him, out of fear that he would see conflict with the neighbors as a further excuse to get me to sell up and move to a retirement community. I was left with only one choice: Eleanor.

To my surprise, she arrived in my flat in less than two hours, explaining that she'd rescheduled her morning appointments because I, apparently, "came first." She showed up in a taxi too, which I thought a little extravagant, carrying two takeaway coffees and brownies.

"You shouldn't have," I said, placing them on a couple of plates, but feeling rather glad that she had.

"Oh, we all deserve a little treat once in a while, Mrs. F.," she said, settling into Edgar's armchair. I smiled—I couldn't help myself—I was really starting to grow fond of the woman. "So what's up? You sounded upset on the phone."

"Yes," I said. "The fact is, I need some advice. I'm worried about something but am anxious about interfering in case I cause myself, or others, unnecessary difficulties."

"All right," she said, and I could see her medical training coming to the fore when she added, "Tell me how I can help."

"And, obviously, I'd prefer if you kept this between you and me."

"Goes without saying."

"Even from Caden."

"Gotcha."

"It's about my neighbors," I told her. "The new family who moved in beneath me."

"Are they noisy?"

"No, it's nothing like that," I said, shaking my head. "It's the man. The father. I think he may be violent. Toward his wife and son, I mean."

She sat back in the chair now and breathed heavily through her nose. An expression crossed her face that suggested to me she was not inexperienced in this area, and I felt immediate relief, reassured that I had chosen the right person to confide in.

"Tell me everything," she said.

I did as instructed. I told her all that I had witnessed in as much detail as I could recall and, to her credit, she sat quietly as I spoke, not interrupting once or questioning me, which I appreciated.

"There's something not right about the man," I concluded. "And then, this morning, something else happened."

"Go on," she said, sipping her coffee.

"I went downstairs to check my post-box," I told her. "You might have seen, as you came through the front door, the five boxes on the wall to your right. There's one for each flat. I almost never receive letters anymore, but I like to check it every morning, just in case. I wasn't snooping, I promise I wasn't, even though I know that it will sound like I'm just an interfering old busybody, but the boxes are so close to the Darcy-Witts' front door that it's almost impossible not to hear if there's any sort of commotion going on in there."

"And there was?" she asked.

"Yes."

"An argument."

"Alex was shouting at the boy," I told her. "He was saying some terrible things."

"Such as?"

I flushed a little. It was upsetting to remember.

"Just say it," said Eleanor in a kindly tone. "I'll understand better if I know."

"He was shouting that if he ever wet the fucking bed again, he would put him through that fucking window," I said, looking down at the floor as I spoke. I hated hearing such words emerge from my mouth, but it was important, I felt, to give Eleanor a full flavor of the man's anger. "He told the boy that he was nine years old now, not a fucking baby, and he shouldn't have to be hit by the stink of fucking piss when he goes in to wake him every fucking morning. I could hear the boy crying and then there was a terrible sound, a scream, before everything went quiet."

"What kind of sound?" asked Eleanor.

I looked around. There was only one way to explain it. I stood up, walked over to the side table and slammed the palm of my hand into the center of the woodwork, making her jump, before returning to my chair.

"He hit him?" she asked.

"He must have done. I was too frightened to stay downstairs, I was afraid he would come out and discover me there, but I didn't want to leave things as they were either. So I went back upstairs, put on my shoes and coat and left the building, walking down the street toward the bus stop, the one that Henry and Madelyn use every morning when he's on his way to school. I had to wait there a good twenty minutes but finally he emerged—the boy, I mean—on his own, walking toward me with his head down. When he reached me, I said his name and he looked up, startled, utterly terrified. He'd been crying, that much was obvious. And there was a red mark on his cheek. Awful to behold."

"That bastard," said Eleanor, her hands clenching into fists. "And did you speak to him? To Henry, I mean?"

"I asked him whether he was all right and he simply nodded and said nothing. It was obvious that he didn't want to talk. I would have pressed him on it, only the bus arrived just at that moment and he leaped on board, going directly to the backseat, while I stood on the street, staring at the back of his head. But as the bus pulled out, he turned around and looked at me with . . . with . . ."

I couldn't help it. I started crying. Eleanor rushed over to me and sat on the side of the chair, placing her arm around my shoulders. It felt so comforting to be held. I don't think I had felt another human being's arm around me since Edgar's death.

"It's all right," she said. "It's good that you told me."

"I don't know what to do," I told her, retrieving my handkerchief from my pocket now and drying my eyes. "I'm certain that he's mistreating them both, but I'm frightened to tell anyone. He has a very threatening nature, you see. You won't tell anyone, will you?"

"Not if you don't want me to," she said. "But I know a little bit about this subject. I have a friend whose husband was a bit too handy with his fists, and it took her years to build up the courage to leave him."

"But she did?" I asked, looking up at her hopefully, thinking that Madelyn might do something similar, and take Henry with her. "She left him in the end?"

"Yes," she replied.

"Well, that's something, I suppose."

"Only he came after her and put her in a wheelchair."

I jolted in my seat. The idea of such violence frightens me, terrifies me, in fact. It drags me back in time.

"Promise me you won't tell anyone," I said.

"If you don't want me to, then I won't," she said. "But we can't just let him keep hurting them. We have to do something."

"I know, but I need to think about it. And until I decide how best to handle the situation, I don't want to take the risk of him coming after me. I can trust you, Eleanor, can't I?"

"You can," she said. "I promise."

"What I told you," I said tentatively. "That day in Fortnum & Mason. About why I was in the hospital for that year when Caden was a boy. You didn't tell him, did you?"

"No," she replied. "I told you I wouldn't, and I don't break my promises."

"Thank you, dear," I said. "I knew I could trust you. The truth is, I hate dredging up the past. There's nothing but torment to be found there."

FOUR

I fell for David in a different way than I had fallen for either Kurt, who'd represented my introduction to desire, or Émile, who'd offered an opportunity to escape my claustrophobic existence with Mother.

But David had nothing in common with either of them. Where they had both been intensely serious, he was, to my delight, immense fun, and I had known precious little of that to date. He didn't sit around talking politics or history but lived entirely in the moment, refusing to discuss the past or the future. We went to the theater together, to concerts, to comedy shows. We saw Eddie Fisher play the London Palladium and, on my birthday, Jo Stafford sing at the Royal Albert Hall. Although we both worked for Harrods, we never talked about our jobs outside of work as gossip bored him, as did the private lives of our colleagues. He had his own flat, a small but comfortable top floor of a house in Clapham, and after our nights out, he always took me back there to bed. He had no compunctions about sex, was neither shy nor anxious in the way that other young men were, and embraced with enthusiasm the physical part of life. Having almost no experience of that world, I did not quite know what to expect from a sexual relationship, but it wasn't long before I craved his touch. Even with my naïveté, it was obvious that here was a young man who knew exactly what he was doing.

"How many girlfriends did you have before me?" I asked one night after a particularly enthusiastic bout of lovemaking. He was sitting up with a pillow behind him, smoking a cigarette, while I lay next to him.

"You really want to know?" he asked, smiling a little as he leaned his head back and blew perfect circles of smoke in the air.

"If you want to tell me."

"It depends whether you mean actual girlfriends or just lovers."

"Is there a difference?"

"Of course. There are only three girls who I count as having been official girlfriends. Outside of them . . ." He thought about it for a few moments. "I don't know, maybe a dozen others who I've gone to bed with?"

Perhaps there were some girls who would have been put off by this admission, but it didn't bother me in the slightest. On the contrary, I liked the fact that he was so experienced, and not just because it meant that he knew how to satisfy me but because, in his company, I finally felt like an adult. He was so much more worldly than the men among whom I passed most of my time, those nervous boys who worked in the stockroom of the store, the arrogant popinjays who managed the floors and fawned over the customers while debasing the girls under their command, or the timid mothers' boys who held sway in the offices and were clearly more at home with an adding machine than a naked body.

"And you?" he asked, rolling over on one arm to look me directly in the eye. "How many men?"

"Just one," I told him. "And he was only a boy."

"You're not serious?"

"Yes."

"But why so few? You must have had offers."

He seemed neither pleased by my inexperience nor scandalized that I had any at all. Rather, he was intrigued by my innocence, even pitying me for it.

"It wasn't how I was brought up," I told him truthfully, and he shook his head dismissively.

"They all say that," he said. "And it's such a waste of time. Sleep with any consenting adult who'll have you, that's what I say. Life's too short for playing games. If we've learned anything from these last fifteen years, it should be that."

When we went out to pubs for an evening, Edgar, his closest friend, would inevitably tag along, and I didn't mind, for I enjoyed his company almost as much as I did David's, and the pair were very close. Indeed, I suspected that if I even tried to interfere in their friendship, or prize them apart, then I would be the one to lose out and not him.

Wondering why Edgar didn't have a girl of his own, I made careful enquiries one night when we were together in the Guinea in Mayfair.

"There was a girl, a while back," David told me. "Her name was Millicent, or Wilhelmina, or something hideous like that. Edgar, what was that girl's name? The one you were mad about?"

"Agatha," said Edgar, waiting at the bar to order more drinks, and I couldn't help but laugh at how David didn't mind shouting out such a personal question across a crowded room, how Edgar didn't object to answering, and how far wrong my boyfriend had been in his memory of the poor girl's name.

"Agatha, that's right," he said, when Edgar sat back down, placing three drinks in front of us, pints for the boys, a half for me, although I had asked for a pint too and the barman had refused me, threatening to throw us out if I insisted. "Can you imagine crying out the name Agatha in a moment of passion?" continued David. "It would ruin the moment, don't you think?"

Even Edgar laughed. "Truth is, we never even got that far," he admitted. "Agatha didn't believe in sex before marriage."

Trying to appear as worldly as both of them, I decided to chime in with a compliment.

"I don't know how she kept her hands off you," I said, and Edgar seemed flattered by the remark, grinning at me.

"Hey you!" cried David, laughing.

"Well, he's a bit of a dish, don't you think?"

"Totally. I definitely would if I was that way inclined."

This, on the other hand, did shock me, but I said nothing.

"Poor old Agatha," said David. "She wasn't good enough for you anyway. You need someone with a bit more life to her."

"Do you like anyone at the moment?" I asked him and, to my surprise, he blushed.

"Sort of," he admitted.

"You didn't tell me!" said David.

"So why don't you ask her out?"

"She has a boyfriend. The best ones always do."

"So take her off him," demanded David. "Get in there and show her what's what."

"No," he said, shaking his head. "No, I couldn't do that. She wouldn't go for it anyway."

We changed the subject then and it was only when David went to the Gents that I brought it up again.

"It's just that we could go out as a foursome if you met someone," I told him. "That would be fun, wouldn't it?"

"David and I tried that once when I was seeing Agatha," he said. "It didn't go well."

"Why ever not?" I asked.

"She didn't like him," he said. "Couldn't stand him, in fact."

I frowned. I found it hard to imagine anyone not falling for David's charms. He was handsome, worldly, fun to be around.

"She must have been mad," I said.

"Oh, it's the same old story," he replied. "You meet girls like that all over. Chaps too. They don't say much about it, but you know what they're thinking."

"Thinking about what?"

"Well, they don't . . . you know." He looked a little uncomfortable.

"They don't what?" I asked, genuinely confused. I didn't understand what he was getting at.

"They don't like people like him."

"People like him?"

He leaned forward and lowered his voice. "They just don't like Jews," he explained. "That kind of thing has always been around, I suppose. That sort of prejudice. You know how it goes. Bigots everywhere. And the war didn't help. If anything, it seems to have made things worse. Reading about what happened afterward, the concentration camps and so on, it rather got people's backs up. The fact that it's always in the news now. So many people looking for answers. Some say it never happened at all, of course, that it's all been staged, but I don't think that's true that, do you? I've seen the photographs. Read some of the books. Actually, there's going to be a documentary shown at the Empire next week. Are you interested in history? I am. It's my area, you see. I'd like to teach in a university one day. Good Lord, I'm rather dominating the conversation, aren't I? You haven't said a word. Are you all right, Gretel? If you don't mind my saying, you're looking a little peaky. It's not the beer, is it? I could order you something lighter if you prefer."

I shook my head. It wasn't the beer. I had never quite understood the phrase "my blood ran cold" until this moment because, as he was speaking, this was exactly what seemed to be happening. Every sinew of my body became chilled, the tiny hairs on my arms and the back of my neck stood on end, and I feared I was going to be sick. Of course, David was a Jew. If I had not been so utterly stupid, so entirely ignorant of the world, I would have realized this from the start, from his name alone. But it had simply never occurred to me. I had been focused only on my attraction to him and the pleasures he gave me in bed.

"David," said Edgar when he returned and sat down with more drinks. "I was just telling Gretel about that documentary playing at the Empire next week. We should go, don't you think?"

"Oh yes, I'd like that," he said. "I'm not the history buff that Edgar is, of course," he added, turning to me. "But I'd be interested in watching it. Seeing what those fucking Nazis looked like in real life."

"Sorry, David," said Edgar. "I hope I didn't—"

"It's fine," he said, turning back and smiling at his friend. "It's just, well, I hadn't quite got around to telling Gretel about that part of my life just yet, that's all."

"What part of your life?" I asked.

"Another time," he said. "Tonight is only about having fun."

FIVE

For a ninety-one-year-old to have few friends is not unusual—by then, most of our acquaintances have passed away—but for a nine-year-old to be equally solitary is more surprising. Not once since his arrival had I seen Henry in company with a child his own age, and I began to wonder why that was. Did he struggle to make friends in school, I asked myself, or was he simply not allowed to bring anyone home with him?

Regular as clockwork, however, I could find him reading in the garden and, upon looking out of my window a few afternoons following Eleanor's visit and seeing the boy lost inside his latest book, I decided to join him.

"Hello, Henry," I said as I approached him, and he looked up and smiled, putting the book down in his lap.

"Hello, Mrs. Fernsby," he said.

"We didn't get a chance to speak at the bus stop the other day."

He turned away now, perhaps not wanting to recall how strangely he had behaved on that occasion. The mark on his cheek had faded in the meantime.

"I was late for school," he explained.

"You seemed upset."

He remained silent for a moment, unwilling to reply.

"Can I sit with you?"

He nodded and moved a little along the bench.

"There's really nothing I enjoy more than sitting out here in the sunshine," I told him with a satisfied sigh as I sat down. "Living in Central London, we're very lucky that we have this private area, don't you think?"

"I prefer the park," he said, presumably referring to Hyde Park.

"Do you ever go there with your friends?" I asked, and he shook his head.

"I'm not allowed," he said.

"Why ever not?" I asked.

"Who would I go with?"

I frowned. "You must have some friends your own age."

He considered this, his forehead wrinkling. "There's children I'm friendly with at school," he said. "But I only see them there."

"Well, that's ridiculous," I said. "A boy your age should have friends running in and out all day long. A bunch of noisy, irritating rascals for me to complain about to your mother."

I smiled at him, and he laughed a little. He seemed pleased by the idea of being part of a gang of his own.

"How is your mother anyway?" I asked. "I haven't seen her since she came home."

I'd avoided going downstairs to knock on the door of Flat One, and not just because Alex Darcy-Witt had warned me off. I had personal experience of how difficult it could be to make a return to motherhood after an extended spell in the hospital and, while my own internment had proven much longer than Madelyn's, I assumed she felt embarrassed by what had taken place. I also expected that she was under instructions from her husband not to speak with me. As I was, not to speak with her son.

Although I, at least, was ignoring that dictate.

"She sleeps a lot," he said.

"Does she have someone taking care of her?"

He frowned, confused by the question. "I'm taking care of her," he replied.

"But you're just a little boy," I said. "If you're taking care of her, then who's taking care of you?"

He shrugged. In a few years' time, he would doubtless be at an age where he would take offense at that soubriquet and insist that he didn't need anyone to take care of him but, for now, he looked somewhat distressed that he had no one to turn to.

"Henry," I said, glancing toward the windows to make sure that no one was watching us. "I'd like to have a serious conversation with you, if that's all right. And I promise, whatever you say will remain between you and me. But I need you to tell me the truth. Can you do that?"

"I always tell the truth," he said.

"I'm sure you do."

"Or Daddy gets angry with me."

"It's your daddy that I want to talk to you about," I said. He looked away now and I knew that I had to take care in my choice of words, or I might frighten him back indoors. "You love your daddy, I suppose?"

"Yes," he said, nodding his head.

"Is he very kind to you?"

He thought about it. "Once, he took me to Disneyland," he said. "He works with the woman who runs it and I was allowed to go to the front of every queue."

"That sounds wonderful," I said. "I've never been. Have I missed out?"

"Definitely," he replied.

"And is he kind to your mummy?" I continued.

This time, he took even longer to answer. "He says that Mummy is very stupid, that she never listens, and that she needs to learn."

"Your mummy doesn't strike me as stupid at all," I said. "In fact, she seems like a very interesting person, a woman with a great deal going on in her mind. Thoughts she'd like to express but perhaps doesn't get the opportunity to. She wanted to be an actress, did you know that? She was an actress, in fact, when she first met your father."

"Mummies can't work," said Henry. "Daddy says so. Mummies are supposed to stay at home and do what they're told when they're told and not keep asking questions about things that are none of their business."

I frowned. The phrase was such an adult one that he had surely overheard it being said and was simply parroting it back to me in the way that my brother had always done when we were children.

"And what happens when they don't do what they're told when they're told?" I asked.

"There are . . ." He struggled over the word. "Consequences," he said finally.

"I see," I said. "And for you, are there consequences for you too? When you're naughty?"

He nodded.

"What sort of consequences?"

Instinctively, his right hand placed itself across his left forearm and it occurred to me that, even though it was a warm day, he was wearing a long-sleeved T-shirt. I reached over, hoping to roll the sleeve up, but he pulled away.

"Don't," he said.

"Please."

"No."

"Show me," I insisted. "I won't hurt you." I had a firm hold of him now and pulled the sleeve back in one quick movement. There was a large bruise across one arm, one that must have been inflicted a few days earlier, which was turning unpleasant shades of yellow and purple now. "What happened here?" I said. "Who did this to you?"

"I fell," he said, pulling his arm back and dragging the sleeve down to cover the wound.

"You get into an extraordinary number of accidents, don't you?" I said.

"I fell," he repeated, raising his voice, more insistent now.

"What if I said I don't believe you?"

"But it's true!"

"Who did this to you, Henry? Who's hurting you? You can tell me, you know."

"No one!" he shouted. "I fell, that's all."

A door opened at the back of the building and Madelyn stepped outside. I could tell by her expression that she wasn't happy to see me talking to her son.

"Don't tell her I said anything," he whispered beneath his breath.

"But you haven't," I pointed out. I lowered my voice now. "Please," I said. "I need to know. I can stop it from happening if you just tell me."

He jumped off the bench and stood directly before me. From the doorway, Madelyn called out, insisting that he come back inside.

"I can't tell you anything," he said. "He's told us what he'll do if anyone finds out."

"Finds out what?" I asked.

He looked toward his mother and then back at me. "How he hurts us," he said.

I sighed, feeling I was getting him to open up. I wished that his mother would go back inside so we could continue our conversation, but the poor child seemed both terrified and conflicted now. He wanted to run away from me, I could tell, but he also wanted me never to let him go.

"And what will he do?" I asked. "What did he say he would do if anyone found out?"

"Henry!" Madelyn was shouting now, and he turned to look at her. But before he left me, he leaned over and whispered in my ear.

It had been many, many decades since I had last heard something so chilling.

SIX

Naturally, I had no great desire to watch the documentary, but both David and Edgar were keen, and I was still at that point in my relationship with the former where I wanted to be with him every moment. Which was foolish of me as he gave every indication of being devoted to me.

The film was simply titled *Darkness*. Although the war had been over for eight years, it remained a subject much discussed on a daily basis. The first volumes to explore the events of those years had started to appear and historians were only scraping the surface of the research they would undertake in the decades ahead. Edgar, of course, was one of these historians. In time, the Second World War would become his primary area of expertise and his most famous work was a three-volume narrative that won every prize and made him something of a celebrity in academic circles.

When the lights came down, my first thought was that I would close my eyes and try to ignore the action on the screen, but, of course, the voiceover put paid to these plans. I was left with no choice but to watch.

It began simply, with an overview of the years leading up to the Anschluss, then Mr. Chamberlain arriving in Munich to meet Hitler and returning with his naïve confidence in "peace for our time," followed by the invalidation of all passports belonging to Jews and their subsequent reissuing with the letter "J" stamped across them in blood-red ink. *Kristallnacht*. The invasion of Poland. Tanks. Rallies. The mesmeric speeches of the Führer. The audience watched, thoroughly engaged by the recent past, and cheering on the British army whenever footage was shown of them going off to war.

Soon, the action moved to Obersalzberg, the mountaintop location of Hitler's retreat, the Eagle's Nest, and we were shown footage from a film shot by Leni Riefenstahl featuring a number of senior figures in the Reich gathered together for a weekend. Hitler himself, of course. Himmler. Goebbels. Heydrich. Eva Braun. A housekeeper passed around glasses of wine while a young boy dressed in the uniform of the Hitlerjugend carried trays of cheese and crackers. As a whole, the group looked happy in each other's company. Had we not been familiar with who each of these people were, what they did and what they would do in the future, it would have seemed like any cheerful gathering of friends enjoying the fresh air at the top of a mountain and the generous hospitality of a benevolent host. But it was here, the narrator told us, that so many conversations regarding the Final Solution took place. Schematics spread across the screen. Diagrams of huts designed to house the inmates. Sketches of the gas chambers. Drawings of the crematoria.

The audience fell silent now and, from some areas of the auditorium, I could hear people sniffling. One or two stood up to leave, unable to cope with what they were watching. Of course, so many had lost loved ones.

"Are you all right?" whispered Edgar to me at one point, and I almost jumped from my seat in fright, so focused had I been on what I was watching.

"I'm fine," I whispered back. "Why?"

"Your hands," he said, and I glanced down. How tightly I had been gripping the arm rests! Immediately, I felt the pain that I hadn't noticed until now and released them, stretching and unstretching my fingers to allow the blood to flow. Saying nothing, I offered Edgar a small smile and turned back to the screen, as did he.

Soon, we were watching images of trains transporting Jews from different parts of Europe toward their fate, the fear on some faces, the naïve trust on others, the anxiety on those of the children. Footage was shown of them arriving at the camps and being separated into different groups by soldiers, men over here, women and children over there, rifles at the ready should anyone disobey. The desperate longing on the faces of families to remain together.

It was difficult to watch, but my eyes were glued to the screen as I remembered what I had been a part of. The shuffle of the men as they went out on work duty in the mornings, the slow, terrible march into the chambers, where they would spend their final moments gasping for air. The smoke emerging from the chimneys, leaving a ghastly ash to fall across the nearby trees and grass. When I saw the look of despair on the faces of the inmates, I turned away, which was when I noticed that David was weeping next to me. Great tears were streaking down his cheeks, which he wiped away now and again. I reached for his hand, but he shook me off.

And then, to my surprise, the music that accompanied the film changed, growing more cheerful, and I looked back at the screen. The voice of the narrator explained that, from time to time, the Nazis would release propaganda films intended to show the world that the camps were not places of hardship at all but that the "guests" being housed there were, in fact, treated with great kindness. Children were shown skipping from stone to stone, playing games, while men and women smiled and chatted, coexisting in apparent contentment as they read, enjoyed the sunshine, and socialized. As I watched, I felt a growing sense of unease, realizing that the location where this part of the film had been made was familiar to me.

It was that other place.

A memory, long forgotten, stirred in my head of a group of film-makers who had been dispatched to our camp and, in preparation for their visit, some of the healthier Jews had been separated from the others, washed and fed so they could play their parts in the sham with some credibility. I had been fascinated by the film equipment, the cameras, the booms, the lights. It had made me think that I might be a film star myself one day.

And then a new voice could be heard.

Father.

He was offering a voice-over to a scene, English subtitles playing below, as he explained how the inmates were given three hot meals a day, access to a library and the finest health care. A football league had even been set up, he said. One of his own initiatives, as he believed in the importance of keeping everyone healthy and active. As if to confirm this, a scene was shown of a group of young men playing football and a ball being kicked into the back of a net, the goal scorer raising his arms in triumph as he ran to embrace his team-mates. To the foolish, this seemed like normal life being played out before us.

I could scarcely breathe, however, hearing Father's familiar into-nation. He swallowed slightly between sentences, unaccustomed to, and perhaps intimidated by, the microphone.

A moment later, I saw him for the first time when the camera cut to our house. He was seated in his office, working at his desk. I had passed that room many times during our stay there but entered it rarely, for he insisted that it was out of bounds at all times, and no exceptions. A moment later the scene changed again. Now he was in the living room, and my stomach sank in anticipation of what might come.

And there, before an audience of a thousand or more, was my entire family, seated around the dinner table: Father, Mother, my brother, and myself. All four of us raising a toast to our beloved Führer, Adolf Hitler. The camera panned slowly from one of us to the next. First Father, appearing proud and patriarchal. Then Mother, beautiful, serene, exuding an aura of calm. Then me. I was sitting up straight, reveling in the attention, looking beyond the camera, where, if I remembered correctly, Kurt was watching, observing the scene as it played out and undoubtedly wishing he could be part of it. I held my breath. Would either David or Edgar recognize me? Eleven years had passed, of course, and I was just a child in these images, but still, the possibility of recognition terrified me.

Then, as if from nowhere, I heard a low keening sound, like an animal caught in a trap. It was horrifying, inhuman, a sound that no living human should ever make. It appeared to be coming from somewhere nearby and, to my surprise, I noticed people turning to look in my direction.

"Gretel," said Edgar, his voice filled with anxiety, even fear. "Gretel, what's wrong?"

The sound was coming from me, emerging from the very depths of me, as I stared at the screen and observed the cheerful face of my beloved younger brother, wearing a shirt and a woolen tank-top, quietly eating his dinner, his eyes glancing up from time to time, trying not to laugh at the camera.

My brother. My lost brother. Whose name I could not utter.

"Gretel," said David now. "Gretel, you've got to be quiet—"

But it was too late to tell me anything. I had dragged myself to my feet and was stumbling along the row, forcing people to pull their legs back to let me out. Pushing open the doors, I threw myself out into the lobby and, from there, into the street beyond.

A bus was coming my way.

Fast.

No time to think.

I threw myself in front of it.

SEVEN

A nd what was it?" asked Eleanor, leaning forward and taking my hand in hers. "What did the boy say?"

I took a deep breath. For days, the sentence had been stuck in my mind, during which I had felt an unholy mixture of panic, anger, and terror. But the idea of saying such terrible words aloud frightened me just as much as remaining silent. I closed my eyes; I didn't want to witness her expression when I uttered them.

"He said that his father told him that if anyone found out what was going on in their home, then he would wait until Henry and his mother were asleep one night, and he would pour gasoline on them both before setting them on fire."

"Jesus Christ!"

I opened my eyes again. Eleanor had dropped her glass of water on the ground and was holding a hand to her mouth. It took her a moment to notice the spillage, but it had fallen on an old rug, and I waved away her offer to get some kitchen towel to dry it up.

"Mrs. F.," she said. "You have to go to the police. You have to tell them."

"I know," I said. "I know I should, but—"

"There's no 'but,'" she cried. "He's threatened to kill them." Her voice rose now in the way that perhaps only the voice of a woman who has served her time in an emergency room and seen the condition of some of the women and children coming through those doors can. "This is what happens. This is what always fucking happens. Sorry . . . I didn't mean to swear."

"It's quite all right."

"It's just . . . men killing women because they can't control them. Men killing children because they can't bear the idea of their wives taking them away from them. Winning in some way. You have to tell the police and let them deal with it. Otherwise, you know how this will end."

I nodded. She was right, of course. But I hated the idea of becoming even more involved in this dreadful family drama, not just because I worried that any intervention on my part might provoke Alex Darcy-Witt into further violence but because I had avoided having any interaction with the justice system for eight decades and did not relish the idea of making an acquaintance with it now.

"If something were to happen to them," continued Eleanor, "and you said nothing, how could you live with the guilt?"

I stared at her. The poor girl had no idea of the guilt I lived with every day.

"Mrs. F.," she said. "Mrs. F., are you all right? I'm sorry, I'm not trying to frighten you, it's just—"

"It's quite all right, my dear. It's just . . . yes. Guilt. Yes, I see that now, of course."

You say that you live with torment, well, you can ease it now, Kurt had told me that morning in the Sydney café, knowing that I would never turn him in to the police, because it would not only bring an end to his life but to mine too. *You tell me that you're filled with regret, then unburden yourself of it. My life is in your hands.* It had been decades since I'd posted my letter to Cynthia Kozel, and it had come to nothing. As I'd expected, she must have thrown it away.

And so, despite all my reservations, once I had confided in Eleanor, there was really no possibility of turning back. I found myself walking, or being marched, toward Kensington Central Police Station, where Eleanor briefly described to the officer behind the desk the nature of our concern and we were invited to take a seat in the waiting area, where we remained for the best part of an hour, before a young man came out and politely invited us to follow him along a barren corridor. He took us into a small interview room, where we sat on one side of the table, while the officer, who introduced himself as Detective Kerr, sat on the other.

"Let's start with your names," he said, and we offered them. "And your relationship to each other?"

"Miss Forbes is to be my daughter-in-law," I told him, hearing an unexpected note of pride in my voice as I related this information. "She's marrying my son in a few weeks' time."

"And do you work, Miss Forbes?" he asked.

"I'm a heart surgeon," she replied, and he raised an eyebrow for a moment and looked suitably impressed.

"And I assume you're retired, Mrs. Fernsby?"

"I'm ninety-one, Detective, so yes, you assume correctly."

He noted down our addresses and phone numbers and then smiled. "So," he said. "What's brought you in to see us today?"

It was difficult to know where to begin, but I felt that I should start at the very beginning, with the death of Mr. Richardson and the arrival of Alison Small, of Small Interiors.

"I don't think you need to go back quite that far, Mrs. F.," said Eleanor gently, but Detective Kerr shook his head.

"The more detail you give us, the better," he said, which made me more confident in my ability to tell the story, and so I narrated it, rather thoroughly, detailing everything I could remember about my every conversation with all three Darcy-Witts, as well as my various observations of them, their injuries and interactions. As I talked, I could see that the policeman was growing more and more concerned, especially when I reached the part where Heidi emerged from Madelyn's bedroom and, in a moment of total clarity, instructed me to summon an ambulance. When I reached the end, I found I could not utter the terrible words that Henry had whispered into my ear, and asked Eleanor to say them instead. When she did, the detective flinched and looked at me, clearly troubled.

"Is that right, Mrs. Fernsby?" he asked. "Is that precisely what the boy said?"

"Almost," I told him. "Only Eleanor said *he would burn them all*; it was actually *he would pour gasoline on them both before setting them on fire*. It means the same thing, I suppose, but I assume you'd prefer me to be as accurate as possible. And 'all' includes him, of course. While 'both' refers only to his wife and son."

"Yes, that's an important distinction," he said, making a note of this. "And you're absolutely sure that those are the words the boy used?"

He was looking directly at me, and I knew what was going through his mind. He was wondering whether I was the Miss Marple sort, constantly in search of a mystery and delving into the heart of any that I discovered. Or maybe I was just a lonely old woman, making up an outrageous story in order to garner a little attention. It seemed perfectly reasonable that he would think this way. He would not be doing his job, I told myself, if he didn't. But I knew what I had seen, what I had witnessed, and what Henry had said to me.

Detective Kerr continued to write in his notebook while Eleanor and I sat in silence. I threw her a look and she smiled encouragingly before squeezing my hand. And then, as I knew he would, the detective moved onto another line of questioning, the one that I dreaded the most.

"Perhaps you could tell me a little bit about yourself, Mrs. Fernsby," he said.

"Of course," I said. "What would you like to know?"

"For a start, where were you born? Here in London?"

I hesitated only briefly. On the way to the police station, I had decided that I would be absolutely honest. I would not offer any unnecessary information, but nor would I lie.

"No," I said. "I was born in Berlin. In 1931."

"Oh," he said, raising an eyebrow in surprise. "I'd never have guessed. You don't have any accent."

"I left Central Europe when I was fifteen," I said, hoping he would not ask why I was using such a general location rather than specifying a country or city.

I could see him making some rapid calculations in his head and decided to save him the bother of asking.

"When the war ended," I told him. "My mother and I, we got away as soon as hostilities came to an end."

"My grandfather fought in the war," he said.

"Did he indeed?" I asked. "I hope he survived it."

"He did, yes. He was in the RAF."

I nodded but didn't pursue the subject. I had no interest in comparing war stories.

"Anyway," he said finally. "So you came to England in 1945? Or 1946?"

"Not quite," I said. "Mother and I, we spent some years in France once peace was restored. After she died, I relocated to Australia. For a fresh start, I'm sure you understand. But it wasn't for me. I didn't even make it through a year there."

"Might I ask why?"

"Have you ever been to Sydney, Detective?" I asked.

"Can't say that I have."

"It's very hot," I told him. "I found it overwhelming. And the food didn't agree with me."

He seemed to believe this and made some more notes.

"And your family," he asked carefully. "During the war—"

"Is any of this really relevant, Detective?" asked Eleanor, remaining polite but sounding a little frustrated. "Surely it can't have anything to do with what's going on with Mrs. Fernsby's downstairs neighbors?"

He thought about it. He did not look like the sort of man who would be put out by a woman questioning him and, after a moment, he nodded.

"Yes, I suppose you're right," he said. "Sorry, I just like to get a bit of background knowledge, that's all. I'm a bit of a history buff, as it happens. The war especially."

"So was my husband," I remarked, breaking my promise not to offer unnecessary information.

Detective Kerr narrowed his eyes and thought for a moment. "Your husband wasn't Edgar Fernsby, by any chance, was he?" he asked, and I nodded.

"He was, as it happens," I said. "You know of him?"

"Of course. I have all his books. He was a brilliant historian."

"How very gratifying."

"I met him once, in fact," he continued. "At a literary festival. He signed a book for me."

"Detective . . ." said Eleanor, frustration seeping into her tone, and I rather wished she hadn't interrupted. I would have been happy to hear this young man sing my late husband's praises for a little longer yet.

"Yes, sorry. Back to business," said Detective Kerr, sitting up straight now and clearing his throat.

"What's important is making sure that this Darcy-Witt man is not a danger to his family," Eleanor continued, and I hoped that she wouldn't press the issue.

"I'll talk to him, of course," he said.

"Will you be able to keep my name out of it?" I asked, leaning forward. "I'd rather have as little involvement in all of this as possible."

"I'll try, certainly," he said, replacing the cap on his pen. "But I can't guarantee anything. Do you feel in any danger yourself?"

I thought about it. The truth was that I did, but I had no intention of having Alex Darcy-Witt force me out of my home into some sort of "safe house" or whatever the detective was considering. I had changed my name quite enough for one lifetime.

"None at all," I said. "I have secure locks on my doors, and I won't let him in if he knocks."

"I think that's for the best," he said, standing up. "You did the right thing coming to see us."

He shook both our hands and walked us back along the corridor, using his security pass to open the doors at the end.

"And your father?" he asked. "I suppose your father had some involvement in the war too?"

I shook my head and smiled. "My father died when I was just a girl," I said, nodding goodbye and making my way out onto the street.

I had promised not to lie and, even at the end, I felt I had remained true to this resolve.

EIGHT

When I awoke, I found myself in a hospital bed with no memory of what had brought me there. I tried to sit up, but moving my body felt too painful and so I settled for trying to turn my head instead to look around. There were five other beds in the ward but only two were occupied and the women in both were asleep. Clearing my throat, I woke Edgar, who, it turned out, had been asleep in an armchair next to me.

"Gretel," he said, an expression of relief on his face. To my surprise, he took my hand, which was lying atop the sheets, in his, then quickly released it.

"What happened?" I asked, confused and anxious. "What am I doing here?"

"Hold on," he said, jumping to his feet and marching out onto the corridor. "Let me fetch a nurse. She'll explain everything."

I tried to keep my body still. Any movement at all was almost too much to bear and, a few moments later, he came back with a young nurse.

"Miss Wilson?" she said. "My name's Nurse Fenton."

"Where am I?" I asked. "What happened?"

"You had an accident. Do you remember any of it?"

"A little," I replied, the memory of our visit to the cinema slowly returning to me, as was my unexpected reaction to it.

"Fortunately, no serious damage was done," she continued. "A broken ankle and a few broken ribs, that's all. Your wrist is strapped too. You were very lucky. Apparently, the bus swerved just in time, or it might have killed you."

If only it had, I thought to myself, I could have been done with this hell once and for all. She made some notes on a chart and told me that Dr. Harket would be around to see me soon.

"How long will I have to stay here?" I asked.

"A couple more days, I should think," she told me. "No more than that."

When she left, I looked up at the ceiling for a few moments before realizing that Edgar was still standing by my bedside. Why him? I wondered. Where was David?

"David had to work today," he told me, anticipating my question. "We've been taking it in shifts."

"Taking what in shifts?" I asked.

"Sitting by your bedside."

I smiled at him, grateful for his kindness but nevertheless surprised that he would put himself out like this for me. David; yes, of course. He and I were courting, after all. But Edgar?

"You're very kind," I said.

"Not at all."

"I'm sure you had much better things to do with your time."

"Nothing seemed more important than this," he said. "I was terribly worried about you."

I smiled at him, and he reached across and squeezed my hand once again, until he grew a little self-conscious and pulled away.

"What happened anyway?" he asked me, his voice quiet and sympathetic. "Why did you run out on us like that? Were you ill?"

"The film," I told him. "It upset me, that's all."

"It upset all of us. Particularly David, but—"

"I can't witness such suffering," I continued. "I can't look at it, I mean."

"I understand."

"Tell me," I said. "I remember turning to David at one point during the film. He was deeply upset."

"Of course." He paused for a few moments, and when he spoke again it was with some hesitation. "He's told you, I presume?"

"Told me what?"

"About his family."

"Not much," I replied. "I know he's an orphan but, other than that, he's never really spoken about them. I've asked, but he's very reticent."

"Then it's probably not my place to say."

I stared at him, feeling a growing sense of unease.

"Whatever it is," I said, "I'd like to know."

He stood up and walked over to the window, looking out onto the street, his brow creased, while I remained silent, unwilling to rush him. Finally, he returned to me and sat down again, this time on the side of the bed, a more intimate gesture than I had expected. I moved my legs beneath the sheet to accommodate him. Edgar exuded compassion. David was trickier to be around.

"David isn't English," he said at last. "You know that much at least, yes?"

"No," I said, surprised to hear it. "I always assumed he was a Londoner."

"For the most part, he is, but he was born in Czechoslovakia. He got out just before the Nazis rolled into Prague. He was only a boy at the time, eleven or twelve, I suppose. His grandparents were leaving, they could see what was coming, and they took him with them. His older sister was in the hospital, having her appendix removed, and so his mother and father waited, intending to follow with her a few weeks later. But, of course, they didn't make it."

"What happened to them?" I asked, although any fool could guess the answer.

"Treblinka," he replied.

I nodded, turning away, and glanced toward the sleeping women, wishing that I was as disconnected from the world as they were.

"Anyway, his grandparents brought him up here," continued Edgar. "He really doesn't remember much about his early years. Or, if he does, he doesn't talk about it. Or not to me, anyway. He only told me this a few years ago and it's never come up again. I've tried to speak to him about it since, once or twice, but he just shuts down. I've often wondered whether you knew."

"I didn't," I said, uncertain whether this was the truth. Had there been a part of me that had suspected all along and simply didn't have the courage to confront it?

"Perhaps I shouldn't have told you," he said. "Only, seeing how emotional you were after the film, I thought I should explain. If it had been him, I could have understood. But you? You could have died, Gretel. Why did you do it? One of the bystanders . . ."

He paused now and shook his head.

"What?" I asked. "One of the bystanders what?"

"She said that it appeared as if you did it deliberately. That you threw yourself in front of the bus. As if you . . . as if you were hoping to get run over."

I looked up at the ceiling again, which was a depressing shade of gray-white and cracked in a hundred places. It seemed a foolish thing to focus on at a moment like this, but all I could think was that it must have been a long time since it had been painted. I felt tears forming in my eyes and, a moment later, they started to trace paths down my cheeks. I wiped them away as quickly as I could.

"It's not true," I said at last. "I was disoriented, Edgar, that's all. And overwhelmed."

"I hoped that was the case," he replied, sounding relieved. "Why would someone like you try something like that?"

"Someone like me?" I asked.

"Someone so wonderful," he said. "You're intelligent, funny, beautiful. Endlessly fascinating. There's no reason why you wouldn't want to live. Unless there's something I don't know, of course?" He stared at me now, sounding a little embarrassed. "What a ridiculous thing to say," he added when it was clear that I had no intention of replying. "I barely know you at all really, do I? There are a thousand things I don't know about you." He hesitated, his voice cracking a little. "A million. I'd like to, though."

I looked at him again, surprised by the intimacy of the line, and I could see it immediately in his eyes. *Oh Edgar*, I thought, turning away. I had never seen that expression turned on me before, not by Kurt, not by Émile, not even by David, but I recognized it well.

And it never did anyone any good.

NINE

The parcel was sitting outside my front door, enclosed in what appeared to be very expensive wrapping paper, with a ribbon around it and a bow affixed elaborately to the top. A small gift tag was attached and written upon it in an unfamiliar hand were the words *Gretel Fernsby*. I picked it up and stared at it, uncertain who might have left such a thing there or why. It wasn't my birthday—that was several weeks away yet—and I couldn't recall having done a good deed for anyone of late. I took my keys from my bag and was about to let myself in when Heidi's door opened and she poked her head outside.

"Gretel," she said, her tone breathless. "At last. I've been waiting for you."

"What is it?" I asked. "Is everything all right?"

She ushered me inside and I followed her reluctantly. I had been looking forward to relaxing in front of the television, but it was impossible to refuse her. I put the gift, whatever it was, on a side table and followed her into the living room, where she was pacing up and down fretfully.

"Whatever's the matter?" I asked.

"It's Oberon," she said. "He says I can't come to Australia with him after all."

"But that's a good thing, surely," I said, sitting down and indicating to her that she should do the same. "You didn't want to go."

"Yes, but he says he's going to go without me. So who'll look after me?"

"Do you think that he looks after you as it is?" I asked.

"Well, he comes to see me," she said, forever disinclined to hear even the mildest criticism of her grandson.

"Not very often, as far as I can tell."

"But he's all that I have," she said. "You and Edgar are very kind, of course, but—"

"Edgar isn't with us anymore, Heidi," I said. "Remember?"

"Oh, that's right," she agreed. "He's at a conference, isn't he? In New York?"

I nodded. There was nothing to be gained by telling her the truth.

"I'll miss him terribly, and I'm just worried, you see," she continued.

"Well, of course," I told her. "It will be an adjustment. But you'll be fine, I promise. We'll take care of each other, you and me. We won't let anyone drag us out of Winterville Court against our will. Caden tried the same thing with me not so long ago, you know, and I sent him away with a flea in his ear." And a check for £100,000, of course, but I chose not to mention that.

She didn't seem particularly reassured, but there was little more that I could do.

"Anyway, he's decided that I should do a home conversion," she said after a moment.

"Who has?" I asked.

"Oberon."

I frowned, looking around the room, which hadn't changed much in all the years that I'd been popping in and out. Why on earth, I wondered, did he want her to convert her flat? And convert it into what?

"I don't understand," I said. "Is he offering to repaint it? Or buy some new furniture?"

"No," she said, shaking her head. "Now let me see if I have this right. He says that I can sell the flat to something called a Third Party and give some of the money to him so he can buy his new home in Sydney, but I can still live here until I die, and I won't have to pay anyone a penny. It'll still be mine. That's what he told me, anyway. Does that sound right?"

"A home reversion," I said, correcting her, for I'd read about such schemes in the newspapers and always thought they were the domain of fraudsters and scoundrels. "And this was his idea, was it?"

"He said it's a good way to retrieve one's . . ." She scrunched up her face, trying to remember the word.

"Equity?" I suggested.

"That's it, yes. A good way to retrieve one's equity."

"And give it to him."

"I'm not money-minded," she said, shrugging her shoulders. "Would you talk to Edgar about it and tell me what he thinks? I know this makes me sound rather old-fashioned, but I do think men are so much better at this sort of thing than women, don't you?"

"Not really, no," I said. "But if you'd prefer to take his advice, then of course, I'll be happy to speak to him about it and I'll let you know what he says. That said, I think it rather unlikely that he'll approve."

"Thank you, Gretel," she said, and we both stood now, and she led me toward the door. "You're a good friend. You've always looked out for me, haven't you? Ever since the day you moved in."

And it was true. I had made a point of it.

"I'd be lost without you," she added, a little wistfully.

Unusually for me, I reached over and gave her a kiss on the cheek before crossing the hallway and returning to my flat, where I put the kettle on for some tea. Strolling over to the window, I looked out, expecting to see Henry seated on one of the benches below, reading, but the garden was empty. I did, however, hear the door that led to it open and waited to see whether he might appear, but no, it was Madelyn who stepped outside, wearing a bright yellow tracksuit. Our paths still hadn't crossed since she'd returned from hospital, and I hadn't dared stop by their flat since making my report to the police a few days earlier.

I watched her as she made her way into the center of the garden, where she stopped, threw back her head and closed her eyes as she appeared to breathe in the fresh air. She stretched her arms out wide and slowly began to spin, once, twice, a third time, before growing unsteady on her feet—dizzy, I suppose—and sitting down on the ground in the lotus position, placing her hands on her knees and remaining very still. I assumed she was practicing yoga, something I had never tried myself. I found myself watching her, wondering what it would be like to be young and supple again, until I heard the button on the kettle click and I turned away, returning to the kitchen to heat the pot.

It was only when I sat down a few minutes later that I remembered the unexpected parcel that had been deposited outside my flat earlier and that I had left it behind at Heidi's. Reluctant as I was to return there, I was eager to see what it contained and so stepped across the corridor once again and knocked.

"I think I forgot something," I said when she opened the door, pointing to the wrapped gift on the side table.

"Oh, Gretel," she said, looking pleased to see me. "I'm so glad you called in. I've been very worried. It's Oberon, you see. He says I can't come to Australia with him after all."

"Yes, I know, dear," I said with a sigh. "We've had this conversation. I'm going to speak to Edgar about it, remember?"

"Oh yes," she replied half-heartedly, disappointed that I was already turning away to return to my own flat. Trying not to feel too guilty, I said my goodbyes once again and disappeared back indoors.

Sitting down, I removed the bow and ribbon and began to open the wrapping paper carefully. It was so luxurious that I thought I might hold on to it for when I next had a gift for someone. I wondered whether Caden might have sent it but decided no, because then the gift tag would have said *For Mother*. Then I thought about Eleanor but was certain that she would have written *For Mrs. F.* However, as soon as the paper was removed and I saw what was inside I knew that it could not possibly be from either of them.

Someone, some unnamed Third Party, to use Oberon's phrase, had sent me a book.

I held it before me, my hands trembling, as I tried to understand what it meant, and read the title carefully: *The Final Solution: Hitler's Plan to Exterminate the Jews*.

Nervously, I opened it and flicked through the pages. It was not a work of popular history, the sort that Edgar had written, as much as an academic text, although it had two sets of photographs of eight pages each, placed one third and two thirds of the way through the volume. Scanning them quickly, it did not take long before I was confronted with my father's face, and I slammed the book shut so hard that the noise startled me. And at that precise moment, my telephone rang. I stared at it, hoping that it would stop, desperate to be left alone to understand the meaning of this extraordinary message, but it kept going, the ringing so insistent that I had no choice but to answer.

"Hello," I said angrily into the receiver, and there was a silence for perhaps ten seconds, then the sound of someone clearing their throat, before a voice spoke.

"I just wanted to check you got my gift," said Alex Darcy-Witt. "I thought it might bring back some happy memories for you."

TEN

On the morning that I was due to be released from hospital, David arrived with a bunch of flowers and a broad smile on his face. He'd visited regularly, as had Edgar, but with his work hours, and the difficulty of private conversation within the ward, it had been almost impossible for us to spend any real time together. I remained in some discomfort, and Dr. Harket, who I found condescending and indifferent to my injuries, had reluctantly given me a course of painkillers, but when I sat up in bed to kiss David it was as if my soreness disappeared entirely. I longed for us to be back in his lodgings together, in bed, the place where I always felt that we were at our best.

"I've had an idea," he said, looking rather less confident than he usually did. "I don't think you should have to look after yourself while you're still healing. You need proper care."

"Oh, I'll be fine," I told him, waving away his concerns for my well-being. "I'll be back in work in a week or so anyway. Are they asking after me?"

"Every day, but there's no need to worry. I've been told to tell you that you must take as long as you need to recover. So, I thought, in the meantime, perhaps you'd like to move in with me?" he said, and

I looked at him in surprise. His face betrayed a certain bashfulness, an anxiety that I might refuse him.

"Really?" I asked.

"Yes."

"I wasn't expecting you to say that."

"Well, you know me. I'm full of surprises."

I thought about it for a moment.

"But we're not married," I told him, and he shrugged his shoulders.

"Does that matter to you so much?"

The truth was, it didn't. Having witnessed all that I had in my life, I could scarcely think of anything so trivial as a piece of paper confirming my legal relationship to David, or anything as unimportant as the moral disapproval of strangers.

"What about the other people in your building?" I asked. "Won't they have something to say about the matter?"

"So what if they do? They can go whistle, for all I care. It's 1953, for heaven's sake, not the 1800s. Anyway, if we are to get married one day, then don't you want it to last forever?"

"Of course I do."

"Then it makes sense that we give it a try first. See if we're suited to each other. You never know, I might drive you crazy with how I eat or laugh or snore."

The idea of moving in together delighted me, but it was tinged with anxiety because, so far, we had both chosen to hide much of our pasts from the other. I wasn't sure that I could make a decision as important as this without being completely honest with him. I had never told the truth to Émile, to Cait. And I had certainly never confided the horrors of my past in someone who was Jewish.

Indeed, the only person I had had an honest conversation with upon this subject was Kurt.

"What's the matter, Gretel?" asked David, sensing my hesitation.

I think he had expected me to throw my arms around him and jump at the chance of our playing house together. I had given every appearance, after all, that I hoped for a future together.

"Nothing," I said. "It's just—"

"Just what?"

Before I could say another word, Nurse Fenton appeared to tell me that Dr. Harket needed a further word with me before I could be discharged. David nodded and, looking a little wounded that I had not been more enthusiastic at his proposal, made his way out onto the corridor, while I sat unhappily in bed, wondering what to do for the best. A few minutes later, the doctor arrived.

"Miss Wilson," he said, pulling the curtain around the bed for privacy's sake, although it was a rather pointless exercise as our conversation could easily carry to the women in the other beds. "How are you feeling? Ready to go home?"

"Much better," I said, sitting up straight and trying not to wince at any pain I felt in case he insisted that my stay be extended. "My ribs are still a little sore, but not as bad as they were yesterday, and my leg—"

"We'll give you a crutch as you leave," he said. "You won't need it for long, but it might help you move around as the bone heals. Who's the young man in the corridor, if you don't mind me asking?"

"Does it matter?"

"Yes, or I wouldn't have asked," he said, his tone surprisingly sharp.

"A friend," I said, uncertain why David's identity mattered so much to him.

"A boyfriend, you mean."

"Yes."

"I see." He glanced back in that direction, although the curtain prevented him from seeing out to the corridor. "And you're not married, you and this friend?"

"No," I said. "Why? Is there a problem?"

"Only that it appears you've been rather free with your virtue, haven't you, Miss Wilson?" he said. "So many of your generation are, of course. Everything's gone to hell since the war ended. But I'm not here to judge."

I stared at him, completely ignorant as to what he was talking about. He recognized my confusion and rolled his eyes, apparently annoyed by my naïveté.

"You're pregnant, Miss Wilson," he said with a sigh. "You're going to have a baby."

I remained silent. This was the last thing I had expected him to say.

"You didn't know?" he asked, raising an eyebrow. "You hadn't guessed?"

"No," I said.

"I wondered whether all of this"—he gestured vaguely at me—"had been some ham-fisted attempt to get rid of the child."

"Of course not," I said, my voice low and quiet, trying to work out what this might mean for me, for David, for our future together. "I promise it wasn't."

"It's just that most women can sense when they are with child. There are the obvious physical changes, for one thing."

"Well, I didn't," I said, growing irritated now. "How far along am I?"

"A few months," he replied. "Plenty of time left for that young man to make an honest woman of you and legitimize the child. Nurse Fenton will make an appointment with an obstetrician for you. You'll need to see him rather soon, of course. You were very fortunate, Miss Wilson, that the baby was not injured in your reck-lessness. Or unfortunate, perhaps, depending on how one thinks about these things."

He opened the curtain again, glancing out toward David, who rose from his seat in the corridor eagerly. He looked so handsome to me as he stood there, the flowers still held tightly in his hands. Years later, when I discovered I was pregnant with Caden, I would, for some reason, recall those flowers when I told Edgar our news. They were dahlias. And I've hated dahlias ever since.

"Would you like me to tell him?" Dr. Harket asked. "It might be better coming from another man, don't you think? We wouldn't want him to start shouting at you on the ward. There are the other pa-tients to consider, after all."

"Why would he start shouting at me?" I asked, baffled.

"For your sheer bloody stupidity," he said.

Had I been in my full health, I might have slapped him. Of course, he believed that this was all my fault, that I had somehow managed to conceive a child alone, to seduce a poor, innocent man, who, prior to my appearance, hadn't known one end of a woman from another. But I couldn't focus on my anger toward the doctor right now. In-stead, I simply felt ill. I had sworn to myself that I would never have children, that it was incumbent upon me that I bring my father's line to an end.

"Thank you, but I'll tell him myself," I replied, steely-voiced, and he looked at me disapprovingly.

"As you wish," he said, walking away, and David returned to the ward.

"Can we go then?" he asked.

"Yes," I said, pulling myself to my feet. "Just give me a few min-utes to get dressed."

"Back to mine?" he added hopefully, and I thought about it.

"To mine first," I said. "There's something we need to talk about. Quite a bit, in fact. And after that, if you still want me to move in with you, then I will. Is that all right?"

He frowned. "Sounds important," he said.

"It is. But let's wait till we're alone."

"Of course," he said. "But I promise you, Gretel, there's nothing you can say to me that will make me not want to be with you. There are things I need to share with you too. About my past. About my family. I know I haven't always been very forthcoming about them, but it's a difficult subject for me. I'll tell you my story and you can tell me yours. And after that, we can start afresh. Begin our new lives together. How does that sound?"

I nodded, hoping that it might prove to be as simple as he described, but knowing in my heart that the world did not work in that way.

I had no choice; I had to confront him.

I woke early and went for a long walk in Hyde Park to clear my mind before dressing as if I were preparing for an appearance in a courtroom, where I was the prosecuting barrister and he the accused standing in the dock. Examining myself in my bedroom's full-length mirror, I looked as self-possessed and strong as a woman in her early nineties can look and felt rather pleased with the effect, wanting to give the appearance of strength tinged with just the slightest whisper of vulnerability. Whatever Alex Darcy-Witt knew about me, or thought he knew, it was imperative for my own survival, not to mention the survival of Caden, that he should not be allowed to share what he had discovered with anyone.

The door to Flat One was opened by Madelyn, who seemed inexplicably pleased to see me. To my dismay, she threw her arms around me in a tight embrace. I'm not a fan of physical affection at the best of times, and my body froze as her much taller frame enclosed me.

"Gretel," she cried, when she finally pulled away, and I ran my hand along my dress to smooth out any creases she might have left in her wake. "It's so good to see you! I've been meaning to come up-stairs and have a good old gossip."

"It's nice to see you too, Madelyn," I replied, wondering whether this excessive display of bonhomie was chemically induced. I didn't exactly have a history of sitting around, drinking wine, plaiting a friend's hair, and discussing celebrity divorces. "But actually, it's your husband I came to see. Is Mr. Darcy-Witt at home?"

"Not right now," she said, looking around and putting a finger to her lower lip, as if she wasn't entirely sure whether this was even the truth or something he had simply told her to tell visitors. "But I'm expecting him at any minute. Would you like to come in and wait?"

I decided that I would. Returning to sit alone in my flat would leave me too anxious and I would only waste time standing by the window, watching for his car or taxi to pull up. Besides, it would give me a chance for a few words with her. I stepped inside and, once again, the flat so resembled the vestibule of an art gallery that I wondered how she possibly moved from room to room during the day without disturbing anything.

"Sit down, please," said Madelyn, and I did as instructed, taking the sofa I had adopted on our first encounter.

"You're feeling better then?" I asked as she sat in the armchair opposite me.

"Oh yes," she said, nodding furiously. "The thing is, Gretel, it was all a terrible misunderstanding. I'm just so sorry that you had to get involved. I feel so embarrassed. Alex says I'm an awful fool for not realizing that I'd taken so many sleeping tablets. It's because they weren't acting fast enough, you see. That's why I took more and more. I rather lost count in the end."

"He's all heart, isn't he?" I remarked. "You'd think he might be a little more sympathetic toward someone who's just been discharged from hospital."

"Alex says that I should get one of those little boxes, you know the ones, the plastic ones with the days of the week printed on them," she continued, ignoring my comment. "You separate your medication into each compartment, so you never get mixed up."

"I know them," I said, nodding. "I have one myself."

"You're ill?" she asked, looking deeply concerned.

"I'm ninety-one," I said with a half-smile. "It takes a certain amount of help to get a woman of my years through the day."

"You're not old, Gretel," she insisted, and I rolled my eyes.

"I am the very definition of old, Madelyn," I said. "Let's not pretend otherwise."

She stopped laughing now and looked wounded.

"Alex says I talk too much," she said after a moment.

"Can a person talk too much?" I asked. "After all, if you have something to say, then—"

"Alex says that I should think before I speak."

"Alex says a lot of things, doesn't he?"

"And that no one wants to hear every half-baked idea that pops into my head. That I embarrass myself and embarrass him when I just start chattering away like some kind of lunatic. He's right, I think. I'm trying to be better at things like that."

A noise from the hallway and Henry appeared, barefoot and wearing shorts and a T-shirt featuring the jacket image from a paperback edition of Jules Verne's *Around the World in Eighty Days*. He looked startled to see me and well he might, for he was sporting a black eye. I'm sorry to say that I wasn't in the least surprised to see it.

"Henry, I told you to stay in your room," said Madelyn, standing up and marching over to him.

"Hello, Mrs. Fernsby," he said, looking at me with a distressed expression on his face.

"Hello, Henry," I said. "I see you've been in the wars again. But then, when are you not? You're like a medieval knight, forever getting into scrapes with peasants along the road."

His hand instinctively reached up to his left eye, which looked tender, and he resisted touching it, returning his hand to his side and staring down toward the floor.

"He was sleepwalking," explained Madelyn. "And he walked into the bathroom door. Can you believe it?"

"Not for a moment, no," I replied.

"Go back to your room, Henry," she said, but he ignored her and pointed at his T-shirt.

"Have you ever read this book, Mrs. Fernsby?" he asked.

"I have," I told him. "Many years ago. I've also read *Twenty Thousand Leagues under the Sea* by the same author."

"I like that title," he said.

"Actually, I may have a copy upstairs," I said. "I'll take a look later and, if I do, you can borrow it."

"Henry, go to your room," repeated Madelyn, raising her voice unnecessarily, and this time he obeyed. I heard the sound of his bedroom door shutting.

"There was no need to shout at him, dear," I said. "He was just talking, that's all. It's good that he enjoys books, don't you agree? Most of the children I see on the streets these days have their heads stuck in their phone all the time. It's encouraging to see a child who likes reading."

"He just won't do what he's told," she said, rubbing at her eyes, apparently exhausted with her son, with her life, with this entire disappointing universe in which she had been condemned to pass her days. "Alex says that he needs to learn discipline and that I'm too soft on him."

"I don't think I can agree with that," I said. "With either statement, I mean."

"You don't understand what it's like," she muttered.

"I understand exactly what it's like," I told her. "I have a son of my own, remember."

"Children are different today," she said. "Alex says that when he was a boy, if he stepped a foot out of line, his father would make him regret it, and it's that sort of strictness that made him the man he is today."

"And what kind of man is that?" I asked.

She looked up at me and frowned. "What do you mean?" she asked.

"It's a simple enough question. What kind of man is your husband? A good one?"

She stared at me, utterly lost for words.

"I only ask," I continued, "because you seem rather frightened of him."

"Frightened of him?" she asked, laughing now, bringing all her skills as an actress to the fore, and, if I am to be honest, they were not the sort that would win any awards. "Why on earth would I be frightened of him?"

"Well, Henry gets injured rather a lot, doesn't he?" I asked. "And shouldn't he be at school now? It's eleven o'clock on a Tuesday morning, after all."

"Alex said to keep him at home until his eye gets better."

"Does a black eye preclude the boy from learning?"

"He just wants the swelling to go down, that's all," she said, looking away, her hands wrapped tightly around each other, her fingers intertwining constantly.

"First a broken arm, then a series of bruises, now a black eye," I said. "Oh, and there was a burn too, wasn't there? And, of course, you've had your own share of mishaps, haven't you?"

She looked up again and shook her head. "I'm fine," she said.

"I don't believe you," I told her. "I imagine that if you were to remove that jumper, which is much too heavy for this good weather, I'd see bruises running up and down your arms. I'm not wrong, am I?"

Before she could reply, there came the sound of a key in the door and Alex stepped inside. He paused for a moment, looking from one of us to the other, before sighing a little, as if he felt there had been a certain inevitability to this moment.

"Mrs. Fernsby," he said, looking exhausted that I was, once again, in his field of vision. "How nice to see you. Visiting. Again."

"Mr. Darcy-Witt," I said, standing up and raising myself to my full height. "I wanted a word with you. In private, if that's at all possible."

He seemed almost to admire my fortitude.

"I expect I have little choice in the matter," he said. "A stroll in the garden, perhaps?"

"Perfect," I replied, marching past him and leading the way to the back door. He didn't follow me immediately and I could hear low voices from behind, his and Madelyn's, locked in conversation. I longed to know what they were saying but continued on my way. As I opened the door, the sun broke through, momentarily blinding me. It was a beautiful spring day, the sort that should be filled only with happy memories.

TWELVE

It was difficult to know where to begin, but I chose Berlin, the city of my birth and the place where I had lived for twelve years until a dinner guest and his lady friend arrived one evening to inform Father of his new posting, and my life, and that of my entire family, changed forever.

"Berlin?" asked David, collapsing into an armchair in my bedroom. I sat across from him, on the bed, trying to stop myself from trembling. I didn't want to look at his face as I spoke. I could not bear the idea of watching his love gradually disappear. It was easier simply to tell my story aloud, as if to an empty room. "But you said you were born in France."

"I know, but I lied. The truth is, I didn't set foot in France until 1946, a few months after the war ended."

"But you lived in Rouen, yes? That much was true?"

"For about six years, yes. Later. But during that first year, Mother and I remained in Paris. We only moved to Rouen when it became impossible to stay in the capital any longer. And I left for Australia almost immediately after Mother died."

"All right," he said, nodding his head. "So, you're German then." There was a hint of suspicion to his tone, disapproval laced with fear.

"Yes," I admitted. "Although I haven't been there since 1946. Nor do I have any plans to return."

"And during the war, did you stay in Germany?"

"Not all the time, no."

He looked relieved. "So you got out," he said. "You weren't part of it. That was brave on your family's part. If you'd been captured—"

"David, wait. Just hear me out."

"But I know something of this myself," he said, leaning forward and trying to take my hand in his, but I pulled away. "I know I haven't told you much about my family, but I really should. It's important that you know what happened to them."

"I already know some of it," I told him. "About your parents and sister, anyway. About Treblinka."

He stared at me in disbelief.

"How did you—"

"He meant well; you must believe that. He only told me because he knew that I was concerned about you, about how you never talked about them or what had taken place. And then, that night, when we went to see that terrible film—"

"Who meant well?" he asked, raising his voice a little. "Who told you all this?"

"Edgar," I said.

He stiffened slightly and his expression mingled disbelief with anger. "Edgar told you about my family?" he asked.

"Not everything," I replied. "Just the basic story, that's all. I'm so sorry that happened to you, David."

He remained silent for a time, considering this. "He shouldn't have done that," he said finally. "It was not his story to tell."

"He's your friend. He cares about you."

He let out a small grunt. I could tell that he wasn't happy but did not want to pursue the subject right now. He stood up and walked toward the window, then noticed the Seugnot jewelry box on my nightstand.

"This is nice," he said reaching for it, perhaps eager to change the subject entirely.

"Don't," I said, my voice rising in fright, for I did not want him to see the photograph it contained. If I could not look at it, then neither could he. "It's fragile."

He turned to me, no doubt surprised by the insistence in my voice, but left it alone.

"Tell me what he told you," he said, returning to his chair, and I repeated what Edgar had said, that his grandparents had taken him to England when they sensed the Nazis were about to invade and that his parents had been due to follow but had failed to do so.

"And my sister," he said. "You forgot my sister."

"Yes, her too," I said, trying to keep my tone as sympathetic as possible. "She was in the hospital, that's what he told me. An appendix operation, is that right?"

"No," he said, shaking his head. "That's what I told him, but it wasn't the truth."

I waited for him to continue.

"I didn't want to tell him what my parents did. How foolish they were."

Again, I remained silent.

"My sister's name was Dita. Did he tell you that at least?"

"No."

"She played piano," he continued, smiling at the recollection. "She was very gifted. I have no skills in that area at all. My father hoped I would, but I'm tone deaf. Dita, however, she could hear a song once and just sit down and play it, note perfect. She played concerts all the time—children's concerts, of course, but everyone could tell how skilled she was and what an extraordinary future lay ahead of her. She was due to play an important recital, one that would have established her reputation even further, and my parents insisted on her staying to perform in it. My Bubbe and Zayde told them they were crazy, that we should all leave together, but they refused. My mother, I think, would have given in, but my father, he was a stubborn man. A proud man. He wanted to hear his daughter play before a large audience. So, the three of us left, and they were due to come to England four days later. But they never arrived. I don't even know if the concert took place. Bubbe tried for a long time to discover what had happened to them, but both she and Zayde went to their graves knowing nothing. It was only afterward, when the records at Treblinka were released and what families remained were contacted, that I learned their fate. Although I had assumed it."

Tears ran down his face, but he wiped them away quickly. I could barely bring myself to look at him. The guilt I felt was building in a place deep inside me, threatening to break me in two.

"I still dream of them," he said, smiling a little through his grief. "I say dream," he added, "but of course I mean I have nightmares. I'm there with them, naked in the gas chambers—"

"David, don't," I pleaded.

"Burning in the fires."

"David!"

"I don't even feel human in those dreams. But that's how they made us feel, isn't it? Like we weren't people at all."

A memory—my father in his office—"Those people? Well, they're not people at all. At least not as we understand the term."

"I'm just a spirit floating across the skies above Poland, an idea rather than a person. A collection of random thoughts mingling with the clouds."

"Stop! Please stop," I begged him, my hands clenched into fists now. I wanted to scream out loud. This was the reality of what my family had done and what I had been hiding over all these years.

He let out a deep sigh that emanated from the very depths of his being. I said nothing. When he did speak again, his voice was so quiet that I had to strain to hear him. He did not look at me.

"You're going to tell me that he was a soldier, aren't you?" he asked. "Your father. You're going to say that he fought. For them."

"Yes," I admitted. I could not pretend any longer.

"I guessed as much. I hoped, perhaps, that I was wrong."

"He was a soldier," I said. "But he didn't fight."

"Well, that's something, I suppose," he replied, a spark of hope crossing his face. "Office staff, then? Something like that? A driver, perhaps?"

I said nothing and the silence between us became so overwhelming that when he leaped from his seat and walked to the window I jumped in fright. He kept his back to me, looking down on the street below.

"Forgive me, Gretel," he said at last.

"Forgive you?" I asked, standing up and walking toward him. Somehow, without intending to, I found my hand involuntarily going to my stomach to protect the baby growing inside me. "What can I possibly have to forgive you for?"

"For all this anger inside me. I find it hard to talk about any of this. About those people. About what they did. I want them all dead. They're still out there, you know. In Europe. In South America. In Australia. So many of them still awaiting justice. Sometimes I think that's how I should spend my life. Hunting them down. Ending them."

He turned to look at me. His face was etched with pain.

"My problem is that I still love you," he said, and it seemed as if he found it torturous even to admit this. He reached out for me, then pulled his arms back. For now, he did not want to touch me, the first time in our relationship when he had been able to keep his hands from my body. "It's not your fault, any of it. So, your father was some, I don't know, humble functionary in an office somewhere. What else could he have done? I can't blame you for that."

"It's more complicated than that."

"But I can't think about it now. There's so much to take in and consider. If, one day, we were to have a baby of our own, for example, what we would tell him? Or her? How would we explain what their grandfather did?"

"Would we need to?" I asked.

"Of course," he said, beginning to pace up and down. "I couldn't live with secrecy or lies."

"But what good would it do?"

He shrugged his shoulders, perhaps uncertain too.

"I need some time," he said eventually. "Just to work it through in my mind. You hate him, I suppose?"

"Who?" I asked.

"Your father."

I thought about it. To share only a fraction of the truth was to share none at all. "I loved him very much when I was a girl," I said. "He's been gone for eight years now but . . . I can't help it, there are times that I still miss him. I know what he did, how he lived . . . but he loved me very much, David. I can't explain it. If I could have him back, just for a day, if I could talk to him for even an hour—"

For a moment, I thought he was going to strike me. He breathed quick and fast, shut his eyes tight.

"I should go home," he said. "I can't discuss this with you right now. I don't blame you, Gretel, I swear that I don't. I understand that you would love your father, it's only natural, but—"

"David, you haven't even heard what I need to tell you," I said, my frustration growing as the conversation veered away from my own story. "You've told me about your family. Now I must tell you about mine. If we really are to have a future together, which is what I want more than anything, then it's important you know every detail."

"There's more?" he asked, looking distressed. "What more could there be? What could be worse than knowing that your father was some low-level functionary for those animals?"

I sat down on the bed and buried my face in my hands.

"Sit down, David, please," I said, and he did as I asked. "There's something I need you to do for me, and if you do this, I promise I will never ask anything of you in this life again."

"What is it?" he asked.

"I just want you to let me tell my story from start to finish without interruption. And when it's over, when you've heard it all and know me better than any person alive does, then you can decide whether you want to stay or go. Will you do that, David? Will you hear me out?"

He nodded. "I will," he said.

"Then I'll start again," I replied quietly. I swallowed, took a deep breath and began.

"I was born in Berlin in 1931," I said. "I lived with my father, my mother and, three years after my own birth, my brother was born. We lived happily. My father was not a humble office worker, as you have suggested, but an officer in the Reich. A senior officer. Of course, I was just a child and knew very little about what he did on a day-to-day basis. The war was going on, he was rarely at home, but it didn't seem to affect us very much. And then, one afternoon, my brother and I came home from school and we were surprised to find Maria, our family's maid, who always kept her head bowed and never looked up from the carpet, standing in my brother's bedroom, pulling all his belongings out of his wardrobe and packing them into four wooden crates, even the things he'd hidden at the back, which he had told me belonged to him and were nobody else's business."

THIRTEEN

I had a visit from the police," said Alex Darcy-Witt when he joined me in the garden. I was pacing slowly from one end to the other and he fell in step with me. Two perfectly ordinary people enjoying a stroll in the sunshine, and not the daughter of a concentration camp commandant and a man who habitually beat his wife and son.

"Did you indeed?" I asked, keeping my voice perfectly calm.

"I did. But then I expect you know that."

"I imagined they'd come calling, yes," I told him. "But I didn't know that it had happened already. I suppose they have no reason to keep me informed."

"They didn't tell me it was you who reported your suspicions to them," he continued. "But I assumed it was. I'm not wrong, am I?"

"No," I said, doing my best to keep my voice controlled, which, to my surprise, was not as difficult as I had expected. "I only wish I'd gone to them sooner. It might have saved Henry from receiving his latest black eye. And from hearing the terrible things you've said to him. That poor boy lives in a state of constant terror."

"He was sleepwalking," insisted Alex. "And he walked into—"

"Alex," I said with a sigh, raising one hand now to silence him. "Let's not. Just let's not."

He smiled a little and nodded.

"They didn't come here, you know," he told me after a moment. "The police, I mean. They didn't show up at Winterville Court. Do you know where they showed up?"

I shook my head. "I haven't the faintest idea," I said.

"My office in Soho. Unannounced. They marched up the stairs like, oh, I don't know, let's say a group of SS officers, and told one of my assistants that they needed to speak to me. I was on a call to LA at the time, with someone very famous. Would you like to know who it was?"

"I'm afraid the fact that you work with film stars doesn't impress me in the slightest, Alex. So no. Don't waste your time."

Honestly, I thought. Did he expect me to care about such trivialities? For heaven's sake, I wanted to tell him, I once shook hands with Adolf Hitler and kissed Eva Braun on the cheek. I'd played with Goebbels' children and attended a birthday party for Gudrun Himmler.

"My office," he repeated. "Where all my deals are done. Where my staff gossip about every little thing that happens. And a police detective and his sidekick, both younger than me, arrived without any warning and said they wanted to question me about my relationship with my wife and son and said we could either talk there or they would frogmarch me down to the local police station."

"And which did you choose?" I asked.

"Does it matter?"

"I'm just interested."

"I chose the station. To keep things formal. And to give my solicitor a chance to show up. One of them, one of the officers I mean, was Jewish. That probably bothers you. The irony is, I have no such prejudices at all."

"No, you reserve your aggression for women and little boys. Do you mind if we sit down?" I asked as we approached the bench. "Well, I'm going to sit anyway. You must do as you please."

"I'll sit with you," he said, throwing himself onto the seat next to me. "You received my gift?"

"I did, yes. But I'm afraid I didn't quite understand the significance of it."

"Gretel," he said, smiling now, delighted at being able to throw this line back at me. "Let's not. Just let's not."

"I have a great interest in history, it's true," I continued, ignoring this. "Perhaps Henry told you that, when we first met, I was reading a biography of Marie Antoinette? And my late husband, Edgar, was a very well-known historian. But I tend to avoid books about the war. Having lived through it, you know."

"Right at the fiery heart, one might say."

I turned to him now, deciding that there was no point playing games any longer.

"You know everything, I assume?" I asked.

"I do," he said, nodding in an almost courtly fashion. "And, quite honestly, Mrs. Fernsby, Mme Guéymard, Miss Wilson, or shall we go with Fräulein—"

And here he employed the surname that I had been born with, my father's infamous name, and one that I had not used since Mother and I had boarded the train for Paris from Berlin in 1946.

"You can just call me Gretel," I said with a sigh. "It's probably simpler."

"Quite honestly, Gretel, all other things aside, I must confess that I'm utterly fascinated," he continued. "I do have a great interest in that period, as you might know from watching some of my films, and for me to be sitting here with you, with someone who was actually there—"

"It's such a very long time ago," I said.

"I never get starstruck, there's no point in my line of work. But I am genuinely starstruck."

"What a ridiculous thing to say."

"I'd like to talk about it with you."

"I never talk about that time in my life."

"Never?"

I thought about it.

"Only twice," I said.

"And who did you tell?"

"A man named David Rotheram, many years ago, in 1953. And then, of course, the man who became my husband. Edgar."

"And their responses?"

"Are none of your concern."

"Please tell me about it."

"No," I said.

"Why not?"

"Because it doesn't matter anymore. It's all in the past. How did you find out anyway? I'm ninety-one years old, and no one ever has before. So, you'll forgive me if I'm intrigued."

He shrugged his shoulders and looked into the center of the garden. "It's what I do," he said. "Or rather what I have people do. Research. Digging into stories, people's backgrounds. And, of course, the world is very different now than when you were young. Nowadays, all you have to do is sit at a computer, put in a little time, and you can discover so much about your enemies. I'm a very influential person, Gretel, and I have contacts in many areas. In the beginning, I just wanted to know more about you, that's all, since you seemed so concerned with what was going on in my home. But one story led to another, and then another. When one researcher hit a dead end, I passed it onto the next."

"So no one else knows the full details?" I asked.

"No. I received each part of your life in different sections. Then I pieced them all together myself. I couldn't believe what I'd stumbled across. I went to the British Film Archive and found an old movie, *Darkness*. Do you know it?"

"I saw it in a cinema once," I told him. "Afterward, I ran out onto the street and threw myself under a bus."

He seemed taken aback by that.

"I'm glad you didn't succeed," he said.

"Really? Why?"

"Because, by rights, you should die in a prison cell."

I thought about it. I could not dispute it. "I'm aware of that," I said quietly.

"I suppose you wish you'd won the war."

I raised an eyebrow. "Oh, Mr. Darcy-Witt," I said, as if I were explaining something obvious to a child. "No one wins a war."

"But don't you feel guilt?" he asked.

"You, of all people, are asking me this question?"

"You can't compare my behavior to yours."

"I was just a child," I told him.

"That would be a more credible response if you had presented yourself to the authorities when the war ended," he said. "You could have helped bring so many to justice. Just think of all the people you might have identified! The stories you might have told! All those lost lives, those millions of people gassed, you could have avenged them in some small way if you had chosen to. You could have brought some peace to their families. But no, instead you chose to put your own safety first."

"We all do that," I said.

"Don't you feel guilt?" he repeated, and I stood up and walked quickly toward the other side of the garden. I pressed my head against the cold wall, my eyes closed. I could feel the blood rushing through my body, my breathing growing strained. He came up behind me and I turned around to face him.

"What are you going to do with this information?" I said. "I don't ask for myself, you understand. If you tell people, yes, I will suffer, of course I will. But there are others—"

"With one phone call," he said, "I could make you the most famous woman on the planet."

I nodded. "I know that," I said. "But I have a son." And there was something else. Caden and Eleanor had called over to see me the previous evening to tell me some unexpected news. "And he's about to become a father," I added. "His fiancée is the most wonderful woman. Neither of them expected this, they thought they were too old, but they're thrilled. So you won't just destroy me, you'll destroy him, her, and my grandchild. All of whom are entirely innocent."

"It's tricky," he said, stroking his chin. "I'd like to expose you, I would. I do believe that you should die in prison. But I have to think about myself too. These allegations you made to the police—"

"Are you going to deny them?" I asked. "You have your poor wife in a state of mental torture. She can't think straight most of the time. She's high on whatever it is people get high on these days so they don't have to face the realities of their lives. She's sacrificed all her ambitions because you can't stand the idea of her having a life of her own. And you hurt her. You hurt her, Mr. Darcy-Witt. You beat her."

"But she can be so annoying," he replied, throwing his arms in the air as if this were a perfectly rational reply and one that any reasonable person should understand. "You have no idea how annoying that woman can be. She doesn't listen. That's her biggest fault."

"So, you hit her?"

He shrugged. "I'd do the same to a dog."

"And your son?"

"Needs discipline."

"You broke his arm."

"I'll admit, I went too far there."

"And the black eye? The burn."

"He spoke back to me. I won't have it. This is my family, Gretel. They belong to me, just like yours belonged to your father. I won't let anyone interfere with that. Least of all a person like you. If you are a person at all. You can look at me with as much contempt as you like, but reflect just a little of that disgust back at yourself, why don't you?"

I said nothing. What could I say in response to this? He was not wrong.

"So, I have a proposition," he said.

"Go on."

"You've heard the phrase 'mutually assured destruction'?"

I nodded. I remembered it from the days of the Cold War. How pointless it would be for America or Russia to dispatch their nuclear bombs in the other's direction; they'd only wipe each other out and everyone would die.

"I have," I said.

"Well, that's the position we find ourselves in here. I can destroy you and you can destroy me. So, it might be simplest if we simply agree to leave each other in peace from now on. I might even sell the flat and take Madelyn and Henry somewhere else. But in the meantime, you have no contact with us, you don't seek any further information about us. We're just a family that lives in the flat beneath yours. Nothing more, nothing less."

"And in return?"

"I'll keep your secrets. Even after you're dead. I'll leave your son and grandchild alone. None of this is their fault, after all. What do you say, Gretel, do we have a deal?"

I looked away and considered it. I glanced up toward the windows, where Heidi was staring down at us with a look of concern on her face. She could probably tell that all was not well between Mr. Darcy-Witt and me. But I ignored her and turned back to Alex, my hand outstretched. What choice, after all, did I have?

"We have a deal," I said.

When he hit her again, I think it was not so much to hurt her as to taunt me, to see whether I would stick to our agreement. It was late on a Saturday evening, and I was starting to think about bed when I heard voices rising from the flat below and the sound of an argument. I closed my eyes, hoping that it would end quickly, but within a few minutes there was the sound of a door slamming and small feet running across the floor toward the back of the building. I stood up and made my way to the back window, to see Henry sitting in the half-light in a corner of the garden, his knees pulled up to his chin, his arms wrapped around them, face buried in his hands. I wanted to leave him alone, to stay out of it, as I had sworn that I would, but I couldn't. I had witnessed too much suffering in my life and done nothing to help. I had to intervene.

Defying every instinct of self-preservation, I made my way down-stairs, trying to ignore the shouting that was going on in the Darcy-Witts' living room, and stepped out into the back garden. Henry looked up, immediately anxious, I assume, that it was his father ap-proaching, then looked relieved when he saw that it was just me.

"Henry," I asked. "Are you all right?"

"I hate him," he replied, starting to cry, and I sat down next to him, put my arm around his shoulder, and instinctively he buried his body into mine. I had not sat this close to a small child since Caden was a boy. "I wish he was dead."

Perhaps anyone else would have chastised the child for saying such a terrible thing, but I knew something of the traumas that fathers could inflict on their offspring.

"Why is he angry with you now?" I asked.

"I was supposed to be doing my homework," he said. "But instead, he caught me reading and he was furious."

"They used to burn books, you know," I replied quietly.

"Who did?"

"It doesn't matter."

"Who did?" he repeated. "Why would anyone burn a book?"

"Bad people," I told him. "All long since dead. Well, most of them anyway. They were afraid of them, you see. Frightened of ideas. Frightened of the truth. People still are, I find. Things don't change that much."

"Stupid people," said Henry, snuffling a little.

"Very stupid people. He hits you often, doesn't he?"

He nodded, almost imperceptibly, and I pulled him closer.

"Is there no way to make him stop?" I asked, and I wasn't asking this of the boy, who could not, of course, provide an answer, but of the universe. The man had somehow managed to convince the police that there was no case to answer. I daresay he had flattered them and used his celebrity, or at least his celebrity contacts, to prevent them from doing any further digging into what was going on at Winterville Court, and so he believed that he could simply go on and on and on. And, as I had often read in the newspapers, this is what men so often did when the world turned a blind eye to their behavior. Until the moment they killed their wives and children, that is, at which point the neighbors would feign surprise and say how he had always seemed like such a quiet, pleasant man.

From the doorway, Madelyn emerged and looked at us both. There was blood on her chin, just below the left corner of her mouth, and her eyes seemed glazed.

"Henry," she said. "Come back in. It's late. You should be in bed."

"I don't want to," he said. "I'm never coming back in."

"Come in!" she roared, suddenly furious, the words so loud that both of us jumped. The boy leaped off the seat and ran as fast as he could inside the building. I stood up after a moment and looked at her.

"He'll kill you one of these days," I said. "You realize that, don't you?"

She let out a deep sigh. "Please let it be tomorrow," she said, turning around and following her son inside.

I remained where I was for a few minutes, angry with myself, hating my neighbor, even despising his wife for allowing this to continue, although I knew that he had her in such a state of terror that she simply could not stand up to him. Unsettled, I made my way back inside and, to my horror, I saw Alex Darcy-Witt standing outside his door, waiting for me. His sleeves were rolled up, his fists clenching and unclenching by his side. He was perspiring but looked like he was enjoying whatever trauma he had inflicted upon his family.

"You just can't stop yourself, can you?" he asked.

"I'm sorry," I said. "But I saw the boy outside and he was so upset. I needed to comfort him."

"I told you to stay away from him. From both of them."

"It won't happen again," I said. "I promise."

He stepped closer to me, and I could smell the whisky on his breath. I wondered how much he'd drunk before he'd attacked them. Whether it made the violence easier for him.

"What am I going to do with you, Gretel?" he asked quietly. "You just won't listen to reason, will you? I have a friend, you know. Well, I have a great many friends. But an important journalist. Always on the look-out for a good story. If I can make you the most famous woman on the planet, I can probably make him the most famous journalist. I wonder should I give him a call. Remind me, what's your son's name? Caden, isn't it? An unusual name. He won't be hard to track down. I can just see all the news trucks camped outside his house now. The reporters shouting questions at him. Should I call him, Gretel? What do you think? We could end this right now. Or will you stay away?"

"I'll stay away," I said.

"Good," he said, stepping back toward his flat. "Because this is your last warning."

He went inside and I heard him call out Henry's name and then, a few moments later, the sound of the boy screaming as he hit him once again. I ran to the door, but there was nothing I could do. I pressed my hands to my ears to block Henry's cries. And then I made my way back upstairs, almost stumbling over the step at the top. I rather regretted not falling. How easy it would be for me simply to tumble backward and fall to my death. A woman my age would never survive it. Truly, I understood Madelyn's wish to pass from this world to the next, no matter what punishment might lie in store for me there.

FOURTEEN

David did exactly as I asked of him. He remained completely silent while I told him the story of my life. It took more than an hour to impart it all but, even then, I did not tell him everything. I did not reveal, for example, my part in my brother's death. It was the only thing I could not speak aloud, in the same way that I could not speak his name.

When I finished, the silence between us seemed infinite and I did not dare look at him. Finally, I could stand it no longer.

"Speak," I said. "Say something, David, please."

When he replied, his voice was soft and low. "What can I say?" he whispered. "Where should I find the words to respond to this?"

I looked across at him. His face was pale, but he seemed composed.

"What are you?" he asked. "Are you even human?"

"I'm Gretel," I told him, desperate to believe that I had not lost his love. "The same Gretel with whom you fell in love."

"Not the same, no," he said, shaking his head.

"I was born into that life," I explained. "I didn't ask for it. I didn't choose it. I cannot help who my father was."

"But his blood runs through your veins."

"It doesn't mean that I'm like him."

His face suddenly took on a look of abject horror, his body seemed to go into spasm, and he turned his head away and, without warning, vomited on the floor. I jumped up, startled, as he reached for a cloth from the table to wipe his face clean. This is what I had done to him.

"I'm sorry, David," I said. "But I fell in love with you and—"

"Don't speak my name," he said, waving his hands before him and, as I took a step in his direction he stumbled backward in fear, his shoe slipping in the pile of sick, and he tumbled over, falling onto the floor, his hands stretched out before him in terror. "Don't come near me," he begged. "Don't touch me."

I was weeping now. People had looked at me with contempt before—Émile on the night that we had slept together, my Parisian neighbors when they had cursed me for my past, even Kurt when we met on that final morning in Sydney—but no one had ever seemed frightened of me. It was as if David thought that it would take only one word from me and all the demons of the past could be summoned from the underworld to drag him to a fate that he had somehow been lucky enough to escape. I stepped back, hoping he would understand that I meant him no harm, and he shuffled away from me toward the wall.

"You can't blame me for this," I said, pleading with him. "My mother suffered as much as any mother—"

"Your mother cared only for her own. But what about the children of others? Everyone who died was someone's child. She didn't care about them, did she?"

"I don't know," I said impotently.

"And you?" he asked. "Did you care?"

I thought about it. There was no point in lying. "No," I said. "No, I didn't. Not then."

"Even when he took you there," he asked. "When you saw what was going on?"

"I was twelve!"

"That's old enough to know the difference between freedom and imprisonment," he replied, standing up now. "Between hunger and starvation. Between life and death and right and wrong!"

"I know," I whispered, for I did. I had known for many years.

"By doing nothing, you did everything. By taking no responsibility, you bear all responsibility. And you let me fall in love with you when you know what you were part of."

"I didn't know that you would—"

"You knew that I was a Jew! You knew that much!"

"Not at the start, no. Perhaps that was naïve of me, I don't know. But it never even occurred to me until Edgar told me, and by then—"

"What, it was too late? Had you known from the beginning, you would have stayed away?"

He walked past me, making sure to keep a safe distance between us.

"David," I said. "Please listen to me. I love you. I can't change the past, but I can promise to live a better future. You must let me. I want that future to be with you, if you'll only allow it."

He shook his head and stared at me as if I were insane.

"If you think I would ever touch you again, then you're just as mad as your father was," he said. "I don't want to be in the same city as you, Gretel, don't you understand that? Let alone the same room. You're as bad as all of them."

"It's not true," I cried, sinking to the floor. "I'm not."

"I must go."

"Please don't."

I considered telling him about the baby growing inside me but didn't dare. He was so horrified by my revelations that I feared he would grab a knife and cut it out of me himself.

"I thought my nightmares could never be added to," he said as he opened the door and stepped outside. "But you, Gretel, have done the impossible. You have made them even worse. They will never go away now."

I stared at him, one final time, pleading with him to stay.

"What do you want of me?" I asked. "What would you have me do?"

"One simple thing," he said, looking directly into my eyes. "Alongside your father, your mother, and your brother, just this: burn in hell."

And with that he was gone. I would never see him again.

It was exactly five months to the day when Edgar and I next met, at his instigation.

He'd tried to visit before—David had told him everything, of course—but I'd found myself unable to face him. And so he'd written to me, time and again, telling me how David had left for North America to begin a new life there. In reply, I had put the story of my early years down on paper and told Edgar to do with my confession whatever he would. Give it to the police. Publish it in a newspaper. I didn't care anymore. But it was greeted with silence and, while every day I expected a knock on the door from a policeman or Nazi hunter, to my astonishment, none ever came.

Now, we sat together in a small coffee shop close to where I lived, sipping cups of hot tea, and he was the same kindly Edgar as ever. I was honest about everything but refused to prostrate myself before him. The life had been sucked out of me by my last encounter with David. I could not go through that again.

But, to my surprise, he did not hold me as responsible for the crimes as his friend had or as others might. After reading my letter, he had wanted to hate me, not just for my past but for what it had done to David, but, despite himself, he found himself unable to alter the feelings he had toward me. And so, he had waited as long as he could before deciding to find me and ask whether I would consider letting him into my life with a view to marriage one day. He had not expected to find me heavy with child, he admitted, but this made no difference to him. He would bring the child up as if it were his own.

For right or wrong, I accepted him because I was lost and lonely and frightened and knew him to be a kind man who would sooner die than hurt me. And, in time, we did marry, and we were happy. No man could have treated his wife with as much tenderness as he did.

There was only one thing that I insisted upon when I agreed to build a life with him. And that was regarding the child that I was carrying. I had already arranged to give that baby up for adoption, I told him, for I did not want it to be infected with the horrors of my past. At first, he protested, but I assured him that I had made my mind up and that if he could not accept that, then he could not accept me. And besides, I added, with the assistance of the hospital, I had found a childless couple who longed to bring up a baby in a loving home and I had made a promise to them that I would not renege upon.

The child was born shortly before Christmas 1953.

A little girl.

"Will you name her before you give her away?" the midwife asked me. "The adoptive parents have said that they would like you to do so, to thank you for the gift you're giving them. They're so very grateful to you."

I thought about it. I had not expected to be offered this opportunity but was happy to accept it.

"Thank you," I told her. "You can tell Mr. and Mrs. Hargrave that their daughter's name is Heidi."

FIFTEEN

I t's difficult to know who was more surprised: Alex Darcy-Witt receiving an invitation for a drink in my flat, or me, when he accepted.

I wrote the invitation on a luxury embossed card, off satin, that I found in my writing desk and used a silver fountain pen that had been so long out of use that I was forced to run the nib under the hot tap to unblock it. It had been many, many years since I had composed anything so formal. It took me back to a time when people communicated in this fashion. Now, I imagined, the only person who might write a letter in such a way was the Queen.

I invited him for 7 p.m. on a Tuesday evening, the night before Caden and Eleanor were to be married, and, at that precise hour, as the minute hand reached the appointed time, there was a knock on my door and there he was, standing outside, wearing an open-necked shirt and carrying a bunch of flowers, like a suitor of old.

"How kind of you," I said, accepting the flowers—my despised dahlias—and carrying them into the kitchen, where I threw them by the sink. I would dispose of them later in the compost bin, when this filthy business was over.

"Don't be too flattered, I didn't buy them myself," he said, sitting down in Edgar's favorite armchair. I knew he would choose that seat, for it dominated the room and he was the type to assume a position of authority. Fortunately for me, it also kept his back to the kitchen. "I got my assistant to do it. Do you like dahlias?"

"I loathe them."

"Even better."

"Still, it's the thought that counts," I said, returning to the living room with a smile. "Now, what can I get you to drink? A glass of whisky, perhaps? A gin and tonic?"

"A cold beer will do very nicely if you have one," he said pleasantly, and I nodded.

"I do indeed," I said. "I like to be prepared for all eventualities."

I went back into the kitchen and opened two bottles of beer, poured each into a glass and carried them out on a silver tray. We clinked glasses and I sat opposite him with only the coffee table separating us.

"Well, this is very civilized," he said, taking a lengthy sip and smiling as the alcohol entered his bloodstream. He, like me, had probably had a long day. In his case, dealing with film stars; in mine, preparing for the following day's excitement.

"Just because we don't like each other doesn't mean that we can't be polite," I said. "After all, we're neighbors, aren't we? We may have to know each other for many years yet. If you don't sell up, that is."

"Not that many, I shouldn't think," he replied. "You can't have that long left in you, surely? I mean, you look good for your age, but you must have one foot in the grave."

I smiled as I sipped my drink. "You have such a charming way about you, Alex," I told him. "I can see why Madelyn fell for you."

He opened his arms wide and grinned. "I am a product of my father," he said. "And you, I imagine, might say the same thing about yourself. It's something we have in common."

"Possibly," I admitted. "Although I've spent my entire life pretending that I'm nothing like him when, the reality is, I can't change the fact that I'm his daughter. Complicit in his crimes. You, on the other hand, you could have been a different man to your father entirely."

Alex nodded. "I'm sure there's a reason for all this," he said. "The invitation, the drinks, the polite chit-chat. Are you going to tell me what it is? I don't really want to stay any longer than is necessary."

"I suppose I wanted to talk to you about guilt," I said, leaning forward. "You asked me about it before, do you remember?"

"I do."

"And I've been thinking about it a great deal ever since. I should have asked you the same question, you see. Whether you feel any."

"Are we speaking honestly now?"

"Of course," I said. "There's only you and I here."

He thought about it for a moment, his tongue bulging slightly in the side of his mouth. Finally, he spoke.

"It's not that I enjoy hitting either of them," he said. "You mustn't think that I get any pleasure from it. Perhaps I wasn't cut out to be a husband or a father. I just can't bear the idea of anyone else having access to Madelyn. On a stage, for example. Or a cinema screen. I want her for myself."

"But why?" I asked. "We can't belong to others."

"That's where you're wrong," he said. "We can. We should. My wife belongs to me."

"Like a possession."

"You say that like it's a bad thing. But don't you treasure your possessions? I do."

I remained silent, uncertain how to respond to this.

"I treasured Madelyn from the start," he continued. "Gave her everything she wanted."

"Except a voice."

"But, you see, I'm not interested in her opinions," he said, looking at me as if this were the most natural thing in the world. "The truth is, she's not that intelligent. And, don't get me wrong, it's not that I'm an unreconstructed misogynist, I know plenty of women who are smarter than me and who I could listen to talk all day long. But Madelyn? No. She has nothing worth saying. But to look at her . . ." He smiled. "Well, you've seen her. You understand me. I could sit before her and look at her all day. If she'd just remain silent."

"You describe her like a painting," I said. "Or a statue."

"A statue, yes," he replied, nodding his head. "Yes, thank you. That's true. But, having said all that," he continued, "it's hard not to feel that she's lost so much of her spirit in recent years. It makes me feel cheated. Sometimes I wonder whether it might not be easier to divorce her, but I'm worried that I might feel resentful if she found that old luster again without me. I couldn't bear that, you see. So, I'm stuck with her. And she with me."

"And Henry?" I asked.

"Henry will grow up strong," he said. "And one day he'll understand why I treat him the way I do. I'm making a man of him."

"I think we have very different ideas on how to define that word."

"Perhaps."

"And he's such a gentle boy."

"But that's exactly what I'm ridding him of, don't you see? That gentility. I can't bear to see him as he is. He's an embarrassment to me. I've seen your son, coming to visit you. Overweight, unhealthy, no sense of style. Don't you feel ashamed of what he's become?"

"I was a bad mother," I admitted. "I didn't deserve him. Any faults he might have are of my own making. The truth is, I'm lucky he turned out as well as he did. I have my late husband to thank for that."

"The sainted Edgar," he said.

"Not a saint, no," I admitted. "But a very good man. The best I've ever known."

"Even better than the commandant?"

"We both know that my father was a monster," I said. "It may have taken me many years to accept that, but it's the truth. It would have been better if his mother had drowned him at birth."

"Then you wouldn't exist."

"A small price to pay, wouldn't you agree, for saving so many millions of lives?"

He shrugged his shoulders. "If it hadn't been him, it would have been someone else," he said. "The Holocaust didn't begin and end with your father. Don't overestimate his influence."

"But he played an enormous role in it. And I've reached the fine old age of ninety-two without having paid any price for his crimes."

"I thought you were ninety-one?" he asked.

"It's my birthday today," I told him.

He laughed. "Happy birthday," he said. "And you're spending it with me. How flattering. Doesn't your son mind?"

"No, he's getting married tomorrow, actually, so I'll see him then. The truth is, I wanted to spend this special evening with you."

His smile faded a little and I sensed that our repartee was coming to an end.

"I'm sure there's something you want to tell me, Gretel?" he asked at last with a sigh. "Otherwise, you wouldn't have called me up here. You're going to try to persuade me to be a better man, am I right? Perhaps offer a lecture about the evils you've seen in your life and how I need to separate myself from all of that."

"Not at all," I said. "I know you'll never change. You'll go on hurting your wife for as long as she's with you, but in the end, I daresay she'll succeed in killing herself. At which point you'll put on a public show of mourning for as long as seems appropriate before finding another unfortunate girl to terrorize. And poor Henry, what will happen to him then? A boarding school, I expect. And a small, sensitive boy like him won't thrive there, will he? It'll be sink or swim. And he'll sink. I can see it in him. I had a brother who died when he was his age, you know."

"I know," he said. "I saw the pictures, remember."

"Of course."

"What happened to him?"

"There was a second boy," I said, recalling the day that Father had taken me into the camp. "A Jewish boy, his own age. I met him in the camp. There were so few children there that it was a surprise to discover him. But some were kept alive, of course. For medical experimentation and what have you."

"You speak like this is a perfectly natural order of things."

"No, there was nothing natural about any of it," I told him, shaking my head. "I found him in the warehouse one day. Where they kept all the striped pajamas."

"The what?"

I shook my head, forgetting that this was a phrase peculiar to my brother and me. "The uniforms, I mean," I told him. "The one the inmates wore. You know the ones I mean."

"Of course," he said, understanding now.

"He told me that he had a friend, a boy who came to visit him at the fence every day. And I knew that my brother, being my brother, so full of adventurous spirit, would one day enter the camp wearing one of those outfits. And he did. Later, when we found his clothes in a pile by the fence, I understood what had happened, although, of course, I could never admit my part in his death to my parents. I've never forgotten that boy. His name was Shmuel. A beautiful name, don't you think? It sounds like the wind blowing. If only I'd told my parents, then everything might have been different. I've blamed myself for that for eighty years now, which is a long time to have something on your conscience."

"Your conscience is an overpopulated land," he said.

"You're not wrong there," I admitted, smiling as I stood up and returned to the kitchen but speaking loudly enough for him to hear me. "I've lived a very long life, Alex, and been mistress of many terrible secrets. I've been partly responsible for the deaths of who knows how many people and I certainly feel responsible for the death of my brother. How am I supposed to atone for any of that?"

I opened a drawer and withdrew the box cutter that I had bought on the day that I had first learned that Mr. Richardson's flat was being put up for sale. It was sharp to the touch, and I slid the button so it opened, its long blade extending from the metal handle, which I gripped tightly in my hand.

"I haven't been able to save anyone," I called out. "Not once. And I might be too late to save your wife. But by God, I intend to save that little boy. I intend to save Henry. And then, at least, I might find some redemption for my sins."

He snorted and I left the kitchen, approaching him from the rear. He didn't even bother to turn as he addressed me.

"It's a nice idea, Gretel," he said. "But I think you're fooling yourself. We've been through this, after all. If you expose me, I expose you. Mutually assured destruction, remember? We can't keep going back and forth on it."

I stood behind his chair now.

"Quite a few people in my life have used a phrase when leaving me," I said. "I thought it would never come to pass, but now, I think they might have been quite prescient. The only thing I can do to make up for my crimes, even in a small way, is to make their wishes come true. Do you know what it is they said? You said it yourself, in fact."

"No," he replied. "Remind me."

"That I should die in a prison cell," I said.

Epilogue

The wedding was a simple but joyous affair. Caden looked remarkably smart in his suit and had even lost a few pounds in recent weeks to ensure that he would fit into it. Eleanor wore an unpretentious cream dress, her makeup understated, her fingernails painted a pale shade of pink. Although it was the third of my son's four weddings that I attended, it was my favorite by far, possibly because I had grown so fond of the bride.

It took place at a registry office and the only other guests were Eleanor's parents and a cousin who introduced himself to me as Marcus and said that he worked in the dog-grooming industry. I was unaware that such an enterprise even existed, but he assured me that it was, in fact, a thriving initiative and that he had almost a dozen vehicles on the roads that called at houses on appointment, took dogs into the vans and give them a wash, a haircut, a pedicure, and a full groom.

"How extraordinary," I said, wondering who had come up with such an idea. It struck me that it would have saved me a lot of time and energy over the years if a similar service had been provided to humans too.

At the dinner afterward, which was held in a very nice restaurant,

Marcus introduced me to another young man, whom he referred to as his partner, and I understood that he did not mean that in a professional sense. It brought me back to Cait Softly and our brief time together in Sydney. I did not think of Cait often, but I hoped that Sydney had proved a good home for her and that she had forgiven me for leaving without saying goodbye.

"What's the latest, Mrs. F.?" Eleanor asked when she joined me in the Ladies to touch up her makeup.

"The latest what?" I asked.

"The goss."

I stared at her, uncertain what she was referring to.

"The man downstairs," she said. "The wife-beater. Any word from the police?"

"Ah," I said. "Yes, I did get a call from Detective . . ." I racked my brain, trying to remember the man's name.

"Kerr," said Eleanor, whose memory was obviously better than mine. "Detective Kerr."

"Yes, that's it," I agreed. "He told me he'd investigated the matter and spoken to Mr. Darcy-Witt, and everything was in order."

Eleanor frowned. "Why would he say that?" she asked.

"Who knows?" I asked. "It's difficult to build a case against a man like Alex Darcy-Witt. Powerful friends, and all that. I wonder did he think I was just looking for attention."

"You don't strike me as someone who seeks attention, Mrs. F.," she said. "On the contrary, you seem like a person who values her privacy."

She was right, of course. A truer word had rarely been spoken of me.

"Anyway, we both know he'd never have stopped doing what he was doing," I continued, "and the police would never have intervened until it was too late, so I decided to put an end to his behavior myself."

"How?"

There was a part of me that wanted to tell her the truth, just to see her reaction. *I slit his throat with a box cutter,* I might have said, *then dragged his dead body into the spare room. The one that Edgar and I used to share. I imagine I'll have to deal with the consequences reasonably soon as it'll only be a day or two before he starts to smell. But I wanted to get through today first. As you know, Caden never quite forgave me for skipping his last wedding.*

But, instead:

"Persuasion," I said. "You'd be surprised how persuasive I can be when I feel passionately about something."

Eleanor seemed unconvinced. "Well, I just hope she finds the wherewithal to leave the bastard," she said. "If she doesn't, it's only a matter of time before a real tragedy strikes."

"Let's not worry about it today," I told her. "After all, it's your wedding day. We should just focus on positives. But actually, now that I have you to myself, there's a small favor I want to ask of you."

"Of course. What is it?"

"Well, obviously, I'm not getting any younger and I might not be around for too much longer. My neighbor, Heidi—you've met her, I think?"

She nodded.

"Would you keep an eye on her if anything happens to me? She has good days and bad days, but she needs someone to look in on her from time to time. Just to check that she's coping. And I feel you're the one person I can absolutely trust to do that."

"Of course," she said. "You have my word on it."

"Thank you, my dear," I said, kissing her cheek. "Now come along, let's not linger in here. This is your wedding dinner. You should be out there, in the restaurant, mingling with your guests. It's a day for happiness, nothing else."

We returned to the party. Caden thanked me for coming and, when I grew tired, he ordered a taxi to take me home. It wasn't late, only ten o'clock, but I don't have the energy for long nights anymore and was looking forward to getting into my dressing gown, making a cup of tea and watching a little television before bed.

While avoiding the spare room, of course.

As I ascended the staircase to my flat, the door to Heidi's flat opened, and Oberon appeared. He looked at me, a little shamefaced, and I gave him a brief nod.

"Been somewhere nice?" he asked, noticing how I was dressed.

"My son's wedding," I told him. "His last wedding, I hope. Well, the last I'll have to attend anyway."

"I suppose I should tell you," he said, "that the whole Australia thing is off."

"Oh dear," I said. "Why is that?"

"They refused to pay any of my relocation fees and, frankly, I didn't see why I should have to shell out the best part of £20,000 for the luxury of moving down under. And with Granny refusing to sell her flat—"

"She said you were thinking of forcing her into a home reversion?" I said.

"Hardly forcing her," he said snippily. "I just thought it would be a good idea, that's all. Anyway, when the company I was talking to changed their mind about the moving fees, I got a little angry with them. Words were exchanged. In retrospect, perhaps I should have been more considered."

"I see," I said, smiling. "So, you'll be staying in London then?"

"Yes," he said. "Probably better off anyway. My skin blisters in the heat something terrible."

"I'm glad to hear it," I told him. "Not that your skin . . . well, you know what I mean. And your grandmother will be pleased too."

He nodded and continued on his way down the stairs.

"And Oberon," I called after him, and he stopped to look up at me.

"Yes?"

"Flat Three will all be yours in time, you know. You just need to have a little patience, that's all. And you might be surprised by how much you'll miss her when she's gone."

He looked at me for a moment and I wondered whether he was going to say something unkind in reply, but no, he simply nodded his head.

"I know it," he said. "Let's hope that's not for a long while yet."

"Indeed," I said, taking my key from my bag and letting myself into my flat, closing the door behind me. A very pretty boy, I thought, my great-grandson, but not a lot going on upstairs.

Alex Darcy-Witt suggested that he could make me the most famous woman on the planet and, while his death did not bring me anything like that level of notoriety, I did become one of the best known in England for a time. It's not every day, after all, that a ninety-two-year-old lady of comfortable means slashes the throat of a successful film producer, gets a good night's sleep, attends her son's wedding, gets *another* good night's sleep, and then calmly calls the emergency services to admit what she's done and offer herself into custody.

Inevitably, it came out that Alex was a cruel, violent man, and there were some who said I'd done the world a service by ridding it of his presence. But, of course, the truth is, I didn't do it for the world. I did it for an innocent nine-year-old boy.

To save him.

The newspapers made a great deal of the fact that I looked like such a harmless old dear. They speculated that I had gone doolally, which annoyed me enormously. My barrister told me that I should go along with this narrative, but I refused. It felt important to me that people knew that I had understood exactly what I was doing, that I had planned the entire thing and executed it—and him—perfectly. If there's one thing I've learned over ninety-two years, it's that it's pointless to keep denying the truth.

The judge, however, aware of the extenuating circumstances, sentenced me to the lowest-security women's prison that could be found, and, while not perfect, it is essentially the retirement village my son had wished upon me. Caden and Eleanor visit often, and it's been a joy to watch her pregnancy grow. Naturally, I won't be able to have any relationship with the child, but at least he or she will grow up ignorant of their terrible lineage. And, of course, I signed my flat over to Caden. To my surprise, however, he has not yet put it on the market. In fact, he's talking of moving in. Which makes me rather happy.

Heidi, my eldest child, comes to see me occasionally, accompanied by Oberon, who always seems fascinated to find himself in a prison and by the fact that I've ended up there. He sends me books and magazines quite regularly, because he's not a bad boy really. I've altered my will to leave a little something to him. Perhaps it will get him to Australia in due course. (Naturally, because I'm willful, I've stipulated that he can come into that inheritance only after his grandmother has died.)

"There's been a lot of drama at Winterville Court since you left," Heidi told me on her last visit when he left us alone for a few minutes. "You'll never believe it, but the man in Flat One was murdered!"

"I know," I told her. "I'm afraid I was the one who did it."

"No, it wasn't you," she said, shaking her head. "It was the woman living across the hall from me. I don't blame her, as it happens. He was a nasty piece of work. He treated his wife and child terribly."

I let it go. There was no point explaining. She wouldn't be able to remember it all anyway.

I have neither seen nor heard from Madelyn or Henry since my sentencing but, if they ever do visit, it's hard to imagine what they might say. I suspect she will look better than she has in a long time but that Henry will be scarred by his loss. He may have wanted his father dead, as he told me, but I imagine he feels ambivalent about that coming to pass. I hope I have not unintentionally damaged him even further. This is a concern that weighs upon me greatly.

Prison itself, however, doesn't bother me too much. I've made some friends and am generally treated with respect by both the inmates and the guards, on account of my advanced years. The food is terrible, of course, and I miss enjoying a glass of wine in the evenings, but one can't have everything.

Lights out is my favorite time, when the hallways fall quiet and I lie in bed, thinking of my family and telling myself that my punishment is a shared one. Some nights, I pray for forgiveness. Most nights, I don't waste my time.

I will say this, however: I am sorry. Not for Alex's death—that doesn't bother me in the slightest—but for the rest of it. The words are too simple, I know, and will be of little comfort to anyone, but I mean them.

I am so sorry.

And then, before I fall asleep, there is one last thing I do.

I was permitted to bring a few small items from home with me to decorate my cell. A rug that Edgar bought for our tenth wedding anniversary that my bare feet land on every morning when I struggle out of bed. Some books that I love, including *Treasure Island* and, a late choice, *Around the World in Eighty Days*, retrieved from Flat

One, where Henry had left it before departing. I re-read them and imagine myself in far-flung places, cities I never had an opportunity to visit, but where I might have lived very different lives, with yet more surnames, enjoying singular adventures while being buried beneath the same traumas. I think of Henry when I read them.

But, most importantly of all, I brought the antique Seugnot jewelry box that I'd kept in my wardrobe for decades and that I had not dared to open since leaving Germany in 1946. It contained only a single item, the photograph that Kurt Kotler took of me on that sunny day so many years ago, outside our house in that other place.

I opened it on my first night in my cell and removed the picture in order to affix it to the wall next to my bed. I looked at myself in it, all of twelve years old, so innocent and so filled with longing for the handsome boy poised behind the lens. But, to my surprise, I realized that I was not alone. In fact, there were several other people in the picture, people I had never noticed were there before.

In the background, outside the gates, stood Father and Mother, locked in conversation. In the far corner was a man dressed in a uniform of striped pajamas, wheeling a barrow, bent over, frightened, aware that he would get into trouble if he did not move quickly enough.

In the top-right corner, a small hemisphere, the edge of Kurt's finger obscuring the lens.

But my greatest surprise was seeing the person who filled the frame on my left. He is sitting on a tire that had been attached to a rope which has, in turn, been hung from the sturdy branches of a tree. He is in mid-swing, his legs flying out before him. His hands clutch the ropes. His face is filled with joy.

My younger brother.

For eighty years, I have not dared to speak his name aloud lest the emotion of those two syllables proves too much for me and causes me to break down at the memory of the terrible experiences of which we were both a part.

But now, his name is the last word on my lips every night as I fall asleep, when I pray that, before dawn breaks, I will be taken from this earth at last and find myself running into his arms, reunited. When I can tell him how sorry I am.

When I can tell them all how sorry I am.

I whisper it now as the lights turn off, my eyes close, and the cells sink into quiet.

The name of the boy that I loved more than any other.

More than Kurt, more than Émile, more than David, more than Edgar, more than Caden.

My brother.

Bruno.

Author's Note

I first conceived the idea for *All the Broken Places* in 2004, shortly after completing the final draft of *The Boy in the Striped Pajamas*, and I knew immediately that I would write it one day. For many years, I kept a file on my computer titled *Gretel's Story*, in which I would make notes about Bruno's older sister, who she might become in later life, and the experiences that might shape her adulthood.

My intention had always been to write the book toward the end of my life, perhaps in my eighties or nineties, when my creative engine, along with the rest of me, was finally grinding to a halt. But then the pandemic happened, and lockdown happened, and I found myself in my back garden ready to write something new; and the isolation of the moment made me think that now was the time. And so, I began.

Revisiting characters from an earlier work can be a risky but exhilarating experience for a novelist, particularly if those characters come from the best-known book of one's career. But it was fascinating for me to return to Gretel after almost twenty years and discover, through the writing, what might have become of her. And also, to rediscover some of the other characters from that earlier book and examine how their actions during the war might have shaped their lives in the years that followed.

When I give talks to creative-writing workshops, I always ask this of my students: without referring to the plot, tell me, in a few sentences, what your novel is about. If I were to answer this question about *All the Broken Places*, I would say that it is a novel about guilt, complicity, and grief, a book that sets out to examine how culpable a young person might be, given the historical events unfolding around her, and whether such a person can ever cleanse themselves of the crimes committed by the people she loved.

These are themes that run through many of my books and about which I have written time and again. Having grown up in Ireland in the 1980s as part of a generation whose childhoods and teenage years were tainted by those who were entrusted with our education, perhaps it's not surprising that I have less interest in the monsters than I do in the people who knew what the monsters were doing and deliberately looked away.

I've been fascinated by the Holocaust ever since I was fifteen, and it's played a big part in both my reading and my writing life. From my first encounter with Elie Wiesel's *Night* in 1986—a book that ignited my interest in the subject—through decades of novels, non-fiction, films, and documentaries, it's a period of history that has always left me hungry to learn more. Like all those who study that era, I'm hoping for answers in that vast library of literature that has been produced over the last seventy-five years. Nonetheless, I'm conscious that my search is a fool's errand, for there are none. In trying to understand, I can only hope to remind, to remember.

Although she is the central character in my story, I am not trying to create a sympathetic character in Gretel. In common with most of mankind, Gretel is replete with flaws and contradictions. She is capable of moments of great kindness and acts of appalling cruelty, and I hope the reader will think about her long after finishing the book, perhaps questioning what they might have done in her place. After all, it is easy when one is far removed from a historical episode to claim that one would not have acted as others did, but it is far more difficult to show such basic humanity in the moment.

Outside of the present day, I chose three eras in which to revisit Gretel. The first is Paris in 1946, and I am indebted to Antony Beevor and Artemis Cooper's scholarly *Paris After the Liberation, 1944–1949* for the insights that book gives into the period. The second is Sydney, Australia, in the early 1950s. As a passionate Australophile who's visited the country many, many times, I chose it not just because it's a city I love, but because it is effectively as far away from Europe as one can go without coming back again; I felt this was something that might appeal to Gretel, who is desperately trying to erase her past. And finally, London in 1953, with a new queen on the throne, a woman of a similar age to Gretel, whose father has also played an important, if substantially more humane, part in the war. Here, peacetime has delivered a generation of young Jews whose families have died in the most horrific ways and who bear terrible scars. I wanted to discover what Gretel would do when faced with such trauma, how she would respond to their pain and whether she would take any responsibility for it.

Writing about the Holocaust is a fraught business and any novelist approaching it takes on an enormous burden of responsibility. Not the burden of education, which is the task of non-fiction, but the burden of exploring emotional truths and authentic human experiences while remembering that the story of every person who died in the Holocaust is one that is worth telling.

For all the mistakes in her life, for all her complicity in evil, and for all her regrets, I believe that Gretel's story is also worth telling.

It is up to the reader to decide whether it is worth reading.

John Boyne
Dublin, 2022

Acknowledgments

For all their advice and encouragement throughout the writing of this book, I'm grateful to Bill Scott-Kerr, Patsy Irwin, Larry Finlay, Eloisa Clegg, and all the team at Transworld Publishers in the UK; to Pamela Dorman, Marie Michels, and everyone at Pamela Dorman Books in the US; and to my agents Simon Trewin and Laura Bonner at WME.

Thank you, too, to my international publishers for their support over many years and, of course, to all my readers.